Award-winning broadcas
written two works of non-f
The Tobermory Treasure, an   novels, *The Wayward
Tide* and *Sweet Exile*, both translated into nine languages. Her
latest novel, *After Shanghai* is published by Macmillan. She lives
near the sea, in Fife, Scotland.

ALISON McLEAY

THE
DREAM
MAKER

PAN BOOKS

First published 1994 by Macmillan

This edition published 1995 by Pan Books
an imprint of Macmillan General Books
Cavaye Place London SW10 9PG
and Basingstoke

Associated companies throughout the world

ISBN 0-330-32433-0

3 5 7 9 8 6 4 2

A CIP record for this book is available from
the British Library

Typeset by Cambridge Composing (UK) Limited, Cambridge
Printed and bound in Great Britain by
Cox & Wyman Ltd, Reading, Berkshire

ACKNOWLEDGEMENT

With thanks and good wishes to all those people of Manitoba, Canada – in Winnipeg, at Norway House and in Churchill on the shores of Hudson Bay – who so generously offered their help and hospitality during my research for this book.

AUTHOR'S NOTE

Throughout this novel I have endeavoured to use the versions of place-names familiar in the early nineteenth century. For instance, although in 1900 the Geographic Board of Canada officially confirmed the name of its great inland sea as Hudson Bay, I have, like the Hudson's Bay Company itself, retained the earlier form.

PART ONE

November 1819

CHAPTER ONE

I

Flora Elizabeth Louise de Montfort St Serf peered from the doorway into the dismal rain lashing Gough Square, and realized she was about to get very wet indeed. With a little gasp of impatience, she pulled her shawl more tightly round her thin shoulders.

In better times four years earlier it had been a good shawl of Lyons silk, but the fringe was frayed now and loose threads had dragged among the flowers. Yet at least it hid the two silver candlesticks which Flora hugged awkwardly to her chest beside her father's enamelled snuff-box, the great punch-ladle with the St Serf arms on it, and a heavy silver inkstand whose crystal bottles threatened to rattle out at any moment.

Flora already regretted the inkstand. By any standard it was an ugly brute of a thing, and if she'd been able to reach the silver tea-caddy without being seen, she'd certainly have taken that instead. But there'd been no time for picking and choosing. As it was, only the hysterical scenes in the drawing-room had allowed her to reach the front door unnoticed.

Cautiously, she searched through the deluge for the bailiffs' horse-van. To her surprise the square was empty: the rain had even driven the lame beggar from his post in the doorway opposite. Only a grimy, two-wheeled hand-cart waited at the bottom of the steps to the St Serfs' lodgings, its shafts tilted skywards like two black horns.

Flora let out her breath in a hiss of contempt. So much for the pride of the St Serfs! Not even a four-wheel wagon to snatch away the little that remained.

For a moment she hesitated, hitching up her shawl with its troublesome burden. London rain seemed to tumble like scour-water into the brick slot of the square, feeding the pools which lay for ever on its slimy flags.

But there was no help for it: she had to go, or be discovered. With sudden decision she darted, head down, from the shelter of the doorway, cursing the trailing hem of her gown, dashing by instinct down the three stone steps which led into the street.

Under her shawl the contraband silver clanked and squeaked, inviting the interest of every passing rogue. The sooner it was all safely stowed beneath her friend Lydia Seaward's bed, the better. Under Lydia's bed . . . For an instant Flora's brow cleared, and a smile twitched the corners of her lips: *Let's hope Mamma never finds out how her silver has been saved from the bailiffs.*

The pointed taper-snuffer of the inkstand had already begun to jab unpleasantly into Flora's ribs, and at the foot of the steps she picked up her skirts to run. Deafened by the rain, she was quite unaware of the purposeful footsteps approaching from the direction of Three-Leg Alley, where a dark, stern young man had turned into the square, bending his beaver hat against the storm, intent upon reaching Fleet Street before his well-cut wool coat was soaked through.

In another second he'd collided painfully with a flowered Lyons shawl hiding something exceedingly sharp in its folds.

'Oh!'

With a resounding clatter, the contents of Flora's bundle cascaded to the flagstones – candlesticks, snuff-box, inkstand, ladle and all – everything but the taper-snuffer, which had pierced the fine wool coat like a stiletto.

For a moment they stared at one another through the downpour – Flora hastily scrabbling for the last of her silver, and the dark young man startled, winded, and now hatless.

Then Flora glanced back in alarm towards the still-open door of her home – and that single glance was enough. In the first few confused seconds the stranger had taken her for a young lady, caught out in the rain: her wet, inky curls tumbled round a face of such delicate paleness that her shining eyes seemed to swallow it up; her hands flew like frail moths in the rainy dimness; she seemed airy, poised for flight . . . All at once the young man's gaze fell on her frayed shawl and shabby cotton gown, and his expression hardened. With stunning swiftness, he stepped forward and grabbed her firmly by the arm.

'So that's your game—'

'Let me go!' Flora tore frantically at the fingers which held her. 'How dare you! Let go of me at once!'

'I will not.'

With his free hand, the young man pulled the snuffer triumphantly from his coat. The woollen fabric was drenched and glisten-

4

ing, and rainwater ran in rivulets from his hair, but the excitement of his capture had done away with any thought of discomfort.

'Whose plate is this?' He thrust the taper-snuffer under Flora's nose. 'Your master's? Or did you sneak into that house and steal the first things you saw?'

'I'm not a thief!' Flora thrashed wildly at his unyielding fingers, panic bringing the blood to her cheeks and making her voice shrill. 'Oh, can't you see you're ruining everything?'

He was holding her with both hands now, tightening his grip as she struggled frantically to be free. If this wretched stranger insisted on dragging her back to the house to make enquiries . . . Suddenly swinging her foot in its cracked satin slipper, she kicked him as hard as she could on the shin.

'Oh – confound you!'

For a second the young man lost his grip, and Flora wrenched herself loose. Already fear had turned to outrage; she pulled her soaking shawl disdainfully round her shoulders exactly as she'd seen her mother do when she was obliged to pass the street-women of Covent Garden.

It was a superb gesture, somewhat spoiled by her rain-soaked hair and the muddy clutter of silverware at her feet.

'What do you take me for?' she demanded frigidly. 'Don't you know a lady when you see one?'

'A lady?' The young man peered at her through the rain, rubbing his injured shin. 'You're hardly more than a girl, for all you kick like a parson's hack—'

'I'm sixteen years old,' Flora informed him, vaguely regretting having kicked quite so hard.

The young man scrutinized her more carefully. There was colour in her cheeks now, like a bright stain under the delicate skin, though her eyes were encircled by great hollows of weariness.

She hadn't run off – and even in that gloomy yard there was enough proud, defiant light in the girl's face to raise a doubt in his mind.

'I beg your pardon,' he conceded after a moment. 'I suppose I might have been mistaken.'

'You *might* have been mistaken?' Resentfully, Flora crouched down to retrieve her scattered treasures from the slops of the gutter. 'Oh, you were mistaken, sir – there's no doubt about that!' Relief made her sharp-tongued. 'Why, if there were an officer here, I'd give you in charge. Laying hands on a respectable lady in broad daylight—'

'And since when have respectable ladies run about town with their arms full of silver plate?' Crossly, the young man retrieved the punch-ladle from a puddle.

'That's my business, I think.' Flora straightened up, cradling her candlesticks. 'Your hat, sir.' She held out the dripping beaver.

'And your ladle . . . Miss—' Curiously, he turned the huge spoon to inspect the coat of arms engraved on its handle.

'Miss St Serf.' Flora snatched the ladle. 'Miss Flora Elizabeth Louise de Montfort St Serf. One of the Hampshire St Serfs, of Chillbourne Park. I imagine you've heard of the family.'

'Ah . . . those St Serfs.'

The young man studied Flora intently for a moment, then turned to gaze up at the bleak building from which she'd escaped. Clear above the drumming of the rain, gruff male voices were growling behind the windows, doggedly resisting a chorus of female scolding. Doors slammed; a heavy object grated across a floor; then the male voices growled again, drowning out the furious soprano.

The young man's gaze had shifted to the official black hand-cart waiting in a puddle at the bottom of the steps.

'Bailiffs . . .' He turned back to Flora. 'So that's what this is all about! You were running off with as much as you could carry before the sheriff's men could take it.'

'Nonsense!' Flora prayed that the rain would cool her burning cheeks. 'I was simply taking some plate to – to the bank vault for safety.' Hastily, she began to wind the candlesticks into her soaking shawl, flustered by the searching stare which followed every movement.

Of course the bailiffs had come to the house! Was the fellow a fool, not to have realized sooner? Scornfully, Flora stole a glimpse at her assailant. It was all very well for men of his sort to go around arresting people. From the looks of his clothes, he'd never had to fend off bailiffs in his entire life.

'Don't forget your snuffer, Miss St Serf.'

The young man held it out in his wet palm, and Flora took it with as much grace as she could muster, venturing a swift glance at his face. He was dark – almost as dark as Papa – yet his eyes were quite startlingly blue, and she wished he wouldn't stare so. He still hadn't put on his hat, she noticed, gallantly remaining as bare-headed in the rainstorm as she was herself.

6

That was something to be said for him, at least. Under cover of gathering up her shawl, Flora considered the rest with all the critical severity of her sixteen years. His figure was good, she decided reluctantly, and his legs were straight and smoothly muscled – even if he had taken care to show them off in the latest tight trousers.

Unfortunately the young man chose that moment to spoil whatever good opinion Flora might have been forming of him.

'I don't blame you for trying to save your belongings, Miss St Serf. In your place, I hope I'd have the courage to do the same. And yet—' He struggled to be fair. 'You can hardly blame tradesmen for trying to get their money.'

'Tell that to the bank!' hissed Flora furiously, binding up her ink-bottles. 'It's the bank who've done this to us – Elder's Bank, creeping hypocrites that they are.' She paused to struggle with the knot of her shawl.

'Everyone knows how the Elders let the royal dukes run up debts of hundreds of thousands – they say old Mr Elder goes crawling on his knees with gifts to keep the Regent happy. And yet the moment they heard Papa was in trouble they wanted their money back at once, and sold us up without a second thought.' Tossing her chin, she added contemptuously, 'As soon as a man is pulled down, the Elders will have his throat cut for a sixpence.'

'Though I dare say the bank has a right to its money.' With a brisk gesture the young man tipped the rainwater from his hat and set it firmly on his head.

'The Elders had no right to drive an innocent man to despair,' retorted Flora hotly, 'yet they did it all the same.'

He was staring at her again; and all at once Flora realized what a picture she must make, with the curve of every limb made voluptuously plain under her soaking gown. Embarrassed, she pulled her shawl-covered bundle over her bosom, and for an instant their eyes met across its silken flowers.

'You shouldn't be out alone in this part of town.'

Flora worked her fingers awkwardly into the folds of the shawl, wondering if he could tell that her stomach had suddenly squeezed up under her ribs – and that the feeling was strangely exciting.

She wriggled her shoulders, and saw his eyes follow the movement.

'"This part of town" is my home now. You'd be surprised how well I know it.'

'At least let me see you safely to wherever you're going.'

'Oh, no – you can't possibly—' Plunged into panic, Flora snatched at the first words to come into her head. 'Don't worry, I shan't be robbed – though you might.' Oh *drat* – his expression showed nothing but genuine concern: at once Flora regretted her sharpness. 'But thank you for offering, all the same.'

There was a moment of disturbing intimacy as they gazed at one another through the veil of rain. Then all at once the sound of raised voices from the windows behind them made Flora tighten her grip on the shawl.

'I must be off.' She hesitated, took a couple of paces towards the entrance to a nearby alleyway and then glanced back over her shoulder. Lydia would certainly want to know the young man's name.

'You never gave me your name, though I told you mine.'

Her captor paused. 'It's Smith.'

'Good day to you then, Mr Smith.' Flora's eyes travelled nervously to the black mouth of the alley before returning to fix him with a brief, valiant smile. 'Don't drown on the way to your carriage, will you?'

Without waiting for an answer, she turned and hurried away.

For a full half-minute the young man watched Flora's small, retreating figure, trailing its sodden fringe of blue Lyons silk. She walked swiftly down the alley, bowed over her treasures, ignoring the pools which had collected among the cobblestones, and as long as he waited, she never looked back.

London rain, he reflected, was hard and unforgiving, no matter who one might be.

2

'He said his name was Smith.' Safe by the side of Lydia Seaward's fire, Flora pulled a handful of pins from her thick, soaking hair, and went on with the story of her morning's adventures.

It was already past noon, but Lydia was still in bed, as Flora had expected. If she was alone, Lydia never rose before two: if the Captain was with her, she didn't get out of bed at all, except to put a white wooden wig-stand in her window as a sign to friends that she was otherwise engaged.

Fortunately there had been no white shape behind the panes overlooking King's Head Court as Flora scurried gratefully up the narrow stairway, leaving a damp trail wherever her sopping slippers had passed.

'Mercy on us – what *have* you been doing?' Lydia reared up on one elbow as the door banged open, her eyes full of sleepy astonishment. 'You've robbed a pawnshop—'

'Of course not!' One by one, Flora set out her treasures on the cluttered table. 'Two horrible bailiffs came this morning with something called a "distraint order", which said they could take away anything they liked – and I suppose I've broken the law by smuggling these away, though I don't care in the least. Will you keep them safe for a day or two?'

'The bailiffs are no friends of mine.' Scratching at her tousled, silver-blonde head, Lydia drew her legs clear of the bedcovers, lowered her feet to the floor and stretched voluptuously, smoothing her cheek against her shoulder like a waking cat.

At last, Flora felt her own strained nerves begin to ease. Here in Lydia's rooms, everything was so reassuringly chaotic – a hopeless muddle of discarded petticoats and forgotten trinkets, of open jars of this-and-that, of half-eaten loaves and odd shoes, and ribbons and chicken-bones and trampled hats, and in the middle of the floor, Lydia's magnificent French bed, looted by her soldier lover from the baggage train of one of Bonaparte's fleeing *maréchals* and now a tumble of frowsy sheets and heavy, bullion-fringed brocade.

'But you're utterly drenched. Here—' Lydia padded across the room, dragging an embroidered cover from the bed. 'Give me that dreadful shawl, and put this over your shoulders. You look like a drowned rat instead of my pretty Flora.'

'Hah!' muttered Flora scornfully. As always, Lydia's bright presence made her abruptly conscious of her own dark solemnity. At twenty-two, Lydia Seaward had the succulent charm of a cherub; her face was a marvel of gently rounded cheeks and soft, full lips above an acquisitive little chin, of sleepy innocent eyes which suggested the helplessness of a baby in the body of a mature woman. Flora could easily understand why men found her irresistible: Fate had dowered Lydia with the face of a ruined child – soft, capricious, and knowing.

And for the hundredth time, she wondered why talking with Lydia was so easy when talking with anyone else seemed to involve such evasions and misunderstandings.

It wasn't as if she'd had many friends at the house in Richmond before they'd been obliged to leave it for Gough Square. For a while she'd shared lessons with Mary Collington, whose father was Captain of the *Lion* – and there'd been Jane Pugh, the Rector's youngest girl, whose red wrists stuck out of her sister's cast-offs, and whom Mrs St Serf had thought not quite *comme il faut*.

In Gough Square, of course, there was no one even remotely *comme il faut* – certainly not Miss Lightsome Harkiss, the undertaker's daughter from Shoe Lane, who wore a ring on every finger and passed thereabouts for nobility. And since according to Constance St Serf no one was good enough to keep company with her daughters, even without a shilling to their names, she'd decreed that in future Flora and her sister Sophie would be sufficient company for one another, and that to be seen chattering to any of the tradesmen's girls would be punished by a week of gruel and water in their cheerless bedroom.

And so, precisely at an age when she longed for someone to share in all the pains and perplexities of ripening womanhood, Flora had found herself with no confidante but Sophie, two years her junior. And Sophie was . . . well, Sophie – temperamental, self-absorbed, and no help at all.

Then, on a day of depressing exploration soon after the family's arrival in Gough Square, Flora had discovered Lydia.

King's Head Court was even smaller and gloomier than Gough Square, and at that particular moment it had rung like an organ-pipe with the voices of quarrelling women as Lydia hurled down curses from her window at her landlady below.

'You're a pig, Sara Harkiss,' Flora heard her shout. 'Captain Bellarmine's coming tonight, and when I tell him what you just called me, he'll stuff every damned penny of the rent money down your husband's ugly throat!'

'He might – if he has it!' the undertaker's wife shouted back, taking a short clay pipe from between her teeth. 'You tell your precious Captain from me—' She prodded the air with a finger as thick as a washing-paddle. 'You tell him there's six weeks owing, and if I don't see some of it by tomorrow noon, I'll turn his precious strumpet into the street where she belongs – just see if I don't!'

From the window came renewed screeching, and a hard little shoe whizzed down into the yard; but Mrs Harkiss was nimble for one of her size, and skipped safely out of the way.

It was only after the short, fierce battle was over and the crowd had melted away that Flora noticed the slipper at her feet – a tiny shoe of figured blue silk with a ribbon bow at its toe and a peak at its heel like a waterman's lantern. It was a lost shoe, crying out to be reunited with its twin; and without a thought for her mother's warnings, Flora picked it up, rubbed away a smudge of dirt with her sleeve, and set off for the stairway to Lydia Seaward's rooms.

At the top of the stairs she'd discovered the mate of the lost shoe, and in Lydia an instant comrade. Six years older than Flora and a century wiser in the ways of the world, Lydia had gazed at her with the sympathetic eyes of an outcast, and had seen a spirit she recognized.

Now, warming her chilled toes by Lydia's fire, Flora wondered what would have become of her without that forbidden refuge, that disordered paradise for a lonely, uprooted, bewildered young creature who understood only that life had suddenly conspired against her happiness.

The silver inkstand on the table caught her eye, and she sighed.

'All because of a court martial, Lydia . . . To lose our home – and now this.'

'I know, I know,' agreed Lydia, who'd heard the story countless times before.

'Life's so unfair!'

'It has its ups and downs,' confirmed Lydia, picking among the gristle of a cold chop-bone with an expression of seraphic concentration. 'Though even today hasn't been all bad.' She paused to gnaw at a tuft of grey fibres with strong, cat-like teeth, hunching her plump shoulders over her task, her bosom shivering as she tore at the shreds. 'Your Mr Smith sounds an interesting find.'

'He's hardly *my* Mr Smith,' objected Flora, her cheeks warming at once.

'Why not, if you want him to be? He offered to come along here with you, didn't he? Well, then – he wouldn't have given a toss for your safety if you'd been a yellow old maid with false hair and a crimping-board for a chest.'

'I dare say he was only being civil.' Flora avoided Lydia's eye.

'Civil my arse!' Lydia made a farting sound with her lips like a wind-cherub from an old map. 'How old are you, dear heart? Fifteen – or is it sixteen now?' She snorted derisively. 'Then it's high time you learned the truth about gentlemen, my innocent dove, before one of 'em gets the chance to teach you. Don't you ever listen to anything I say?'

'I listen to every word,' Flora assured her truthfully.

'Well, then.' Lydia waved her clean-picked bone. 'If you don't have a penny in the world – like me – nor yet a taste for governessing or stitching garters for twopence a time, then there's only one way to get a living, and that's to find some fellow to pay for it.'

Flora stuck out her lower lip. 'He took me for a common thief, Lydia!'

'But you liked the look of him, didn't you? He was handsome enough, by all accounts.'

'In an icy sort of way, I suppose.' Flora studied her toes.

'And his waist was his own, as far as you could see? I can't abide stays on a man,' added Lydia darkly. 'They creak at all the wrong moments. Look at their bums – you can always tell.'

'I didn't look at his . . . rear,' insisted Flora helplessly. She felt herself colouring once more; even after years of friendship, she was still shocked by Lydia's forthrightness. After a moment she admitted in a small voice, 'His legs were good.'

'There you are then!' cried Lydia triumphantly. 'And he liked what he saw of you, depend on it.'

'Lydia, I know absolutely nothing about him! He might be the greatest monster that ever lived – he might kidnap poor girls and sell them for white slaves . . .' Flora's eyes flew open, the exact limpid green of the great twist at the centre of a sheet of spun glass, clear and profound; then her long, soft lashes swept down to veil them. 'At any rate, Mr Smith seemed a great deal too sure of himself, if you ask me. And besides,' she added with finality, 'I've no idea who he is, or where he lives, and I shall probably never see him again.'

'He knows where *you* live,' Lydia pointed out. 'And if he walked through the square once, this Mr Smith of yours, he can walk through it again. Good gracious – you're as good as introduced to him now! Another word, and you can count yourself an old friend.'

'I don't want to be his friend!'

'Well, you *should* want it.' Lydia puckered her forehead into an absent frown. 'As I keep telling you, sweetness – rich men marry rich women, and poor men, too, if they can manage it. So you see, penniless drudges like you and I must look out for ourselves.' She leaned forward to make sure of Flora's attention. 'All I'm saying is, in your position I'd keep my eyes open and forget about white slaves for the present.'

The rain had stopped by the time Flora returned home, lecturing herself as she went in a tone distinctly like her mother's. What nonsense Lydia talked, to be sure – as if there were nothing else to life than men, and the getting and keeping of them. All the same, she couldn't resist glancing about her as she hurried down the alley towards the glistening cobbles of Gough Square.

A few paces short of the alley-mouth, she halted in astonishment and pressed herself into a nearby doorway. The bailiff's hand-cart had gone, certainly, but its place had been taken by a gigantic black travelling-coach, which, together with its four horses, had somehow squeezed into the square as tightly as a hat in a hatbox.

The coachman wore a blue livery, like the groom hastily folding down the steps for his returning passengers. Flora knew that livery of old. Long before the carriage door had been thrown open, she knew it would bear the red-and-gold flash of the St Serf arms with its proud scroll of 'God Sharpen My Sword'. Wonder of wonders, Grandfather St Serf had called – General Bayard St Serf, veteran of Mysore and Assaye, scourge of Mahrattas and tremulous subalterns, descendant of a hundred generations of warriors.

Even as Flora watched, the General marched down the steps of the house, straight as a pikestaff, his silver head shining like St George's helmet, while the soundly bonneted figure of Mrs General St Serf tramped at his heels.

On the shoulders of the St Serfs, the General was fond of declaring, rested the honour of the nation. Since the days of the Conqueror, countless St Serfs had sanctified greedy little wars with their presence, serving their monarchs by turning petulant brawls into the holiest of crusades. The St Serfs had been above criticism, the self-appointed conscience of kings – until the day of Major Edmund St Serf's disgrace.

The General had sworn never to speak to his elder son again, and yet now – inexplicably – after four years of silent contempt, he'd taken it into his head to call.

Flora watched her mother linger at the top of the steps while the iron-shod wheels ground on the cobbles, and the enormous vehicle rolled out of the square, clearing its narrow archway by some miracle of navigation. There was a precoccupied expression on Constance's face as she stood there, pinching her nostrils with a lace-edged handkerchief against the stench of mouldy flagstones. As soon as she caught sight of Flora her brows flew into an angry knot.

'And where have you been, I'd like to know? Come inside at once – you look like a beggar.' Constance stared defensively round the square, searching for watching eyes. 'And where are my candlesticks, may I ask? And your father's inkstand, and the punch-ladle—'

'And the snuff-box too,' Flora finished for her. 'They're quite safe, I promise you.'

'I'm pleased to hear it.' Constance closed the door with a bang, shutting them both into the shadows of the panelled hall.

'I thought you'd be happy I'd saved something from the bailiffs,' Flora pointed out.

'And so I am.' Constance gave a brisk nod, like the peck of a bird. 'And I'm pleased to see you showing a little common sense for once. But where have you left them? That's what I want to know.'

'Do you know the house where the laundrywoman lives?' Flora was amazed by her own glibness.

'You left my silver with the laundrywoman?' Constance's mouth hung open in horror.

'With someone the laundrywoman knows.' This at least was true: everyone knew Lydia Seaward. In any case, since Constance didn't care to deal with the laundrywoman in person, she'd probably never discover the truth. 'What did Grandpapa want?' asked Flora curiously.

'You left my silver with a total stranger!' Constance ignored the question. 'You'll go back and fetch it first thing tomorrow.'

'Of course. But it's perfectly safe, I'm sure.' Flora gazed round the hallway as if expecting some sign of change, some evidence of the momentous event which had just taken place. 'Why did Grandpapa come here?' she asked once more. 'I thought he'd sworn never to speak to Papa again. Had the bailiffs gone when he arrived? Oh, gracious—' She clapped a hand to her mouth. 'Did Grandpapa see the bailiffs going through all our things?'

'The General caught them with my mother-of-pearl fan in their dirty hands, and my diamond studs, too. All to satisfy that devil of a tailor.' Constance made a furious little sound. 'He should be grateful the Major gave him business at all, wretched snipper that he is!' Pettishly, she picked at the bodice of her gown. 'The General paid the bailiffs what was owing, and made them put everything back where they found it.'

'Grandpapa *paid* them?' Flora gave a whoop of delight. 'But that's wonderful! I knew he'd come round in the end. Oh, Papa must be so pleased!' And she set off for the staircase which led to their first-floor rooms.

'Unfortunately not.' Constance's voice was as dry as the stirring of old leaves. 'The General seems as set against your father as he ever was. He only came because he'd heard of our debts, and considered them a further disgrace to the family.'

'But it isn't Papa's fault!' protested Flora. 'It was Elder's Bank who brought us to this! Everybody knows how they've hounded Papa. If Grandpapa would only pay what we owe the bank—'

'Maybe he will,' conceded her mother, 'one day. For the present, he has something else in mind.'

'Oh. Well, at least he came here, which is better than nothing.' Once more, Flora made as if to go upstairs.

'Wait, Flora.'

Constance hesitated, drawing her lips up under her nose in an expression Flora had learned to dread. Then she took a breath, and began in a rush, 'The General has proposed – to me, since he still refuses to speak to your father—' She drew another breath. 'He has proposed that in order to salvage something from our present . . . difficulties, he should take over the future upbringing of one of our daughters – which of course means that one of you girls, at least, would be raised as a young lady should . . . but it would also mean that before long we might *bring him round* again to giving back Papa's allowance, do you see?'

'Not really,' admitted Flora warily.

'The General seems to remember . . . many years ago, apparently, when you were just a child—' Constance pressed a hand to her temple. 'Though I really can't recall the occasion myself . . . It seems he saw you on the lawn at Richmond with Papa's sword in your hand, drilling the under-gardeners, and the incident has stayed in his mind. "I feel something may be made of Flora," – that's what he said today. "In the proper surroundings, we may make a St Serf of her yet."'

'But I'm a St Serf already, surely.'

'Well, of course you are.'

'Then I don't understand what Grandpapa means.'

'It really doesn't matter whether you understand or not.' Tension was making Constance snappish. 'All you need to know is that in three days' time you'll be leaving Gough Square for good. In future, Flora, you're to live with the General in Hampshire.'

'Flora always gets what she wants! Never me! None of you cares the least bit about me, and that's the truth.'

Sophie was standing in the drawing-room doorway, her pretty face dark with mutiny and a wild light in her eyes. 'I might as well be dead – and then you'd all be sorry.'

She kicked savagely at a door-panel, gulped back the pain of her bruised toes, and fled from the room, slamming the door hard behind her.

It was no more than Flora had expected. Almost since babyhood, Sophie's tantrums had exploded without warning, like summer storms crashing out of the bluest of skies, driving governess after governess to despair. Thwarted, she could scream herself ill, collapsing at last in hysterical exhaustion, her skin milk-pale and her eyes sunk to pools of silent reproach.

Now the governesses had departed along with the airy house in Richmond, and Sophie's inconsolable howls could be heard all through the six rooms they rented in Gough Square.

'You little idiot!' In the privacy of their shared bedroom, Flora confronted her sister crossly. 'Do you think I want to go off to horrible Hampshire? Do you imagine I'll *enjoy* living with Grandpapa?'

Flora had passed a miserable night. No matter what her mother might say, she knew perfectly well the kind of life which awaited her in her grandfather's house. As far as the General was concerned, females – girl children – were a very poor substitute for sons. Sons could be taught to carry the standard, to believe, to conquer or lay down their lives for an honourable cause. However soldierly Flora had looked with Papa's sword in her babyish hand, the fact remained that she was still a girl, and her grandfather would expect her to be demure and submissive, and to run when she was called, like his horse or his dog.

Gough Square and its alleyways might be sunless and narrow, but at least there she had freedom to come and go almost as she liked, and to think her own thoughts without interference. What was there in Hampshire for Flora?

Sophie sat resentfully on the end of the bed, her fine-featured face blotched with weeping. In looks she resembled her mother – bright, rippling hair and a smooth, porcelain face tapering to a sharp little chin, on which the features seemed to be painted in enamel. Now her prettiness was marred by the tears which left glistening paths across it.

'It was you Grandpapa chose,' she muttered at last, impatiently brushing back a damp strand of hair. 'He chose you, which means he didn't want me. Nobody ever wants me – not even Mamma and Papa.'

'Oh, for goodness' sake, Sophie!' Flora, curled up against the bolster, frowned at her sister severely. 'I do wish you wouldn't invent things, just to make a fuss. You know perfectly well you're Papa's favourite – his "little miracle" – the fairy princess who used to sit on his knee and play with the braid on his uniform coat.'

Sophie sniffed, and tugged at a blonde curl. They'd cut off her hair, all those years before, when she'd tossed and shivered in the grip of fever, racked by the delirium of pneumonia. The Major had been certain the tiny life was lost, and declared it a miracle when she recovered. Ever since, he'd feared for Sophie's health, writing home from campaigns to enquire whether she was eating enough, and keeping herself warm, and being preserved from 'disturbance' – by which he meant being given her own way whenever possible.

'I want to go to Hampshire with Grandpapa,' she insisted now. 'I want to live with him at Chillbourne.'

Crossly, Flora twisted the button on the big bolster until it slipped through her fingers and wriggled back into place. 'The General only asked for me because of some silly thing he remembered from the old days at Richmond, when I was playing at being a soldier. He hasn't set eyes on me for more than three years, so he can't have the least idea what I'm like.'

'He set eyes on me yesterday afternoon,' retorted Sophie, 'yet he still asked for you. So did Grandmamma, even though I curtseyed like anything and asked if her rheumatism was better.'

'Oh, Sophie, do stop this nonsense. I've no patience with you when you speak like this. Besides – I've told Mamma I don't want to go.' Flora pulled up her knees and hugged them.

'But you hate living in the city.' In her astonishment, Sophie forgot to be resentful. 'You've always said you couldn't wait to get away from here, and go off and explore the world.'

'The world,' agreed Flora readily. 'But not Hampshire.'

She gazed round the bare grey room whose single window looked out on the sooty wall of the adjoining building.

'It's true, I hated this place at first. I couldn't believe so many people lived packed in together, like rats in a barn . . . and there were so many beggars . . . and the boys running down the street behind the carriages, scraping up after the horses . . . and the gingerbread-seller with his filthy bandages and his little stove – and never a blink of sun from one day to the next. But now . . .' She frowned vaguely, unable to put her present feelings into words.

For two months the previous year she'd nursed a wild passion for the handsome young man who sold oranges at the corner of Fetter Lane. None of Constance St Serf's scolding had altered Flora's heart in the very least, but, in any case, her adoration had died a natural death with the end of the orange season; one day the young man had been there on his corner – and next day he'd gone, leaving Flora's life as empty as one of his own bitter orange-rinds. Yet a memory of the churning confusion he'd wrought in her heart had returned to disturb her.

'Anyway,' she added firmly to Sophie, 'I'd be like a bird in a cage, cooped up in Hampshire. I'd run away after a week.'

'Well, I think you're mad.' Morosely, Sophie traced a pattern on the floor with the toe of her shoe. 'I'd give years of my life to get out of this place! When Mamma said we were going to live in London, I thought she meant somewhere like Curzon Street, where Great-aunt Sybil lives – somewhere we'd give dances, and keep a carriage and a barouche for the park. I never dreamed she'd bring us to a broken-down corner like this!'

She gazed round the room, and shuddered.

'I hate the smallness of it, and the darkness, and the filthy smells – and Mamma and Papa having rows all the time. They never used to argue at Richmond.'

'I suppose it's been hard for them both, always being in debt and having to scrape by on so little. Mamma hates it, I know – and it upsets Papa to hear her complain. But what's done is done, and we must make the best of it.' Flora reached out a hand to touch her sister's shoulder, only to see her twist away.

'But it need never have happened!' All at once, Sophie's eyes blazed, and she wound her fingers together in her lap. 'Why couldn't Papa have done as Wellington told him, and given the order to fire on that horrid town? It was Bonaparte's fault if the people were killed, surely, not Papa's. And they could have surrendered, couldn't they? They could have opened the gates, and let the English soldiers go in.'

'They were trying to save their homes, Sophie,' murmured Flora, remembering the bailiffs' heavy tread on the stairs the day before.

18

'But Papa must have known what would happen if he disobeyed an order. He must have known what would happen to *us* – to you and me, and Mamma – and yet he didn't care. A pack of enemy Frenchmen mattered more to him than his own family.'

'It wasn't like that. I'm sure it wasn't.'

Yet how had it been? Even now, four years later, Flora understood very little of the events which had led to her father's disgrace.

Wellington himself had described the Major as 'a perfect soldier' – never one of those idle swells who lounged round parade-grounds under umbrellas, leaving the business of soldiering to their sergeants. As a young subaltern he'd insisted on staying, wounded, with his gun-battery at the battle of La Nivelle, and had been rewarded with a post on Wellington's staff when the Duke went to Paris as Ambassador in the autumn of 1814. In a year or two more, it seemed, nothing would stand between Edmund St Serf and high command; yet, not nine months later, he'd flatly refused to bring his guns to bear on the French town of Péronne, which had shut its gates in defiance of the victor of Waterloo.

Wellington had been on his way to Paris, and in no mood for delay. Péronne – known as *La Pucelle*, 'The Virgin' – was swiftly deflowered by the English Army, and the Major found himself under guard, awaiting court martial at his commander's pleasure.

General St Serf had written at once to Wellington on his son's behalf. The poor fellow was clearly ill; four years of Peninsular sun had addled his wits. But the prisoner refused to say a word in his own defence, except to insist there had been innocent civilians in Péronne, and it had been morally wrong to attack them.

A soldier's duty was to obey – not to think. The General had made this brutally clear as soon as his great black carriage could carry him up from Hampshire, but the Major refused to be intimidated. With his eyes fixed on some distant prospect beyond the window, he resolutely repeated his argument: there had been blameless women and children in Péronne *La Pucelle*, and it had been wrong to fire upon them.

'BOSH!' roared the General at the top of his voice. 'FRENCH women and children, dammit. The enemy, Edmund, or had you forgotten? Blast your eyes, you've made me the laughing-stock of England for a handful of Bonaparte's peasants.'

This time the Major turned his head, and regarded his father for a moment in angry silence. Then, without another word, he strode out of the room.

Flora, twelve years old at the time, knew only that Grandpapa had lost his temper and had suddenly made them poor. Papa would never inherit Chillbourne now, and worse still – his income from the St Serf estates had been cut off from that moment.

Yet Papa had come home safely, and could still be persuaded to make daisy-chains with his daughters in the garden, and to listen to the songs their governess had taught them, even if there were moments when Flora could sense his thoughts drifting away to a place where she couldn't follow.

But Major St Serf had been a soldier, never a man of business; and soon Flora's mother was forced to rise from her tea-table to take an interest in the family finances. She swiftly discovered that apart from her own small quarterly income, they consisted of nothing but debt.

The Major owed a great deal. He'd had a position to maintain in society, and like most men of any style, he'd done so largely on credit. It was good business for banks to encourage men with expectations to get into debt – and, of course, in the past there'd been the prospect of Chillbourne. Now, suddenly, everything was different. As soon as they heard of Major St Serf's disinheritance, Elder's Bank sold his notes-of-hand for a pittance to a Whitechapel attorney, and the hounding began.

The news spread – bringing the tailor, the wine merchant, the saddler, the hatter, the gunsmith and every tradesman within a radius of ten miles sprinting to the door with their reckonings, presenting them more and more offensively as time went by.

Yet with every passing day the Major retreated further into melancholia, until, in desperation, Constance held a sheaf of bills under her husband's nose and demanded to know how he meant to pay them. For several seconds he gazed at her, blank-eyed.

'You decide,' he said at last, and turned back to the fire.

Constance set her jaw, and decided. The house in Richmond had been mortgaged, and the bank had already ordered its sale: now the travelling-chaise disappeared, and the carriage-horses, and the powdered coachman who'd sat on the box, and the knife-boy and the gardeners, until at last the family retreated to six shabby rooms on the first floor of the crumbling house in Gough Square, barely a rat-scuttle away from the busy traffic of Fleet Street.

Now there was only one servant left – steadfast Maggie, who swept like a dervish, and cleaned the grates, and made up fires, and carried coals up the steep and winding stairs, fetched water-jugs and emptied slops, trimmed lamps, and carried plates down from the dining-room to be scoured in icy water in the green-veined stone sink in the kitchen.

For her father's sake, Flora had tried to accept their new life with a good grace, occupying her time with trips to the bake-house or to the laundrywoman who starched the Major's neckcloths at a penny for six. But Sophie would never go with her, claiming that it tired her to walk so far on the uneven cobbles.

'Sophie may stay with me,' the Major would insist, stretching out a thin hand to his favourite. 'You know she isn't strong, Flora.'

'Yes, Papa.' And Flora would set off dutifully into the echoing lanes, telling herself it was only fair that Sophie should be indulged and cosseted: goodness only knew what might become of her sister's fragile health if she were made to do something she disliked.

And now, most of all, Sophie wanted to live at Chillbourne.

'I can't imagine why you don't want to go away with Grandpapa,' she told Flora for the twentieth time. 'I'd have gone with him at once, if he'd ever thought of asking me.'

'No, you wouldn't, Sophie. Papa would die of unhappiness if you left him – you know that.'

'I *would* have gone!' Sophie muttered resentfully. 'I know I shall only get ill again, if I have to stay here for much longer. The soles are almost out of my black satin slippers from going up and down the stone stairs – and yesterday's milk was quite blue because they water it so much here. Ismene-Maria thought so too.'

Ismene-Maria was Sophie's doll, another Sophie in every way, who suffered as Sophie did and shared her guiltiest longings, confided in whispers after dark in the furthest corner of the bed they both shared with Flora.

It wasn't as if Ismene-Maria was especially lovable. She had a round, pinched wooden head, accusing eyes, and eyebrows which were no more than a whisker-stroke. Her angular wooden limbs were jointed with unyielding leather, yet as often as not Ismene-Maria was the only one to hear a word from Sophie during her dreadful week-long sulks, the only creature in a pitiless world who'd never betrayed her.

'Ismene-Maria would like it in Hampshire,' said Sophie with conviction.

In vain, Flora pleaded Sophie's case with her mother. The country air would be good for her sister's health; Sophie was neat and domestic, while she was a dreamer; Sophie loved fine clothes, while Flora didn't care about fashion; and above all, Sophie longed to go to Chillbourne, while she, Flora, could hardly bear the thought of the place.

In his chair by the fire, she heard her father draw in his breath with a hiss of alarm. In her despair she'd forgotten he was there, let alone that he might be listening.

'Sophie's too young,' he said with sudden vehemence. 'Be guided by your mother, Flora.'

At two o'clock on the afternoon appointed for Flora's departure, she dragged her small leather trunk with her cipher *F. E. L. deM. StS.* on the lid out into the hall for her mother's inspection. These days Flora's wardrobe only half-filled its camphor-smelling interior, lined with marbled paper.

'So little . . .' Constance St Serf frowned down at the empty space which remained. 'Still – I dare say it's all to the good, since your grandmother will feel obliged to make up any deficiencies.'

'Oh, Mamma—' Flora burst out suddenly, 'it still isn't too late to let Sophie go to Chillbourne instead of me.' She reached out, trying to capture her mother's hand. 'I want so much to stay here – and Sophie is so desperate to go.'

Constance St Serf whisked her fingers out of her daughter's reach.

'Don't argue with me, Flora. My goodness, girl – the General's offering you the kind of opportunity most young women would die for. Now, call Maggie to fasten your trunk, and then go and tidy yourself up. Your grandfather will be here at three, and you know how he hates to be kept waiting.'

Flora frowned at herself in the looking-glass as she tied on her bonnet. Now that the time for departure had almost arrived, her removal from Gough Square seemed horribly final and irrevocable. If she ever returned, it would no doubt only be under the eagle eye of her grandparents: she'd probably never again see the two secret friends who'd made her life there bearable – Lydia Seaward and Achille Dédalon, the automaton-maker of Shoe Lane.

She'd sent Dédalon a note of farewell by way of Lydia, but now that the moment for leaving was almost at hand, the scrap of paper seemed poor thanks for all his kindness. With half an hour to spare before her grandfather's arrival, Flora slipped out of the house and ran quickly through the alleys to Shoe Lane. At that hour she was certain of finding the automaton-maker busy at his bench, and Lydia settled on his shabby sofa, stretched out in a mass of flounced muslin, her cupid's mouth full of sweetmeats and the grossest gossip of the gutters.

No child could pass Dédalon's window without stopping to stare at the miraculous clockwork conjuror which advertised his trade. Even at rest in his bower of roses, the masked harlequin was a wonder to behold. But when the key was wound – oh, magic – the moon-pale face swayed like a flower and the tragic eyes swung round, while two slender hands began to flourish shells above the velvet-covered table.

Voilà! – a half-sovereign was revealed. *Voyez!* – the coin had miraculously changed places, only to become a Moor's grinning head a moment later, and then to vanish again altogether, leaving the table empty and the harlequin nodding with satisfaction at his own cleverness.

Dédalon had fled from Paris, he'd told Lydia, to save himself from the vengeance of the '*miquelets*', the royalist gangs who'd emerged after Waterloo to hunt down Bonapartists and liberals. Not, he insisted, that he'd been a Bonapartist – at least, not after Bonaparte had allowed his armies to terrorize the poor countryfolk of Europe. Dédalon was an *automatiste*, a maker of mechanisms, a creator of illusions . . .

'A winder-up of dreams,' Lydia had declared astutely, presenting him to Flora like a Moor's head she'd just conjured up herself.

At first, Flora had felt awkward in Dédalon's presence. It was all very well for Lydia to haunt his workshop in Shoe Lane: the automaton-maker neither judged her nor desired her, which was unique in Lydia's experience of men, and though she didn't understand a tenth of his 'fancy philosophizing', she adored the sound of his rich French consonants rumpling the English language, and let the rest flow over her head.

Flora was less confiding by nature, and yet from that first meeting Dédalon had taken such kindly interest in her that before long she'd found herself chatting to him like a life-long friend.

*

Someone had wound up the clockwork conjuror. As Flora pushed open the door, his sleepwalker's face turned for a moment towards her, the eyes as blank as her father's under a bower of dusty roses.

'Sweetness! And don't you look smart!' From the gloom of the workshop Flora heard Lydia's voice, and tugged self-consciously at the strings of her old white satin bonnet. If the bonnet looked at all trim, it was a trick of the firelight, like everything else in that cave of chimeras.

Disconcerted, she peered into the darkness, at first seeing only the two points of light – the fire, and a deepset, murky little window in the opposite wall, over the bench where Dédalon carried out his most intricate work. Round the hearth, the firelight flickered on a carpet of wood shavings and torn paper and scraps of leather soaked in stinking glue, where the flesh of Dédalon's creatures emerged from moulds of papier mâché *cartonnage*.

As her eyes became accustomed to the gloom, she saw the giant scissors which dangled their legs from the roof-beams, and the sheaves of iron wire hanging like drying herbs; on the walls, ranks of pincers and gouges emerged from the shadows, and on the bench, a skeletal torso stood impaled on a spike, its single tiny hand reaching out beseechingly for nothing at all.

Dédalon glanced up from his work, his head on one side, as full of fierce life as one of the dusky crows among the chimney-pots.

'Flora! But I thought you'd left us.' His domed temples gleamed in the silvery dimness of the window: unfashionably, Dédalon kept his thinning black hair dragged back and tied with a scrap of string at the nape of his neck, where it dangled over the waistcoat which served him for an apron. Somehow it made him seem smaller than he was – stooped forward until his head was no higher than Flora's, except when he perched on the tall stool at his bench. She'd never dared to ask his age: older than Papa, certainly, but still not as old as the General.

The thought of her grandfather brought her back abruptly to the present.

'I'll soon be gone,' she said. 'Very soon.' She sank down on the end of the sofa where Lydia had drawn up her feet to make room. 'My grandfather will be here in half an hour, but I couldn't go without saying a proper goodbye. I can't bear to think I may never see either of you again.'

'Well, then – run away!' declared Lydia recklessly. 'Become an independent woman like me—'

'Listen to our Semiramis!' The automaton-maker's voice rasped like one of his own metal files. 'Look at her, cold-hearted beauty that she is! Could the Assyrian queen have looked any sweeter, as she sent her husbands to their deaths? Those eyes promise everything – even eternity – but observe that firm little chin. Madame Lydia could make a man bleed if it suited her.' He cocked his head to the opposite side, considering the effect. 'If only I could make a face like that, here at my bench . . .'

'Oh rot you, Dédalon, you disgusting old man!' Lydia pretended to be indignant. 'I'm the mildest of creatures – Flora will tell you.'

'Mild as vitriol,' agreed the automaton-maker. 'Come then, clever Semiramis – surely you can think of a respectable way of keeping Flora here in London with us?'

'You said your sister would gladly go to the country in your place,' Lydia reminded her.

'Mamma won't hear of it.' Restlessly, Flora rose and walked towards the fire. 'It's all so stupid!' she burst out. 'Here I am, desperate to stay, while Sophie's longing to go – and yet we're both going to be made miserable.'

'And what does the gallant Major have to say about it all?' At his bench by the window, Dédalon kept his eyes on the spindle he'd been fitting to a metal plate, though his hands had become suddenly still. 'Always, you say *Mamma has decided*.'

Flora shrugged helplessly. 'Papa doesn't seem to be able to make any decisions.'

'What – none at all? Not even when it concerns his daughters' future?'

'He must be off his head!' declared Lydia flatly. 'Here's Flora about to be dragged off to the depths of the country, and he doesn't care!'

'I can't tell whether he cares or not.' Frowning, Flora examined her bonnet-strings. 'Though I'm sure he'd rather see me go than Sophie. Sophie has always been his favourite.'

'Not you, my dear?' The automaton-maker picked up his pincers once more. 'I'm surprised to hear that.'

'It's because Sophie was so ill.' Loyally, Flora rushed to excuse her father's preference. 'She almost died, you see, years ago, when she was hardly more than a baby. And ever since, he's worried that she might fall sick again. Not that she has,' she added truthfully.

'But don't you mind Sophie having all his attention?' Lydia wanted to know.

'Sometimes I do.' Flora stared down at the rubbish-strewn floor. 'Though Sophie was very ill, you know, and I daresay it's left her weakened.'

'Ah . . .' Dédalon laid down his pincers and turned back towards Flora, knotting his fingers between his knees. 'And if your grandfather suddenly changed his mind and decided to take Sophie off to the country with him . . . How would her papa feel then?'

Flora frowned again. 'He'd be wretchedly miserable, I should think.'

'Sad at losing his pet,' murmured the automaton-maker. 'As sad as I'd be if I lost my Solomon.'

He'd raised his voice a little as he spoke the name, and immediately the shadows by the hearth were disturbed by a swift scrabbling followed by the light rattle of a chain. With the suddenness of a gunshot, a small, thunder-coloured monkey leaped up to crouch on the lid of an old chest, his pale fur cowl creamy in the firelight under a black skull-cap of hair.

'Solomon, you demon—' Dédalon snapped his fingers. 'Can you hear your name in your sleep, then?'

For a moment, the monkey surveyed Flora with bright, resentful eyes.

'Che-e-e-eet!'

'Solomon, Solomon – *que tu es méchant!*' Dédalon wagged a finger in the animal's direction. '*Voilà la "sagesse de Salomon",*' he added reprovingly. '*Mais, c'est Flora! C'est notre amie, tu sais.*'

The monkey continued his implacable stare.

'It's the bonnet, you understand. He doesn't know it.'

Flora untied the ribbons and squatted down, letting the white satin bonnet dangle back from her shoulders. Cautiously, Solomon reached out to lay a dusky knuckle against Flora's cheek.

'There you are, silly boy. You knew me all the time, didn't you?'

Flora held out her arms, and the monkey sprang up to cling contentedly round her neck, curling his tail over her wrist as if she were a tree which had obligingly welcomed him into its branches. His fur gave off an earthy, bitter smell which was strong but not unduly unpleasant.

From the sofa, Lydia Seaward regarded the transaction with distaste.

'I don't know how you can bear to touch that dirty animal. I've seen him scratching away in his corner there. He must be alive with vermin.'

'I've seen you scratch too, my little queen.' Dédalon's glare was as implacable as the monkey's. 'If you want to know, I'd sooner share a bed with Solomon.'

'Well, that's one choice you'll never have to make.' Crossly, Lydia spread her skirts over the toes of her shoes.

The monkey hooted softly at Flora's ear, ribbing his pale, fuzzy brow in an expression of mild astonishment which changed in an instant to a furious scowl as if some long-standing grievance had entered his mind.

'Do you know, Solomon, I believe you have a look of the General.' Flora reached up to rub gently at the quizzical head. 'He has silvery fur, just like yours – and he scowls exactly as you're doing now. If your eyes weren't quite so dark . . .'

'They might be cousins,' Dédalon finished for her. 'And why not? Why is it so hard to imagine a tribe of man-monkeys, when the world was young, who first learned to walk on two legs, and then went on to give birth to you and me?'

From the sofa, Lydia snorted in derision. 'My dear Dédalon, the Bible says clearly that men were made men, and monkeys were made monkeys. That's good enough for me, no matter what your clever French philosophers may think.'

'And yet,' persisted the automaton-maker, 'if I were to take away the ape's hairy skin, would he look so different from Flora's grandfather without his?'

'Dédalon, you're altogether revolting,' complained Lydia. 'How can you talk of skinning people like that?'

'Because it makes us all the same.' The automaton-maker spread his hands. 'Take away the silks and jewels and dressed hair, and who can tell the crossing-sweeper from the general?'

'Or take away their heads,' crowed Lydia. 'That's what you Frenchmen do when you start talking about *equality*.'

'It was done,' the automaton-maker admitted softly. 'The guillotine made us all the same in the end.'

'Even your King and Queen.'

'To prove they were no different from the rest,' repeated Flora dutifully. 'Isn't that what you always say?'

The automaton-maker smiled. 'You've learned your lesson well, my little republican.'

'My grandfather would have a fit, if he could hear us.' Flora continued to scratch the monkey's head with an exploratory finger. 'Grandpapa would tell you that God made men to be masters of animals and women, and kings to be masters of men. And then God made my grandfather a general, because Grandpapa knows what's best for everyone else.' She sighed heavily. 'And now Grandpapa's decided to make me a lady, by all accounts. It's just as well he can't see me at this moment.'

Dédalon turned suddenly to fix Flora with his curious lopsided stare.

'Is it? Are you so sure of that?'

CHAPTER TWO

I

It was past three o'clock by the time Flora appeared again in Gough Square, hurrying a little awkwardly with her hands folded over a bosom grown curiously stout.

The General had already arrived; his great black carriage had once more managed to squeeze itself into the square, no doubt at the instant his watch rang three. Flora quickened her pace. Behind the grimy first-floor windows Constance St Serf would be searching for her daughter, her lips drawn up like a buttonhole and her eyes hard with annoyance.

Yet half-way to her door Flora halted, her errand completely forgotten and her mouth sagging open in dismay. At that very moment, not twenty yards away, a vigorous male back was disappearing into the gloomy gully of Bolt Court, intent on reaching Fleet Street.

Flora's heart began to flutter like a captive finch. She knew that back: she knew its front even better, and for a few startled seconds she gaped after the departing Mr Smith, astonished at the turmoil the mere sight of the man had set up inside her.

Lydia had been right: Mr Smith had made it his business to cross Gough Square once more, with that confident stride of his. And with her heart still thudding in time to his retreating footsteps, Flora began to wonder how much it had mattered to her, to be there to see him when she did. One thing was certain – there would be no Mr Smith in Hampshire.

With renewed courage she set off for the ordeal ahead.

Upstairs in the drawing-room, Constance St Serf sat with her back to the door, her shoulders rigid and her face precisely to the front. Flora read the signs at once: her mother was agitated, angrily aware that the Major had pulled his armchair right up to the fire as if nothing which went on in the room that day could be of the slightest interest to him.

At the far side of the table, his parents had commandeered the only two gilt beechwood chairs to have survived the move from Richmond. General St Serf sat on one, massively square in his blue wool coat and old-fashioned breeches, his chin thrust out like a military ram, his silver soldier's whiskers foaming over his no-nonsense neckcloth. Next to him sat his wife, shiny in brown silk and an immense bonnet of pink *gros de Naples* trimmed with blonde lace and foxtail feathers.

The General's expression indicated a man as unbending in spirit as he was in the flesh – and proud of it, too. Heart-searching and shilly-shallying were the weaknesses of poets and book-writers. Firmness maketh the man, and a firm man, thank heaven, made an iron-bound wife. Individually, General and Mrs St Serf were formidable: in battle order they were more than enough to destroy a desperate daughter-in-law trying to make up for the intransigence of her husband.

'Ah! And about time too!' The General saw the door open, and scowled across the table. 'Well, Flora, this is a poor beginning, I must say. A poor beginning.'

Beside him, his wife's brows met in a frown. Admittedly, Mrs General St Serf hadn't set eyes on her elder granddaughter for several years, but she remembered Flora as being a slight little creature with too much of the polecat about her to give hope of a fashionable embonpoint. There'd certainly been no hint of the remarkable bosom which was now straining the fastenings of her granddaughter's mantle.

'Come in, child! Don't dither in the doorway!' Constance St Serf resisted the temptation to look round. 'Where in the world have you been?' she hissed out of the corner of her mouth, her gaze still fixed brightly on the General.

'I had to say goodbye to a friend.' Flora advanced into the room and waited behind her mother's chair, uncomfortably aware of her grandmother's eyes suspiciously probing her chest. Self-consciously, she clasped her hands across it. The General was still glowering like a model for the Wrath of God, and for the first time Flora began to doubt the wisdom of the plan which had seemed so splendid not five minutes before. Determinedly, she fixed her mind on a vision of Mr Smith, coolly gallant in his elegant coat: surely such a man must eat generals for breakfast.

'I told you most particularly not to keep your grandparents waiting.' Constance St Serf's voice was thin and clear. 'If I told her once, General, I'm sure I told her a hundred times. "Whatever you do," I said, "don't keep—"'

'To small effect, it seems.' The General swayed a little in his chair, and Flora distinctly heard his corset creak. 'Her behaviour will have to change.'

'Writing to her friends will do perfectly well,' agreed Constance.

'In moderation,' growled the General. 'If her friends are suitable and her letters are short. Long letters are a sign of a flighty mind. Say what you want, and have done with it.'

'*Just* what I always say! Isn't that so, Edmund?' Covertly, Constance kicked the back of her husband's chair, only to be met with resolute silence.

To fill the vacuum Constance smiled sweetly at the General, while Flora glanced quickly round the room for Sophie. To her dismay, she realized that her younger sister was probably still sulking in their bedroom. This was an unforeseen difficulty: Sophie was an important part of her plan, and, to make matters worse, Flora had begun to feel her bosom wriggle alarmingly.

'Do you know your catechism, child?' demanded the General suddenly.

'I believe so, Grandpapa.' Under cover of coughing, Flora tightened her hold on her mantle.

'Then tell me, child – what should be the fruit of the spirit?'

'Love, joy, peace,' began Flora automatically, 'long-suffering, gentleness, goodness, faith, meekness and temperance, Grandpapa.'

'I'm pleased to hear you say so.' The General combed his whiskers with the tips of his blunt fingers. 'And punctuality, my girl – add that to your list – and submission to the guidance of your future husband, which is God's judgement on women for being first in transgression—'

From the far side of the table, Mrs General St Serf had continued to watch her granddaughter's chest intently, moving to the very edge of her chair and raising the lorgnette which hung on a chain round her neck. In her vast pink bonnet she looked like a curious oyster, with the foxtail feathers nodding like weed on its shell.

After a moment or two, while Flora's attention was fixed on the General, a small, dusky hand with lithe, intelligent fingers slid from the overlap of her mantle and began to tug at the nearest button.

'General—' said his wife sharply.

'You will write to your mother each Sunday,' the General rumbled on, 'and to your father, if you think it's necessary.' He glared at the

Major's chair-back. 'Madam—' Constance snapped to attention in her seat. 'Kindly inform my son that Flora will only be permitted to visit this house when her grandmother and I judge it appropriate, and not otherwise.'

'General—' his wife interrupted again.

'Let him understand—'

'Understand . . .' repeated Constance, nodding and frowning with the effort of transmission.

'I do not intend the benefits of Chillbourne to be squandered by frequent visits to such a neighbourhood as this. Or by allowing Flora to spend time in her father's company. Edmund is clearly unbalanced. Goodness knows what ideas he's put into her head as it is.'

'Goodness knows . . .' Constance repeated vaguely, her brow furrowed even more. 'Are you saying, General, that you wish to have sole control of Flora?'

'Once she leaves this house, Constance, I intend that Flora shall be my child in all respects. I shall feed her, clothe her, and bear the considerable expense of raising her. You will be entirely relieved of the burden of a daughter. Surely you don't expect to have the direction of her upbringing as well?'

'Well – no. No, of course not . . .' Constance glanced quickly at her husband.

'Heaven knows,' growled the General, 'I tried to do my best for Edmund.' He paused impressively and extended his gloved hands, resting on the gold knob of his cane. 'I bought him his commission – I gave him a generous allowance – and he flung it all back in my face.' The General raised his voice, to be sure the Major would hear. 'Flung it all back in my face, he did, damn his eyes!'

'I'm sure he would thank you most humbly for it *now*,' said Constance hastily, 'if you were to offer it to him again.'

Seven inches below Flora's chin, slender grey-pink fingers had at last succeeded in easing their button from its hole, watched in utter disbelief from under the pink bonnet. Just as the General drew breath to pronounce upon the question of restoring the all-important allowance, a creamy little head capped in black popped out of the front of Flora's mantle, and a curious pale face stared round the room.

Mrs General St Serf lurched back in her chair with a shriek. Too late, Flora made a grab for the bosom of her mantle, where Solomon, like a dark demon, was wriggling free to explore his new surroundings. This wasn't at all what Flora had planned: a glimpse of her 'pet' at the right moment would have been more than enough – but

Solomon had ideas of his own. Taking Flora's chest for a springboard, he leaped for the table, landing on all fours among the Madeira glasses under the astounded eyes of the General and his wife.

'Take it away!' shouted Grandmamma St Serf, lashing out at the incubus with her gloved hands. Half rising, the General tried to sweep Solomon from the table with his cane, but only succeeded in hurling Flora's mother from her chair and sending her scrambling to the questionable safety of her husband's side.

Crouched like a giant insect among the rolling glasses, the monkey let out a series of terrified screams.

'Don't hurt him! He doesn't mean any harm.' Plunging forward, Flora thrust the cane aside and snatched at the end of the animal's chain. With another angry screech Solomon leaped for the tall pole-screen, sending it crashing down as he flew on to a perilous foothold on the chimneypiece. From the chimneypiece he sprang to a nearby dumb-waiter, and from there – by skipping nimbly along the back of Mrs General St Serf's chair – to the heavy brocade curtains, plucking a handful of pink foxtail feathers as he passed.

The General was on his feet now, thrashing his cane and bellowing, 'Hold him! Seize him there, I say!'

Flora ran to the curtains and shook them gently, calling 'Solomon – it's me, Flora. Do come down.' But her pleas were ignored. Solomon, his bright black eyes fixed on the cane in the General's hand, simply retreated to the curtain-rail, from where he scolded his pursuers in a series of ear-splitting screams and flung pink feathers at the General's head.

'Oh, please leave him alone.' Flora tried to squeeze between her grandfather and his quarry. 'Can't you see he's frightened?'

The General snorted and pushed her aside. 'I shall deal with you, my girl, when I've finished with this vermin you've brought in. Constance – send down for my pistols. I'll shoot the creature.' In a hail of pink feathers, he jabbed at the curtain.

'No! You mustn't shoot him.'

The General wheeled round. 'Edmund!' he roared. 'Will you take this confounded child out of my way? Your mother's been attacked by a wild beast, and now I'm being told what to do by an impudent girl.'

A sudden silence fell as the General realized that in the excitement of the moment he'd spoken directly to his son for the first time in four years.

'Constance,' he blustered, 'send down at once for my pistols.'

But Constance was crouching at the Major's elbow. 'Edmund, do *something*, for pity's sake!'

Very slowly, the Major leaned over the arm of his chair, and surveyed the room. His gaze swept down towards his wife.

'Tell my father that if he leaves the animal alone, it may well leave him alone too.' Without another word, he turned back to the fire.

'Hah!' shouted the General, vindicated. 'I might have known Edmund would have some milk-and-water suggestion to make. Frenchmen and monkeys get off scot-free, in Major St Serf's book. Dammit, Adelaide, how did I ever come to sire such a spineless runt of a creature?'

At that moment the door opened and Sophie walked into the room, the picture of flower-like innocence with her hair loose and childish laced slippers on her feet.

'Hrrmph.' The General cleared his throat and lowered his cane, tapping it noisily on the floor.

'Why, Sophie!' exclaimed her mother, struggling to her feet.

Grandmamma St Serf looked up from her inspection of the ruined bonnet to peer at the newcomer.

'Remind me of who you are.'

'I'm Sophia, Grandmamma.' Sophie's guileless gaze flicked round the room. The General was angry – angry with Flora and her parents, no doubt; the fact that there was a monkey on the curtain-rail, warily watching all that went on, was most probably something to do with Flora and the odd friends she kept sneaking off to see. If Sophie was at all surprised by the situation, she was astute enough not to show it.

'Ah – Sophia.' Mrs General St Serf examined her second granddaughter through her lorgnette, and then turned to glare fiercely at Flora. 'The *younger* sister.' Majestically, she returned to Sophie. 'You do not also keep wild animals hidden in your clothing, I hope?'

'No, Grandmamma.'

'The monkey does not belong to Flora—' Mrs St Serf put in feebly. 'We would never permit—'

'Your daughter's pet has utterly ruined my bonnet!' Mrs General St Serf held out the spoiled brim for inspection. 'Do you see what the brute has done?'

Sophie was already by her grandmother's side.

'How dreadful!' She reached out a dainty hand and stroked the tattered brim like an injured bird. 'And how upsetting for you, Grandmamma.'

34

'You'd like that, would you?'

'More than anything, Grandpapa.'

'Well, then, it's decided.' Firmly, Mrs General St Serf tied the ribbons of her bonnet. 'Edmund, we shall take Sophia. Clearly, we should have chosen her in the first place. How long will it take you to pack your belongings, child?'

'Not long, Grandmamma. Not long at all, and I'll start directly.'

'No.' The Major's voice cut through the commotion like a pistol-shot, turning all heads towards him. Pale and drawn, he leaned forward in his chair to stare at his younger daughter. 'No,' he repeated. 'You shan't take Sophie.'

'But, Papa!'

'Sophie is too young to leave her mother.' With painful dignity, the Major rose to his feet. 'And her health is fragile.'

'But, Edmund!' Constance was frantic with despair. 'Sophie wishes to live at Chillbourne – I know she does. And it would be such a benefit to her.'

'I do not wish her to go.'

'But I *must* go with Grandpapa and Grandmamma,' cried Sophie desperately.

'Your daughter seems to know where her best interests lie,' observed the General, his composure restored. His chin thrust forward once more, bristling his whiskers.

'Sophie!' murmured the Major reproachfully.

'I want to live with Grandpapa and Grandmamma.'

'Even your children wish to leave you, it seems.' The General stuck out his corseted chest.

'That isn't true!' At last Flora found her voice. 'We both love Papa, whatever he's done.'

'Silence, miss!' snapped the General at once. 'No one wants your opinion. You've done enough damage for one afternoon.'

'I'll deal with you later, Flora.' Constance shot her daughter a ferocious glance.

'I want to live at Chillbourne in future,' Sophie repeated doggedly. 'I don't want to live here any more.'

'I won't permit you to go.' The Major's face was grey, except for the blanched white rims of his nostrils. 'You're too young and too delicate to leave home.'

'Nonsense—' the General interrupted him. 'Everyone knows that pure country air is by far the best thing for a weak constitution. And besides . . . there could be other benefits to my taking Sophia.'

A crafty expression had appeared on the General's face; he swung his cane experimentally between his finger and thumb, and regarded Constance with thoughtful care. 'In addition to providing Sophia with an excellent and health-giving home, I would also be prepared to clear your debt at Elder's Bank. You owe them five thousand pounds, I believe.'

'Five thousand and forty-six,' Constance corrected him hastily.

'Five thousand and forty-six pounds, then . . .' proposed the General in a voice like spider-silk, 'on condition Sophia comes to live with me at Chillbourne.'

'I do not sell my children,' snapped the Major.

'You were ready to give the other girl away gratis.'

'Flora is . . . older.' The Major avoided Flora's eye.

'But Edmund,' wheedled Constance, 'if Sophie really wants to go . . . would you stand in her way?' She laid a dimpled hand on her husband's arm. 'I know how fond you are of Sophie – of course I do – but that should make you all the more anxious to do what's best for the dear child . . . And just imagine the relief of not being in debt to the Elders any more!'

'I believe I should be happy at Chillbourne,' said Sophie softly.

Major St Serf gazed at his younger daughter in bewilderment.

'But, my dear – aren't you happy here with me?'

'No, Papa. Not any more.' Sophie stared at her feet, her shoulders tense with the effort of betrayal.

'Oh, Sophie . . .' murmured Flora. All at once the Major looked so lost that she longed to run to him and throw her arms round his neck. 'Sophie . . .' she repeated instead. 'How can you say such things?'

'Because they're true! Aren't we always supposed to tell the truth?'

'Tell the truth, and shame the devil!' barked the General exultantly. 'Well, Edmund? Did you hear what your daughter said?'

'I heard what she said.' The Major's voice had dwindled to a whisper. He turned away towards the chimneypiece, but his body proclaimed a surrender to despair. 'If that's what Sophie wishes, then I suppose she must go.'

'Oh, Edmund, thank you!' Constance St Serf clapped her hands with relief. 'Sophie – did you hear? What a blessing, what a godsend! And you'll pay off our debt at the bank, General, did you say? Five thousand and forty-six pounds, if you remember . . .'

'You shall have a draft on my own bank in the morning.'

'Edmund, did you hear that? The General has been so generous – so generous! Say what you will, one can always rely on family in a crisis. Though Sophie will miss us, I'm sure . . .'

She glanced round, but Sophie had already fled from the room – no doubt, thought Flora, to share the wonderful news with Ismene-Maria.

It took Sophie no more than a few minutes to transfer her meticulous store of clothing and shoes to a trunk for the journey to Hampshire. When she came downstairs in bonnet and cloak, her face was luminous with joy, and her radiant smile never faltered as she said goodbye to her parents.

The Major bent gravely to have his cheek kissed, and let his hand linger for a moment on Sophie's golden head. A step away, Flora watched the parting, marvelling at the completeness with which a lifetime's bond had been broken. Sophie's farewell to her father was as brief and formal as her leave-taking of poor Maggie, who sobbed into her apron at the top of the basement stairs.

'Goodbye, Flora! I'll write to tell you all about Chillbourne,' she promised, taking her sister's hand between her own cool palms. 'And you can tell me how you came to bring that perfectly *dreadful* animal into the house,' she added in a whisper. 'Did you mean this to happen? Oh, Flora, thank you! I promise from now on I'll be really, really happy. I'll never forget what you did for me today.'

As the wheels of the black coach ground ponderously out of the square, Flora tried to stifle a sense of unease. She should have been happy: Sophie was going to Chillbourne, and she was not. Yet she couldn't help feeling that more mischief had been done that day than she had ever intended.

2

Solomon had come down from the curtain-rail by the time Flora returned to the drawing-room. Finding the room empty, he'd descended to the table and was crouched there, draining the dregs of the General's Madeira, when Flora appeared in the doorway. He glanced up at once with the glass in his hands, caught in the act of dredging the lees with a bent finger.

'Don't be afraid, Solomon, it's only me.' Crossing cautiously to the table, Flora held out her arms, and, reassured by the sound of his name, Solomon leaped into them, dragging his tangled chain.

'There now – do you see?' Flora turned to face her mother, who'd followed her into the room. 'He's really very tame. If Grandmother hadn't screamed and frightened him, he'd never have run off like that.'

'The General's right – I believe you are mad.' Mrs St Serf edged into the room, her back against the wall. 'Keep the brute away from me. Look at his teeth. He'll fly at me if you let go of that chain – I can see it in his eyes.'

'You're being silly, Mamma. Come and scratch his head like this . . . See how he likes it?' The monkey had arched himself back against Flora's finger, his eyes half-shut and unfocused.

'I wouldn't dream of touching him.' Constance had reached the sanctuary of the fireplace, and her voice became stronger. 'You . . . wretched girl! I believe you planned this whole business from the very first. You brought that filthy creature into my house, insulted your grandmother and infuriated the General – just when I was trying to persuade him to restore Papa's money . . . And all for your own selfish purposes.'

'You'll have five thousand pounds tomorrow,' objected Flora. 'Isn't that a great deal of money?'

'But we *owe* a great deal of money!'

'Well, at least Papa will be able to pay his debts at the bank.'

'With thirty pieces of silver.' The Major appeared in the doorway, his face patched with resentful crimson. 'Well, Constance? Are you satisfied with your price? Was it a fair exchange, do you think, for my daughter?'

'You needn't glare at me like that!' shrilled his wife. 'Sophie went to Chillbourne of her own free will. Nobody made her go.'

Flora saw her the muscles of her father's jaw tighten in pain.

'You haven't the slightest notion of what you've done.' The Major's voice rose, angry and bitter. 'You heartless wretch, you've sold our daughter – sold her for a few pounds to buy off the bank.'

'I've done *something* – which is more than you've ever achieved,' snapped Constance, tears of rage springing to her eyes. 'I've managed to gain us a little time before we're thrown out on the street – and I've given one of our daughters, at least, some future to look forward to. And if it hadn't been for you and this selfish, obstinate girl here, I might have done even better!'

The Major opened his mouth to reply but closed it again in silence. As swiftly as it had come, his new resolve had withered away, destroyed by the fierceness of his wife's defiance and his new, aching loneliness.

'You still have me, Papa,' Flora reminded him gently. 'I know I'm not Sophie, but I'll try to take her place.'

'Flora . . .' Wearily, the Major pressed the hand she held out to him, and managed a grateful smile. 'Bless you for that, my dear.'

'And you needn't worry yourself about Sophie.' Briskly, Constance gathered up the scattered Madeira glasses. 'Sophie's quite clever enough to realize that the General will do far more for her than her own father could. You may call me all the names you like, Edmund, but what was I supposed to do? Do you want me to stand aside and see my daughters turned on to the streets to sell themselves for their bread?'

With a start, Constance remembered that one of those daughters was standing behind her, watching her mother in silent horror. Catching sight of the expression in Flora's eyes, she became savage.

'As for you, Flora – you'll stay in your room until I can bear to speak to you again, but first of all you'll take that filthy brute back to wherever it belongs. Where did you get it from, anyway?' she demanded. 'I don't know of any menagerie round here.'

'I borrowed him from . . . a friend.'

'Oh?' Her mother's eyes narrowed intently. 'What sort of friend keeps a wild beast in his house?'

'A Frenchman in Shoe Lane,' Flora admitted uneasily. 'He makes mechanical figures – clockwork people and animals, and singing birds that pop out of boxes. Solomon lives in his workshop.'

There was a sudden movement by the fire, where the Major, who'd flung himself down in his usual chair, leaned forward suddenly, his eyes devouring his daughter's face.

'A Frenchman, you say?'

'Yes, Papa.'

'And he makes birds that sing?' The Major's hands opened to release an invisible bird, then he shook his head dazedly. 'I knew of a man, once . . . in Paris. He worked for Breguet the watchmaker . . .'

Suddenly the Major's whole attention was fixed on Flora; fear had begun to gather in his eyes like thickening darkness, and when he spoke again his voice was barely above a whisper. 'What is his name, this maker of birds?'

'The man you knew in Paris?' Deliberately, Flora pretended to

41

misunderstand. 'You never told me his name, Papa, though I'm sure he must have been—'

'The man who owns the monkey!' The Major struck the arm of his chair. 'The Frenchman in Shoe Lane.'

'What does it matter?' demanded Constance. 'Flora will take the animal back, and that's the last time—'

'His name! Tell me his name.'

Silently cursing herself for her carelessness, Flora confessed, 'His name is Achille Dédalon, Papa.'

'Again.'

'Achille Dédalon.'

'Dédalon.' The Major repeated the name softly, testing the syllables as if their sound reassured him. 'It means nothing to me . . . You're certain that's his name?'

'There's a sign over his door. *Achille Dédalon, Automaton-maker*.'

The Major leaned back against his cushions, his eyes closed. 'It isn't the same man,' he murmured.

'Well, of course it isn't!' Constance shook her head in disgust. 'What's the matter, Papa? Are you ill?'

'No . . . I'm well enough. But for a moment I thought . . .' Without opening his eyes, the Major waved aside Flora's anxiety. 'Don't concern yourself, my dear. Old soldiers sometimes have these strange fancies.'

'I understand, Papa.'

Yet Flora didn't understand. If there was one thing she was sure of in all she'd seen that day – in her father's bloodless lips, and his face blue-shadowed like a frightened child's – it was that she didn't understand any of it.

42

CHAPTER THREE

I

Five thousand and forty-six pounds: the General's draft arrived at ten the next morning in the hand of a Coutts' messenger, and for the rest of the day Constance wore it in the bodice of her gown, relishing its dry chafing against her skin. As darkness fell she lit the candles early, rather than lose sight of its precious script, and the following morning, in a seedy broker's officer in Exeter 'Change, the magical paper was turned into gold and bills and banknotes infused with the tart smell of the menagerie on the floor below.

'Why should the Elders have my money?' Constance demanded of the elephant as she passed. 'Why should I let the Elders swallow it all as if it had never existed?'

The elephant curled his trunk and watched her through spiky lashes.

'If the Elders can wait for the Prince Regent's cash, they can wait for mine,' Constance concluded, stepping out, her head held high, into the streets of London.

For a few more days Constance St Serf was a lady with a sum of money at her disposal. Then, little by little, tradesmen began to nibble like ants at its edges. The coal merchant was paid and passed word of his windfall to the wine merchant, who sped round to Gough Square as fast as his legs would carry him. In less than an hour the good news had reached the silk mercer, the linen draper and the staymaker, who all presented their bills, until Constance found herself handing out sums to all and sundry – so much to the fishmonger, so much to the liveryman for stabling the Major's single remaining saddle-horse, so much for the rent . . . so much, so much.

But the bank could wait: that would teach the Elders to issue impertinent demands for their cash. It was far more important, reasoned Constance, to repay loans begged from friends, so that at last she could resume calling on former acquaintances, and look them once more in the eye.

Yet now she discovered, too late, that her hundred guineas borrowed here and there had brought with it a new coolness on the part of the lenders. A friend in need is an embarrassment; Constance St Serf might have repaid her debts, but her calls were not returned and no hostesses sent invitations to her rented rooms in Gough Square.

Before long Constance had learned a hard lesson: to lose sixty thousand at cards might be delightfully dashing, but to be short of twenty-five shillings for the rent was nothing less than social suicide.

Meanwhile, in the bed she'd shared for more than two years with her sister Sophie, Flora lay alone between the cold, much-darned linen sheets, and tried to believe matters had taken a turn for the better.

Five thousand and forty-six pounds: in a matter of minutes she'd seen a price offered and agreed, and a young woman change hands like a laying hen or a joint of beef. The enormity of it had stunned Flora, and the speed of it had taken her breath away. Could the paupers who sold their children for chimney-boys have made a faster bargain? Yet Sophie had wanted so desperately to go . . .

In her imagination Flora pictured Sophie's shoes arranged in a painstaking row at the bottom of an elegant japanned wardrobe, satin slippers to the left, coloured kid shoes to the right, their toes aligned to a whisker, laces in neat coils inside. By now Sophie would have a nightgown drawer and a stocking drawer, and another for caps, and a fourth for belts – for there must be endless drawers and cabinets at Chillbourne, though no starched maid would ever keep them as tidy as Sophie.

Flora and her sister had shared a maid at Richmond, a former nursery-maid who'd graduated with them from the boiled-milk-and-camphor-smelling world of the nursery. Mary had been eight years older than Flora, but for all that she was still a child in many ways, and there had been times when Flora, gravely watching Mary and Sophie giggling together over a stocking-toe puppet, felt she was by far the oldest of the three.

As long as Flora could remember, their young world had revolved around Sophie and her fragile health. Mary had been Sophie's slave, Papa her protector, Mamma her example, and Flora . . . her older sister, a solemn-eyed mystery, proof against both charm and tears.

Flora wasn't naturally withdrawn, but with the attention of the household given wholly to Sophie it had been easy to grow into the habit of silence. Yet there were certain advantages to life in her sister's shadow. People tended not to notice when Flora came and went, or to ask what she was thinking – or even to assume she should be thinking anything at all. But Flora thought a great deal, storing up everything she saw and heard, turning the memories over in quiet moments, trying to fit them together into the great puzzle of her life.

And now one large piece of it had been carried off suddenly to Chillbourne.

Sophie's first letter arrived a fortnight after she'd left Gough Square, and her mother pounced on it at once. Constance still smarted from being dropped by her former friends, and saw Sophie as her last remaining hope of keeping a toehold in society.

'"Dearest Mamma,"' Constance read aloud, '"I am well." Well, I should think so, too,' she grumbled. 'London is the place for fevers, not Hampshire!'

'Go on, Mamma – please.'

'"The weather at Chillbourne has been fine, but cold,"' Constance continued, '"though of course, we have very big fires in all the rooms, and Grandpapa employs three men just to cut wood and bring it to the house."'

Constance halted for a moment, glancing enviously at her own small grate.

'"I have the most charming room you can imagine,"' she read on at last, '"much bigger than my old room at Richmond, with a view over the lake and the little temple on the island. Grandpapa has engaged a governess for me, Miss Meagle, whose papa is rector of an important church in Worcester. Miss Meagle plays well, especially hymns, and so Grandpapa has ordered a pianoforte for the breakfast-room so that Miss Meagle and I may practise. He was surprised to hear I had never been made to try."'

'And be asked to play for all the dances?' her mother demanded. 'And never be able to step out with a partner of her own?'

'She should be safe enough if she keeps to hymns.' Flora tried to examine Sophie's letter over her mother's shoulder. 'What else does she say?'

'"Tell Flora"', Constance continued reluctantly, '"that Grand-mamma has given me the prettiest leather work-box with brass mounts, all divided up inside and lined with quilted satin. Almost too elegant to use! She says I must now wear my hair up, though not in curls, and that my ribbons are sadly faded. Do you know, Grand-mamma gave twenty guineas for the bonnet Flora's monkey tore? I think I shall like living here.

45

'"I hope you and Papa and Flora are well. Your loving daughter, Sophie."'

Ten minutes later, Constance St Serf sped off to her milliner to buy several yards of mulberry and lavender ribbons, which she was assured were the colours absolutely à la mode, to send off in a packet to Chillbourne.

'Grandmamma said it was kind of you to send ribbons,' announced Sophie blithely in her next letter. 'She said it was a pity you had not sent better ones in the new Armonzeau, but that your circumstances had no doubt prevented it. However, it does not matter, since Grandmamma and I went up to London last week and bought a great deal at Shears' and Swan & Edgar, and at Nicholay's in Oxford Street who make her winter furs. So don't trouble to send more, Mamma, as I have all I want now, including a swansdown muff with a gold chain. Your loving daughter, Sophie.'

Mrs St Serf sat for a long time in silence after this, her lips gathered up tightly and her eyes studying the cheap 'Persian' floor-cloth at her feet.

'They came all the way to London,' she observed at last, 'and never called on us here!'

'I expect they'd no time for social calls,' suggested Flora hopefully.

'Yes, of course – I dare say you're right.' Constance brightened a little. 'I'd forgotten how long it takes to come up from Chillbourne. Assuredly, that's why they didn't call.'

2

Sophie, it seemed from her letters, had thoroughly enjoyed her first Christmas at Chillbourne.

'Can you imagine, the celebrations went on for almost three days! Uncle Greville St Serf came down from London with two fearfully dashing officers from his regiment and took me out to call on all the houses round about, where the ladies made a tremendous fuss of the handsome soldiers, as you can imagine. He has taught me to skate on the lake, and even persuaded Grandpapa to have an old sleigh brought out for rides round the park. Uncle Greville told me Grandpapa will give him anything at all, he has only to ask.'

'That's Greville's reward for treating the old man like God Almighty,' muttered Constance. 'Your uncle will do anything for money,' she added unthinkingly. 'It's quite disgusting.'

She returned to Sophie's letter. '"Grandmamma has given me a set of amber buckles cased in gold, and a beautiful Turkish pelisse with an ermine collar."'

For a moment, Constance dropped her hands to her lap, and the letter too. Then, with a great effort, she tried again.

'"Grandpapa gave me the dearest little rosewood writing-table, with ever so many compartments and a secret drawer—"'

Constance broke off with a cry and fled from the room, dropping the letter as she ran.

Three weeks went by before Sophie wrote again. Then a month passed, and as the spring of 1820 began to replace winter, her letters became shorter and less frequent. Before long she'd stopped asking about Flora and her parents, until her letters were no more than a list of where she'd been and whom she'd seen there, and whatever Grandpapa and Grandmamma had given her since her previous note.

At last, in May Sophie wrote to announce she would call – briefly, and with Grandmamma – on the following Tuesday afternoon, which happened to be her fifteenth birthday.

Constance plunged instantly into a frenzy of preparation.

She bought two pounds of the best beeswax candles in case the visit lasted into the evening. She purchased – for cash – a pound of fine pekoe and a boxful of dried fruit and nuts, dressed the nuts in silver paper leaves, rejected the result as vulgar in a china bowl, and flew out to buy a crystal sweetmeat glass to show them off to better advantage.

But overwashed fabrics look dull beside the sparkle of crystal, and so a new apron had to be bought for Maggie, not to be put on until two minutes before she served tea, plus a new turban for Constance in striped silver gauze with a feather, a new muslin handkerchief for Flora's neck and gloves for the Major.

In the event, Sophie and her grandmother spent a total of twenty minutes in Gough Square, including the time they took to pass through the dirty wainscot of the hall and climb the stairs to the floor above. As soon as Sophie set foot in the house, Flora saw her glance this way and that, transfixed by a kind of furtive shock. *Did I really come from this?* her eyes demanded. *Was it as cramped and dark when I lived here? Did Mamma really look such a scarecrow, and Papa so tired and old?*

In the drawing-room she perched on the edge of a chair in her flounced muslin pelisse and dazzling O'Neill hat.

'You look so *well*, my love!' cried her mother, enraptured.

'Thank you, Mamma,' replied Sophie coolly, and Constance drew back her outstretched arms as if she'd touched a hot kettle.

The Major had made a point of rising early that day in order to shave and dress immaculately in honour of his daughter's visit. Flora had helped him straighten his cravat, realizing with a start how little care he'd taken with his appearance during the months since Sophie's departure.

However, today was different. Today the Major stood by the chimneypiece, devouring his younger daughter with his eyes.

'I hope you're keeping up your lessons, Sophie.'

'Sophia's studies are progressing satisfactorily.' Grandmamma St Serf inclined her head towards her granddaughter's. 'How shall a woman learn, Sophia?'

'"Let a woman learn in silence, with all subjection,"' recited Sophie at once. '"Suffer not a woman to teach, nor to usurp authority over a man, but to be in silence."'

'Quite so,' agreed the General's wife. 'Now give us something in French, Sophia.'

'*Mais oui, si vous voulez, Grandmère.*' Sophie took a breath. '"*Aide-toi,*"' she recited mechanically, '"*et le ciel t'aidera.*" God rewards honest endeavour.'

'*Très bien,* Sophia. That will do.'

'*Merci, Grandmère.*'

Constance's eyes gleamed. 'Sophie also plays the pianoforte now, I believe.'

'She plays tolerably.' Mrs General St Serf gazed round the little chamber. 'If you had an instrument, I'd ask her to play for you. But I see you don't.'

If she'd said 'no glass in the windows' Constance couldn't have been more mortified. 'We are . . . between pianofortes,' she explained quickly. 'Between our Richmond instrument and . . . the one which is to come.'

'No matter.' Grandmamma St Serf waved a dismissive hand. 'The improvement in Sophia is quite obvious. All that was required was

guidance. No doubt if you'd taken a stricter line with the other one—'
She glared across the room at Flora. 'We should not have had that
unpleasantness with the monkey.'

With an effort the Major rose to his feet, crossed the room, and
placed a hand on the back of Sophie's chair.

'Sophie—' he began.

'Yes, Papa?'

'Tell me – are you really happy at Chillbourne? I want to know
the truth, my dear. Don't be afraid.'

'Of course she's happy at Chillbourne!' snorted the General's
wife. 'Aren't you, Sophia?'

'Sophie, my child,' the Major persisted, leaning on the arm of her
chair. 'Are you quite certain you don't want to come home? Because
no one will make you stay at Chillbourne against your will. Not for a
moment.'

'Papa, I am truly happy at Chillbourne,' Sophie assured him. She
glanced apologetically towards her grandmother. 'Grandmamma and
Grandpapa have become like parents to me, and I have Uncle Greville
too, when he's at home.' Awkwardly, she reached out to touch her
father's frail hand, but pulled away at once when he tried to catch
hold of her fingers. 'You mustn't worry about me, Papa. I have
everything I could possibly want.'

After that, for the rest of the visit Sophie sat complacently on the
edge of her chair – exactly, it seemed to Flora, like Dédalon's
clockwork conjuror, waiting to be wound up again to show off her
accomplishments. Flora tried to take pleasure in her sister's obvious
happiness, but she couldn't blot out the sight of their father, still
standing by Sophie's chair with the quiet dignity of despair.

Had Sophie no sense of his pain? Didn't she care at all that the
person who'd loved her best in the world now waited at her side,
bereft and comfortless?

Constance had taken a small leather box from the drawer of her
work-table. She hesitated for a moment, stroking the familiar leather
between her fingers as if reluctant to let go of it.

'I've been keeping this for your birthday, Sophie dear.' With a
sudden movement she held out the box. 'I do hope you like it. My
mother wore it, and generations of Clantavish ladies before her. It's
quite an heirloom.'

Delicately, Sophie opened the box, and Grandmamma St Serf
inclined her head to gaze at the big silver brooch which lay inside.

'Very pretty,' observed the General's wife. 'My Scotch cook has one just like it.'

The next day Mrs St Serf went out and bought a Broadwood cabinet-pianoforte for forty-five guineas.

'I know I shouldn't have bought it!' she snapped when Flora protested. 'Who knows better than I do what we can and cannot afford? But what if Sophie calls again, and there's nothing for her to play on?'

Constance didn't dare to say more: for the truth was that Sophie was gone; her own pride was gone; and now the five thousand and forty-six pounds was gone too.

3

'I shall write to Scaurs,' Constance announced firmly. 'My brother has the castle now, after all – and the land, and the river-fishing. It's high time he put his hand in his pocket to help his sister in her time of need.'

'I'm sure Uncle Archibald will help,' Flora agreed, wishing she could say it with more conviction.

Constance never tired of recalling the brilliant assemblies of her Scottish girlhood, a glittering procession of beaux in silver buckles and feathered bonnets, and of silken ladies in sedans. Yet Flora suspected that if life at Scaurs had seemed lavish, it was only because the poor beyond the castle walls were very poor indeed. Uncle Archibald's tenants in the village of Strowie were said to scrape by on a diet of herrings, oatmeal and potatoes; to such people even a few hundred gold sovereigns must seem like the riches of Croesus.

Archibald Clantavish's reply, when it came, sent his sister to bed for three days.

Life at the Castle of Scaurs, complained the laird, had become a sorry business compared with the happy extravagance of their youth. Moreover, Archibald Clantavish had a daughter to dower and the estate to preserve for his heir – and altogether his finances were even more strained than the last time his sister had asked for a loan.

'To be blunt,' he added, 'if our father had known of the difficulties which lay ahead for me, I'm persuaded he'd never have left you a penny in settlement . . . For any sake, Constance, can your husband not restrain your spending? You were anxious enough to marry him, as I remember.

'I enclose a small matter of twenty-five pounds English . . .'

Now at last Constance was forced to think of Elder's Bank, whose letters she'd hidden for six months, unread, at the bottom of her work-table. The rent might have been paid and their other debts satisfied, but the Major's debt to the bank was as large as ever, and the coming months loomed ahead with no income but Constance's tiny allowance. Perhaps if she were to call on old Mr Elder himself, it might be possible to ask for a small sum on account . . .

Constance tied her best bonnet over her prettiest cambric cap and set off for Fleet Street, confident that if necessary she could charm an army of cashiers and Fair Cashbook Writers, and Keepers of the Bill Book and old Mr Elder himself into seeing the justice of her case.

'Flora – you will come with me as far as the Front Office.' In spite of her determination, Constance's voice was tense and shrill.

Flora had never been permitted to enter the bank before, and as she walked through the tiled lobby into the legendary Front Office of Elder's Bank she wondered if her mother felt as small and insignificant as she did.

She found herself in a room the size of a modest ballroom, but without the least hint of gaiety. Drab brown wainscot rose like a tidemark on walls of such mould-coloured dullness that the room seemed like a fish-tank. A mahogany counter faced the door; beyond it, on either side of a central aisle, ten slab-like brown desks were occupied by ten unsmiling men in black who raised their eyes towards her with the impassive stare of lizards.

Flora, left to wait on a hard wooden chair, stared back.

Gradually, she became conscious of a thin, dry stink hanging over the room, and after a second or two she recognized it as the smell of dirt and rank metal which clings to the palms after handling coins, a combination of brass and tobacco, liquorice and pork-rind, and all the pungent smells of the pockets of London. There in the Front Office of Elder's Bank the mixture clung to the walls and floated like dust in the air – the sour, sullen scent of money.

Almost as soon as Flora had made her discovery, her mother returned in a fury, her face redder than the cherry-coloured bow at her chin, her hard heels smacking the floorboards.

'The impertinence of those Elders!' she muttered, wrapping herself tightly in her shawl. 'Impudent creatures!' Constance turned to glare at the room in general, and then added, 'Who are the Elders, may I ask, to read a lecture to a St Serf? To a woman with generations of Clantavish blood in her veins? And what is the business of a banking-house, pray, if not to lend money to those who temporarily have none?'

'Old Mr Elder scolded you for being in debt?' asked Flora in surprise.

'Not at all. Mr Elder was at least a gentleman – but he has retired from banking, it seems.'

'Ah – so it was his son Felix who scolded you . . .'

Now Flora began to understand. She'd seen Felix Elder for herself one day in Hyde Park, when the Major still owned a carriage and her mother had made a point of driving out in it. Felix was the banker's first son and seventh child, a large man with round cheeks and round eyes, and hands like the soft round pouches used for storing sovereigns. All the same, Flora was surprised to hear that he'd now been left in charge of the bank. Lydia always swore Felix spent as much time playing cards as he ever passed behind a desk, well known for drinking the night away in the Coal Hole among the raffish theatre set. More than once, it was said, the Chief Clerk had found him with his head sunk on a ledger, snoring the morning away in consequence.

'Felix Elder, indeed—' snapped Constance, straightening her bonnet with angry fingers. 'And his damnable brother Darius!'

'But surely Darius Elder's been in India for years.' Flora tried to draw her mother towards the door. 'At least, that's what I heard.'

'Well, clearly Mr Darius Elder *isn't* in India any longer, since I've left him not a moment since! Though I tell you, Flora, it's a pity his family didn't leave him in India, since that's where he seems to have abandoned his manners. Can you believe it, he sent for all the cash-books, and had the clerks running hither and yon until he had my whole life spread out in front of him – all written up in guineas and sixpences!'

'Why should he want that?'

'To humiliate me, why else? "I see there's a large sum outstanding, Mrs St Serf." Well, of course there is – because, not so long ago, the Elders couldn't wait to lend it to us. "And you've made no provision to clear the debt." But how does he expect me to clear it, with no money coming in? *Feckless* – they actually used the word *feckless*! Oh, Flora, I had to sit there and let myself be spoken to like a naughty child!'

'Darius Elder called you feckless?'

'One or other of them . . . Perhaps it was Felix who actually used the word, but what does it matter? They're both Elders, aren't they?'

'Indeed, they are.' Flora tilted her chin indignantly. 'To think that a vulgar horror like Felix Elder should *presume* to hound our family for money. And now this nasty brother of his – what did you call him – Darius?' She made a furious little sound, and then remembered the object of her mother's visit. 'But will they let us borrow a little more, do you think?'

'Will they?' Almost at the door, Constance gave a moan of despair and pressed her gloves to her face. 'Not a penny,' she mumbled indistinctly. 'Not a single penny-piece!' Her eyes rose, tragically, above her gloved fingers. 'Old Mr Elder might have listened to me, but these two . . . Felix said the old man had underwritten half of London by not pressing his friends to repay. Oh, Flora what shall we do?'

'The General was right – the Elders aren't fit to associate with decent people.' Flora allowed herself a last glance round the mould-green room. 'They're beneath contempt,' she declared with reckless loyalty. 'If only I were a soldier like Papa – oh, I'd make them so sorry!'

Her eye was caught by a movement in the centre aisle. Felix Elder himself, his fashionable cravat rising almost up to his nose and ears, was advancing through the Front Office – and at his side, tall and darkly glittering, was Flora's Mr Smith.

Flora froze, her mouth a silent 'O' of consternation. Thirty feet away among the rows of desks, Mr Smith halted suddenly, staring in Flora's direction with the dismayed expression of a man who has remembered, too late, something he ought not to have forgotten.

'Oh, poor Mr Smith!' gasped Flora, suddenly breathless from the thumping of her heart. 'Felix Elder's frowning at him like a thunder-cloud. Perhaps he owes the Elders money too. Oh, poor man—' Across the room, she hung on that blue, blue gaze.

At Flora's side, Constance peered round like a querulous tortoise.

'Smith?' she demanded. 'That fellow's name isn't Smith, you goose! Haven't I just been telling you? That's Darius Elder, wretch that he is!'

A few seconds later, for the second time in their brief acquaintance, Darius Elder watched Flora's retreating back with a feeling of gnawing disquiet. He'd known that Constance St Serf had daughters: yet it had been months since business had taken him near Gough Square again, and somehow he'd failed to connect that knowledge with the memory of a pale, half-drowned, fleeting figure whose pride had burned like a lamp in the gloom of a rain-soaked morning.

For a moment, he considered following Constance and her daughter, and trying to explain – to offer some compromise, some way of easing the distress he'd seen in the girl's face when she'd recognized him . . .

'What's the matter, brother?' At Darius's shoulder, Felix rubbed his damp palms down his waistcoat. 'You look as if you've lost a guinea and found sixpence.'

'I wish it was as simple as that.'

'Great heavens, don't tell me you're sorry for the St Serfs, all of a sudden? Darius, my boy, they've spent a lifetime looking down their long noses at usurers like us. Let them see how it feels to be bottom of the heap for a change. Besides,' he added, slapping his brother on the back, 'our business is to make money, remember – not to lose it. Or did they teach you something different in India?'

4

'No wonder he told you his name was Smith!' Lydia, in her chemise, knees wide apart, was sucking an orange with such gusto that dimples appeared in its sides. 'And all the time the creature was an Elder!'

'An Elder, and a liar,' confirmed Flora grimly. It was the morning after her dismaying discovery at the bank, and she was supposed to be in Shoe Lane, buying the cheapest ox-cheeks she could find for dinner.

'My dear, *everyone* lies.' Lydia regarded her solemnly over the shrinking globe of the orange. 'Sometimes it's the only way. Take this Princess What's-her-name who's to be married next week – now, I know for a fact she's had herself made a virgin all over again by that Italian surgeon who takes a couple of stitches . . . Come the wedding night, she'll be sore and her husband will be happy – every bit as happy as the little dragoon who had it the first time. Now, is that a bad lie or a good one?'

Flora shook her head, amazed as usual by Lydia's knowledge of scandal, and if the truth were told, more than a little horrified.

'How do you know all these things?' she demanded.

'George tells me.' Lydia squeezed the orange flat between her palms, then drew the back of her hand across lips grown plump with the effort of sucking. 'All the scandal goes round George's club, or the regimental mess. Men are far worse gossips than women, you know.'

'Men are despicable!' Flora burst out. Mentally, she summoned Mr Darius Elder to account for himself: arrogant, overbearing – a member of a family which fawned on the rich as zealously as they bullied the needy – narrow, suspicious . . .

'He told me a downright lie,' she said bitterly.

'Oh, for any sake, sweetness – he's a human being, not a marble saint. And more human than some, if what I hear is true.' Lydia pressed her lips together and looked wise. 'Don't you know what they say in White's about Darius Elder?'

'I have no interest in the man whatsoever.' Flora began to tease out the tangled fringe of one of Lydia's shawls, her head bent low over her work. After a moment she added, 'I suppose it's something to do with a woman.'

'Naturally it is. What other kind of gossip is interesting?'

Flora sighed. 'You'd better tell me, then.'

'Oho! So you *do* still care about him, Elder or not!'

'No, I don't! Oh . . . bother this tangle!' In a sudden passion, Flora flung down the shawl and tilted her face to the ceiling, trying to stem the tears of frustration which welled in her eyes. 'Oh, Lydia, it makes me so flustered, just to see him . . . and I hate to feel like that – all hollow and confused – yet I can't seem to stop thinking about him.'

Angrily, she wiped her eyes on her sleeves, then shook her head in despair.

'I feel so ashamed when I remember how dreadfully the Elders have treated Papa. And yet somehow that only makes it worse . . .' Her voice trailed away. 'I can't help wondering about him, you see.'

'Wondering's no sin, in my opinion.' Lydia stretched out her legs and contemplated her bare feet, dimly translucent like smooth white fruit.

'But is this *love*, Lydia? Surely it can't be – I've hardly exchanged a dozen words with Darius Elder in my whole life. Is this dreadful muddle what being in love means, or is love something else entirely?'

'I'm not the one to tell you that, sweetness.' Lydia gazed at Flora with the eyes of a troubled angel, and then added quickly, 'Though

55

I'm a mistress, mind – not a whore. I've not looked at any man but the Captain for nigh on three years now. Well—' she corrected herself, 'that's to say I've looked at a few, but I've never done anything.'

She sighed profoundly, and returned to the contemplation of her rosy toenails.

'You see, my dear, when I was just a little thing – eight, or maybe nine years old – there was never a penny to spare in our home, save what we children could get for ourselves. And there was a street nearby – well known it was – where gentlemen would come and give you a shilling for . . . touching them. I never did anything else, mind, though I was sometimes asked. Just touched them, where they wanted it.' She sighed again, and slid her hands down her thighs.

'I used to despise them, you know – for wanting it so badly. I used to look at them and think *You poor wretch – does it take so little?* I saw what a woman could do, if she keeps her head.'

She glanced up, and met Flora's eye. 'So don't ask me about love. Perhaps it's when that kind of thought doesn't come.'

'Oh, Lydia . . . I'm sorry.'

'Sorry? Sorry for what?' Lydia shrugged elaborately. 'Be sorry for yourself, dear heart – don't waste your sympathy on me.'

She stood up suddenly, snatched the shawl, and swirled it over her crumpled chemise like a robe of oriental splendour. She regarded Flora over one rainbow shoulder.

'Shall I tell you now what they say about Darius Elder in White's?' Her lips curled seductively over their secret. 'They say . . .' She drew up the shawl dramatically. 'They say he was sent home from India – *sent home*, mark you – because of a scandal over a lady. A native lady, moreover – the daughter of one of the Indian princes. What do you think of that, my dear?'

'No doubt he promised her everything, and then abandoned her. That's how the Elders behave.'

'That isn't what they're saying in White's, according to my George. They say—' Lydia sat down again, and leaned forward intently. 'They say he discovered this woman one day by chance, on his way from one place to another—'

'Calcutta,' supplied Flora. 'He went out to Calcutta to learn about foreign trade with the East India Company, so I heard.'

'Perhaps he did.' Lydia waved away the interruption. 'But at any rate, he discovered this young woman, marooned by the roadside where her sedan-carriers had left her when they ran away from a tiger or some such wild beast. As I say, she was the daughter of one of the native princes, and normally he'd never have seen her, because the Hindus keep their women veiled and locked away from strangers.

'But the important thing is – he immediately fell in love with the lady, and she with him. And after he'd taken her safely back to her father's palace they managed to meet in secret and pass messages to and fro, until finally they decided to run off together. He was set on marrying her, so they say, but the girl's father wouldn't hear of it.

'Still, by all accounts the young couple had planned their escape very well. They were almost clear of the palace when they were caught.'

'Caught?' Despite herself, Flora's eyes grew round with alarm.

'Caught – and dragged back in chains.' Lydia held out her wrists, bound with invisible shackles. 'Of course, because Darius Elder was an officer of the East India Company, the prince could only hand him over to the Governor-General and demand that he should be punished. But there was nothing Darius could do to rescue the poor little princess. Her father shut her up in a room with no windows and precious little food, and they say she died of a broken heart.'

'And that's when he was sent back to England?'

'Not just then, according to the fellow who brought the story back from Calcutta.' The shawl slid, unnoticed, from Lydia's shoulders. 'No – Darius Elder was packed off to the frontier and warned never to show his face in the district again. But before very long he was in trouble once more. Some army officer made a careless remark about the dead girl – you know how they can speak of native women – and Darius challenged him to a duel, which of course is strictly forbidden by the Company. The officer was shot and very nearly died of the wound, and your Mr Elder was put on the first ship home.' Lydia leaned back, her hands on her knees. 'What do you think of that?'

There was a moment of silence while longing and disbelief battled in Flora's heart.

'Oh, Lydia, are you certain? You said yourself that gentlemen's clubs are full of made-up gossip.'

'It isn't all made up, my dear.'

'Then perhaps Captain George has mistaken the name of the man involved. I can't believe Darius Elder would ever run off with an Indian princess, or fight a duel for her honour. No – it's impossible.'

Flora shook her head, as if trying hard to dislodge the notion. Then she hesitated, and a wistful expression came into her eyes. 'It is impossible, isn't it, Lydia?'

'George seemed quite certain of his facts, I must say.' With her head on one side and a soft, sad expression on her face, Lydia watched Flora struggle with her warring emotions. 'I don't suppose any of this has helped to solve your problem,' she concluded at last. 'But, sweetness, it does seem that your Mr Elder isn't at all the man you thought he was.'

5

In Gough Square, autumn revealed itself in a dwindling of daylight and a scattering of yellowed, wind-borne leaves from the ancient hawthorn by the Rolls chapel a couple of streets away. Yet the soft melancholy of the season did nothing to ease the confusion in Flora's heart; though almost a year had passed since their first rain-drenched meeting, the bewildering image of Darius Elder haunted her still, and the more she gave herself up to dreams, the more disloyal she felt.

One afternoon, on her way back from buying butcher's tallow candles in Shoe Lane, she yielded to the temptation of stopping at the automaton-maker's workshop. At that time of day she'd find not only Dédalon, hunched over his bench, but Lydia too, stretched out on the shabby sofa, half-asleep and full of comforting philosophy.

The workshop was darker than ever in the late-autumn gloom. From somewhere beyond the pedal-lathe she heard the irregular scrape of a file, and from his place by the fire, the chink of Solomon's chain; but the sofa was empty, and Lydia nowhere to be seen.

The smooth dome of Dédalon's brow rose above the pedal-lathe as he looked to see who'd come.

'Ah.' He settled down once more on his stool. 'Mademoiselle Lydia's gone to buy a hat. Captain George won a few guineas at cards last night, and Semiramis has run off to spend them before they wither and die.' He laughed softly. 'So today, my dear, you can be queen of the sofa. Sit down and speak to me. Tell me what new dramas have overtaken the St Serfs since I saw you last.'

'I'd rather watch you work, if I may.' A contrivance of levers and wire lay on the bench before him, no bigger than a snuff-box. 'What are you making, Dédalon?'

'A singing bird for Kingsley the clockmaker. A finch to live in an enamelled case and rise up at the touch of a spring to sing among golden trees with leaves of diamonds. Something to fill the empty minutes while the hands move round the clock-face.'

The automaton-maker lifted the mechanism between finger and thumb, and turned it to reveal a tiny bellows.

'This will give my finch a voice – do you see how it opens and shuts? By tomorrow his little bird-organ will be finished, and he'll be ready to receive his feathers. Then he goes to his perch in the clock.' The bellows folded with the faintest of sighs, and Dédalon smiled. 'I like to think of him singing about fat worms and beetles in his bower of diamonds.'

Flora thought about this for a moment. 'My sister can only sing about diamonds.'

'Ah – the stolen sister.' The automaton-maker took up a pair of finely pointed pincers. 'No, not stolen,' he corrected himself. 'The bought and paid-for sister.' For a moment there was silence while he concentrated on hooking the end of a spring to an almost invisible eye. 'Does he still mourn the loss of his favourite, your papa?'

'It's true – you'd almost think Sophie was dead, from the way he speaks of her. Sophie was always . . .' Leaning back against the lathe, Flora groped for words to describe the relationship between the two. 'Sophie was always so entirely Papa's – as if somehow she only recovered from her illness for his sake, and then lived for him, and needed his protection . . . Now that he's lost her – after everything else – it's as if he has nothing left at all.'

'Ah . . .' The automaton-maker worked on in silence for a few minutes, patiently fixing the bellows into place on the brass frame.

'To possess another human being,' he observed suddenly, 'to see another living creature walk and talk and speak entirely for your pleasure . . . It's very seductive to exercise such power. And between fathers and daughters there is always possession and power.' Dédalon's head was bent over his work, his face in shadow as he examined the tiny apparatus through an eye-glass.

'I had a daughter once,' he murmured. 'But she died.'

Flora opened her mouth to murmur words of sympathy, but the automaton-maker had already moved on.

'The bellows must fit the wind-chest exactly.' With infinite care, he tested the connection. 'And the spring must fall against it *so*.'

Satisfied Dédalon laid the pieces on the bench and gravely surveyed them.

'It's more powerful than hunger, this longing to create a live creature, utterly of one's own. Not just a machine of springs and cams, and gear-wheels and clock escapements, but as much alive as you or I.'

He gave Flora a sidelong glance.

'Nothing to say, then? Do you find the idea so incredible? Yet show me an artist who's never lingered over his work in the half-light, dreaming that by some miracle his paint has become warm flesh and blood, or an eye has begun to shine with real understanding.'

His head on one side, Dédalon measured Flora's reaction.

'A painter or a sculptor would certainly need a miracle to achieve such a thing,' he continued softly. 'But for an automaton-maker – for a builder of mechanisms – it could be more than a dream.'

'To make life?' Flora stared at him, appalled. 'To make an actual, living creature out of all this?' She indicated the bird-organ on the bench.

'Did you ever hear of a man by the name of Vaucanson?' Dédalon watched her with bright, unblinking eyes. 'Vaucanson died many years ago, but he was one of the greatest of all automaton-makers. He believed that the creation of life itself was within his grasp, if he could only make a perfect copy of the systems of the body – not just bone and muscle, but the digestion of food and the circulation of the blood. And his dream drove him to make three wonderful figures – a flute-player, a gypsy drummer, and a duck.

'I never saw the two musicians. But I saw the duck.' Dédalon paused, absorbed by a vision far beyond the walls of his workshop. 'The bird stood on a box – big, like this—' His hands described the dimensions. 'And when a lever was pressed, the duck began to move his head, looking round – so – and to spread his wings, little by little, unfolding every feather . . . Then he lowered his head to eat grain from a dish, and when the dish was empty he'd straighten his neck and blow out his stomach, wagging the feathers of his tail, and – *voilà* – from his backside . . . you understand?'

'But that's impossible!'

'Not at all! The grain was digested, dissolved by acid in the bird's stomach and made to pass through.' Dédalon sighed, and took up his pincers once more. 'There were four hundred moving parts in each wing. Each of the feathers was made of gilded copper . . . The bird was exhibited everywhere. Vaucanson's Duck. Emperors demanded to see it.'

'And what happened to it?'

Dédalon shook his head. 'Vaucanson sold it. He squandered his dream and became a maker of music-boxes and catch-penny toys. After he died the duck became broken, and no one but its creator could mend it. I have no idea where it is now.'

Flora considered the story for a moment. 'But the duck was never really alive. Not properly, like you and I.'

'Ah, but Vaucanson only possessed the knowledge of his own time.' Dédalon made a minute adjustment to the tiny bellows. 'Nowadays we know more. I've studied for years to understand all the human mechanisms – all the tendons and muscles, the digestion, the breathing – and I've found nothing which couldn't be copied in another form. And if we copy all the mechanisms, it follows that we must create life.'

Flora felt the air chill around her, as if someone had opened a door to let in a draught. Lydia had told her about Dédalon's 'studies' – carried out among the corpses piled up by the Terror which had followed the revolution in France. Through all the madness and death the automaton-maker had pursued his dream of creation, picking like a crow among the unclaimed leavings of the guillotine, dissecting and learning. With a shudder, Flora tried to push the picture from her mind.

'But surely there's more to us than simple flesh and blood!' she burst out. 'What about the soul? What about the part of us which loves and hopes, and cherishes our dreams? What about pity, and laughter? How could you ever make those?'

'Why should I try?' The automaton-maker tossed down his pincers. 'Let me tell you, in all my experience of dissection, I never once found any sign of this *soul* people make such a fuss about. Not in the heart, not in the brain – not in the smallest toe. Not once! And yet the priests promise us the soul is something which will endure, even when our bodies are dust.'

He tapped on the bench with a hard finger.

'They're afraid to admit we're only collections of tubes and rods and hinges, no different from horses and dogs, or monkeys like Solomon there. Yet all the evidence proves we're just simple machines.'

Dédalon reached out to take Flora's hands in his own; incapable of resistance, she allowed them to be held.

'You see, *ma petite*, we aren't masters of the world at all – just small parts of its huge mechanism. Give me a little time, and I'll make you another sister, better than the last. I'll make you a lover who'll be your slave – anything you want . . .'

An expression of pure horror had crept over Flora's face. At the sight of it Dédalon sat back and released her hands.

'But not today. Not yet. Even Vaucanson's Duck had no heart.'

CHAPTER FOUR

I

For the rest of that year the little household in Gough Square lurched
on somehow from one day to the next, spinning out Constance's
quarterly allowance as far as it would go, and launching into a frenzy
of economies when it finally ran out. Early in 1821 they gave up two
of their six rooms in order to reduce the rent, banishing faithful
Maggie to an empty store-cupboard next to the kitchen, and con-
demning Flora to a half-share in her mother's bedroom. Uncomfortably conscious of her shrinking world, Flora waited to see who would
arrive to fill the two rooms they'd vacated.

She was hoping for a shopman to whistle on the stairs, or a clerk
to stand on the front steps, jingling the change in his pocket –
someone young, at any rate, to lighten the gloom of her home. Every
day now, the Major seemed to retreat further into that place of pain
where no one could follow, the bones of his face standing out lividly
among the blue shadows of sleeplessness. After dark his nightmares
closed in, and his cries woke Flora and her mother in the next room,
startling them from sleep, convinced the house was on fire.

Within a fortnight, Flora's hopes were dashed when a stout
middle-aged man named Theodore Wesley moved in.

'He's a gentleman, at least.' Constance had established this fact
from their landlady, Mrs Moss. 'Came into a great deal of family
money once upon a time, but nowadays sadly reduced.'

Mr Wesley, it seemed, had even set about losing his inheritance
in a gentlemanly way. Inspired by the gossip of his club, he'd
promptly withdrawn his funds from dreary government loans and
lodged them instead in Irish banks paying a sparkling ten per cent.
Raising a mortgage on his house, he'd bought shares in up-and-
coming Patagonian canals and the dock schemes of Lower Gothnia:
but almost as soon as he'd completed the deals, his Irish banks failed,
his Patagonian canals ran into quicksand, and the Gothnian dock-
builders were wiped out to a man in a civil war.

Now, having lost his house, his servants and his admirable stable,
he was reduced to boiling his own morning kettle in his little parlour,

toasting his late-night supper before the fire, and walking in fair weather or foul to a nearby tavern for his daily dinner.

Yet the shreds of faded glory still clung to Mr Wesley: even his smile displayed gentlemanly teeth – the expensive kind, of carved ivory with exquisite gold springs which kept them fidgeting while he spoke. His boots might have been worn, but they shone like glass, and he'd a decent horror of being seen in broad daylight, carrying home his own parcels. Whenever the tea merchant refused to send round a quarter-pound of floor-sweepings to Gough Square, Mr Wesley, with neither carriage nor footman to convey it, tied his tiny purchase to his coat buttons and strolled back, festooned like a hatstand but with his hands respectably empty.

'I was badly advised, Mrs St Serf,' he confided. 'Badly advised, and that's the truth. One moment those fellows at Elder's Bank were all crying "Invest, invest" – and then in the next breath they told me I'd been deplorably rash, and went back to their port and cigars.'

Constance St Serf pricked up her ears at the sound of the hated name.

'Won't you come into the drawing-room, Mr Wesley?' she suggested. 'I'll tell Maggie to bring us some Madeira.'

Lydia's verdict was straightforward. 'Your Mr Wesley should have married some wealthy woman while he was able. That's what a sensible man would have done with his money.'

'Perhaps he couldn't find a lady he liked.'

Lydia flung up her hands. 'What has *liking* got to do with it? Money marries money, there's nothing surer. Good heavens, I've seen a sixteen-year-old girl with half a dozen English counties to her name handed over to a half-blind, drooling old devil, simply because he could load her down with diamonds! And crying her eyes out at the altar, too, for love of some penniless cousin left at home.'

It was a prophetic conversation. One morning not long afterwards, Flora discovered Lydia shut up in her rooms behind drawn curtains, stretched in anguish across her monumental bed. A few garbled sentences were enough to reveal that the disaster Lydia had always feared had finally come to pass: Captain George Bellarmine's family had found him a bride.

'She's five years older than George,' mourned Lydia, 'and plain as a cow's backside. But her father's the man who keeps the Navy in rope, and she's very rich – rich enough to keep the dear boy in the comfort he deserves.' Lydia broke off in a series of gulping sobs, and then tried again. 'She's given p-poor George her picture in a little gold frame – all covered with diamonds and seed-pearls . . .' Lydia took a great breath, and finished the sentence in a howl of despair, *'to wear round his neck!'*

It was the parting of the ways. For three years Lydia had been faithful to her George, and he, as far as could be determined, to her; but rich brides, Flora knew, expected a period of sinless behaviour.

Then suddenly Lydia vanished, and for almost four days was nowhere to be found. By the time she returned, Flora had begun to fear the worst, imagining Lydia's face, drifting like a flawless pearl below a green veil of river water.

Yet when Lydia returned she looked amazingly well. Not only was she dressed to the hilt in a new gown of rose-coloured satin, but her skin was lustrous, her eyes sparkled, and a little smile of satisfaction twitched at the corners of her lips.

'He's married you!' guessed Flora in delight. 'Captain George has married you after all, in spite of the rope-maker's daughter.'

'I should think not!' Lydia kicked off a rose-coloured shoe, sending it spinning into the air like a shimmering bird. 'No, George Bellarmine will go like a lamb to the altar, bless him, and I hope he finds some happiness there. What good would it do him to marry a woman like me? I'd never let him consider it. We'd starve inside a week.'

'Then where on earth have you been?'

'I've been to see the regiment,' Lydia declared with pride. 'George's regiment, on parade. George put me up in an inn near the barracks . . .' Lydia slid her hands up to the nape of her neck, and stretched luxuriantly. 'And he bought me all this.' Tucking in her chin, she peered down over her tightly strained bodice. 'Poor boy, it cost him a fortune. Just as well his future bride is so rich.'

Lydia smiled serenely and raised seraphic eyes to the ceiling.

'I don't suppose I'll ever see the dear fellow again.'

'But what will you do now?' Bewildered, Flora threw delicacy to the wind. 'I mean . . . how will you live?'

'Live? Oh, I intend to live very well in future.' Slowly, Lydia trailed her fingers down over the blushing satin of her gown, tracing a winding path to her thighs. 'George has introduced me to his colonel. Such a handsome man, with a large fortune of his own . . .' She wriggled contentedly. 'Oh, I *do* like soldiers . . .'

Before long, Lydia's colonel had whisked her from the grim

shadows of King's Head Court to a small, pretty house in Park Street with its front door between an oil-shop and a pork-butcher's. Unfortunately, Park Street was almost two miles from Gough Square.

'I could write to you there,' suggested Flora. 'And you could send your replies to Dédalon's.'

'I've never learned to write, my love. I can manage my name, but I can't write well enough for letters.' Lydia gazed sorrowfully at Flora. 'The Colonel has spoken of having me taught, but I doubt if I'll learn it as quick as all that.'

She thought for a moment, and then her face brightened.

'We could meet at Dédalon's, though, from time to time. It isn't much, but it's better than nothing.'

Piled into a hackney-carriage, with her hatboxes at her feet, Lydia trundled off in the wake of the carrier's cart bearing the *maréchal*'s bed towards her new home in Park Street.

Lydia had escaped, and had taken a great deal of the shabby familiarity of the neighbourhood with her in her carrier's cart. Now that the refuge of Lydia's home was closed to her, it seemed to Flora that the quarrelling voices rang more aggressively through the warren of courts which surrounded Gough Square, and the loitering beggars watched her more carefully with their wolfish eyes.

Dédalon seemed unmoved by Lydia's departure.

'Semiramis has gone on her way,' he remarked without turning his head from his work. 'And she'll go far – you'll see – now she understands how it can be done.'

'How what can be done, Dédalon?'

'How to make her way in this hard world of ours.'

'By falling in love with George Bellarmine's colonel? That was a lucky chance, certainly.'

This time Dédalon turned his head, and gave Flora a disbelieving stare. '"Falling in love"? Is that what you call it? Good business, more like.'

'Oh, I know—' Flora waved his cynicism aside. 'You're about to tell me there's no place for love among the gear-wheels and clock escapements you say we're made of.'

The automaton-maker shrugged. 'What is love, when you dissect it under a magnifying lens? Nothing but two monkeys coming together to make a third monkey. Anything more is illusion. At least Lydia has realized it's better to choose rich monkeys.'

'Oh, you're impossible, Dédalon!'

'My dear—' Dédalon laid down his tools and turned to face Flora squarely. 'My dear, listen to one who knows the truth. Illusion is my business. As Lydia says, I'm a winder-up of dreams – I make the tick-tick-tick which hides under the silver paper.'

'I won't listen to any more of this!'

'As you please, *ma petite*. Wait until you're older, and there are no longer stars in your eyes.'

'I hope that day never comes!' declared Flora passionately, and silently vowed to herself that in future she'd leave the automaton-maker alone with his scorn and his clockwork. Yet the truth was that without Dédalon she'd have had no one at all to talk to, and the automaton-maker could talk in a way which filled the hungry spaces of Flora's mind, neglected since the last governess had departed five years earlier.

For a long time she'd felt only relief at being free of the schoolroom; but now whenever Sophie returned, full of accomplishments and speaking with the pedantic voice of Miss Meagle, Flora was reduced to awkward silence to hide the depth of her ignorance. In desperation she turned to Dédalon, who owned a great number of books, in English as well as in French.

'Ah – so now you want to learn!' Dédalon turned on his stool and knotted his long fingers between his knees. 'But what exactly do you want to learn?'

He regarded her sternly. 'If you're looking for the fruits of reason, *ma petite*, we'll see what can be done for you. But don't ask me to discuss Lord Byron and his overheated romantic nonsense. Illusion! Nothing but illusion, as I said.'

'Nothing of Lord Byron's, then.'

After that, each afternoon, while the Major stared from his bedroom window and his wife and Mr Wesley polished their gentility in the drawing-room, Flora slipped away to Shoe Lane. There the automaton-maker read to her from Rousseau's theories on the nature of mankind, translating as he went; he picked out passages from Lamarck's *Histoire Naturelle* on the transformation of species, or from Cabanis' pamphlet on the animality of man; and from journals of exploration describing creatures stranger than anything Noah could have imagined.

'Science – science will explode all the mysteries, given time. Science will write the new gospels.'

Yet for all the automaton-maker's teaching, thoughts of Darius

Elder kept slipping under Flora's guard of *reason*, beguiling her with feelings of the softest, wildest, most elemental kind. It couldn't be love, of course: Flora was sure of that now, since such a thing did not exist in the world to which Dédalon had led her. But still the man would not let go! Persistent devil, his image clung to the margins of her consciousness like . . . like an Elder – what else?

2

But while the St Serfs lived in constant fear of the bailiff's knock, fashionable London was searching for witty, diverting and expensive gifts to please its new King, George IV, whose coronation had been set for 19th July 1821. As the date drew nearer, the city was plunged into a frenzy of extravagance. Dédalon's harlequin conjuror was soon sold, to a gentleman who never even blinked at its price; the jewelled singing bird was swiftly completed and sent off, while in Shoe Lane, Rousseau and Cabanis had been set aside so that the automaton-maker could work at full speed on a life-sized peacock which would strut and spread its tail at the touch of a switch.

Sophie was going to the coronation. That fact emerged soon after General St Serf was summoned from Hampshire to put his military mind to the arrangements for the royal banquet which would follow the ceremony. It was a minor task, but enough to guarantee the General and his family a place in a scarlet-draped box in Westminster Abbey; accordingly, he put aside his doubts about his sovereign's character, and rushed up to London to do his duty.

With two weeks still to go, Sophie was in a frenzy of agitation over what she should wear on the great day.

'Absolutely everyone who matters will be there,' she assured her mother in one of her rare letters; Flora saw a tear blot the line as Constance read it.

'I'd hate to sit for hours in the Abbey,' she told her mother, 'but perhaps we could wait outside to see the procession.'

'And make it plain we weren't invited?' demanded Constance, quickly sweeping the back of her hand over her eyes. 'Absolutely not. I shall pretend to be out of town when it happens.'

For the life of her, Flora couldn't see why standing in a crowd should be so much more disgraceful than suffering a court martial. Even to see the pageantry from a little way off would be almost as good as being part of it: and lately, since Lydia's departure, the walls of Gough Square had pressed in on her more cheerlessly than ever.

Lydia had returned three times to Shoe Lane, and on each occasion Flora had tried to pretend that nothing had changed, and that Lydia was the same carefree, immodest creature who'd hurled shoes at her landlady from her window in King's Head Court and wept salt tears over the Captain's marriage. But it wasn't true – and the difference wasn't simply that Lydia was dressed more expensively and in better taste than before, or that there were now enough pearls at her ears and throat to occupy a whole bed of oysters.

A subtler change had also taken place, a change which Flora would have struggled to describe. If anything, Lydia was even more beautiful than before; a faint touch of rouge had made her strange, bewildering, lapsed-angel charm more poignant than ever, and yet . . . Had that selfish little chin become a trifle firmer, or her eyes more watchful? Impossible to say, and yet the sense of change remained.

'Semiramis has decided to honour us with a call tomorrow,' announced the automaton-maker one June afternoon when Flora looked in to see how the peacock was progressing. He held out a single page which had been sealed by a wafer. 'This arrived today by hackney-carriage, no less. If she can afford to pay a man to take her correspondence across London, then Milady Lydia must certainly have gone up in the world.'

Flora unfolded the sheet of paper. Two lines of uncertain letters crept across it: *Coming at two tomorrow. Tell Flora.* Underneath, scrawled with more confidence, was the name *Lydia*.

'So the Colonel's having her taught to write after all,' remarked Dédalon, peering over Flora's shoulder. 'She'll soon be able to send notes to her lovers, just as a lady should.'

'But Lydia's devoted to the Colonel – you know that.'

'And to making her way in the world. I understand that too.'

Certainly, when Lydia stepped into Dédalon's workshop the following afternoon, there was no doubt that Park Street was having a wonderful effect on her.

'My sweet!' she exclaimed without any preamble. 'How would you like to go to the coronation after all? Not to the Abbey, you understand – but the dear Colonel has taken a place for me in one of the galleries right outside Westminster Hall, overlooking the procession. He's taken two places, in fact, at twenty guineas apiece, which is *highly* obliging of him, so I can have a friend to keep me company.

Of course, the gallery is perfectly respectable and we shall be quite safe alone.' She clapped her hands in anticipation of the treat. 'We're sure to see the King very close by – and oh, Flora, I do want you to come!'

'I'd like to come, but . . .' Flora hesitated, and the silence became doubly profound after the babble of Lydia's excitement.

In the gloom of the workshop, she saw Lydia straighten her shoulders.

'No . . . Well, never mind, dear heart, I can quite understand that you don't care to be seen out in public with someone like me . . . Don't give it a thought, I shall find another friend to go with me, I'm sure.'

'No, Lydia, wait—' Now, at last, Flora understood the nature of the change which had overtaken her friend. Lydia was no longer the carefree voluptuary of King's Head Court, but a sinner who'd recognized and accepted her disreputable portion in life. Immediately, Flora felt a rush of affection for her.

'Oh, Lydia, of course I'll come with you, no matter what Mamma says. I don't know how it can be managed, but I'll arrange it somehow.'

In the event, hardly any arranging was needed. Constance chose the day of the coronation to visit a cousin's grave in St Paul's burial-ground, confident that anyone who mattered *there* would be in no position to sneer. Mr Wesley decided to go with her for the pleasure of the walk, and Flora was to be left in her father's nominal care.

Shortly after nine in the morning, as soon as her mother's best bonnet had disappeared into the entrance to Bolt Court, Flora sped on winged feet to Dédalon's workshop, where Lydia had arranged to meet her in one of the hackney-carriages she adored.

It was fortunate they'd set out early. Even at that hour their hired carriage had to force its way through the packed streets round Westminster, propelled by the driver's curses and the frantic plunging of his horse. Everywhere, gold-tasselled coaches of the nobility were marooned in an ocean of bobbing heads; their coachmen hallooed and lashed with their whips while liveried footmen tried to clear their masters' way like powdered prophets trying to part the Red Sea.

A platform more than twenty feet wide had been built from Westminster Hall to the Abbey to give everyone a good view of the procession. Once in their places at the front of the gallery, Flora and

Lydia found themselves on a level with the soldiers guarding the route; a jostling crowd had already filled the space between gallery and platform, scrambling for the best vantage-points and peering between the sentries' legs for any sign that the monarch was on his way.

Flora gazed dutifully wherever Lydia pointed, admiring the parading dandies and their fashionable ladies, and wondering how it was that Lydia, who a year earlier had been a virtual prisoner in King's Head Court, suddenly knew all these modish creatures by name. More amazing still, one or two of the unaccompanied men nodded or removed their hats in recognition of her wave.

'Oh, well, you know how it is.' Lydia shrugged her silken shoulders and fanned herself rapidly with a tiny ivory fan. 'The Colonel has taken a box for me at the Opera, and gentlemen *will* come in to introduce themselves. Sometimes it's all I can do to hear the singing,' she added innocently.

'I suppose it must be.' Flora suddenly felt desperately dowdy in her three-year-old muslin, and in spite of her republican ideals, began to long for a single face in all that vast multitude which she herself could recognize.

Without any warning, trumpets blared out from Westminster Hall.

'Why, there's the King!' Gratefully, she caught sight of a gold canopy swaying out into the sunlight. 'Look, Lydia – King George is here.' She felt quite triumphant; what were a clutch of viscounts and sugar-barons, compared with a single glimpse of the monarch himself?

All the same, Flora almost expected the King to sweep off his plumed hat to Lydia as he passed, so impressed was she by her friend's social success. Lydia was still happily pointing out Lord This and the Marquess of That long after they'd gone on their way in their suffocating robes, and the King's enormous star-spangled train had at last been borne off to the doorway of the Abbey.

Illusion, thought Flora, recalling Dédalon's lessons. Feathers and silver paper, to enchant the crowd . . . Yet a memory persisted of crimson velvet and white satin trunk-hose and tights; of bishops waddling like fat white geese, and officers of state gingerly carrying a crown like a garish toy; and of the perfume of scattered lavender and rosemary sprigs, bruised by the trudging of a hundred feet, rising up like the balm of a garden after rain.

Lydia had brought cold chicken and champagne, and the time

passed very merrily until, with a blast of trumpets, the procession returned, this time with the King in his tinsel crown, and the peers in coronets which slipped and slithered over rakish wigs and ancient, wobbling heads.

At last, a little nervously, Lydia and Flora descended the steps into the sea of people flooding away from the Abbey.

'What we need is a hackney-coach.' Lydia clutched her basket and peered hopefully into the throng. But the coaches were waiting at the edge of the crowd; there was nothing for it but to push determinedly forward, trying to keep their heads above the currents which whirled them to and fro.

All of a sudden, astonishingly near and distinct above the throng, Flora caught sight of two faces she recognized.

She'd never have dreamed of asking such men for help, but the mere sight of one of the faces was still enough to fill her with more intoxicating, breath-snatching excitement than a dozen coronations could have produced. The passing months had had no effect at all: his image had stayed before her, as clear and as vital as the man himself. Immediately she pointed the two figures out to Lydia.

'Look – over there – in the curricle. There's Darius Elder and his brother Felix. Trust the Elders to look after themselves!'

'So that's your friend Mr Elder!' With difficulty, Lydia shaded her eyes to examine him. 'And his brother Felix in blue. I'd know that coarse face of his anywhere.' She staggered as the crowd pressed about her, hoisting her for a moment off her feet.

All at once Flora felt a small, hard body wriggle against her own; there was a scuffle and a wrench, and a glimpse of an undernourished back burrowing like a rat among the legs and arms of the crowd. A faint ripple of craning heads on the surface of the human ocean marked the path of the burrower towards a nearby side-street.

'My purse!' Frantically, Flora snatched at thin air. 'Oh, Lydia, that boy has taken my purse! Stop! Hold that thief!'

But nobody in the crowd cared for anyone but himself; no one even turned a head to see who'd been careless enough to leave a purse dangling from her wrist as she was carried along in that ebbing wave of sightseers. There had been little enough in the purse – five shillings, put by in case of emergencies – but it was all Flora had, and its loss was a disaster.

'Too late!' yelled Lydia in her ear. 'He's long gone, the little brat. You've seen the last of your money, my dear.'

A disturbance had broken out round the curricle. Over the heads of the crowd, Flora saw Felix Elder alone on the pitching leather seat while a groom clung for dear life to the heads of his horses. A space quickly cleared as the crowd fell back from the milling hooves – and in that space stood Darius Elder, grasping a small, thrashing figure by its filthy shirt-collar and holding up a slender, netted-silk purse.

'My purse!' St Serf or not, Flora clawed her way through the stream of people, desperate to reach the spot before someone else could claim her property. 'It's mine! Wait! I'm coming!'

With Lydia toiling after her, Flora emerged, gasping and dishevelled, at the side of the curricle. Only then did she remember who it was that had rescued her five shillings.

'I believe that purse is mine, Mr Elder.' Hastily, Flora smoothed her crumpled skirts and brushed a trailing strand of hair behind one ear.

Darius Elder was still holding the spitting, clawing child against his side, pinioning the boy's arms to prevent his escape, and for a moment he failed to look up.

'This is our young robber, I think.' He gave the boy a shake, and the child twisted round with a snarl.

Now at last Darius raised his head. His eyes swept over Flora, and widened in surprise.

'Miss St Serf,' he declared, straightening up. 'It is, isn't it? Miss Flora St Serf – I saw you in the bank once, with your mother . . . And you were the young lady with the candlesticks – in Gough Square, in the rain.'

For a fleeting moment Flora's heart soared at the thought that he'd remembered her; then almost at once her joy was swept aside by a memory of bailiffs, and debts, and the humiliating circumstances of that meeting.

'I really don't recall the occasion.' Yet a treacherous warmth was rising in her cheeks to reveal her lie. Quickly, she held out her hand. 'But thank you, all the same, for saving my purse. It was foolish of me to let it be stolen.'

Darius Elder ignored her outstretched palm.

'But you must remember that day! You were wet through, with your arms full of silver, and I took you for a thief.' He paused. 'Do you really not remember?'

He seemed genuinely disappointed; then he added casually, 'I still carry the scar of your taper-snuffer.'

'But that's impossible! It was hardly—' Too late, Flora realized she'd given herself away.

'So you do remember.' He smiled, exploring her face with his eyes as if searching for the ardent, quicksilver creature he'd discovered that day.

All at once the boy struggling in Darius's grip took advantage of the distraction to stamp cruelly on his toes.

'Dammit – you little – I beg your pardon, Miss St Serf.'

The tiny thief, having got his man off balance, suddenly wriggled out of his shirt like a sloughing snake, and scurried away into the crowd.

'For God's sake, Darius!' exploded Felix from the curricle, 'you've let the young rogue get away from you.'

For a moment Darius stared after the departed boy. Then he turned back.

'Miss St Serf,' he said formally, 'may I present my brother Felix? Felix, this is Miss St Serf – of Gough Square – who has temporarily lost her purse.'

'Gough Square, eh?' Felix knitted his brows and stuck out his lower lip. 'What – a daughter of the Major who—'

Flora noticed Darius Elder silence his brother with a frown, and felt a reluctant surge of gratitude.

'It was Felix who spotted your robber running towards us,' Darius admitted, 'though I'll take the credit for catching the young wretch.'

'And for letting him go,' grunted Felix.

'He's welcome to his freedom, the little weasel. What would you have done with him, anyway?'

'Handed him over to Townsend and his Runners.' Felix pouted righteously, running a finger round the rim of his extravagant cravat. 'A spell of hard labour would have fixed his nonsense soon enough.'

'Fixed him, or killed him.' Darius Elder turned thoughtfully to Flora. 'What do you say, Miss St Serf?'

Flora made a slight gesture with her hand, once more uncomfortably aware of being examined from head to toe.

'There were only a few shillings in the purse,' she murmured. 'It would be harsh to send a boy to prison for so little.'

Darius Elder glanced up at his brother. 'There's your answer, Felix. The lady has declined to prosecute.' He turned back to Flora. 'But how do you come to be on foot in all this crush, Miss St Serf? Have you lost the General's carriage?'

Just at that moment Lydia emerged from the nearest part of the crowd, glowing from her exertions and her hat fetchingly askew.

'Gracious, sweetness – are you safe, then?' She laid a dainty hand on Flora's arm. 'I thought I'd be carried all the way to St James's before that fellow in the mason's apron put me down.'

With a speed which belied his stoutness, Felix Elder slithered down from the curricle to land at Lydia's feet, his little eyes bright.

'Mr Felix Elder, and Mr Darius Elder,' said Flora reluctantly. 'Miss Seaward.'

At once, Felix took charge of Lydia.

'I've seen you at the Opera, with Colonel West,' he breathed, absorbing every detail of Lydia's fashionable person. To Flora's dismay, the very attitude of Felix's body proclaimed all that his brother might need to know about Miss Lydia Seaward: he was leaning back against the side of the curricle, his stomach thrust out and his chin drawn in – his face slack with desire and his eyes hot behind their half-shut lids.

When Darius turned back to Flora, she was conscious of a change in his manner. He was staring at her almost angrily, though somehow she sensed he wasn't so much angry *with* her as *for* her – angry with the world and its ways.

'Miss Seaward is a good friend of yours?'

'I've known Lydia for some time,' Flora admitted. 'She used to live near us.'

'In Gough Square.'

'Yes.'

'But you don't live there any more.'

'Certainly, I do! You must know that.'

'I know your parents live there.'

'And so do I! Where else would I live?'

'Nowhere else, indeed.' Darius's frown cleared, and he seemed relieved. 'You live at home, of course. I'm pleased to hear it.'

He glanced across to where Felix had just leaned forward to chuck Lydia under the chin, and a dreadful suspicion suddenly began to form in Flora's mind.

'Mr Elder—' she began heatedly.

'Forgive me—' Darius raised a hand in a gesture of apology. 'You understand . . . I know times are hard for you at present – and when I saw you with Miss Seaward I didn't know what to think.'

Flora stared at him, appalled – and found herself blushing to the roots of her hair, on Lydia's behalf as well as her own.

'You thought . . . You assumed I was . . .'

'With good reason, you must admit. And I have begged your

pardon, Miss St Serf,' he added stiffly. 'Perhaps for your own sake you should choose your friends more carefully in future.'

'My friends are none of your affair!' Losing her temper, Flora snapped her fingers. 'It will be a sad day when I have to learn respectability from an Elder! Lydia,' she called abruptly, 'I'm sure the crowd is thinner now. We should be able to find a hackney-coach quite easily. 'Mr Elder—' Her voice had the icy sharpness of sleet. 'I'm grateful for your assistance – and your brother's too.'

'I'd have offered to take you both home . . .' With chill formality, Darius indicated the two-seat curricle. 'But, as you see, we have the wrong carriage for company. However, my groom shall find you a hackney.'

'How very kind!' Lydia, bubbling with gratitude, treated Darius to a glittering smile and resumed her tête-à-tête with Felix. To her dismay, Flora found herself left alone with Darius Elder in the frigid silence of two people who can think of nothing remotely polite to say to one another.

And yet even to be furious with him – to be outraged by his coolness, and to know he was equally maddened by her – was thrilling in its way . . . Flora breathed in deeply, relishing the tingle of battle, and under cover of searching for the returning groom, she stole a sideways glance. Darius Elder's eyes stared determinedly before him, but they were glowing with the blue-green intensity of burning salt; his profile was sharp, every inch of his body taut and defiant. With a shudder, Flora turned her head away and closed her eyes, trying to repress the sensation of being examined in her turn.

Let the groom come back . . . Oh, let him come back soon, leading the shabby sanctuary of a hackney-coach . . .

Illusion, illusion – but what kind of illusion could ravage the reason in this way? What kind of mirage had the power to sweep judgement aside – to explode good sense in a shower of rainbow stars?

Her hand was still trembling shamefully as she grasped the strap of the hackney to haul herself aboard.

'Miss St Serf – your purse.'

Lydia was leaning from the window, blowing coy kisses to Felix. Crossly, Flora reached past her, and succeeded in accepting the blue netted-silk absurdity from Darius Elder's hand without glancing into his face. The purse was painfully, obviously light; Flora pressed herself back into the rank-smelling darkness of the coach, and prayed for the driver to set his horse in motion.

'Good day, Miss St Serf.'

'Good day to you, Mr Elder.' It was as much as Flora could manage through gritted teeth.

'Well – what a man!' Lydia kicked off her shoes and swung her feet up on the opposite cushion.

'Why do you say that?' Flora's mind was so full of Darius that it was several seconds before she realized Lydia was referring to Felix.

'Did you ever see such a rake? Did you ever see a man so in love with himself?' Lydia pulled out her fan, and began to ply it with brisk little shivers of the sticks.

'You seemed happy enough in Felix's company.'

'My dear – that was business. If you have to live at the whim of a man, it's only sensible to keep one or two of the creatures warm in case of accidents.'

Flora fixed her gaze on the window, but Lydia leaned over to tap her on the knee with her fan.

'And what about his brother Darius, then! Oh, my dear – it's easy to see what attracted you to *him* . . .' Rapturously, Lydia wriggled her bottom.

'If you'll take me as far as Fetter Lane, Lydia, I'll run home from there.'

Flora's voice was so sharp that Lydia sat up at once, her eyes flying open in surprise. 'What's the matter, sweetness? Have I said something wrong?'

'No.'

'Is it something Darius Elder said, then?'

'No,' lied Flora. How could she describe her pain at being mistaken for exactly what Lydia *was* – a woman who was no more than a plaything for a man, obliged to blow kisses to wealthy boors who might one day come in useful.

Uncomprehending, Lydia persisted.

'Is it something to do with your purse being stolen? You got it back, didn't you?'

'Oh, Darius Elder saw to that.'

'Indeed he did.' Roguishly, Lydia tapped Flora's knee once more. 'No wonder a Hindu princess fell at his feet! Lovers like that don't grow on trees.'

'You don't know anything about him.'

'Sweetness – I know *men*. It's almost the only thing I do know about, God help me. And I can tell you, if you pass up a peach like Darius Elder, you'll be sorry.'

'Lydia, I promise you that whatever I may or may not think, Mr Darius Elder certainly doesn't want me.'

'Make him want you, then.'

'Nonsense!'

'I mean it, Flora. If you're waiting for a man to declare his love for you, you'll die an old maid. Love is what you call it when you've brought him to heel. Besides, from the look of him he's half-way there already.'

'Rubbish!'

'Very well. Have it your own way.' Stiffly, Lydia fanned.

'Thank you – I shall.'

Silence descended while the carriage rattled along the Strand and Flora fiddled with the wretched purse. Unthinkingly, she slid aside the brass ring which closed it, and felt for her five precious shillings. After a moment she withdrew her fingers in astonishment, pulling with them a piece of folded paper. In the dimness of the carriage, she examined it closely. It was unmistakably a five-pound note.

Lydia glanced across.

'Well, that's the first time I've seen a stolen purse come back with more than it had when it disappeared.' Lydia regarded the note with approval. 'You must have put it in there for safe-keeping, and forgotten all about it.'

Bewildered, Flora shook her head. 'I've never seen it before.'

'You must have done. Five-pound notes don't make themselves out of thin air. What a piece of luck!'

'No – you don't understand. The note wasn't there when the purse was stolen, I'm certain. In our house, five-pound notes are too precious to mislay.'

'Are you saying someone put it in there?' Lydia stopped fanning and stared at the note.

'But the only person who's touched this purse since it was stolen is—'

'Darius Elder,' Lydia finished softly. 'He's rich enough, certainly, and you gave him an excellent chance to do it. Oh, my dear . . .' Her eyes sparkled with wickedness. 'You may not want Mr Elder at any price, but I strongly suspect he wants *you* . . .'

CHAPTER FIVE

I

In the darkness of the night, while her mother slept soundly at the other side of the room, Flora lay awake, alternately boiling with anger and cringing with shame. Every few minutes, her fingers crept under the pillow to feel the stiff edge of the folded paper and confirm what her mind almost refused to accept. Darius Elder had somehow managed to put a five-pound note into the blue silk purse before returning it to her.

It was the only explanation – since the little thief certainly hadn't put it there. From the starved look of him, even Flora's five shillings would have been riches beyond imagination.

Darius Elder.

Flora repeated the name aloud, and heard her mother stir in her sleep. 'Edmund . . . why . . .' – and then the sound of limbs tensing, and subsiding again in slumber.

Flora slid her hand into the cool smoothness beneath her pillow, and touched the note once more.

There was only one explanation. With a shiver, Flora recalled the slow passing of those blue eyes over her body: Darius Elder must have intended the note as a message, as a sign of what a mistress could expect of a lover on twenty thousand a year – or whatever his income might be.

For a moment, Flora was furious enough to consider rising from her bed and going instantly to the Elders' house in Curzon Street to tell him otherwise. To be invited to become Darius Elder's mistress . . . To be installed, she supposed, in a discreet little house in a quiet street . . . to give intimate dinners for his friends . . . to lie, perhaps, in a lavish bed like the *maréchal*'s, drowsy in silk and fine perfumes, while the taut, fierce body she'd secretly examined by the curricle extended itself, naked and insistent, next to her own—

Flora stretched out her head on the pillow, drowning in the guilty darkness. What would Dédalon say, if he could see her now, rolling like a lustful cat at the first sign of a man's desire?

It was all Lydia's fault. Lydia had caused her to think like this, to run her eyes over a man with as much relish as if she'd rippled her fingers in rich figured silks – and then to calculate the price of his attentions.

Commerce, or the blind instinct of the species: never a word about love, except to dismiss it as a nonsense dreamed up by the Romantics to fill their overheated poetry.

Flora scowled in the darkness, and felt for the note once more.

Oh, there was a rotten, cynical world beyond the gentle Richmond garden where her daydreams had lived.

2

The next morning, while Mr Wesley and her mother conferred over which seamstress would remake his frayed shirt-collars at the smallest cost, Flora slipped away towards Fleet Street.

For the second time in her life, she walked through the tiled lobby into the sea-green world of Elder's Bank, where the lizard cashiers eyed her from their desks with blank reptilian stares. Almost at once, Flora felt her outrage begin to dissolve, cooled by the icy ceremony of that green gloom. She hesitated by the counter, uncertain what to do next.

'America Stock!' declared a voice at her ear, and a messenger clutching a tape-bound packet was directed to a desk at the rear of the room. 'Papers from the Navy Office!' A clerk at the side raised his hand. Flora waited, clutching the five-pound note, wondering if she should hold it up and shout 'Insult Returned!'

The nearest teller was dealing out sovereigns with a copper trowel. After a moment or two, Flora's silent hovering seemed to disturb him, and he signalled to a nearby desk where a studious figure arose, adjusted his spectacles, and slid forward to attend to her.

'Second Fair Cashbook Writer at your service, Miss. How may I help you?'

'Will you please tell Mr Elder – Mr Darius Elder – that Miss Flora St Serf wishes to say a few words to him.'

'I shall ascertain whether Mr Elder is available, Miss St Serf. In the meantime, if you'd care to sit . . .' The Second Fair Cashbook Writer indicated the row of hard chairs by a window, bowed again, and set off down the aisle of desks towards a tall and distant doorway, walking on the sides of his feet to keep them silent on the wooden floor.

For what seemed an age, Flora perched on the edge of a chair watching the bank go about its business. Every part of that business seemed to begin or end in the submarine Front Office, where the high ceiling echoed to the eternal mutter of voices and the shuffling of paper. Groups of gentlemen murmured in corners, their heads tilted inwards like the spikes on an iron railing; Flora's eye was caught by a stout little man in an old-fashioned white tie-wig who'd set down a row of green bottles on the edge of a desk in order to count out his banknotes. Almost at once, his powdery shoulders disappeared among the crowd of messengers answering cries of 'West Walk, if you please!' or 'South Walk here!' like a cloud of flies in that sea-green grotto.

'If you'll kindly walk through to the Debenture Office, Miss.'

Soundlessly, her guide had reappeared at her side, his hand held out towards the tall door at the rear of the room. Flora rose from her chair, lifted her chin, and set off down the long aisle in the direction he'd indicated.

The Debenture Office turned out to be smaller than the one she'd left, but though the walls were the same dull green in colour, they were broken by classical pilasters and gilt-framed portraits. The door stood open, and from the corridor Flora could see Darius Elder leaning on one of the two desks it contained, listening intently to the man who sat behind it. He was staring down at the ledger spread open before him, too absorbed by it to notice her coming, and a treacherous little part of Flora felt disappointed.

'Miss St Serf . . .' He straightened up at once, formally polite. 'This is an unexpected call. Normally it's your mother who comes here.' He indicated the other two men in the room. 'May I present our Chief Clerk and his assistant . . .'

Cool! Cool as an iceberg, quite unruffled by the presence of the woman whose favours he'd tried to solicit. Gracious heavens, but the man must be an accomplished seducer – to present his victim to his Chief Clerk without batting an eye . . . The arrogance of the creature! Such sheer, shameless immorality . . .

Once more Flora rehearsed the words she meant to say as soon as she and Darius Elder were alone – until it dawned upon her that he had no intention of interviewing her alone.

'I presume you're here on business, Miss St Serf?'

'Business . . . of a kind, I dare say.' She glared at him, stressing the words so that he should be left in no doubt of the 'business' she had in mind. The clerks had tactfully bent their heads over their desks.

'I came to return this, Mr Elder.' Flora held out the five-pound note accusingly. 'It's yours, I believe. *You must have lost it yesterday when you caught the boy who took my purse.*'

Flora squared her shoulders and stared Darius straight in the eye. Behind his desk, the Chief Clerk began to shuffle papers with ostentatious zeal.

'You must be mistaken, Miss St Serf.' Darius Elder's face was expressionless. 'I'm not aware of having lost any money.'

'Oh, I'm not the one who's mistaken, Mr Elder. I assure you, I know exactly how the note came to be in the place where I found it – *and why.* Naturally, I brought it back at once.'

'I'm certain the note is yours.'

'The note is *not* mine, Mr Elder! It never was mine. I didn't want it – I don't intend to earn it – and I haven't the slightest intention of keeping it. *I trust you understand what I mean.*'

And since he wouldn't take the note from her hand, Flora slapped it down squarely on the Chief Clerk's desk at his side.

'The money isn't mine, Miss St Serf, I assure you.' Darius Elder slid the note back along the desk towards her. 'And since you don't know the owner, I'd say you have a perfect right to keep it.'

'I will not keep it!' Angrily, Flora slid the note towards him again. 'And if you thought I would – then you chose the wrong woman, sir!'

'I'm sure you could find a use for it, nevertheless.' With a hiss, the note made its way back across the desk.

'Never, Mr Elder!' Flora promptly returned it.

The Chief Clerk's eyes were rolling in their sockets, fixed on the note as it slid to and fro under his nose. The eyes came to a bulging halt as two hands, pushing at the same moment, collided and clasped one another; instantly they flew apart again, leaving the crumpled five-pound note to lie accusingly between them.

'At any rate, I've made the matter plain to you.' Flora tugged at her fingers as if she could still feel the warmth of Darius Elder's flesh.

'I still don't see why you won't keep it.'

'You don't see? *You don't see?*' Flora lowered her voice to a furious hiss. 'Mr Elder, are you blind and deaf – or just blindly, insufferably arrogant? Do you imagine you've simply to snap your fingers, and any woman in London will do your bidding?'

The Chief Clerk, staring at her in astonishment, suddenly suffered a paroxysm of coughing and returned hastily to his papers.

'Get back to your work!' he snapped at his assistant.

'Miss St Serf – I've simply suggested you should keep the note you found.'

'Oh, I know what you suggested, Mr Elder. You made it quite plain what you wanted – though I dare say you thought you were being extremely subtle.'

All at once, realization dawned in Darius Elder's face, widening his eyes and draining some of their colour.

'Surely you don't think . . . You can't seriously believe . . .' He glanced quickly at the bent heads of the two clerks, who were no longer even pretending to write. Seizing Flora by the arm, he steered her towards the door. 'If you'd care to come this way, there are some pictures on the walls of this passage which might interest you . . .'

Half a dozen paces beyond the firmly shut door, he halted in the empty corridor.

'Now, Miss St Serf—' He faced her squarely, only to find himself suddenly tongue-tied, taken aback by the pride which shone, fierce and splendid, in her eyes.

'Miss St Serf,' he began again, 'you've just attacked me quite infamously. I hope you realize how unjust you've been.'

'*I've* been unjust! When you deliberately tried to – to—'

'I tried nothing of the kind!' Darius Elder's indignation rose to match Flora's. 'You know perfectly well I apologized for the mistake I made yesterday – and you also know why I made it.'

'All I know is that one moment you were looking down your nose at poor Lydia for letting herself be kept by a man – and the next you were secretly pushing five pounds into my purse. What was that, if it wasn't a *proposition*? And don't try to deny you put it there!'

'But for heaven's sake – that was something entirely different! How was I to know you'd think . . .'

'So you did do it!'

'Of course I did it – though now I wish to blazes I hadn't.'

A clerk scurried down the passage from the Front Office, and began to climb a nearby staircase. They waited, glaring at one another, until the man's footsteps had died to a faint patter overhead.

'It never crossed my mind for a moment that you'd be so stupid!'

83

Darius Elder tried to keep his voice low. 'You actually believed I would offer you money for . . . so that you'd . . . God in heaven!' He threw up his hands in a gesture of futility.

Flora stared at him, the wind suddenly drained from the sails of her outrage. 'But—'

'Let me assure you, Miss St Serf, I do not go around stuffing money into young women's purses in order to lure them into my bed. At least give me credit for a little finesse!' A bloodless spot had appeared high on either cheekbone. 'And even if I did, you aren't at all the kind of woman . . .'

He waved a hand, dismissing the very idea. Any fool could see that, even furious and mistaken, Flora St Serf existed as far above such petty intrigues as a shining star above a cattle-pen.

Misunderstanding, Flora's lower lip trembled a little. 'Then if you didn't . . . didn't want me – why did you put the money in my purse?'

'I acted without thinking. I felt . . .' He stopped, apparently embarrassed by the impulse which had seized him.

'You felt sorry for me!' Flora's voice was anguished: this new indignity was almost worse than the other. 'You saw me in an old, crumpled gown, pulled about by the crowd – and you remembered all Papa's debts – and you *pitied* me! Oh, how could you!'

Flora was almost in tears now, but they were tears of rage and frustration.

'At least you realize there was nothing improper—'

'Gracious heaven, can you not understand yet? To be pitied by you, of all people . . .' Wretched with shame, Flora lost her temper.

'How dare you feel sorry for me!' she burst out recklessly. 'The conceit of you Elders – just because half of London's in debt to your bank! You toss me five pounds, just as you might throw a penny to the crossing-sweeper – as if I was a beggar, scrambling in the gutter for crusts. Well, I'm not a beggar, Mr Elder, I'm a St Serf. And the St Serfs do not need your pity – or your charity.'

'You've made that perfectly clear.' Darius Elder's sympathy had turned to cold anger, and the two livid spots on his cheekbones remained. 'I'd forgotten you held my family in such low regard, Miss St Serf, simply on account of our profession. There was a time when I, too, disliked the idea of the bank and all it stood for, but now that circumstances have brought me into the family business, I must say it seems to serve a useful enough purpose in the world. At least, I can't see why it should deserve the curses you pour upon it.'

Stiffly, he held out a hand to indicate that she should walk to the Front Office.

'And as for my clumsy attempt to give you money . . . It was a stupid mistake, and I apologize for causing you offence. I shall take care not to do so again.'

They were almost at the tall doorway which led into the Front Office, and with the end of the interview in sight Flora had begun to regret her outburst. His eyes – one could grow to dislike those eyes, but that mouth was dangerously weakening.

'I dare say you meant well,' she conceded lamely.

'An Elder – mean well?' Darius Elder's voice was frigidly ironic. 'Impossible, Miss St Serf. Money-lenders have no hearts – surely you know that.'

'I didn't say that.'

'Oh, I think you did.' Darius allowed Flora to pass ahead of him into the Front Office, then halted with scrupulous ceremony at the final line of desks. 'Good day to you, Miss St Serf. It was so kind of you to call. After this I'm sure we both know exactly where we stand.'

A few moments later Flora found herself once more in the brightness of Fleet Street, her heart filled with a deep and inexplicable agony.

3

Since she could hardly hate Darius Elder for not having tried to buy her body, Flora decided to hate him for his pity, and spent countless hours in voluptuous self-torment, thinking of all the things his five pounds might have bought. Six yards of the best India muslin and silk gloves to match . . . New boots to replace her poor, cracked soles . . . Enough pekoe to fill her mother's pot a hundred times over . . . No! Not for all the pekoe in the Orient! Proudly, Flora embraced her misery like a lover.

Constance had already discovered her secret visit to the coronation; now, feeling quite heroic, Flora could see no harm in telling her mother how a St Serf had flung an Elder's charity-money back in his face.

Constance was mending a glove which had burst at the seam, though since every stitch pulled a new hole in the worn white kid, the glove was no more complete than when she'd started.

'So you think I was right to do as I did?' Flora had been surprised to find her mother so little offended by her story.

'Right to take Darius Elder's money back to him? I dare say that was proper, my dear – though I wish you'd consulted me first. I hope you weren't rude.'

'Rude?' Flora stared at her mother in amazement.

'No doubt Mr Elder meant it kindly.' Constance peered at the white kid. 'Five pounds is nothing to a gentleman of that family. It was nothing to us, once,' she added sadly, snipping with tiny scissors at her futile stitching.

'Once, perhaps,' agreed Flora heatedly, 'before the Elders hounded Papa into the ground! Surely we aren't reduced to begging from them now.'

'I suppose not . . . Though you said yourself Mr Elder refused to take the money back, and swore at first he'd never put it into your purse.' There was a pause, while Constance struggled with her pride. 'Isn't it possible – just possible – that it really was five pounds of your own which you'd overlooked?'

'There was nothing but a few shillings in the purse when I left home!'

'But you can't be sure of that, Flora.' Constance raised reproachful eyes to her daughter. 'The note was folded up, after all.'

'I don't see how—'

'And perhaps if you couldn't be *absolutely* sure . . . then you should have kept it after all, just to be safe, and not gone bothering Mr Elder about it.' Constance held up the glove, and for the first time Flora saw the faded, hungry expression in her mother's eyes. 'We could have done a great deal with five pounds.'

'And let Darius Elder treat us like street beggars?' exclaimed Flora in a passion.

'You can't be certain,' her mother persisted doggedly. 'It might have been yours. What a happy discovery, a lost five-pound note!'

'It wasn't lost. It was never mine.'

'All the same, I wish you'd asked me. The St Serfs would never take anyone's charity, naturally – but if the note was ours all along . . .' Constance regarded Flora severely over the abandoned glove. 'Yes, decidedly – you were very wrong to give it away.'

Now at last Flora understood how far the family had fallen. The signs had been there before, but she'd failed to notice them, beguiled by her mother's insistence on everything being *comme il faut* despite their straitened circumstances. In the months that followed the return of the note she began to notice familiar possessions disappearing one by one, quietly sold in order that the family might live. Without explanation, the silver punch-ladle went missing from its place, and then the inkstand which Flora had saved from the bailiffs; soon after, they were followed by the Major's military greatcoat, and the silver spoons, replaced in twos and threes by cheap horn.

Maggie had been sent out to sell the Major's sword, she confessed one day, and his silver-mounted sword-belt. Maggie had come to London from Scaurs when Constance was married, and her loyalty to the family of Clantavish went far beyond that of maid to mistress.

'Maggie,' asked Flora, 'when did you last get your wages?'

'Oh, my dear lassie, how can I take money from the mistress when she's in such sair straits? What would I buy with wages, anyway? There's barely room for a bed in my wee cupboard by the kitchen.'

After that Flora could hardly sit down to dinner without wondering which treasures had been sold to put food on her plate. What ring or chain had been transformed into the piece of greyish ham which curled on its dish between the smoking butcher's candles? It seemed to Flora as if she was eating the family's substance with every mouthful, swallowing up house and home as she cleared her plate, and she glanced at her parents, wondering if they felt the same revulsion.

Sophie called in September, splendid in the wide silk sleeves which had become all the rage. And Flora, who'd thrown Darius Elder's five pounds in his face with such disdain, was left to dress up her pride in much altered white muslin, while the flesh melted from her bones on a diet of vanished greatcoat and coarse brown bread.

In December the duns began to arrive again, hammering on the street door at six in the morning, or marching into the drawing-room and refusing to leave until the Major made them uneasy by staring at them with burning, haunted eyes.

Then one day when the duns were at their worst, a tear-stained note arrived from Sophie to say that Uncle Greville St Serf, the dashing dragoon, was dead, and the house at Chillbourne was plunged in the deepest despair imaginable. Worse still – with dreadful irony – it appeared that the General's second son, after surviving the dangers of countless battles, had died of trying to swallow his sword at a rowdy mess dinner.

'Will you go to the burial, Papa?' Flora enquired, thinking of the missing greatcoat.

The answer came after a long silence. 'No.'

'But surely—'

'No.' After a moment, he repeated it more loudly. 'NO!' And Major St Serf rose furiously from his chair, pushed his daughter aside, and banged out of the room.

A few minutes later, Flora heard a muffled sound like the moaning of an animal in pain: after a moment she realized it was coming from her father's bedchamber, where the Major had locked himself in to suffer alone.

4

The 7th February 1822 was Flora's nineteenth birthday.

Sophie sent a letter to say that she couldn't call because of still being in mourning for her uncle, but enclosed a tortoiseshell and soft leather reticule in the latest style, perfect for the social calls which Flora never made. Constance presented her with a handkerchief she'd embroidered, kissed the air by her cheek, and went off at once to the basement kitchen 'to give Maggie her orders'.

So much, thought Flora, for her nineteenth birthday – until, at ten in the morning, one of Dédalon's apprentices brought a parcel to the door. Long before Maggie had time to climb up the stairs from the kitchen, Flora had carried off her package to open it in secret in a freezing corner by the earth-closet behind the house.

Dédalon's gift was all the more precious for the hours which must have gone into its making. At first it seemed no more than a dainty box made of papier mâché, painted with scenes of woods and hills, which Flora guessed must have been drawn from the French country-side. But when the box was opened, wonder of wonders, music began to play and a papier mâché dancer rose up from a concealed panel to pirouette slowly to the tinkling tune.

The face of the dancer was as exquisitely painted as a miniature portrait. For a moment, Flora wondered if the little creature was meant to be herself, but the hair was fair and the skin too sallow. Yet by some miracle of Dédalon's art the face seemed full of life, so ready to speak and to laugh that Flora could hardly tear her eyes from it. *Give me a little time, and I'll make you another sister*, Dédalon had promised her once – and indeed, the tiny dancer had a look of Sophie, with her arms held in a graceful arc and one leg bent for a leap into the air which she'd never make.

Carefully, Flora wound the mechanism and listened once more to the melody. She recognized the tune of a French country dance she'd often heard Dédalon whistle under his breath; now the notes fell like a shower of ice crystals in the frosty air, as bright and as clear as the morning itself.

Flora had barely reached the top of the stairs with her booty when she heard her mother call from the hallway below.

'Flora! Flora, do you hear me?'

'Yes, Mamma.' Flora put her head over the balustrade and peered down.

'Can you imagine—' Constance's voice floated up to her, shrill with indignation. 'That wretch of a laundrywoman has sent round to say she'll sell Papa's good cambric neckcloths if I don't pay her everything that's owing – the impertinent creature. You must go with me, Flora, since I can't possibly go alone and Maggie has the dinner to see to.'

'In a moment, certainly—'

'Now, my girl! It may be your birthday today, but you aren't a lady of leisure yet. Here – put this shawl round your shoulders.'

Constance was waiting below, the shawl held out. Searching hastily for a temporary hiding-place for her music-box, Flora's eye fell on an old Windsor chair by the drawing-room door, its wooden seat covered by a cushion her mother had embroidered in the easy days at Richmond. Quickly, Flora propped up the cushion and thrust the box out of sight behind it. As soon as she returned, she'd hide Dédalon's gift where it wouldn't be found and give rise to awkward questions.

With a heavy heart, she set off with her mother to the laundry-woman's home several streets away. Constance, she knew, meant to lecture the laundress, who'd complain in her turn about folk who gave themselves airs and never paid their bills – and the whole episode would dissolve into threats and ill-feeling.

Yet the scene at the laundrywoman's was nothing compared to the wailing and commotion which greeted them on their return to Gough Square. In growing alarm, Flora and her mother pushed their way through the curious crowd at the foot of the steps to find Maggie flat on her face in the hallway, shrieking with grief, and Mr Theodore Wesley at the head of the stairs, supporting a weeping Mrs Moss and murmuring 'A bad business, a very bad business,' through his lustrous teeth.

Flora and Constance flew up the stairs in time to see an elderly man emerge from the drawing-room in a bobbed medical wig and low-crowned beaver hat, a pair of nose-spectacles swinging from his neck on a cord.

'Not a spark,' he intoned in Mr Wesley's direction. 'Not a chance, I'm afraid – not the slightest flicker. Are you a brother, perhaps?'

Mr Wesley shook his head sombrely.

'Nothing I could do,' the doctor declared to the company in general. 'Dead before his nose hit the table, I'd say.'

'Doctor—' Clutching her skirts in both hands, Constance St Serf hurried towards him.

'Ah!' The doctor eyed her with some relief. 'The widow, no doubt. My condolences, Madam – your husband is thoroughly dead. My bill will follow. Good day to you, gracious lady.'

As the doctor pushed past her, cramming his hat more firmly over his dirty wig, Flora's eyes flew instinctively to the Windsor chair and to the embroidered cushion which had hidden her musical box.

The cushion lay as flat on the seat as a penny-piece. Her hastily hidden birthday gift had gone.

CHAPTER SIX

I

The Major had shot himself through the right temple with the pocket pistol he'd carried at Waterloo, killing himself thoroughly, as the doctor had said – the last efficient act of a perfect soldier. By his hand stood Flora's music-box, open and silent, the dancer frozen in a shocked arabesque.

For a long time, it seemed, Flora stood in the doorway, as motionless as the little figurine, trying to absorb the fact that her father was there, before her, slumped at the table – and yet not there: she'd never again hear the sound of his voice, or see his eyes come to rest on her with wistful affection . . . It was an affection she'd returned as love, but which hadn't, in the end, been enough to prevent tragedy. *How could his life have become so worthless to him, when it was still so precious to me? Oh, Papa, if you'd only explained . . . I'd have done anything. Anything at all . . .* Tears of helplessness rolled down her cheeks.

Round its core of stillness the room began to fill with people, whispering and murmuring so as not to disturb the dead. Constance was overwhelmed by a flurry of women, and soon all Flora could see of her father was an elbow shrouded in white cambric, motionless in a thickening stain of blood. No one had thought to close the music-box, her birthday gift from the automaton-maker.

'I must see – stand aside there—'

Impatiently, Constance parted the protective arms which encircled her, shielding the table from her gaze.

'Ah . . .' She stood silently at the dead man's shoulder, staring down. Her face was pale, and there was a tightness round her eyes, but she seemed . . . frustrated . . . pitying . . . as if a favourite pet she'd nursed through a long illness had died in spite of all her trouble.

What did she see? A man, Flora guessed, who'd deprived her of the home and social position which had been her whole life, for some unfathomable ideal of his own – yet, in the end, a man broken by an even greater loss than hers.

'His uniform coat . . .' Constance extended a hand to stroke the blue wool, and Flora, standing by the door, realized that, in her own frugal way, her mother had once loved a soldier.

Constance's gaze had moved on beyond the slumped figure, and had come to rest on the music-box. Its presence didn't seem to puzzle her any more than the sight of her husband lying in a pool of his own blood.

'Sophie . . .' Constance's face brightened as if she'd opened a door to find her younger daughter waiting on the threshold. 'Sophie . . .'

From the table the shining dancer smiled gaily back at her, just as she'd smiled at the Major.

Sophie – Flora had noticed the likeness herself. Silent in the doorway, she cursed herself for her carelessness in leaving the box where he could find it and be reminded once more.

It was Flora who wrote to break the news to Sophie and the General, disturbed by her mother's strange mood.

'I pray you will allow Sophie to visit us in London now,' she added firmly at the end of her note to her grandfather, 'since I believe Mamma should have the company of both of her daughters at this sad time.'

Both of her daughters: yet it was Sophie for whom her mother asked continually, as if only Sophie's return could set a seal on what had happened. It was Flora who'd sent for the layer-out, and Flora who'd persuaded the doctor to certify 'accidental death while cleaning a firearm', thus saving her father from being buried in unconsecrated ground without so much as a billet of wood to mark the spot. It was Flora, too, who'd haggled with the undertaker over the cost of the funeral – but it was Sophie whose face Constance wanted to see, and no face but hers.

On the morning after her father's death, Flora took the music-box to a toy-seller a mile away in Regent Street, and used the money he gave her to pay for a simple iron cross for the Major's grave.

Sophie, at Chillbourne, wasn't allowed to read her sister's letter. Instead, Miss Meagle was asked to break the dreadful news as gently as she knew how – and being a passionless woman, bluntly informed Sophie that her father had died of a pistol-ball to the brain inflicted by his own hand, and that in the circumstances she was excused pianoforte practice for the rest of the day.

The General brooded over Flora's letter in the wintry dimness of his study, and began to fear a future which had escaped from his control. In a single year the mighty citadel of the St Serfs had become a thing of the past; the sons and grandsons who were to have carried his standard bravely through the coming centuries had vanished like a mirage.

For the first time in his life, after sixty-five years of resolute health, General Bayard St Serf fell ill. Overnight, gout claimed one foot and palpitations rattled his heart; he became liverish, and the stomach which had thrived on battlefield rations now refused anything stronger than egg custard. Robbed of a future, the General found himself abandoned in the past, with nothing to hold him back from the darkness of the grave but a not-quite-seventeen-year-old girl.

Sophie must be allowed to visit her mother: it was her duty to go, and in the General's mind duty was still paramount. Yet what if she never came back? Disturbingly, the General discovered that the yellow-haired child who stared at him with hungry eyes when she sat with him after dinner had become an infinitely precious part of his existence. Suppose the Clantavish woman insisted on keeping Sophie with her in London? Suppose Sophie herself agreed? For who could tell how Edmund's wife might poison the girl's mind against her grandparents?

The General shook his head uncomprehendingly, past events no longer sharply focused in his memory. The single, overwhelming thought left in his failing mind was that Sophie – the last hope of the St Serf line – should return as soon as possible to live with him at Chillbourne.

The fear showed in his face when he spoke to her.

'You won't go off and forget about me, will you?' he begged awkwardly when she came to say goodbye. 'Naturally, it is your duty to comfort your mother at a time like this, but I shall worry about you, far away in the city instead of safely here at Chillbourne.'

He reached out a papery, liver-spotted hand to cover Sophie's where it lay on the arm of his chair.

Sophie stared down at the alien skin, then raised her eyes to examine her grandfather carefully, disconcerted by the strange wheedling tone in his voice. Was the old man ill? Sophie became uneasy, as if the very earth were trembling under her feet.

Sensing her alarm, the General tightened his grip. With a gasp, Sophie pulled her hand away, appalled to discover her tower of certainty, her remote, infallible, godlike grandfather, pleading for the affection of a sixteen-year-old girl. This was no longer the grandfather she knew, the grandfather whose word had governed every moment of her life in his house. She'd come to be given orders, to be told what was expected of her – not to be petted and cajoled like a spoiled lapdog.

Confused, she struggled to make sense of the moment.

'I'm definitely to come back here, then, Grandpapa? I'm not to stay in London with Mamma?'

'If you wish to come back, my dear.' The General gazed at her anxiously, suddenly afraid to insist. 'Your grandmother and I are old now, and dull companions for a young girl. But this is a large, empty house for two elderly people . . .'

The General paused, as if the exact form of words eluded him. 'It would give us very great pleasure, if you wished to stay with us at Chillbourne – but we'd never keep you against your will.' With an effort, he added, 'You must choose where you want to live, Sophie.'

Sophie, not Sophia! Desperately, Sophie groped for direction.

'Then . . . you *expect* me to come back to Chillbourne.'

'No, no, I don't expect anything.' The General looked troubled. 'I simply hope you'll come back to us. Out of . . . affection, perhaps.'

Sophie stared at her grandfather in horror, suddenly seeing his face overlaid with her father's, wordlessly begging her to forgive him for being a frail and imperfect mortal, pleading with her to stay with him and to understand.

'It is . . . my duty to go to Mamma,' she concluded uncertainly. 'You said so, Grandpapa. But then . . . surely it is also my duty to come back to Chillbourne. You and Grandmamma have been so very kind to me, and after all, Mamma still has Flora to care for her. My duty lies here, with you.'

'Out of duty, then,' the General conceded with a sigh. 'As long as you come back to us, child.'

A few minutes later, for the first time in months, Sophie fetched Ismene-Maria from the back of the cupboard in her room, and packed the doll into her hatbox for the journey to London.

Sophie, her maid and Miss Meagle were to stay with the General's widowed sister, Mrs Ivory, in Curzon Street.

Mrs Ivory received her great-niece kindly but with the brisk unsentimentality of a widow of long standing, and promptly placed her chariot at Sophie's disposal so that she might be driven to Gough Square whenever she chose.

Mrs Ivory, thought Sophie regretfully, was just like her brother, the General, in better days – direct, forceful, and unwavering in her beliefs.

'Meagle will turn you into a hunchback,' she warned Sophie on the second evening of her stay. 'Too much sitting over books ruins the eyes of a growing young woman, and too much pianoforte warps the spine. Doesn't she know anything but hymns? Playing for hymns blunts the fingers – it's a scientific fact. All that *bang-thump, bang-thump*! Play nocturnes, my dear, if you must play at all. Think peaceful thoughts, and your hands will grow beautiful too. I shall tell Meagle so when I see her.'

Sophie's thoughts, had Mrs Ivory only known it, were anything but peaceful. At ten that morning, her father had been buried with as much ceremony as Flora had been able to contrive after selling the dead man's watch and boots. Two empty hired carriages had followed the bier, and Mr Theodore Wesley and Undertaker Harkiss had walked ahead as chief, and only, mourners.

Sophie had gone to Gough Square in Mrs Ivory's chariot at two in the afternoon, and felt the old, sour chill invade her bones as soon as the carriage turned under the last archway.

If she'd hated the old house before, she hated it now with a passion almost beyond reason. The mere sight of its narrow, wainscoted entry was enough to choke her throat like a cancer; the smell of boiling vegetables from the kitchen and tom-cats from the stairs made her head swim, and she knew that to go once more into the dark, poky cupboard which her mother insisted on calling the 'drawing-room' would take every ounce of her resolution.

However dismayed she'd been by her grandfather's pitiable state, Sophie knew beyond doubt that she'd never again be able to live in the house in Gough Square. To be shut up in that mean brick yard, day after dreary day, was more than she could ever endure. And the guilt of not being able to endure it, and of having escaped from the prison which still held her hollow-eyed sister, only added to her profound distress.

Flora greeted her alone in the shadows at the top of the stairs, drawing her into a wordless embrace. After a moment, Sophie disengaged herself, and peered anxiously round the little hallway.

'Where's Mamma?'

'She's resting. We won't disturb her yet.' Flora's eyes were red-rimmed from recent tears, and she seemed uncomfortable, glancing all the time towards the closed door of her mother's bedroom.

'I thought Mamma might want to see me. But not if you think she's too upset, of course. I'll call again tomorrow.' Sophie half-turned, ready to leave again.

'No – wait . . .' Flora trapped her by the arm. 'Mamma does want to see you. Very much. It's all she speaks about.' Flora's gaze swept once more towards the bedroom door before returning anxiously to her sister. 'But I wanted to talk to you before she does. To explain.'

She gestured towards the drawing-room door. 'If we stand here Mamma will hear us talking.'

'But isn't that where—' Sophie caught at Flora's sleeve, her eyes round with alarm.

'Yes, it's where we found Papa.' A weary irritation had crept into Flora's voice. 'But since we only have four rooms, we can't very well afford the luxury of shutting one of them up for good.'

Sophie allowed herself to be led towards the drawing-room. Once inside, she glanced round apprehensively, reassured by the sight of the table and chairs standing in their accustomed places on the worn floorcloth.

Fluttering a gloved hand over her eyes, Sophie sank down on one of the chairs.

'I'm sorry, Flora. You can think me a great fool if you like – and I'm sure you do, since you're such a down-to-earth, practical person. But I'm so glad I wasn't here when – when it happened.'

Flora examined her sister closely. Sophie's black bonnet and black velvet pelisse were enough to make any complexion seem pale, but there was a leaden whiteness to the skin about her eyes, an ominous transparency Flora remembered of old. Frowning, she searched for words of reassurance.

'It was awful at the time, of course. I kept thinking of things I might have said or done that could have made a difference . . . But afterwards, when the shock had worn off a little, I realized it was almost as if Papa had been dying for ages – dying inside – and the moment had finally come. I suppose that deep down I'd given up hoping he'd ever be his old self again.'

'And yet . . .' A faint frown creased Sophie's pale brow as she tried to disentangle her feelings for her father. 'I mean – Papa didn't have to be miserable. He wasn't ill or anything, and the court martial was over and done with years ago. Why did he have to mope about it for so long?'

Flora shook her head. 'I wish I could tell you that. If I'd understood, perhaps I could have done something to help.'

Sophie had perched herself on the edge of one of the gilt beechwood chairs like a blackbird about to fly off at any moment. She tugged at her pelisse with black-gloved hands, and her umbrella clattered to the floor. Flora held up a finger for silence, her head cocked in the direction of their mother's room.

'Have I wakened her?' Sophie turned anxiously towards the door.

'No – I don't think so.' Flora let her hand fall back to her lap and studied it there intently. 'Mamma is very . . . upset,' she explained, choosing the word with care. 'But not in the way you'd expect.' She paused again. 'I don't think either of us ever realized how dreadful it was for her to have to leave Richmond and all her friends, and to come to live here and be so poor. It became an obsession with her, and in her heart she blamed Papa for making it all happen.'

Flora glanced up to find Sophie watching her, the pupils of her eyes as huge and black as the buttons of her pelisse.

'Papa couldn't help it, of course,' Flora said quickly. 'I don't suppose he wanted to be poor any more than we did. Imagine being so miserable that you've nothing left to live for.'

Sophie stared slowly round the narrow little room. 'I can imagine it,' she murmured. 'If the last hope were gone. If everything suddenly became meaningless.' Her huge eyes came to rest again on Flora. 'I know how Papa felt, you see – but not *why* . . .'

'My darling child!'

Anything further Sophie might have said was lost when the drawing-room door was thrown open and Constance rushed in with a cry of delight to embrace her younger daughter.

'Sophie, my dear!' For a moment Constance's eyes devoured Sophie's immaculate ensemble before returning fondly to her daughter's pale face. 'It does me so much good to see you. It's been my one comfort in the last few days, to know I was able to send you away from all this.'

She reached out to stroke Sophie's colourless cheek, and Sophie almost flinched from her touch.

'I was so sorry to hear about Papa . . .'

Constance's gaze flicked round the room, and the sight of it seemed to spark a memory.

'Until the very end, you know, he wanted you back.' She clasped Sophie's hands possessively. 'Right . . . until . . . the very last moment.'

'Mamma – please.' All of a sudden Flora had seen a flash of fear in her sister's eyes. 'How can you possibly know that?'

'Oh, I'm sure of it.' Constance continued to smile fondly at her younger daughter. 'Why else should he have the box on the table beside him? As soon as I set eyes on the little dancer, I knew.'

'What box?' demanded Sophie wildly. 'I don't know anything about a box! Why should it have anything to do with me?'

'It was a music-box,' explained Flora quickly. 'A toy – nothing at all – but there was a dancer inside with fair hair like yours, and Mamma's convinced it reminded Papa of you.' Out of her mother's sight, Flora made reassuring signs to Sophie. 'I'd have told you,' she whispered, 'except that Mamma came in before I had a chance.'

'Let me see the music-box!' insisted Sophie at once. 'I don't believe the dancer looked like me at all. Why should Papa's death have anything to do with me?'

'He'd have kept you here for ever, you know, shut up with him in this house.' By main force, Constance kept hold of Sophie's hands. 'But you had the good sense to run off to Chillbourne, my darling, and look at you now!'

Sophie gazed at her mother in horror. With an anguished moan she wrenched her hands free.

'That isn't true! I didn't mean to run away from him. It was Flora who sent me away, because she couldn't bear to go herself. If I'd known he was so unhappy I'd have come back at once – you believe that, Flora, don't you?' Sophie turned to her sister in desperate appeal.

'Well . . . that is . . .' Flora made a gesture of helplessness, torn between the plain truth and the obvious pain in her sister's face.

'How was I to know Papa wanted me to come back, if he didn't say so?' Sophie's eyes flashed indignantly, but her trembling lower lip gave away the lie.

'What does it matter?' asked Constance. 'As long as one of my girls is living the life she was intended for.'

'No . . . Don't, Mamma – please!'

'Sophie,' began Flora soothingly, 'Mamma's quite right – none of it matters any more. Poor Papa's beyond caring about anything now, so the reason for it all isn't important.'

'Oh, yes – the saintly Flora!' The skin around Sophie's nostrils had taken on a bluish tinge. 'So you're prepared to forgive me, are you, for living in luxury at Chillbourne while you stayed with Papa in Gough Square? How very, very generous!'

'Sophie!' Flora's voice rose in protest. 'I didn't say anything of the kind.'

Sophie shook her head violently, wrenching the veil she'd raised up round her bonnet.

'You may not have said it, but that's what you were thinking, all the same. "Selfish Sophie, who broke her father's heart." I'm the one who caused Papa's death – that's what you believe, isn't it?'

'Of course not. No one's blaming you for anything, Sophie. You're the one who's blaming herself.'

'You've always been jealous of me, Flora.' Sophie was at the door now, a pillar of black with a haunted, tragic face. 'You had me sent away to Chillbourne because I was Papa's favourite – and now you're jealous of me again, because I have pretty clothes and go to parties.'

'Mamma, please!' Flora appealed to her mother. 'Make Sophie understand what nonsense she's talking.'

'Yes – come and sit by me, Sophie dear, and tell me all the news from Chillbourne. Have you driven out in the sleigh again this winter? Oh, I should so like to see it – you must look so very elegant!'

'I must go.' Sophie stared at her mother in horror. 'Great-aunt Sybil will be wondering what's happened to me.' Groping for the handle, she tore open the door.

'But you've only just arrived! You must take some Madeira – and an almond cake . . . Maggie makes excellent almond cakes. I wonder I never discovered that before.'

Sophie's eyes began to fill with tears. With a cry of despair, she fled from the room.

'Sophie, wait!' Flora hurried after her sister, but Sophie was already at the foot of the staircase. The sound of her swiftly tapping footsteps died away down its echoing well, followed after a moment by the slamming of the front door.

All the way to Curzon Street, Sophie wallowed in wretchedness, pressed into her corner of the chariot, her cheeks wet with tears.

She'd gone to Gough Square with the old guilt already gnawing at her heart, and had returned with her worst fears confirmed. The rattle of the chariot's wheels over the cobbles threw back her thoughts like a curse. Oh, she was selfish and weak – selfish and weak, while Flora was virtuous and strong.

Impulsively, Sophie tore off her mourning gloves, unable to bear their reproachful blackness for a minute longer. Yet somehow the dye seemed to have stained her hands; anxiously, she scrubbed at her fingers and palms, but only succeeded in raising red weals to mix with the greyness which had offended her.

Her misery tinged now with panic, she rubbed her hands down her pelisse – and then realized that the pelisse was as black as her gloves. Was there no escape from that dismal colour? Were her hands to be marked by it for ever?

Ismene-Maria wouldn't care. In the shadowy carriage Sophie began to think longingly of her doll, stiffly comforting in her new chintz dress. Yet what use were fine clothes, when the woman inside them had a heart of straw!

3

By the end of another week there was no comfort at all to be found in the first-floor rooms overlooking Gough Square – and precious little else. If Mr Wesley hadn't offered to hide Constance's sacred pianoforte in his own parlour, it would certainly have been carried away by the swarm of bailiffs and creditors who gathered like flies to pick over the Major's remains.

But the law was clear: a man's wife was no more capable of independent action than the pen in his hand, which meant that the Major's debts were his alone, and died with him. His creditors departed again with what little there was, gloomily scratching the address from their books.

A week later, Elder's Bank sent a gentlemanly letter regretting Major St Serf's death and confirming they'd given up what he owed as irrecoverable. Mrs St Serf's quarterly allowance was paid by trustees for her sole use, and couldn't be claimed to satisfy her husband's creditors. Constance read the letter with satisfaction: her income was small – very small – but everyone knew that a Major's widow could make economies unthinkable in a Major's wife.

Sophie had not returned to Gough Square.

'She'll come back once she's calmed down,' her mother predicted confidently, but instead, Sophie sent a short, impersonal note by one of Mrs Ivory's footmen to explain that her grandfather's health had suddenly taken a turn for the worse, and she was obliged to return to Chillbourne.

With a sigh, Flora sat down to write a long letter of reassurance: Sophie was in no way to blame for the Major's death, and no one had thought of accusing her; the presence of the music-box had been a complete coincidence. The letter had gone off to Chillbourne the next day, but so far there'd been no reply. In the meantime, Flora and her mother set about establishing a new life for themselves.

If they made do with two rooms and the use of the basement kitchen, Constance's allowance would cover the rent and leave a little over. If Maggie were to remain with them – even in two bare rooms Constance shrieked aloud at the thought of washing her own linen or carrying coals – then Flora insisted that Maggie must be paid regular wages out of what was left; however, as soon as she, Flora had found work as an apothecary's assistant or something of the sort—

'My daughter – selling James's Powder for the bowels of rag-men and chimney-purifiers?' demanded Constance. 'I'd sooner starve than see you do such a vulgar thing.'

In the end, it was Constance who discovered a new source of income, when a month to the day after the Major's death, Miss Lightsome Harkiss, the undertaker's daughter, rapped on the door with the handle of the enormous fan dangling from her wrist and demanded to speak to the Widow St Serf.

'Mother has heard', she explained without any preamble, 'as how you have a pianoforty in the house, and wants to know if you'd be so kind as to give us lessons. *Me*,' she corrected herself solemnly.

Constance examined her caller through narrowed eyes. 'Give pianoforte lessons?' she repeated slowly. 'For money?'

'Cash on the nail,' confirmed the undertaker's child. 'No credit asked, no credit given.'

Gravely, Constance studied Miss Harkiss from the top of the monstrous plumes in her five-guinea bonnet to the hem of her twelve-guinea patent lace dress.

'You'd better come inside then, Miss Harkiss, and we'll see what we can do for you.'

Soon Miss Harkiss and several of her friends were coming regularly to learn gentility and 'The Death of Nelson' at a guinea an hour, leaving their fees discreetly under the first volume of *Gradus ad Parnassum* on the drawing-room table so as not to offend against good taste.

Unfortunately, the sight of Miss Harkiss plodding her beringed fingers up and down the ivory keys, her lace cap sliding over one eye with the effort of concentration, only made Flora feel more idle than ever. Yet, thanks to the undertaker's daughter, her visits to Dédalon in Shoe Lane were no longer a secret, nor the books she borrowed there to relieve her boredom.

'*Anatomical Philosophy*,' declared her mother in distaste, holding the volume at arm's length. 'I found it, Miss, hidden under your pillow – full of perfectly disgusting engravings.'

'It simply compares one animal with another. There's nothing disgusting in that.'

'Nevertheless,' persisted Constance, 'it shouldn't concern you whether slugs have backbones or whether they don't. Really, Flora, I despair of you. You're rapidly turning into the kind of woman no right-thinking man would wish to marry.'

'Then I'll just have to hope for a wrong-thinking man,' retorted Flora crisply, 'or better still – stay single.'

Fortunately, another pupil arrived before Constance could think of an answer to this. Defiantly tying on her bonnet, Flora made her way through the rain-swept yards to the automaton-maker's workshop.

4

Dédalon had learned of the Major's death without surprise, though the circumstances of it seemed to fascinate him, and he returned to the subject almost every time Flora called.

'My music-box,' he'd murmur, his head bent low over some piece of intricate mechanism. 'My music-box – found beside a dead soldier . . . Ended . . . Run down . . . Finished.'

'You make it all sound so inevitable.'

The automaton-maker drew out a length of fine string and snapped it with a knife.

'Your father's death was inevitable.' Dédalon concentrated on tying a knot. 'It was time for him to go. Once an animal has made up its mind to die, there's no rational help for it.'

Her nerves on edge, Flora was irritated by the bleakness of Dédalon's philosophy.

'My father was hardly a rat or a lapdog, you know!'

'I make no exception for fathers. Next minute you'll tell me you still believe in ladies swooning over sunsets out of the sheer sublimity of their souls! "A goat will never paint the *Last Supper* or compose an oratorio, therefore man must necessarily be divine. If he kills himself, it's because he has weighed his soul in the cosmic balance, and found himself wanting." Is that what you think?'

'I don't know what to think.'

The automaton-maker threw up his hands. 'And I had hopes of making you a scientist! Already, you've run back to the teachings of the nursery.'

'I didn't say I thought you were wrong. I just . . . don't know.'

'Well, you should know. And you should write to your sister again, and promise her she had nothing whatever to do with her father's death, because we are all – *all*, in this sordid world of ours – concerned with nothing more than our own miserable instincts.' With finality, Dédalon turned back to his bench.

'I couldn't possibly put such a thing in a letter to Sophie! The General would have a fit at such blasphemy, and Sophie's governess would have an even bigger fit. Sophie says her father is rector of a big church in Worcester,' added Flora, and then suggested maliciously, 'Why don't you go and tell *him* he's no more spiritual than the monkeys?'

The automaton-maker gave a short, harsh laugh. 'Solomon!' he called out. 'Make me a bishop! *Un évêque! Allons—*'

Chirping, the monkey swung down from his perch by the fire and strutted awkwardly across the cluttered floor, his chest thrown out, his gnarled little hands clasped across it, and a studious scowl on his face. In his skullcap and cowl he managed a fair imitation of ecclesiastical dignity.

'Bravo, my friend!' cried the automaton-maker as Solomon dropped down to squat at his feet, holding out dark, oily fingers for a reward.

'If it was left to me, you'd have a cathedral tomorrow. You keep your opinions to yourself and think only of the next meal – what more could anyone ask?'

Dédalon broke off a piece of apple and the monkey hunched over it, pressing the fruit to his mouth with both hands. For a moment the automaton-maker watched him in silence.

'Perhaps we should go back to Paris now, Solomon . . . What do you think? Have we finished our work here in London?'

Flora stared at him in dismay. 'Oh, Dédalon – no . . . You wouldn't really go back to France, would you?'

The automaton-maker examined her carefully, his head tilted back. 'You don't want us to go?'

'Of course not!' With the possibility suddenly before her, Flora was consumed with dismay. 'Oh, Dédalon, you've been such a friend . . . so much more than a friend . . .' Helplessly, she lifted her hands, searching for words to express exactly how much more. 'Lydia's so far away now – if you go too, then I've no one at all.'

The automaton-maker rolled his head forward until he was staring at her from under his black brows. Yet his eyes were unexpectedly soft.

'So . . . you will be sorry, if I go.' He pursed his lips and frowned. 'I too . . . I will be sorry.' The admission seemed to trouble him, and for a few seconds he fell silent.

'As I told you,' he continued at last, 'I had a daughter once – a daughter who was stolen away from me, and died.' Slowly, he reached out to touch Flora's cheek. 'But then, when I least expected it, you came to me, and said, "Dédalon – teach me". And it was almost like having my daughter again. What had been stolen was given back to me.'

He considered the hand which had touched her, then let it fall to his side.

'I will stay, my daughter, and watch over you.'

5

Later that day, Flora wrote again to Sophie as the automaton-maker had advised, though she chose her words carefully, knowing perfectly well how Miss Meagle would react to any hint of *Anatomical Philosophy*. A full month passed before she received a reply, and Sophie's answer, when it came, had been franked in Bath, to where Flora's letter had been forwarded.

'What on earth is the girl doing in Bath?' Crossly, Constance hunted in a drawer for her spectacles. 'No one said anything to me of Bath. The General never struck me as a Bath sort of man, nor his wife either.' In a fever of curiosity she slammed one drawer shut and opened the next.

'Well – read the letter, Flora! What are you waiting for?'

Quickly, Flora scanned the first few lines.

'Sophie has been quite ill, she says. The General was so worried that he sent to London for a surgeon, who diagnosed "hysteropathia" brought on by the shock of Papa's death.' Flora glanced up at her mother. 'We should have taken more care, you know.'

'It's Sophie's sensitive temperament, that's all.' Constance continued to rummage. 'She was always a susceptible child.'

'Apparently the doctor prescribed a change of air and spa waters, and so Mrs Ivory carried Sophie off to Bath, where she takes a house each year for her daughters and their families.'

'And why wasn't I informed of all this?' Constance abandoned the final drawer and turned round, flapping her hands in annoyance. 'It's not good enough, Flora – really, it isn't. They drag my child from town to town and dose her with patent remedies, and never think of saying a word about it to her mother!'

'I wish you hadn't told Sophie how much Papa missed her when she went away to Chillbourne. Now she blames herself for his death – I'm sure that's why she became so ill.'

'Nonsense! I only told her the truth.' Constance found her spectacles at last, and began to disentangle the metal legs. 'No – to my mind, it was the General who started the whole business by cutting off your father's income in such a spiteful way. How that man can live with himself, I'm sure I don't know.'

In silence, Flora held out the letter.

'Does Sophie say where she's staying in Bath?' Constance turned the page the right way up and peered at the superscription. 'Royal Crescent, indeed! Well, I'm pleased to see Mrs Ivory knows how things should be done, even though Bath has become a little *passé* in the last year or two. Royal Crescent! Most of the right people will call on them there, I should think . . . And what's this? A concert in the Gardens?' Constance pressed her lips together in disapproval. 'Far too early in the year, I'd have thought, if the girl's as sick as she says . . .'

'Well, I hope it cheers her up,' declared Flora emphatically.

'All this talk of hysteropathia!' Briskly, Constance rustled the page. 'I dare say Sophie caught a chill, coming up in the General's carriage without a foot-warmer. It's high time he sold that draughty old thing and bought a proper post-chaise with sleeping cushions and spring curtains, and one of those clever little baskets for umbrellas. It's the least he can do for Sophie, after driving her poor father to his grave.'

'Dear me—' she added in the next breath, 'what will Sophie think of us here, after all the elegant new people she must be meeting in Bath?'

Sophie returned to London with Mrs Ivory at the end of May, and seemed in no hurry to go back to the dreary saloons of Chillbourne. In London she shopped with Mrs Ivory, paid calls with Mrs Ivory, and took tea with Mrs Ivory's friends; and when Mrs Ivory pronounced it her duty to go in the barouche to take her mother and sister out for an airing, Sophie reluctantly did as she'd been told.

Three months in Bath had done her immeasurable good. With new colour in her cheeks and her fluffy fair hair prettily dressed under a black pagoda parasol, Sophie knew she made a dramatic picture in the stylish carriage, just as she had on fine days in Bath's Sydney Gardens, amid the crowds of fashionable visitors.

Constance urged her to take tea at Gough Square, but Sophie refused outright, barely suppressing a shudder. Mrs Ivory's barouche, she insisted, could never manage the sharp turn under the archway – and, in any case, who could bear to be indoors in such fine weather? Absently, Sophie brushed an invisible mark from her glove. No – they would go for a drive, and then the barouche would deposit Constance and Flora in Fleet Street, near the door of Elder's Bank, from where it was only a few steps to their home.

The sun shone as they swept along, but Constance hardly noticed, entirely occupied in drawing out of Sophie an account of where she'd been in Bath, and whom she'd seen there. For a whole hour Constance listened, enraptured, her lips a little apart and her eyes fixed on Sophie's face.

'. . . And his children, too. And her brother, the Earl? Well, I never!'

Sitting opposite them, with her back to the horses, Flora let the glittering stream of gossip flow over her head, and revelled in the borrowed luxury of the barouche. But as the carriage drew up in front of the old grey bank building, she saw Sophie glance towards its door and her face assume a proprietorial smile.

'There's one of the gentlemen now, Mamma.' She pointed to a

tall figure disappearing at that moment into the bank. 'That's Mr Darius Elder, you know. He and his brother were always so kind to me at the Assembly Rooms. We were quite like old friends by the end of our stay.'

'Where?' Flora, in the opposite seat, craned round at once, but was too late to see more than a broad back vanishing into the shadows of the doorway. *Perhaps he'll come out again . . . oh, please . . . I'd almost settle for his pity now – at least that would be better than being despised for a fool . . .*

'Flora—' Behind her, she heard Sophie's voice, and turned back to see Sophie staring at her intently.

'Do you know Mr Elder, then?' Sophie enquired.

'Not at all . . . That is to say, I've seen him in the bank. With Mamma,' Flora added quickly.

'Nowhere else?' Sophie watched her sister closely, fascinated to discover that at the age of nineteen Flora could still blush so easily, the sudden warmth of her cheeks bringing out the greenness of her eyes. Saintly Flora . . . Loyal Flora, who'd chosen to stay at home with Papa.

'Where could I possibly have met Mr Elder?' Flora's tone was defensive. 'I don't go into society, as you do.'

'No, of course.' Yet Sophie noticed that Flora's heightened colour remained, while Flora's eyes flicked continually towards the door of the bank, as if she hoped Darius Elder might reappear.

'Though I don't need to go into society to see the Elders,' Sophie added casually. 'They have a house near us in Curzon Street, you know.'

'Curzon Street . . .' murmured Constance, a wistful look spreading over her face. 'You do seem to be moving in very elegant circles these days, Sophie. Quite the *beau monde*.'

Sophie trailed her hand thoughtfully over the silk damask cushions of the barouche.

'I'd like to be married some day soon,' she declared. 'Then I could have a barouche of my own, and a town house with servants.' Across the carriage she saw Flora's eyes on her, frankly envious, and couldn't resist adding, 'I'd give balls and parties for all my friends . . . Fashionable gentlemen like the Elders.'

If Flora had only known it, the same subject was being discussed at that moment behind the grey walls of the bank, where Darius Elder had flung his hat on the table in the directors' parlour and taken up a position before the empty hearth, his hands deep in his pockets and his eyes fixed gloomily on the toes of his boots.

'Oh, you're back, are you?' Felix Elder swung his feet off the table and rubbed his sleep-laden eyes. 'Though I can't say it looks as if the Mitre's claret has improved your mood very much.'

'There's nothing the matter with my mood.'

'Not much!' Felix sprawled back in his chair. 'You're miserable – you're restless, and yet you tell me there's nothing the matter with you.' He regarded his brother speculatively. 'I reckon what you need, my friend, is a wife. You want to find some sweet, rich young creature and marry her straight off.'

'I've no intention of marrying anyone, Felix – you know that perfectly well. The last thing I want in my life is a love affair.'

'Because of that unfortunate business in India? Bosh – you're too thin-skinned by half. Good heavens, if all my youthful adventures were ever added up—'

'It wasn't an adventure.' Angrily, Darius rounded on his brother. 'I meant every word I said to that poor girl – every promise I made—' He flung out his arms helplessly. 'Yet look how it all ended.' He returned his hands to his pockets. 'I still see her face, sometimes, in my sleep. I wake up with my heart pounding, remembering her scream of terror as they dragged her away. No—' He set his shoulders. 'Once is enough for any man.'

Felix snorted dismissively. 'Who said anything about love? I said you needed a wife, not a lover.'

'You're a fine one to talk! I don't see you on your way to the altar.'

'It's different for me.' Fastidiously, Felix brushed a hair from his lapel. 'I'm quite content as I am.'

'And so am I, I assure you.'

'What? Pacing around the bank with a face as long as a fiddle, unable to put your mind to anything for more than two seconds? If I didn't know you'd given it up, Darius, I'd swear you were in love again.'

'You're mad. You don't know what you're talking about.' Darius paused, frowned, then shook his head decisively. 'Absolute nonsense,' he declared.

'Not that what you want makes any difference.' Felix lay back in his chair. 'You'll soon have no choice in the matter. Our revered eldest sister tells me she has every intention of marrying you off.'

'Ann?' Darius looked up at once. Lady Maximilian was a determined woman who usually managed, if only by sheer persistence, to
get her own way.

'You won't escape, you know,' continued Felix blandly. 'Sooner
or later she'll find you a nice heiress, if only for the sake of the family
fortune. You might as well give in with good grace, and hope she
finds you a pretty one. Besides,' he added significantly, 'I reckon it's
just what you need. The best cure for restlessness, my boy, is
marriage. Sound medical fact.'

6

'This is what comes of taking Sophie off to Bath and introducing her
to all and sundry.' Back in her Gough Square bedroom, Constance
slipped her mantle from her shoulders and shook out the creases.
'Now nothing will do for her but a country estate, a house in town
and twenty thousand a year to spend on China silk stockings. And
how is that to be managed, I'd like to know?'

'I thought Sophie looked particularly well this afternoon,' murmured Flora unhappily.

'Oh, I dare say she did – in a borrowed carriage and a silk gown
her grandfather had paid for. But what is she worth, when all's said
and done? The poor girl is penniless!'

Constance shook her mantle vigorously once more.

'I hadn't the heart to tell her she'll be lucky to land some hunting
farmer with a few mortgaged acres, who'll expect her to pull off his
boots of an evening and patch his breeches with homespun. That's
my lady Sophie's fate, if I'm not much mistaken.'

A few weeks later, the General wrote plaintively to his sister to
enquire when Sophie would be returning to Chillbourne. Sophie
promptly suffered a relapse of the condition which had taken her to
Bath, and was judged too delicate to be moved from London.

At the end of another month the General wrote again to suggest
that the pure air of Hampshire was surely better for an invalid than
smoke-ridden London. Sophie's health immediately broke down once
more, and Mrs Ivory took the General to task for upsetting his
granddaughter. Surely he could see that London was a livelier place

for an active young woman than the silent acres of Hampshire? And here Mrs Ivory played a master-stroke: Miss Meagle was sent home to Hampshire, and her hymn-books along with her.

The General grew anxious. At Christmas 1822, in a final, desperate attempt to secure Sophie's affection, he named her publicly as his heir. When he died, Sophie would have Chillbourne and its endless acres, just as Greville would have done if he'd lived.

This time Sophie returned to Hampshire for four whole months before rushing back again to London, and the sick old man had himself carried half-way down the carriage-sweep to kiss her cheek before she was finally driven away.

With a whoop of glee, Mrs Ivory threw herself entirely into the game she enjoyed most in the world – the business of finding a husband for her seventeen-year-old grand-niece. Having seen her four daughters satisfactorily settled, Sybil Ivory knew to a nicety what Sophie's inheritance might purchase in the marriage market. The top shelves of the nobility, she knew, were out of reach: those eligible young men had usually run up gambling debts on a royal scale, and had to marry accordingly.

An alliance with *trade* was impossible: the biggest brewer in the country was still a tapster with the smell of malt in his hair. And yet . . . one had to be open-minded. Undeniably, there was a species of trade which every year pulled itself by its bootstraps a little nearer to Society; a powerful caste whose chief men rebuked governments and kept company with kings, and stayed decently far from the grimy-fingered reality of their business . . . Why – any day now, they'd haul themselves into the peerage. There was clearly no time to lose.

On her eighteenth birthday in May, Sophie went into half-mourning of lilac, which conveniently happened to be all the rage that summer. Now she drove out in Mrs Ivory's barouche in a ribboned pelisse befitting the heiress to Chillbourne and General St Serf's large fortune.

Flora wore grey for their drive to the park. It was all she had – a dress which had been made up two years earlier out of cheap green chintz, but which had taken the grey dye badly, producing a mottled, mouldy effect which made Sophie stare with distaste. At once Sophie burrowed under her rugs and pulled out a beautiful shawl of the finest Kashmir, bordered with palm leaves and exotic blue flowers.

'These carriages can be so chilly,' she said, holding it out; but Flora saw her glance away, avoiding her sister's eye, and guessed precisely why the shawl had been offered. Swallowing her humiliation, Flora threw it over her shoulders, hiding her blotched gown from view.

It was a very fine shawl indeed. From her own side of the carriage Sophie admired it, draped about her sister's shoulders, and reflected that the gentleman who'd brought it to the house in Curzon Street had shown undeniable good taste. He was a cultivated man, she'd decided; moreover, he was rich, and likely to be richer. Half the crowned heads of Europe looked on his family as friends and counsellors; it was said they could ruin a man with a wink of an eye in the right quarter.

Sophie allowed herself a contented smile; a little wriggle of excitement shivered the lilac pelisse.

From the opposite side of the barouche, Flora saw the smile, and reminded herself that if it hadn't been for the automaton-maker's monkey and her own infatuation with a handsome stranger, she – Flora – might have been an heiress in a carriage wearing a fussy pelisse with ridiculous ribbon bows. Still – now at last Sophie must be happy. There could be no more guilty resentment, no more imaginary grievances or grudges to be settled – not while Flora sat there in blotchy grey, and Sophie sparkled like an amethyst in a priceless setting. Surely now Sophie must have everything she ever wanted.

'This is a beautiful shawl,' she said, guessing at Sophie's thoughts. 'Did you buy it in London?'

'It was a present.' A malicious warmth began to glow like a coal in the pit of Sophie's stomach. Saintly Flora! Virtuous Flora! See how you like this!

'It was given to me by a gentleman, as a matter of fact.'

'Oh? How lucky!' For a few seconds Flora wrestled with her curiosity. 'An interesting gentleman, was he?'

'Extremely interesting . . . Very handsome, and quite charming, in fact.' Sophie's eyes had become hard. 'He talked to me for almost an entire evening and completely forgot to dance with anyone else, though I know the Rivington girls were dying for a chance at him. Mrs Ivory said everyone's eyes were upon us.'

'Indeed . . .' Flora's hand moved to cover an ugly darn on her skirt. 'And which gentleman would that be, may I ask?'

'Oh, I'm sure you must remember,' said Sophie with deadly innocence, 'since *you* were the one to stay in London with Papa, while I ran off to Hampshire and left him . . .' For a moment, a smudge on her lilac glove distracted her. 'I was talking of Mr Elder, of Elder's Bank.'

'Mrs Ivory let Felix Elder give you this?' In her astonishment Flora ignored the gibe. 'But what was she thinking of? Felix is such a dreadful rake!'

'Oh, not Felix!' Sophie took a deep breath, savouring the moment. 'I meant Mr Darius Elder, his brother. You must remember *him* . . . Well, he's the gentleman who gave me the shawl.'

CHAPTER SEVEN

I

'You can't possibly allow it!' Furiously, Flora confronted her mother across the drawing-room table. 'Sophie marry Darius Elder! An Elder, of all people!'

Sophie, and Darius Elder . . . The very thought of it made Flora dizzy with horror, but not at all for the reason she'd given. *Money marries money* – so Lydia had warned her often enough, and here was the proof of it. As for Flora, she hadn't a penny in the world. All she'd had were her secret, hopeless dreams – dreams of an Elder with gypsy looks and defiant blue eyes, and a mouth like curled petals, even when it quarrelled with her . . . Yet now even those poor dreams were being snatched away.

'After all they've done—' Flora gripped the edge of the table. 'Surely you won't let Sophie marry an Elder!'

What other reason could she give? That she'd willingly have perished for the smile of the very man her sister had chosen, Elder though he was?

Constance smiled absently, and turned to gaze out of the soot-spotted window. Flora knew that misty, wistful expression. With agony in her heart she realized that the same useful process which had gilded her mother's memories of her bleak Scottish girlhood had begun to sprinkle its enchanted dust over Sophie's betrothal.

Constance's obliging memory could transform the worst disasters into triumphs and the ugliest geese into swans, leaving no trace of their past existence. Already, on the slightest excuse, Constance would give a moving account of her husband's heroic death at Waterloo; now, it seemed, the Elder family were about to be shorn of their horns and tails, and be reborn conveniently as saints.

Even the General had been won over to his sister's scheme, afraid to deny Sophie anything she wanted.

'But she can't – you can't—' Flora's voice seemed to echo from the hollow wreckage of her heart.

'Don't dramatize, Flora.' Constance drew in her chin like a self-righteous little peg-doll. 'I dare say you'd have sung a different tune if Mr Elder had come calling on *you*.'

With a cry of anguish Flora fled from the room, and hurling herself on her bed, dissolved into tears of desolation.

2

While Constance had given Sophie up to her grandparents in almost every respect, there was one remaining mother's privilege which she had never relinquished. No matter what those matchmaking ladies Mrs Ivory and Lady Maximilian might have settled between them, Sophie was still only eighteen, and required her mother's consent to marry at all. Now, after six bitter years in the social wilderness of Gough Square, Constance intended to savour her power.

Within a week, a splendidly frogged footman found his way to Gough Square in Mrs Ivory's chariot, bearing an invitation to dinner in Curzon Street for Mrs St Serf and Miss St Serf in a fortnight's time. In curl-papers and with an old shawl thrown over her night-gown, Constance breathed ecstatically over the elegant invitation, tracing the swooping pen-strokes with her finger. An invitation to Curzon Street? No – it was an invitation to the world! The gates of an earthly paradise were about to swing open for her once more, with Sophie as her key.

'There's no help for it, I must have something made up new,' she announced that evening at dinner, raising her lip with a finger to inspect a front tooth in the shiny bowl of her spoon.

In spite of everything, Constance was obliged to admit she'd made a most fetching widow. Everyone said so – or at least Mr Wesley had said so several times, his eyes quite moist with sincerity. But one couldn't live for ever in black. It was such a depressing shade! Even a year of it was enough to make a woman quite miserable, and incapable of enjoying her widowhood. Now Constance was in the mood for change, for a hard, bright armour to carry her magnificently into Mrs Ivory's drawing-room.

'Flora – are you listening to me?'

'I hear you.' White-faced and listless, Flora pushed her plate away untouched.

'Now, fortunately I have a guinea or two laid by . . . though I'm sure a gown will cost every penny of that.' Constance sneaked another sidelong glance at her daughter. 'So . . . you won't mind, Flora, not having something new yourself? After all, it doesn't matter so much for you, since you aren't directly concerned in the engagement.

'Besides,' she added with more confidence, 'I've always thought your satin net *so* becoming. Only yesterday, Mrs Moss said to me, "We haven't seen Flora in her satin net for *years*, though it made her look such a young lady."'

'But my old satin net hardly covers my shins!' Flora gazed at her mother in horror. 'And it's so babyish.'

'Nonsense! I refuse to believe you've grown so much since you were sixteen. And even if you are a little taller, Maggie can always lengthen the hem as much as is needed – or even add a piece, if it comes to that. Once the candles are lit, no one ever sees a dress below the waist – and, in any case, wadded hems are all the rage this year.'

'Even better,' said Flora desperately, 'I shan't go. You said yourself, Sophie's engagement doesn't concern me in the least.'

'Of course you'll go! Do you want to offend them all, and ruin your sister's chances?' Constance bent forward and tapped the table, her nail striking the wood like the rattle of musket-fire. 'All manner of benefits will come of this marriage, I promise you. And if you don't want to end up an old maid yourself, you'd better think of that.'

She leaned back in her chair. 'No, my girl, I shall expect you to go with me to Curzon Street, and wear your old satin net without any more fuss. No one will look at you anyway – they all know we don't have money to spend on frivolous things like new gowns.' Constance dismissed the idea with a wave of her hand. 'If I had a satin net gown like yours,' she added piously, 'I'm sure I should never have needed another.'

Two days later, to her mother's amusement, Flora appeared at dinner wearing a frilled muslin cap tied closely round her head, for all the world like a regular old maid. She clung to the cap for a week and a half, never taking it off unless it was to put on a nightcap, until eventually Constance began to wonder if she hadn't been a little hard on her elder daughter. It wasn't entirely impossible that Flora should find herself a husband one day – though it was unfortunate that she'd have to attend Mrs Ivory's dinner in a childish little dress of net over faded satin which had been made for her years before. Still, as Constance had pointed out, the engagement was really none of Flora's concern.

Mrs Ivory's carriage was to collect them at six on the day of the dinner. At four, Maggie stumped upstairs to help Constance dress, shouting to Flora, shut in the drawing-room, to call her when hooking-up was required.

At fifteen minutes past five Flora left the house with her bonnet tied closely over the muslin cap. She returned – without the cap and a little apprehensively – at five minutes before six; and her mother's shriek of horror as Flora appeared in the drawing-room doorway brought Maggie up the stairs again to see what new calamity had befallen the St Serfs.

'Flora!' Constance pressed her palms to her vigorously rouged cheeks. 'What in heaven's name have you done to yourself? Are you mad? Have you been attacked in the street?' A querulous note entered her voice. 'And where in the world did you get that gown?'

From the doorway Flora gazed back at her, pliant as flame, vivid in a dress of rich red lutestring, her head strikingly small and graceful under a helmet of dark, short-cropped waves.

'Where—' cried her mother theatrically, 'is your hair?'

'I sold it.' Proudly, Flora stood her ground. 'It was all I had to sell, since you wouldn't allow me to earn any money of my own. I went off to the hair-pedlar in Holborn and told him if he left me three inches for myself, he could have all the rest for twelve guineas.

'And then,' she went on before her mother could speak, 'I used the money to buy eight yards of this red lutestring, and Lucy Dawes made it up for only six shillings because I helped her stitch the skirt.'

She held out her arms in a rapturous pirouette.

'Isn't it the most glorious thing?'

'Oh, to blazes with the gown! You look . . .' Furiously, Constance opened and shut her mouth, groping for the appropriate word. 'You look like a maniac from an asylum! As if you've been shaved for lice!'

The happiness fled at once from Flora's face. 'As a matter of fact,' she said quietly, 'I rather like it.'

In truth, confronted with the devastation for the first time in the hair-pedlar's mirror, she'd been almost as shocked as her mother. But by then it was too late to change her mind, and there was nothing to be gained by regretting what she'd done. Anything was better than appearing before Darius Elder and his elegant friends in her detested satin net dress, strained like a bolster across her bosom and with six inches of left-over cotton tacked on to make it reach her toes.

Across the room, the looking-glass over the chimneypiece framed a dryad in the russet of autumn, a shimmering sprite with eyes like dusky moths and a dark, polished cap. Flora smiled, and the dryad smiled back, a little nervously.

'That's Mrs Ivory's carriage now, mistress,' reported Maggie from the window. 'Hair or no hair, you'd best be off, both of you.'

3

Mrs Ivory had spared nothing on Sophie's behalf. By the time Flora and her mother reached Curzon Street, the narrow thoroughfare was already choked with carriages and their fidgeting horses, while a procession of bright silks and gauzes tripped between the rows of livery flanking the entrance. It was quite possible, Flora reflected, that her hair might have come to the party on its own behalf, as the soaring wired loop of an 'Apollo Knot' on one of the more fashionable heads.

Mrs Ivory, powdered and pearl-bound at the doorway, touched her cold, rouged cheek to Constance St Serf's, but gave Flora barely a glance, except to peer in alarm at her clipped head, murmuring 'And you've been ill, you poor child . . .'

Sophie, brilliant in celestial blue, swooped by to gape at her sister's shorn head with an abstracted frown before whirling away again into the throng. Constance plunged at once into a battalion of Elder cousins, leaving Flora to the Ivory son-in-law appointed to take her in to dinner, and for half an hour she endured a lecture on the prospects for the coming winter's hunting while she inspected Mrs Ivory's guests from the shelter of his enormous flanks.

To her annoyance, by the time they went downstairs to dinner, Flora still hadn't caught even a glimpse of Darius Elder. Two hours were to pass – two hours of hound sickness and ten-mile runs – before at last the cloth was drawn, the fruits and jellies and barley-sugar pagodas were disposed of, and the ladies withdrew upstairs once more, leaving the gentlemen to their port and brandy.

In the drawing-room, Constance began to confer once more with Sophie and a grim-faced council of female Elders. Left to herself,

Flora sat down alone between two giant Chinese vases, grateful for the fact that candles had been brought, and she could think her own thoughts in the shadows. At least when the gentlemen came upstairs she should be safe there from her dinner partner and his inevitable pack of hounds.

At long last, on the heels of his father and Sir Digby Maximilian, she saw Darius Elder come into the room, halt just inside the doorway, and gaze round with a preoccupied air. From her corner Flora watched him as rationally as she could manage, trying to calm the thumping of her heart by reminding herself of every indignity she'd suffered at his hands.

No doubt some people would have called Darius Elder extremely handsome at that moment – though Flora immediately noted that his nose was a little too straight and the planes of his features rather too architectural for real elegance. Furthermore, Flora added severely to herself, it was a well-known fact that eyes, to be fine, should be brown – and Darius Elder's were quite strikingly blue.

At that precise moment Darius glanced towards Flora's corner between the vases, noticed her staring, and took it as an invitation to speak.

'Miss St Serf.' He grasped a nearby chair by its back and set it down near her own. 'May I?'

Flora didn't, at that instant, trust herself to speak, but inclined her head instead.

'I thought perhaps you were waiting for someone.'

'Not at all. I hardly know anyone here.'

'Then you must make do with me.'

Darius sat down and for several seconds regarded Flora in silence. With an effort, Flora devoted herself to tracing the pattern on a Chinese vase with her finger, as if her sister's husband-to-be was of less significance than a painted mandarin.

'You don't like me, Miss St Serf.' When she didn't look up, he added, 'For Sophia's sake, I wish you thought better of me.'

This time Flora did stare at him, taken aback. *Sophia*, indeed! Such a cold name for a soon-to-be wife! Did he know so little of Sophie, then? She examined his face, searching for an answer. Did he love Sophie? She saw his lips tighten – that remarkable mouth, which promised that he *could* love, *had* loved, *did* love, perhaps . . . Did love Sophie, even, in which case Flora must genuinely try to wish them well.

To Darius it seemed that she was regarding him coolly.

118

'Sophia seems to think I'll make a passable husband,' he continued, 'yet you and I . . . We can't even exchange a word without quarrelling.'

'The quarrels were none of my making,' Flora insisted at once.

'Then I was entirely at fault, I suppose, while you were blameless?'

'Certainly I was.' *Oh, please – how did we come to be arguing again?*

'I suppose you'd prefer that we never spoke to one another at all!'

'As you wish, I'm sure.' The words leaped out before Flora could stop them.

'Very well, then – let's keep silent. At least it would spare Sophia the distress of seeing her sister and her husband at one another's throats.'

For several seconds they remained united in angry silence. Yet somehow the longer it lasted, the more intimate the silence became, until Darius was compelled to break it.

'You made it quite clear, the last time we met, that you despise my family because of our profession. However, money—'

'Money?' demanded Flora, her voice ringing with distress. 'Is that all you can think about?' Consumed with despair, she plunged on. 'Tell me, Mr Elder – since we're being so honest with one another – would you ever have thought of marrying Sophie if she hadn't been the General's heiress?'

Taken aback, Darius frowned, and then answered with some honesty, 'I don't suppose the question would have arisen.'

Flora stared at him incredulously. 'You admit it? You admit you wouldn't have thought of her if she'd had nothing?' She felt the colour rising treacherously to her cheeks, but she'd gone too far to draw back. 'Don't you love her at all?'

For a moment she thought he might be about to blurt out some violent retort; but when he spoke his voice was cold.

'Affairs of the heart are hardly the way to shape the destiny of families.'

'You haven't answered my question! *Do you love Sophie?*'

His eyes met hers in silent challenge, and then slid away to focus on a distant point, far beyond the chandelier.

'It has been my experience . . . that *love*, if it exists at all, is strongest when it fixes on the most unsuitable people – on the people most likely to bring us pain. It's an indulgence. It becomes a bad habit, like biting one's nails.'

'And you don't bite your nails, I see.'

'I assure you, Sophia and I are perfectly suited.'

There was a flash of celestial blue between the vases, and the businesslike flutter of a fan.

'So this is where you've been hiding, sister – whispering in a corner with my Mr Elder . . .' Sophie smiled delicately, but her eyes glittered over the edge of her fan. 'I'd no idea you were such good friends.'

Darius had risen to his feet. 'Miss St Serf and I have met briefly before.'

'But you must call her Flora, now you're to be related!' Sophie tapped his wrist with her fan. 'Flora would like that more than anything – wouldn't you, Flora?'

She slipped a cat-like paw through the crook of Darius's arm, and leaned her cheek possessively against his shoulder. *Money marries money.* Flora felt the pressure of Sophie's embrace like a constriction in her throat.

'Sophie – don't flirt.' Abandoning her coven in the corner, Constance bore down on them, her hands clasped across her stomach and a satisfied expression on her face. 'Pray don't cling to Mr Elder so,' she added sharply. 'Have the goodness to wait until I've given my consent, and a proper announcement has been made.'

'Yes, Mamma.' Sophie released Darius Elder's arm and primly folded her fan.

'There's something I wish to discuss with Mr Elder,' her mother continued.

'Oh.' Taking the hint, Sophie departed.

Flora lingered at Constance's side, quite unable to drag herself away. Fortunately, Constance hardly seemed to remember her presence, engrossed as she was in some manoeuvre of her own.

'Mr Elder . . .'

'Mrs St Serf.' With a last glance at Flora, Darius Elder inclined his head, recognizing a business meeting when he saw one.

'I've had *such* a delightful conversation with your sister, Lady Maximilian,' Constance swept on, 'and with your cousins, the Miss Mees, and your charming aunt, Mrs Foxlake. Such a pleasant tête-à-tête! And we're all agreed, you know, that you and Sophie make a particularly delightful couple.' Constance simpered a little, her lips drawn up like the neck of her drawstring reticule.

'That being so—' She put her hand to her brow, and all at once her expression changed to one of profound sorrow. 'That being so . . . what I have to say to you now is especially hard. I regret –

though it pains me to say so – I regret that I really cannot consent to the match.'

Only just in time, Flora stifled a cry of amazement, and silently thanked whatever providence looked after penniless girls that her mother had come to her senses.

Darius Elder seemed to take the blow with amazing calmness. He said nothing at all, but continued to regard Constance in thoughtful silence, as if trying to calculate precisely what was afoot.

Breathless with relief, Flora waited for Constance to give her reasons – to declare that such a match would be a hollow mockery, no more a marriage than a bill of sale. But to Flora's astonishment, Constance plunged into her reticule, drew out a lace-edged handkerchief and began to dab her eyes with it, as if the collapse of her daughter's engagement was a disaster almost too great to be borne.

'I take it,' Darius Elder began gravely, 'I take it you've found some obstacle in the way of my marrying Sophia, Mrs St Serf. You do not object to me, personally.' His eyes flicked briefly towards Flora.

'Oh no, Mr Elder!' Constance gave a well-bred sniff and dabbed her eyes again. 'You are in every way a most distinguished gentleman. My objection is not to you in the least.'

Flora gaped. What in the world was her mother thinking of?

'Oh dear – it's so very mortifying . . .' Constance sniffed once more to indicate the extent of her mortification. 'You must understand, Mr Elder, that my daughter Sophie is very dear to me – her welfare, naturally, but also her happiness.'

'Sophia's happiness is my principal concern.'

At Constance's side, Flora was becoming anxious. What obstacle could there be to the marriage, except its utter preposterousness?

'You'll appreciate, then,' Constance continued, 'how hard it is for a mother to realize that she might, one day, be the means of embarrassing her daughter beyond endurance!'

Speeding towards the nub of her argument, Constance fixed Darius Elder with a squirrel-like eye.

'Suppose it came out that *Mrs Elder*'s mother and sister were reduced to living in two bare rooms in a ruinous old house in Gough Square? Two squalid boxes, no more – where our poverty forces us to drag out our days.'

Here Constance's eyes filled with tears requiring further dabbing.

'I cannot allow it! I cannot allow my daughter to risk such humiliation.'

'Mamma!' protested Flora, outraged at the brazenness of her mother's blackmail. Now at last she understood what Constance intended. The marriage would proceed, that was clear. It was merely a case of agreeing on terms – and here was Constance 'talking up her stock' like a horse-trader while her customer listened in a kind of contemptuous boredom.

Flora's heart ached with shame and misery. 'This is insufferable! What must Mr Elder think of us?'

'It's no more than the truth, my dear,' insisted her mother theatrically. 'We are desperately poor, and there's no escaping it. If Sophie were to marry Mr Elder, we should only be an embarrassment to her in our present state.'

Constance favoured Flora with the most tragic of glances – then her eyes lit up with inspiration.

'My daughter Flora, Mr Elder, is living proof of the hardship we endure.'

Seizing Flora by the arm, Constance dragged her forward.

'Poor Flora couldn't bear to shame her sister by appearing in a wretched old dress in such smart company – but we had no money to buy her another, and so—'

'Be quiet, Mamma!' hissed Flora, glimpsing the horror ahead.

'And so—' Constance swept on to a climax, as Flora waited, rigid with humiliation under that curious blue gaze.

'SHE SOLD HER HAIR, Mr Elder!' proclaimed Constance in an awful voice. 'Sold it to pay for the gown she stands in.'

There was a moment of dreadful silence, during which Flora wished the carpet would rise up and swallow her mercifully out of sight. From a great distance, she heard Darius Elder's voice.

'I thought, perhaps, you had been ill.'

She knew he was staring at her shorn head – she could feel his eyes on her like the caress of a hand.

'Something will be done for you, Mrs St Serf,' he promised softly. 'I give you my word.'

Constance's gown rustled as she reached out to take her prospective son-in-law's arm.

'I'm sure you and Sophie will make an excellent marriage,' she cooed contentedly. 'Two people of such *delicate* sensibility.'

On Thursday, 11th September, 1823, Sophia St Serf and Darius Elder were married in the chapel at Chillbourne, the bride being given away by her grandfather. On the following Monday the bride's mother and sister left their two dismal rooms behind Fleet Street for a comfortable house in Montagu Square rented for them by the General at Darius Elder's request.

PART TWO

October 1823

CHAPTER EIGHT

I

An annual income of five hundred pounds went with the new house, and while it wasn't as much as Constance would have liked, it was more than the General wanted to give, which was victory of a kind.

Dédalon had nodded sagely when Flora broke the news of their imminent move.

'That's good,' he declared. 'It's time for you to get away from Gough Square and try out your wings. But come back and visit me from time to time. We won't forget you, Solomon and I.'

'I'll come back – of course I will,' Flora assured him, and immediately felt guilty. The truth was that her visits to the automaton-maker's workshop had become less frequent during the last few months. Little by little, its sepulchral gloom, where pincers dangled from the black eaves like spiders' legs and small, tufted manikins scowled from the shadows, had begun to make her uneasy, like a glimpse of a hobgoblin underworld forbidden to human eyes.

Anything was possible in that workshop of dreams, where monkeys became bishops and a tangle of rods and bellows could produce the heart-melting song of a chaffinch. Nothing was inviolate there, nothing ended life as it had begun. Nowadays Solomon seemed to watch Flora resentfully from his perch, as if he sensed she'd gone over to the forces of propriety, and no longer had any business in that cavern of illusion. Already Flora belonged to the sunlit terraces of Montagu Square, where all was calm and order, and life rolled along on its cosy certainties like the oiled wheels of Mrs Ivory's barouche.

'I'll come back to see you often,' she promised Dédalon dutifully, and tried to believe that she would.

2

Constance was cock-a-hoop, richer by five hundred pounds a year and a five-storey stucco-bound house in a most respectable part of town.

No potato-sellers set up their charcoal stoves against the railings here; no placard-men trooped up and down the pavements, rigged out as patent iron stoves or giant blacking-jars. Knife-grinders came, tugging their hat-brims respectfully, and chimney-sweeps, and before dawn brawny, brown-armed girls who staggered under the weight of their pails and shouted 'Milk below!'

But the beggars belonged to the half-light of Gough Square, and the blind peep-show man, creeping like a sightless snail under the shell of his great canvas booth.

Having secured her house, Constance set about filling it – at the General's expense – with furniture in the fashionable Greek and Egyptian style, heavily encumbered with brass and gold leaf. Even when her rooms began to resemble an auction hall, Constance continued to hunt out the rare and the costly, the sweet scent of vengeance thrilling her as she shopped.

Every winged-lion side-table was a hit on the enemy's camp, a small compensation for her days of enforced poverty. Now the memory of each scowl cost the General a brass candle-sconce, and every hard word a looking-glass or a dinner-plate as Constance paid him back for his harshness in gold-garlanded obelisks and clawed Assyrian stools.

Constance was clearly delighted with the bargain she'd made, yet Flora couldn't help feeling that she, personally, had paid a great price for the clutter of urns and sphinxes which crowded their rooms, and the early morning concerto of doorsteps being scrubbed up and down the square.

Her one consolation was to find herself only a street or two from Lydia Seaward, tucked away in Colonel West's little love-nest between the oil-shop and the pork-butcher's in Park Street. Whenever she could, she slipped away from her mother's vigilance to a new haven among the plump striped sofas and cluttered tables of Lydia's little home.

'I try not to visit Sophie's house in New Road any more than I can help,' she told Lydia sincerely, 'though Darius hardly ever seems to be there when we call. But I really have no interest in anything Sophie does,' she added, trying to believe she meant that, too. 'I hope they're happy together, that's all.'

'Figs to that!' snorted Lydia, propping her delicate, shoeless little feet on a card-table. Beside her, the open window let in the smell of Park Street, and oil, and pork-butchery, and overworked horses clopping dispiritedly over the cobblestones.

'Happy together?' she demanded. 'You don't hope anything of the kind – not inside, you don't. And you know perfectly well Darius Elder will do what they all do in the end – get himself an heir, and then leave his wife to her lovers and go back to his bachelor life.'

In fact, Sophie – with a dreadful, giggling coyness – had already had a room on her top floor distempered and hung with chintz curtains as a nursery for the brood of babies which she confidently expected to crown her triumph as a wife. Yet the months passed, with no excited whispering of events to come. Sophie's smile was more brittle now, and though the possessive note was still there in her voice when she spoke of her husband, there was a feverish glint in her eye which warned Constance that artful enquiries about her daughter's condition would no longer be well received.

At the beginning of the summer, Sophie spent six weeks at Chillbourne for the sake of her health, leaving Darius at the mercy of the servants at New Road.

'That isn't the way to get babies,' muttered her mother, clicking her teeth in disapproval.

September brought the first anniversary of Sophie's marriage, and an agitated consultation in the morning-room at New Road between Sophie and Constance. That evening in Montagu Square, the dinner-table was wrapped in such dismal silence that even the filling of a water-glass split the air with the roar of a cataract.

'I can't think what she's doing wrong!' Constance burst out at last as the serving-girl took the soup-plates back to the kitchen. 'No one in my family's ever had trouble producing an heir – except too many of them, sometimes.'

Suddenly aware she'd strayed into the vexed territory of the mechanics of procreation, she fell silent and fiddled with her fork.

'I don't suppose you know what I'm talking about, Flora.'

'Bearing children, I thought.'

'Not just bearing them, but *getting* them.'

'Oh.'

'You see, there are certain things . . .' Constance stopped, and sighed, and seemed to find it easier to address her remarks to the prongs of her fork. 'Certain . . . *exercises* necessary for the getting of children which may seem highly strange and disagreeable at the time, but which must be borne with fortitude.' Constance finished her sentence at high speed and leaned back in her chair, exhausted.

'And what exercises would those be?' enquired Flora with mischievous innocence. If her mother could have heard some of Lydia's forthright comments on the habits of the male sex, she might have considered her lecture a little late in the day.

'Never you mind!' snapped Constance furiously. 'It's enough for you to know they exist, and there's no escape from them if you're to produce any children. Though Sophie seems to be doing her duty well enough by her husband, from what I can make out – and Darius presumably knows his business in that department. Yet there are still no babies on the way to fill that nursery of hers.'

Flora didn't reply. All the humour had abruptly drained from the situation, banished by the thought of Sophie 'doing her duty' by her husband. Flora would never have found it a duty – no, not in those arms – nor a hollow fantasy, as Dédalon claimed, nor an indulgence, as Lydia insisted. Oh, she despised herself for her disloyalty to her father, every bit as much as she despised Sophie for hers: but the fact remained that the very sting of Darius Elder's glance, of his hard, fierce spirit and the intolerant set of his shoulders, were as precious to her still as the stubborn softness of that strange, diffuse mouth, even as it reproached her.

The thought of those eyes, blue-shadowed in the dawn, opening to the brush of Sophie's lips on their lashes, was almost unbearable, and Flora pushed her plate away, suddenly sick to her soul. Yet Darius Elder was irrevocably Sophie's now, and she had no choice but to learn to accept the fact.

Sometimes Flora examined her face in her dressing-mirror to see if it bore any sign of the struggle taking place inside her. But the glass contained only a pensive young woman – a little wan, perhaps, and with velvety smudges under her eyes, but now quite passably *comme il faut*, with her hair restored to its former dark abundance, and a dress of ruby Indian muslin in the latest, smartest fashion.

3

Sophie's second year of marriage marched inexorably forward, but her nursery remained stubbornly empty. As if the room itself were somehow to blame, Sophie had it scrubbed out and redecorated time after time. Her obsession spread to the house as a whole, until nothing would satisfy her but the redecoration of every part of it; she even insisted on living there while the work was done, suffocating everyone in a fog of plaster dust and distemper rather than allow the tiniest corner to remain unscoured.

Every month, her hopes rose to fever-point; and regularly every month she was hurled into misery by the discovery that the one thing she could not buy – the validation, the triumph of her wifehood – had escaped her once more. Regularly now, her maid would find her bent over her wash-stand, splashing tears into the water as she scrubbed despair from her spotless fingers.

Not only the servants were affected. Nowadays, Flora and her mother could call at New Road without ever catching a glimpse of Darius Elder, who seemed to spend most of his time away from home.

Searching desperately for diversion, Sophie's eye fell upon the example of the great political hostesses, Lady Holland and Lady Melbourne, and she immediately decided to establish a salon of her own. If men of letters or politicians could visit the offices of Elder's Bank, why shouldn't they grace Mrs Darius Elder's drawing-room too?

For a long time Flora managed to avoid Sophie's dinners or supper-parties, always inventing an excuse for refusing. Sophie's 'salons' sounded as ferocious as a Roman circus, and since Flora was no society lion, she concluded she'd only been invited as one of the martyrs.

Besides – Flora had only just discovered a new world for herself in books of travellers' tales, and far preferred to spend an evening poring over James Bruce's adventures in search of the source of the Nile than among Sophie's smart friends. Curled up on one of her mother's Grecian sofas, she could voyage with Humboldt on the inky rivers of Venezuela, or with Cook on the Pacific, or travel with Clarke to the Urals and with Barrow to China. Here, among wonders which Dédalon had only touched upon, Flora searched determinedly for new dreams to replace the ones she'd lost.

'At least go *once* to New Road,' Constance implored. 'Sophie's becoming quite vexed with you, and she's quarrelsome enough as it is. Just once – to please me, Flora dear. After that you may have as many headaches as you please.'

Sophie's supper was quite different from Mrs Ivory's party in Curzon Street. Instead of a stately parade to the dining-table, a higgledy-piggledy brawl broke out as the assembled celebrities scrambled into their places, and throughout the meal, as far as Flora could see, everyone talked with their mouths full or shouted to drown out their neighbours' conversation. And this, apparently, was the cream of London fashion – yelling at one another along the length of the table, braying with laughter at their own witticisms, drinking, nudging, belching, flicking pellets of bread, and falling off their chairs to screams of glee from their friends on either side.

After supper there was no question of the ladies withdrawing. If only to keep the gentlemen from becoming insensibly drunk, the whole company surged upstairs once more to trade gossip or snore in corners or play cards in an adjoining room. A prominent opera-singer was now perched on a newspaper-editor's lap and an archduke asleep on a card-table; to Flora it seemed a good moment to ask for Sophie's carriage to take her home.

After a few minutes searching she found, not Sophie, but Darius Elder, alone in a window recess, staring out into the gathering darkness. She'd managed to avoid him all evening, but now he looked round at her approach, making it impossible for her to pass by.

'Are you bored with your guests already, brother-in-law?' She'd meant to speak lightly, yet somehow the question emerged like a challenge.

Darius turned to survey the crowded room without enthusiasm.

'They're Sophie's guests, not mine. But if she enjoys giving these dinners,' he added defensively, 'if they make her happy – then why not?'

His eyes roamed over the candle-lit faces, and finally picked out the bright figure of his wife, chatting animatedly with a celebrated painter, her hands fluttering, the feathers in her hair swaying like palms in a gale. Then he turned back to Flora, so abruptly that she caught the lingering sadness in his eyes.

'I know you never approved of my marrying Sophie – but I do care about her, I promise you.'

Enviously, Flora followed his glance across the room. 'Sophie seems to be enjoying her evening a great deal.'

'Only *seems* to be?'

'I've known Sophie since she was a baby, don't forget.'

'Then perhaps you can tell me what's troubling her.' He gave a short, resigned sigh, and his eyes sought out his wife once more. 'She dissolves into weeping for no reason at all – or flies into a screaming fit at the least annoyance until she's almost uncontrollable. Two maids have already left, claiming they were afraid of what she might do.'

He was at a loss, genuinely distressed by the enigma of Sophie: Flora could hear the anxiety in his voice, and wished from the desolate depths of her soul that he'd chosen someone else to confide in.

'Have you asked Sophie what's the matter?' she enquired stiffly.

'I've tried.'

'And?'

'She walks away, and won't talk to me. She's miserable, I can see that – but there doesn't seem to be any medical reason for it. The doctor leaves tonics, which she refuses to take, and tells her to spend more time in the open air.' He lifted his hands in a gesture of futility, and Flora felt as if her heart would break.

'I know you think I'm a monster,' he added softly, 'but I swear to you I've never reproached Sophie with anything since the day we were married. She does exactly as she pleases with the house. She goes wherever she wants and buys whatever takes her fancy. I don't ask her to explain how she's spent her time or her money. What more can she want?'

His expression held such silent entreaty that Flora was compelled to look away.

'I don't know what she wants. A child, perhaps.' And then, without being able to help herself, she added in a small voice, 'I never said you were a monster. At least – if I did, I didn't mean it.'

'Didn't you?' Darius was searching her face with such intensity that Flora could hear the blood begin to drum in her ears. All at once she longed desperately to be safe again in Montagu Square with her sea-captains and her explorers.

To her dismay, Darius persisted.

'Then, if you don't think I'm such a monster . . . What do you think of me, Flora?'

'You can't ask me that.' Flora made an effort to sound lighthearted.

'But I want to know all the same.' Unwaveringly, his eyes held hers.

'Please—'

A sudden commotion broke out at the door, and Flora glanced gratefully towards it. A hush had fallen on the room, while all eyes turned to the extraordinary figure framed in the doorway – a tall man,

133

darker even than Darius Elder, and his face made darker still by the curl of hair that fell on his brow and the deep, mysterious moustache which shaded his lips. He paused for a moment in the doorway, his head flung back a little, gathering the folds of a long, gold-brocaded Arab robe.

'Newsome . . .' Darius murmured under his breath.

'Who?'

'Ralph Newsome. *Newsome of Nubia*, they're calling him now.'

'Not Newsome the explorer?' Flora's eyes opened wide as she snatched at the diversion. 'The author of *Newsome's Journals*? Oh, I've read every word of his travels in Persia and Egypt! But I thought he'd gone off to explore Abyssinia,' she added in surprise.

Darius Elder surveyed the glittering figure in the doorway with distaste.

'He seems to have come back.'

At the other side of the room Ralph Newsome advanced into the crowd and was immediately swallowed up by it. Flora turned to Darius, her eyes shining.

'Ralph Newsome – how amazing! Do you know, he's climbed the remotest mountains among hostile tribesmen, and travelled to places where no one else has ever gone?' In her excitement, Flora even placed a hand on Darius's arm. 'Will you introduce me to him – please?'

He glanced down at her hand, a little sourly. 'I don't see why.'

'Because I've read every volume of his journals several times over. I've read *Travels Among the Mussulmen*, and *The Afghan Road* – and oh, you wouldn't believe the wonderful way he has of describing the nobility of the mountains in the evening light . . .'

Impassioned by a splendour beyond words, Flora's hand flew from Darius's sleeve to create fantastic landscapes in the air. When she glanced round again, it was to see Ralph Newsome himself emerging from the crowd in his shining robes, a glass of claret in one hand and a large piece of plum cake in the other.

'Oh, gracious – look, here he comes with Sophie.'

How charming, said Sophie's smile as she approached, but her eyes implied something quite different, flicking suspiciously between the faces of her husband and her sister while her elegant nostrils twitched, scenting the sharp note of conspiracy.

'Well, here you are – both of you!' Sophie's smile was sweeter than sugar-paste. At once, her little cat's paw wriggled itself into the crook of her husband's elbow, as startlingly white against the black fabric of his coat as a 'sold' ticket at a painting exhibition.

'You know my husband, of course, Mr Newsome—'

'My banker? Alas—' The explorer raised his glass. 'Only too well.'

'But not my sister Flora, I think.'

'Delighted, Miss St Serf.' Deftly, Ralph Newsome transferred the glass and the cake to the same hand, and held out the other. For a moment Flora thought he meant to kiss her fingers, and suffered a pang of disappointment at such cheap gallantry. Instead, however, he clasped her hand for several seconds in the warmth of his own, while his eyes consumed hers with an intensity which momentarily took her breath away.

They were the darkest eyes she'd ever seen, long at their outer corners, their pupils lost in irises of velvety blackness which only now and then showed the soft lustre of ancient oak. No wonder Newsome could pass for an Arab when the need arose; years of eastern suns had burned into the skin stretched taut across his cheekbones and jaw, burnishing it to the sheen of copper. No wonder suburban matrons flocked to his lectures and rushed to buy his books, and secluded young women in country rectories sent him locks of their hair, promising him their prayers on his next tour.

'I've read everything you've ever written,' Flora assured him.

'Indeed? I hope not.' The black eyes glittered roguishly. 'That would be . . . a great mistake.'

'Your books, I mean,' Flora said quickly, hoping the heat she felt rising in her cheeks wouldn't reveal itself in blushes. 'All of them. Everything. In fact, I only finished reading *The Afghan Road* this afternoon.'

'My dear Miss St Serf, you must have the patience of a saint, to persevere with my rambling stuff. Next time I find myself marooned in the desert, drinking camel's bath-water and sleeping in a snake-pit, I shall think of your kindness, and find the strength to go on.'

Sophie gave a sudden trill of a laugh. 'Oh, what a rogue you are, to make fun of us poor stay-at-homes! Isn't he, Darius?'

'If you say so.'

'And my poor sister one of your most devoted admirers!' added Sophie slyly. '*Oh, if only I could meet that wonderful man!* She's said it to me so often.'

'Sophie!' protested Flora. 'What on earth will Mr Newsome think of me?'

'I think you show considerable taste, Miss St Serf.'

Ralph Newsome's dark eyes caressed Flora's as a reward for her constancy.

Flora found herself smiling idiotically in response. It was impossible not to admire such a free spirit; here was a man who'd devoted his life to adventure and to unlocking the secrets of distant horizons, who – unlike most Englishmen – could wear an Arab robe with a casual arrogance which gave him an almost piratical air. An image floated irresistibly into Flora's mind of a traveller drowsing by a campfire under the desert stars, contemplating the infinite variety of the planet.

'To be fair,' Ralph Newsome admitted, 'my sister Hester must take a great deal of the credit for my journals. Goodness knows how she manages to make sense of the shambles of notes I bring home!' He smiled ruefully. 'And yet somehow she always seems to get them ready in time for the printer. The latest volume should be published quite soon, made up from my Abyssinian material.'

'With more of your exciting adventures?' Sophie was still clinging to Darius's arm.

The explorer shrugged, and the gold threads of his robe glinted in the candlelight.

'It's tedious stuff mostly – geological observations, some new maps, a few notes on the tribesmen . . . And a page or two on the Forbidden City of Mittur, of course.'

'You've been inside a Forbidden City?' squeaked Sophie. 'Did you hear that, Flora?'

'I believe I was the first European to set foot in the place,' admitted Newsome nonchalantly. He took a large bite out of the lump of plum cake, and waved the glass in an explanatory circle.

'Mind you – it was a pretty near thing whether I ever came back from it again. You wouldn't have thought much of that, Elder, I dare say – defaulting on a loan, without even my carcass to sell as collateral?'

Darius Elder gave a thin smile, and Flora laughed outright. Sophie, delighted at the success of her introduction, began to draw her husband away.

'You must excuse us, Flora, and dear Mr Newsome. One of my other guests is most anxious to meet my husband . . .'

In a moment, they were gone.

'Oh, please tell me about the Forbidden City,' Flora begged quickly, afraid Ralph Newsome might be about to follow. 'I must know why you almost didn't come back.'

'Ah . . . that . . .' Newsome made an expansive gesture with the plum cake. 'If you're certain I won't bore you . . .'

'Oh, never!'

'Well, you see – the only way I could get into the city in the first place was by disguising myself as a Somali camel-trader and going in with my men. Fortunately, no one suspected us – but we'd hardly got clear of the place again when the Amir discovered how I'd tricked him, and got dashed hot about it. Swore to have my head,' he added blandly.

'*Infidel*, do you see – an unbeliever in the Forbidden City. At any rate, he sent some of his cut-throats to chase after us, with orders to creep up during the night and kill us all while we slept.'

The explorer smiled, as if the memory amused him.

'They'd have finished us off, I dare say, if my camel hadn't caught wind of them and squealed loud enough to wake the whole camp. My own damned servant turned out to be in on the plot, and he'd taken my guns.'

Newsome paused for another bite of cake.

'By good luck, however, I still had my razor in my travelling bag – and it's amazing what you can do with one of those when the odds are against you. There was a bit of a skirmish, but the bandits soon took to their heels.'

He gave another self-deprecating little smile. 'You know how it is.'

'Oh, yes . . .' breathed Flora in awe. 'And I can't wait to read about it in your journal. I'm sure you've been far too modest to tell me the whole story.'

Ralph Newsome raised a hand in mild denial.

'When all's said and done, it amounted to very little. One of those risks one has to take in pursuit of knowledge. We're a restless breed, we travellers, and our curiosity makes us outcasts from every society. We become homeless, Miss St Serf. We live by wandering – and because of that we're condemned to wander for the rest of our lives.'

The poignancy of it touched Flora's heart. 'You have no home at all?'

'Oh, I have a house of sorts in Russell Square, where my sister lives. But I wouldn't call it a home.'

'And, of course, you've never married . . . Oh, forgive me,' Flora added quickly, 'I shouldn't repeat gossip.'

Ralph Newsome spread his hands philosophically. 'It's perfectly true. What lady wants a savage for a husband? An outlaw – a nomad . . .'

'Rousseau saw nobility in the savage state,' Flora reminded him encouragingly. 'Man in a state of nature.'

'So . . . You're a follower of Rousseau, Miss St Serf?'

'I've read some of his works.'

'Then I'm afraid the worthy Christian ladies and gentlemen who subscribe for my travels would hardly agree with you about the nobility of the savage. They believe religious instruction is the only way to bring the unenlightened wretch to a degree of civilization.'

'Well, then, *I* do not agree with *them*.'

'You don't?' Newsome regarded Flora with interest.

'I believe there are some ways in which we might even learn from the "wretches" as you call them. For one thing, we might rediscover man's true nature.'

'And what is that, Miss St Serf?'

'Not so very different from the animals.'

'Indeed!' The explorer's elegant, tanned fingers drifted up to explore the fringes of his moustache. 'Indeed . . .' he murmured again. 'You're a young lady with most unexpected views.'

'I beg your pardon. I didn't mean to lecture you.'

'Not at all . . . not at all.' Ralph Newsome continued to stroke the dark foliage which concealed his lips. 'I'm a seeker after knowledge, Miss St Serf, as I told you. I pursue it in any form.'

Yet he continued to study her thoughtfully, leaving Flora with the distinct impression of having been far too forthright.

'When shall we see your Abyssinian journal in the booksellers' shops?' she asked hastily.

'Will you really read it, Miss St Serf?'

'But of course! I'll subscribe for it at your publishers' tomorrow.'

'You're very kind.' Once more, Ralph Newsome caressed her with his modest, self-mocking half-smile. 'But there's no need to go to the trouble of leaving an order. I'll have a copy sent to you on the day of publication, with my compliments. I shall be most interested to hear the opinion of such an unusual young lady as yourself.'

CHAPTER NINE

I

It was Sophie who suggested Ralph Newsome should go in person to deliver his new journal to Montagu Square. To Flora's secret disappointment he arrived without the Arab robe, though even in a close-cut black promenade coat he managed to look a trifle exotic, his rich, cinnamon-coloured skin shining faintly as if it had been massaged all over with oil.

'Extraordinary,' he murmured, gazing round Constance's cluttered drawing-room. 'For a moment there, I thought I must be back in the Cairo bazaar.'

Constance took this as a compliment and managed a fleeting smile. The explorer made himself as comfortable as he could on a gilt Pharaoh's throne.

'Eighteenth dynasty,' he remarked conversationally, tapping a scarab.

'Oh, to be sure. Eighteenth dynasty.' Constance watched him uneasily, as if he were a strange and beautiful python which had followed her daughter home.

Fortunately, Mrs Ivory arrived at that moment, throwing Constance into such a ferment that Ralph Newsome was able to move near enough to Flora to engage her exclusively in conversation.

'My journal, as I promised.' From the pocket of his coat he produced a leather-bound volume. '*An Account of a Tour to Abyssinia and Travels in the Interior of that Country. With Particulars Regarding the Aboriginal African Tribes, together with Notes on Their Respective Customs, and a First Account of the Forbidden City of Mittur.*'

He offered the volume with his thumb in the flyleaf, holding it open so that the words handwritten on the page could be read. *To Miss Flora St Serf, from her servant, Ralph Newsome. 17th December, 1824.*

'Good gracious,' she murmured, taken aback.

'I didn't mean to embarrass you.'

'Oh, you haven't – not at all. It's just . . . It's so very kind of you to bring it here yourself. I really didn't expect so much.'

The explorer waved away her thanks. 'As long as I haven't offended you. To be perfectly honest—' He glanced across to where Constance St Serf and Mrs Ivory were exchanging stilted compliments, and then smiled apologetically at Flora. 'To be honest, I find it hard to put on drawing-room manners again, after the freedom of the wilderness. If I had my way, I'd never go out in society at all. I'm a solitary beast, best left to my own melancholy.'

'And yet you give such wonderful lectures . . .'

'Ah . . . those . . .' He waved a hand in a weary, graceful gesture. 'It's an obligation – the duty of those who travel where no one has gone before. The learned societies expect it. Universities expect it.' He sighed like a man beset with calls upon his generosity. 'And they will keep offering me large sums of money for doing it.'

'And you have ships to charter, I suppose, and hundreds of porters to pay, with their camels and donkeys and what have you.'

'Gracious no – committees find the money for that sort of thing, or the Government does, if it happens to have its eye on some nice little sultanate and wants to know how well it's defended.'

He smiled conspiratorially, and his black eyes showed off their golden glint. 'Like my little jaunt among the Gurkhas, a few years ago. "Take Kathmandu," I said to the East India people, "and you'll have Sikkim and all the lowland country to the west of it." I'm pleased to say they took my advice, and annexed the place.'

'You were spying for the British . . .'

'Hardly that – nothing so heroic. Just . . . reporting what I saw. Like my ramble through Kashmir—'

'You've been to Kashmir!' Flora gazed at him enviously. 'Oh, I should so much like to see Kashmir.'

'Then you should hurry to Kashmir before the Russians take charge of it. Because that's what they're planning, I'm sure. At any rate, that's what I've told the Prime Minister.' He regarded Flora with mock severity. 'I suppose after all this I ought to swear you to secrecy.'

'On my honour, then, I promise,' laughed Flora, placing her hand on the *Tour to Abyssinia*.

'You must say "I swear to keep all Ralph Newsome's secrets" – otherwise how can we talk about anything worthwhile?'

'I shall swear you aren't at all what I expected,' conceded Flora. 'Will that do?'

'Oh . . . for now.' Newsome leaned back speculatively in his chair. 'But then, you yourself are quite unexpected. I can't think of many young ladies who'd agree with what you said to me at your sister's "soirée".'

'And what was that, particularly?'

'Oh . . . about the savage state being superior in some ways to a state of Christian enlightenment.' His hand rose absently to his moustache, where his fingers began to brush slowly to and fro. 'Is that genuinely what you believe?'

'Well, yes – I suppose it is.'

'But that isn't . . . Forgive me for prying, but is that what your mother has taught you, or a governess?'

'Oh, good gracious, no! Mamma would be shocked to hear me say it. She always warns me to keep such opinions to myself, or no respectable man will have anything to do with me.'

Ralph Newsome laughed, showing strong white teeth under the blackness of his moustache.

'My late mother was a most devout woman,' he remarked. 'Every part of her life was ruled by the exact word of scripture. She believed that an Englishman was the most sublime of God's creations, and should live as nothing less than a saint. My sister still holds similar views.'

'Your sister and I might not always agree, I fear.'

'No . . . That's true.' Newsome's restless fingers moved to his ear, a small, lobeless, efficient ear set back tightly against his head. It was quite a different ear, Flora noticed, from Darius Elder's; his were delicate at the rim, curving almost like a woman's to the pink cushions of their lobes. But then, no two ears are ever quite alike – so Dédalon had assured her – not even left and right belonging to the same head, so complex is our construction.

'You wouldn't agree with Hester then, that the earth was created in six days, and man on the last of them?'

Flora removed her gaze from the fascinating sight of Ralph Newsome's brown fingers caressing his brown ear.

'You've seen so much more of the world than I have, Mr Newsome. Do you believe such variety could be created in six of our short days?'

'I asked you for your opinion, Miss St Serf.'

'Then I think . . . that all life forms have developed and changed over millennia – all life forms, including man.'

'You are an evolutionist, in fact.' Newsome's eyes, as black as a bird's, gave no clue to whether he approved or disapproved. 'My sister would say you were also a heretic. A heathen.'

'Miss Newsome may think whatever she pleases,' retorted Flora with dignity. 'You asked the question, and I have given you an honest answer.'

Ralph Newsome flung back his head with a great roar of laughter; on the other side of the room, Constance St Serf and Mrs Ivory swung round in astonishment.

'Do you know, Miss St Serf – you remind me very much of a beautiful Berber girl I once came across in Tunisia. The same proud independence. The same dark hair and fine-boned features. And your eyes . . . What colour are your eyes, precisely?' He leaned forward again to examine them.

'I suppose they're a little greenish.' Piqued by his laughter, Flora lowered her lids and stared at the toes of her shoes.

'There – now I've offended you. Though they're quite light-skinned, you know, the Berber people.'

'I'm not offended in the least. People are people, after all, no matter what colour their skins may be.'

'And people are animals, so you tell me. Man has an animal nature of which he should be proud.' The lines round Ralph Newsome's eyes deepened mischievously.

'You've no right to question me, Mr Newsome, and then tease me when I give you a straightforward answer!'

'Miss St Serf, I beg your pardon. But you must understand that with most young ladies, one can exhaust their opinions in thirty seconds. You are . . . something quite different, in every way. I think perhaps we may have a great deal to talk about, you and I.'

'I'm afraid I've very little experience of the world. Whatever I've learned has come from books.'

'So much the better. The Arabs tell us *a woman without modesty is bread without salt*. You should wear your innocence like a jewel, Miss St Serf. Good heavens – is that the time?' Ralph Newsome consulted a handsome gold watch. 'I'm expected at the Royal Society in fifteen minutes.'

Rising to his feet, he gathered up his hat and ebony cane.

'A pleasure, Mrs St Serf. *Always* a pleasure, Mrs Ivory. And Miss St Serf—' He clasped Flora's hand with the same warm, lingering pressure she'd noticed before, and lowered his voice a fraction. 'I'll call on you again, if I may, to hear your opinion on my new journal.'

'I shall be glad to see you, Mr Newsome.' Behind him, on the table, her eye fell on the book itself, open once more at the flyleaf: *To Miss Flora St Serf, from her servant, Ralph Newsome*.

'I shall be delighted to see you,' she added, 'whenever you care to call.'

2

'And the shepherds in the hills wear wigs, he says – great cauliflowers like the Duke of Wellington's coachmen, but made of sheepskin and grease, and dyed bright red!'

'Really?' said Sophie politely. 'Well, I must say, Flora, you seem to have learned this journal of Ralph Newsome's off by heart. My brain's quite aching with all your talk of daggers and *hukkah* pipes and vultures.'

'Gurgur.'

'I beg your pardon?'

'*Gurgur*. That's what the Somalis call their vultures,' Flora informed her.

'Is it, indeed? Well, all I can say is thank goodness we're not plagued with the filthy things in New Road.' Sophie put her head on one side, and regarded her sister with speculative eyes. 'Mr Newsome seems to have made quite a conquest of Flora, wouldn't you say, Darius?'

Darius Elder, one elbow on his drawing-room chimneypiece, glanced up suddenly, as if his thoughts had been as far away as the Forbidden City itself. Since it was Sunday and sleeting heavily he was at home but determinedly restless.

'I said Mr Newsome seems to have made a great conquest of Flora,' Sophie repeated sharply. 'As she has of him, by all accounts. He's never done telling me what unusual opinions she has.'

'If you say so, then no doubt it's true.' Darius Elder frowned at the spectacle of Flora, sitting between Sophie and her mother, a cup of tea growing cold in her hand while she described the marvels of the *Tour to Abyssinia*.

'Newsome delivered this book himself, did you say?'

'He did – with a handsome inscription in it, too.' Flora's pride defeated her attempt at coolness. 'And he called again the following week to see what I'd made of it. Of course, I told him it was wonderful.'

'Generous of you.'

Darius's tone was so sarcastic that Flora glanced up at him in surprise.

'Oh no – it really is a wonderful book. When you think how long his journey was, and how dangerous . . . The Amir of Mittur would have had Mr Newsome's head cut off at once, if he'd realized he was an infidel in disguise.'

'A great loss, no doubt.'

'If you're going to make fun of him, Darius, then I shan't say any more.' Flora put down her teacup with decision.

'He's quite rich,' announced Sophie unexpectedly. 'Not family money, you understand – his father died when he was only a baby – but he's made a great deal for himself out of his books and his lectures.'

'Oh?' Constance stopped stirring her tea and looked up. 'I thought all these explorers were as poor as church mice.'

'But Ralph Newsome's so famous!' protested Sophie. '*Newsome of Nubia*! Ladies are never done sending him sonnets – and the Society for the Repression of Slavery gave him a huge silver inkstand with the figure of a slave throwing off his chains. I dare say he'll be knighted before very long, if he keeps up this pace.'

For a fleeting second Darius's eyes met Flora's, sharing the memory of another silver inkstand and its pointed taper-snuffer.

'How often has Ralph Newsome called on you?' he demanded abruptly.

Flora stiffened in her chair. 'Does it matter?'

'Yes, why do you want to know?' asked her mother.

'Just curiosity.' Yet his eyes never left Flora's face. 'I simply thought that for a man looking for an opinion on a book, he seems to be making a great many social calls these days.'

'Darius doesn't approve of Ralph Newsome,' said Sophie, making a face.

'I don't like the man, it's true.'

'Because he's handsome, and dashing, and not at all boring,' retorted Sophie, her voice quivering ominously.

'Because he comes to my house dressed up like a Cairo fortune-teller,' snapped her husband. 'He's a mountebank. A showman.'

'He's a world traveller,' objected Flora, determined to be loyal to her new friend. 'You can't expect him to be the same as ordinary people.'

'Especially if he's rich,' added Constance. 'If he's rich, he can do as he pleases. It isn't as if he has a wife to think of, or any—' She stopped abruptly, and stole a furtive glance at Sophie. '. . . children,' she finished lamely.

'I don't trust the man.' Darius Elder kicked the logs in the grate. 'I don't like the way he's sniffing round Montagu Square, making up to my sister-in-law.'

'Well, then, I'm sorry for you,' muttered Sophie mutinously.

'But what can a famous explorer possibly see in Flora?' enquired Constance, turning to gaze at Flora in astonishment.

'This is all utter nonsense, and you know it!' Flora, her cheeks scarlet, faced Darius furiously across the tea-table. 'Mr Newsome has simply been kind enough to give me a copy of his book and tell me something of his travels. I really don't see why it matters whether you all approve of him or not.'

'Over-excited,' muttered Constance in Sophie's direction. 'She's over-excited,' she mouthed to Darius Elder. 'Too many naked tribesmen and camels and so forth. I never think these books are suitable for a young woman's eyes. Do you know—' She leaned forward intently. 'Somali women trample up and down on their men's backs at night, and the men seem to *like* it?'

'Mamma!' protested Flora in mortification.

'Well, that's what he says – and a few other things besides, which young girls have no need to know.'

'For goodness' sake,' cried Flora, 'in a week's time I shall be twenty-two years old! I wish you'd all stop treating me as if I were a child. Mr Newsome is the only one who speaks to me as if I had a grain of sense in my head. At least he seems to believe I'm a grown woman.'

Darius Elder's expression was stony. 'Oh, I'm sure he does. I'm sure he does.'

3

From that moment, Flora became an avid student of the Horn of Africa. Like her mother, she couldn't really believe that Ralph Newsome had any serious interest in her as a person – but there was a void in her life which ached to be filled, and she had a perfect right to choose who should fill it.

For her part, Constance couldn't quite make up her mind whether she thought Ralph Newsome a good thing or not. Darius Elder disliked him, and the Elders were, after all, his bankers; but then, anyone who was *anyone* fell out with their bankers sooner or later, from the King downwards – it was almost a badge of respectability.

'As Mr Ralph Newsome said to me the other day . . .' was a phrase which tripped arrestingly off the tongue – and since he'd no doubt be off on his travels again before long, his usefulness as a social asset wouldn't last for ever. *Ergo* – anything that brought him to Montagu Square deserved to be encouraged.

Constance even accompanied Flora to the explorer's next lecture at the Royal Society, and dozed quietly in her seat while Flora dreamed over every word. The nomad's tale fell on her ears like outlandish music, name after name beating the drum of romance. The Nubian Desert – Bisan – the Dankali Plain . . . In her imagination Flora rode her bad-tempered little Dankali camel southwards at Newsome's side, through the lands of the warlike Gallo, over barren hillsides where myrrh-trees grew and warriors gathered the gum in the boss of their shields. The explorer led her on through the pass at Killulloo to the Plain of Marar, stronghold of robbers, and on to Berberah for the voyage home . . . It was all so wild, so dangerous, and so exotic – which was no doubt why Darius Elder disapproved of it so much.

Surely only the most wooden of men could be blind to Ralph Newsome's heroism? Wooden – or jealous, perhaps . . . Flora allowed herself a certain amount of bitter satisfaction over this possibility; but Darius was Sophie's now, and could be as jealous as he pleased, since Flora had vowed to put him behind her. It was time to look forward – and there in the future, inescapably, was the fascinating presence of Ralph Newsome.

For Newsome was no gentle wanderer of the byways. By his own account he travelled wolfishly, hunting, ravishing and subduing the landscape he passed over. The challenge of each new plain, each lake and each mountain was its defiant intactness: wherever the land lay proud and virgin, Newsome would ache to set his foot, enslaving it for ever. His wanderings were a war with the world's wildness, in which every conquest drove him on to more.

By April, Flora had been to eight lectures, two tea-parties given in Ralph Newsome's honour by bluestocking ladies, and an exhibition of Arab art at the Museum. To her rapturous delight, she'd even received a necklace of silver bells which she rushed to parade in front of Sophie and her husband – much more stylish than a common-or-garden Kashmir shawl as a present for a lady . . .

'There now—' Ralph Newsome had looped the silver links round her neck like a fantastic collar. 'Now you're my Berber girl to the life – proud and wild as a desert mare.' And when Flora turned to thank him, she found him gazing at her with a savage possessiveness she'd never seen before in a man's eyes.

A male, without a blemish, Hester Newsome had called him when she came to Montagu Square, quoting Leviticus. 'Chosen by God to demonstrate the Christian way before the heathen.'

Hester Newsome was a thin woman in blue, a shrivelled inkstain with sunken white cheeks and the fanatical, bulging eyes of a shrew.

'My husband was a soldier,' said Constance. 'Among the St Serfs, duty is paramount.'

'My brother's duty is paramount,' declared Hester Newsome, looking significantly at Flora. She had a prominent edge to her upper lip, like a snail's foot, and the faint sensation of a moustache.

'Where my brother has shown the way, the forces of the Lord can follow. He is divinely inspired, and divinely protected.'

'That must be useful,' commented Constance, who'd only just returned to church-going; during her poverty she'd grudged the pew-rent but refused to stand at the back.

'We are but humble hand-maidens,' continued Miss Newsome sonorously. 'Privileged to minister to such a man.'

'I dare say,' murmured Constance, glancing covertly at her watch.

'What a terrible creature!' she exclaimed as soon as Hester Newsome's narrow blue back had been swallowed up in the maw of her carriage. 'Quite besotted with her brother, like all these dried-up old harridans, and spitting in the eye of any woman who dares to come near him. "Humble hand-maidens", indeed. Goodness knows why she took it into her head to come snooping round here. Does she think we're savages in need of conversion, I wonder?'

'Ten to one, he's going to ask you,' exclaimed Lydia next day when Flora told her of Hester Newsome's visit. '*Mrs Ralph Newsome* – my love, what a catch!' And Lydia threw her alabaster arms round Flora's neck and hugged her ecstatically.

'What's the matter, sweetness?' Lydia stepped back with a frown. 'Isn't that what you want?'

Flora was staring at her with troubled eyes. 'Somehow I never thought he might want to marry me.'

'What? Flora St Serf, I don't believe it! Never thought of such a thing? Why on earth do you suppose the fellow's been haunting

Montagu Square, making small-talk with your mamma? Not for the pleasure of sitting on her Egyptian chairs, I promise you. Oh come, my love—' Lydia clapped her hands together in amazement, 'don't tell me you never, ever suspected he might have come courting.'

'But he's a famous man,' protested Flora. 'And he's so much older than me. At least fifteen years older, I should think.'

'So what if he is?' Lydia shrugged. 'He's in his prime, that's all.' She waltzed across her little drawing-room to collapse like an overblown rose on one of the striped sofas. 'And when it comes to age, my pretty, just remember you're no spring chicken yourself. Twenty-two, and still single.' She shook her head and sucked in her cheeks. 'Twenty-two and a *virgin*, at that. You're probably the last of your kind in London.'

'There's Hester Newsome too, I should think.'

'You can never tell,' objected Lydia sagely. 'Sometimes you find these religious old hens have had the parson and the verger and most of the choir boys too, and consider themselves well blessed in the process.'

'Not Hester Newsome,' said Flora, laughing.

'Ah, well . . .' Lydia made a face. 'Perhaps you don't miss what you've never had. But it wouldn't do for me.'

'Well, I don't think I want to marry anyone.'

'Fiddlesticks!'

'It's true. I shall find a little school somewhere, and teach for a living—'

'And be desperately poor all your life, while you turn into another Hester Newsome.' Lydia banged her hands down on the striped upholstery. 'My dear Flora, that isn't how the world goes for women, and you know it. Is Hester Newsome an independent lady? Of course she isn't! She's in thrall to her brother – his "hand-maiden", as she puts it.'

Lydia beckoned Flora to sit down beside her.

'Flora, dear heart, in the world we have now, a woman without a man to protect her – unless she's a widow – is a woman who doesn't exist. It's all very well to talk about teaching, but even charity schools look sideways at young single women asking for work. And if you can't find work,' she went on, 'what's to become of you? Do you want to be your sister's pensioner for the rest of your life?'

Lydia took Flora's hand in hers, and gave it a comforting squeeze.

'No, my dear – if this explorer of yours offers you a ring, snatch it as quick as you can.' She shook her head again. 'I can't believe it never crossed your mind that he might.'

'Well, it just didn't,' confessed Flora. 'I was . . . I was thinking of something else.'

'Of something else, or some*one* else?' Lydia peered at Flora closely. 'Was it Darius Elder, by any chance?'

'Why should I be thinking of him?' Flora glanced away, unable to meet Lydia's eye.

'I just hope you aren't. Not seriously, at any rate. Now he's married to your sister, I'm afraid you'll have to regard Darius Elder as a piece of rather decorative furniture and nothing else. Admire the upholstery if you wish, but don't think of anything more.'

'Darius doesn't want me to have anything to do with Ralph Newsome.'

'Oh – men are devils, aren't they?' Lydia's face assumed an expression of amused contempt. 'Married men are all the same. They'll take advantage of you if you give them the least chance, and then they'll swear it was all your fault. And Darius Elder will do it as soon as the rest,' she added warningly. 'He'll make pretty speeches when it suits him – but he'll be gone in an instant when difficulties arise. That's why I say to you, my love, if you have a chance of a good marriage – take it. Don't waste your life dreaming about another woman's husband!'

'And what about you and the Colonel?' Flora blurted out. 'Colonel West has a wife and children already, doesn't he? Why are you wasting your life on him?'

Lydia shrugged. 'Because he pays me to, my dear. That's the long and short of it. Oh, he's a kind enough man, and good company, and he's certainly not mean with his money. But if he didn't have that money, I wouldn't be here – depend on it. And one day, when he gets tired of me, he'll turn me out in the street to find another protector. But I don't want that for you, sweetness!' Anxiously, Lydia took Flora's hand again. 'Forget this fellow Elder! Put him out of your mind for good. Believe me – even the best of men can be cruel to the women they've promised to love.'

All of a sudden she let go of Flora's hand, and placed her palms decisively on her knees.

'Come – we'll walk in the park for half an hour, and see if I can't talk some sense into you.'

Her arm linked through Lydia's, Flora allowed herself to be led into the green acres of Hyde Park, and along a footpath towards the eastern limit of the Serpentine. Flora had expected another lecture, yet for some time Lydia said nothing at all, and they walked in silence between the banks of scythed turf which flanked the path, towards the bland sheet of water glittering invitingly between the trees. It was an unfashionable hour for a promenade, and the park was largely deserted except for a few gentlemen exercising their horses in the distance, and a child on a tubby pony being led to and fro by a military-looking instructor.

'This was where the Regent had his great display, after they sent Napoleon to Elba.' Lydia pointed at the sparkling expanse of the Serpentine, its surface ruffled by the light breeze. 'I dare say you were too young to see it – but, oh, what a night that was! Booths everywhere selling porter and pies, a painted castle and enough fireworks to make it as light as day, and a whole fleet of little battle-ships, with sails and flags and guns blazing . . . There never was such a show.' With her hands, Lydia indicated the size of the spectacle.

'The Regent even brought in a squad of little men to crew his model ships – Laplanders, they were, not one of them above three-and-a-half feet tall. And yet when they got here, the Prince said they were still too big by almost twelve inches, and would capsize his boats. Poor little fellows,' she added sadly. 'They cried their eyes out when they were sent home.'

'That's all very interesting, Lydia, but I don't see what it has to do with me.'

'I was thinking of Bonaparte, my dear, and Waterloo . . .'

'I used to ask Papa what it was like at Waterloo,' recalled Flora, 'but he'd never tell me.'

'I can understand why he didn't.'

Flora glanced at her friend in surprise. Lydia's expression was uncharacteristically solemn; she was gazing into the distance with the sombre resolve of a soldier about to go into battle, and her hands in their little lemon kid gloves were clasped tightly under the swell of her bosom.

'Come – let's get away from this place, and walk down to Achilles.' Linking her arm once more with Flora's, Lydia pulled her away in the direction of the distant bronze monument.

'Waterloo again,' remarked Flora as the martial figure reared above a bank of shrubs. 'Wellington's monument – but not Papa's. The battle was like a nightmare for him, which he never threw off.'

'More of a nightmare than you know.' Lydia pressed her shoulder against Flora's in a gesture of fierce sympathy. 'Oh, my dear, I hope I'm doing the right thing by telling you this. Maybe your father will curse me for it, wherever he is – but I want to save you from wasting your life like another young woman . . . Do you understand?'

'No, I don't understand.' For a few seconds the sun passed behind a cloud, and in the sudden faint chill, Flora shook her head. 'I don't understand any of this, Lydia. Tell me whatever it is you know.'

Lydia took a decisive breath. 'Do you remember George Bellarmine?'

'The soldier who paid for your rooms in King's Head Court . . .'

'Captain George – yes.' Lydia quickened her pace. 'Now, you must understand, this isn't my secret. It's your father's, if it's anybody's, and George promised the poor man his family would never find out. I'm only telling you now because . . . because *he* might have told you himself, if he'd been able. But you must swear to keep the secret in your turn.'

'Then I swear,' Flora agreed, mystified. 'I promise I won't tell a soul.'

Lydia nodded, apparently satisfied. She took a deep breath, and launched into her tale.

'George told me all this one day, quite by chance.' Her eyes were fixed on the path, where her little feet emerged one after the other from under the hem of her skirt. 'We happened to be talking about that French town – what's-its-name – Péronne – where your father defied Wellington's order and got himself court martialled for it. George's regiment was there too, just after Waterloo, when Péronne was bombarded and taken. He was in the First Foot, you know, though they call them the Grenadiers these days.

'At any rate—' Lydia took another great breath. 'George was put in charge of the place where they'd locked up your father after his arrest. And somehow during the night the two men began talking about what he'd done. The Major was in a dreadful state – *poor fellow*, said George. And that was when George heard about the little French girl,' Lydia finished in a rush.

'What French girl?' demanded Flora, her mouth suddenly dry.

'She was a young woman from the Marais, apparently, a working-girl who'd caught his eye in a Paris street when he was there with Wellington at the embassy. There he was, a handsome soldier and an officer too, enough to turn any poor girl's head when he came whispering to her of love.' She stole a sideways glance at Flora. 'The girl was much younger, of course – fair-haired and very pretty, so your father told George. Madeleine was her name, and she was a wonderful dancer – as light as the notes of the music itself. But she was a tradesman's daughter, and though they'd exchanged the usual vows of love, I don't suppose the Major gave her another thought after he left Paris.'

Lydia scowled up at the muscular bronze bulk of Achilles.

'Let's walk back along the ride,' she said, 'and leave this fellow to swing his sword as if it was the only important thing in the world. Soldiers!' she said scornfully. 'Fighting was all they could think about in Brussels, I dare say, just before the battle. But your father's poor little Madeleine had good cause to remember her lover. She managed to smuggle a letter to him in Brussels, to say she was carrying his child, but since her papa had disowned her when he found out, she'd had to leave Paris and take refuge with her mother's people in the country. The baby was almost due, her aunt was treating her badly, and she didn't know what to do. She begged your father to rescue her and provide for the child. Perhaps she even thought he might marry her – who knows? She may not have known he had a wife and family in England.'

Lydia paused.

'Go on,' said Flora, her face set.

'Well, it seems your father's thoughts were too full of Bonaparte at that moment to be bothered with a French girl and her problems. And maybe he was a little worried that the story might find its way home to his wife.' Lydia shrugged. 'At any rate, he told George he'd sent back a pretty short answer, claiming he could do nothing to help the girl – and hinting he was by no means sure the child was his. After all, there had been a great many British soldiers in Paris at the time.'

'He would never do such a thing!'

'They can all do it, my love!' exclaimed Lydia. 'But listen to the rest.' She held up a warning finger. 'Sometime during the battle, it seems, your father began to think differently about the whole business. Strange things happen to a man when he knows he might be dead by the end of the day, and all of a sudden the Major began to wonder whether poor Madeleine mightn't have been telling the truth after all. Perhaps he thought of his two young daughters waiting at home, his own flesh and blood. By all accounts Madeleine's baby was just as surely his. And so he swore to himself that if he survived the battle, he'd find a way of looking after her.

'A great many men died that day,' said Lydia with a sigh, 'but not your papa. As soon as the fighting was over, he thought of Madeleine, and of course her letter had told him exactly where to find her. Unfortunately, the town where she lived lay right in the path of Wellington's march towards Paris.'

'Not—'

Lydia nodded. 'Péronne, as bad luck would have it. Good heavens, how could the poor man give an order to open fire on the place, when he knew his own child and its mother were at risk? He'd already betrayed her once. How could he add to his cruelty by firing on the town as Wellington had commanded?' Lydia shook her head. 'But it takes more than one man to stop a war. Péronne was bombarded and captured, and your father was arrested for disobeying an order.'

'And what about Madeleine and her baby?' demanded Flora quickly. 'The child must be almost ten years old by now – my father's child. Didn't Captain George say what became of them?'

Lydia fixed her eyes on the approaching gate.

'While your father was under arrest in Péronne, the girl's cousin came to the window of his prison. He said the baby had been born two days before the Major's reply arrived from Brussels, and the poor little mother went almost mad with despair when she read the letter. Her mother's people didn't want her, her father had told her she'd no home in Paris any more, and she'd nowhere left to go. Late one night she went out, taking the baby with her, and never came back. In the morning they discovered her body in the river, and her child floating nearby.'

Flora stopped walking and stood stock-still in the middle of the park while the breeze played softly with the ends of her veil.

'And my father blamed himself for their deaths.'

'So George Bellarmine said. No sentence from a court martial could have been half as awful as the one your father pronounced on himself.'

'All those years of misery . . . For a drowned girl and her baby.'

'Misery – and death, in the end.'

But Flora had already returned in her mind to the dark, narrow room in Gough Square where her father had lain face-down over the table in a thickening pool of blood.

'The music-box . . . The little fair-haired dancer in the music-box must have reminded him of the poor dead girl . . . Oh, Papa – why couldn't you have told us?'

5

'Don't think too badly of your father,' pleaded Lydia as they parted at the iron gates. 'He wasn't really a wicked man, and he suffered terribly for what he'd done. But, do you see – if your father could do such a thing to a helpless girl, then any man is capable of it. That's why I beg you to accept Ralph Newsome if he asks you to marry him. Be the wife of a good man, instead of wasting your life dreaming of someone impossible.'

'I must have time to think—' Flora put a hand to her brow, as if to be assured, at least, of her own existence. 'And besides – perhaps you're wrong. Perhaps marriage is the last thing on Mr Newsome's mind.'

'Oh, he'll propose, I promise you. Otherwise why should his sister bother to inspect you?' Gently, Lydia took Flora's hands in her own. 'Sweetness – look at me. Please . . . Just look.'

Reluctantly, Flora raised her eyes.

'Flora dear, when you look at me, you see nothing at all. I'm an invisibility. I'm like the little *Parisienne*, except that I continue to live.' Lydia's eyes glistened. 'But I have no position – no claim on a living soul. I'm condemned to please one man after another for the very bread in my mouth. My darling – have you any notion how much I want to please *myself*, just for once?'

And with a final squeeze of Flora's hands, Lydia turned on her heel and walked quickly away towards Park Street.

CHAPTER TEN

I

The first drops of a summer shower had started to mist the air by the time Flora returned to Montagu Square.

Late into the evening, she sat in the drawing-room window, looking out on the still-glistening pavements and trying to come to terms with what Lydia had told her. A copy of the *Tour to Abyssinia* lay open on her lap, but only to stave off conversation: her thoughts had long since strayed from the Plain of Marar to a makeshift prison in Péronne and the disgraced officer who'd been held there. Her father hadn't been a wicked man, nor a cruel one; yet in spite of that he'd caused two needless deaths, and had died in the end of his own, unshared guilt.

Yet with whom could he have shared it? From her post at the window Flora studied her mother, stitching fastidiously by the empty hearth, stabbing her needle precisely through the stretched linen and tugging it taut at once before any untidy loops could spoil her immaculate finish. Appearances were all that mattered.

Wearily, Flora turned back to her window. Had the streets of Péronne been slicked with wet on the night of the little *Parisienne*'s last journey? Madeleine had been beyond caring how she appeared, desperate for any shelter at all for herself and her baby, Flora's half-brother or half-sister – Captain George had never discovered which.

For the fourth or fifth time, Flora tried to apply herself to Ralph Newsome's description of Abyssinian women, with their henna-stained hands and feet and their kohl-bordered eyes. But the image of the fair-haired *Parisienne* would not leave her, wheeling and turning in the embrace of the river to the endless tune of the automaton-maker's music box. Restless, Flora sighed aloud.

'I expect you've caught a chill.'

Flora looked up at once, startled by the sound of her mother's voice.

'Don't imagine I didn't see you picking at your fish tonight,' Constance continued without lifting her eyes from her embroidery. 'You hardly ate enough to feed a sparrow.' She gave a righteous sniff.

'You never give a thought to *my* feelings – neither you, nor your sister. Here's Sophie become so thin I shouldn't see her if she turned sideways, and now I find you poking and prodding at your food as if you expected to find creepy-crawlies in it. Sometimes I think you do it on purpose to vex me.'

'I wasn't very hungry, that's all.'

'You've taken a chill, just as I said, from walking in the park.' Constance raised her head to frown at Flora cross the room. 'In the park, indeed! All alone, like a . . . well, like a woman of no reputation. Flora, what am I to do with you?' Constance tut-tutted over her stitching.

'Sybil Ivory tells me she'd got each of her daughters off by the age of nineteen, and always to some well-set-up young fellow with more than ten thousand a year and good expectations. And why? Because her daughters took the trouble to make themselves agreeable.'

'I wouldn't thank you for any of their husbands,' retorted Flora, recalling the Ivory son-in-law who'd bored her to death with his wretched pack of hounds.

Constance flicked away such criticism with the edge of her embroidery.

'You must learn to be agreeable, Flora, and not always to be putting forward your own opinions.'

In the window, Flora shut her book with an angry snap, but her mother was too immersed in her lecture to notice.

'I took great care, I may tell you, never to dispute a single thing with your father – and I can say *with confidence* that he never looked at another woman in all the years of our marriage. I dare say he loved me too much, poor wretch,' she continued smugly, 'and all, mark you, because I never, ever, argued with him. So you see, my girl, silence got me a husband, and kept him faithful all his life.'

Simmering with fury, Flora rose from her seat in the window, conscious that if she stayed where she was she'd surely break her promise to Lydia that her father's secret would go no further.

Without a word, but weighing Newsome's *Abyssinia* like a brick in her hand, she marched out of the room, slamming the door behind her.

In the days that followed, it seemed to Flora that her mother's criticisms had grown more incessant than ever, and always led back to the same complaint – that, at twenty-two, Flora was still unmarried, the only object in Constance's house which refused to conform to her standards of seemliness.

Flora had begun to stoop, her mother grumbled; she walked in huge strides, like a washerwoman; she wore collars when everyone in fashion had taken up lace; dragged to church on Sundays, she stared about her during the hymns, rustled through her Bible during the sermon, and then set such a rapid pace homeward that none of the young men dallying round the church door had a chance of catching up. Moreover, Flora's fingernails were cut too square, she wouldn't have bows in her hair, and she refused point-blank to tie on half-lemons at night to whiten her elbows. Flora, in short, was a trial and a tribulation to her mamma.

2

At the end of June, Ralph Newsome travelled to Bristol to give a lecture, and then went on to Manchester, Liverpool and Newcastle.

'It's a pity you didn't make yourself more agreeable to *him*,' observed Constance gloomily. 'There was a time when I thought you might have had a faint chance of getting him, too. But now he's slipped away to be swept up by the first blacking-maker's widow with a small waist and a few pounds of her own.'

Yet the explorer returned in August without any suburban widow on his arm, and in a great state of excitement over a new railway system he'd discovered on his north-country travels.

'The possibilities of the railway are—' He threw his arms wide, dominating Constance's drawing-room. 'They are quite without limit. I must have travelled by most overland methods known to man, from ox-cart to stagecoach, but this time . . . This time I believe I've seen the future. The iron rails will turn the wilderness from man's master into his servant.'

'But railway wagons will still need horses to pull them,' objected Flora. 'How will horses survive in the desert, or in the northern winters?'

'Horses? Absolutely not! Miss St Serf, if you'd only seen what I saw at a colliery in Durham – eight miles of iron rails, and wagons running over them without a horse to be found anywhere.'

The explorer bestrode the hearthrug as if it were a stage, his eyes flashing dark fire.

'For almost half of that distance the wagons were pulled by steam locomotives. And in spite of all the canal-men say, there have been no explosions and no disasters. The locomotives have simply trudged on their way like great puffing beasts, devouring their coal and working obediently for their engineers. Oh, I wish you could have seen it for yourself.'

'Indeed, I wish I had. The most exciting thing to happen here since you left was when the milk-seller's horse ran off and overturned his cart, and tipped all his pails out in the road.'

From his post on the hearthrug, Newsome examined Flora carefully.

'It must be a weary life for you, shut up here with your mother.'

'It is. Oh, believe me, it is.'

'Which makes your . . . liberal views . . . all the more surprising. Few young women show such an understanding of the frailty of human nature.'

'I don't know that I ever said—'

'I remember exactly what you said, Miss St Serf. You said that man was merely one more animal among the rest, that reason had led you to think so, and that we're wrong to take the biblical account of creation as the truth.'

'I can't believe I'm alone in thinking that.'

'Alone among ladies of my acquaintance, at least.' Newsome chewed his lip for a moment, while his eyes devoured Flora's face. 'Most young ladies are wedded to the teaching of their Bibles. Yet you, Miss St Serf . . . I do believe you're no more of a Christian than a whirling dervish!'

Flora watched him, disconcerted, trying to decide if this was intended as praise or blame.

'It's true,' she said carefully, 'that I believe science will show us facts which will not always agree with the word of the gospels.'

'Science!' Newsome held up a finger. 'Science, of course.' He stared for a moment at the toes of his boots, and then looked up. 'Do you know, Miss St Serf – I have an idea . . . Speaking of science – I had it in mind to go up to Stockton next month for the opening of this new coal line between Darlington and the Tees. They've promised a steam locomotive for the opening day, and one of the committee members has offered me a place in a wagon if I care to take it up.'

'You're actually going to ride on the train?' Flora's eyes flew wide in amazement. 'But will it be safe?'

The explorer smiled indulgently. 'You're a dear girl, to be

concerned for my safety! But don't worry – the train will be perfectly safe. In fact, I was about to propose that you and your sister and her husband should come to Stockton with me, and make up a party. There's a tolerable hotel in the town, I believe – and I'm sure it would do Darius Elder good to leave his bank behind for a few days, and see what's going on in the world beyond London. What do you say, Miss St Serf? Will you dare to ride with me on the new railway?'

Flora's mouth had formed a round 'O' of astonishment, and it was a few seconds before she could force it to express her delight.

'Oh, I'd like that very much indeed.' Her brow darkened for a moment. 'But I'm not sure if my brother-in-law will agree to the trip. He doesn't like . . .' her voice faded as she tried to find an excuse for Darius Elder's rooted suspicion of his host, 'sight-seeing,' she finished lamely.

'Leave Darius Elder to me – and to his wife. Once your sister hears what I have in mind, I should think she'll make it impossible for him to say no.'

3

Exactly as Ralph Newsome had predicted, as soon as Sophie learned of the outing to Stockton she was frantic to go. Darius, confronted by his wife, her lips trembling and her eyes unnaturally bright, had no choice but to consent. At least the trip would mean a few days' peace from the half-dozen miniature greyhounds which were Sophie's latest obsession – fragile, eel-like little creatures which bounded unchecked over the chairs and sofas and skittered in a pack at their mistress's heels.

Now there was no more need for Sophie to be alone. In the drawing-room the dogs lay adoringly at her feet; in the park they filled her carriage or spilled out to trot at the end of a web of silver chains; even during the night they took it in turn to spring from her bedroom carpet to a favoured spot at the bottom of her bed.

After every outing Sophie ordered the dogs' feet to be washed with scented soap, and the servants objected strongly to the task until Dash bit a footman, who complained and lost his job. At last, Darius, irritably sweeping one of the animals from his dinner-table, remarked that two dogs would have been enough for most people. Instantly hysterical, Sophie refused to eat or speak for an entire week, and was only coaxed out of her room with a gift of six red collars of the softest Spanish leather, one for each of her pets.

After that, as often as not, Darius dined at his club.

At the beginning of September, the proprietors of the Stockton & Darlington Railway Company announced that their grand opening would take place on the 27th of that month. By then Ralph Newsome had planned his expedition down to the smallest detail: a large chaise had been hired, horses ordered ahead, hampers of victuals provided for the journey, and a baggage-wagon arranged to follow with trunks and servants.

It was too late now for Flora to have second thoughts, though she couldn't help wondering how such an oddly assorted party would endure one another's company for several days on end. And as for herself . . . She was flattered, of course, to be included in Ralph Newsome's outing, but puzzled as well. It was impossible, no matter what Lydia said, that a man of Newsome's stature – a national hero – should have any intention of proposing marriage to a complete *nobody* when he had so many adoring ladies to choose from.

For all the time he'd spent in Flora's company, he'd never hinted at such a thing. He'd given her the necklace, of course, and he'd never tried to hide his admiration for her graceful movements and pale, thoughtful face; but when he looked at her it was with the passion of a collector for a piece of cold porcelain, covetous and single-minded. She could imagine him looking at a mountain so.

As Flora had feared, the first night's dinner at their Stockton hotel was a strained affair in spite of the general mood of excitement and Sophie's forced high spirits. They'd left London before dawn, and throughout the long journey north, Darius Elder had said little, leaving Sophie to chatter to Flora about the poor lonely hounds she'd had to leave at home, and Ralph Newsome to frown out of the chaise windows as if something important weighed on his mind.

Sophie was the only one inclined to make conversation at dinner, and she didn't seem to be able to stop. All through the soup and the mutton and capons, she babbled and gossiped about anything which came into her head, recklessly flying from one subject to another as if the only thing that mattered was to keep silence at bay. And while she spoke, her eyes flicked constantly from her sister to Ralph

Newsome, as if she would have given a great deal to know how matters stood between them.

The morning of the 27th brought another early start. The privileged few with seats reserved in one of the railway company's new coal wagons had been asked to gather at nine o'clock by the engine-house below the Brusselton Tower some nine miles west of Darlington. There the wonderful mobile steam-engine 'Locomotion' would be waiting to pull them with its coal and water tender, six wagons of coal and the proprietors' coach 'Experiment', all the way to Stockton in time for a Town Hall dinner at three o'clock sharp.

By the time Ralph Newsome's post-chaise reached Shildon Lane End at the foot of the Brusselton ridge, the sloping fields round about were already thronged with sightseers scrambling for the best view. Down on the track, Locomotion wheezed in her sleep, stout as a wooden hen, the tangle of rods on her back temporarily stilled and a thin trickle of woodsmoke rising from her black chimney.

It was impossible to see anything of her wheels or her tender for the mass of curious humanity swarming all round her, the boldest reaching out to slap the monster's side or finger her joints. The six wagons of coal behind the tender were bright with the holiday clothes of people perched recklessly on top of the load, while company staff struggled through the crowds, guiding ticket-holders to their seats in the high, heavy, sloping-sided wagons allocated to the official passengers.

With the hard eye of a man who'd outfaced desert bandits, Ralph Newsome shepherded his party through the crush, though by the time places were sorted out Sophie and Darius found themselves seated at the opposite end of the wagon from Flora and her explorer. There was no time to make an exchange. All four were immediately wedged into their places by the unscheduled passengers who scrambled aboard, while small boys buzzed round like flies, clinging to the ironwork of the trucks, no sooner brushed off than returning to settle somewhere else.

At last, with a shriek of steam from Locomotion's safety-valve and a great lurch which almost threw Flora from her bench, the train shuddered into motion. A faint breeze touched Flora's cheek as their speed passed walking-pace, a warm breeze, scented with the acrid breath of the locomotive instead of the heavy, sharp smell of straining horses.

There was still a horse ahead of them – but far beyond the self-important funnel and busy piston-rods of the locomotive – where a flag-man cleared their path along the rails. The real wonder of it all was the tons of freight being hauled behind, where a load big enough for countless carts and carriages was following meekly after a single snorting steam-machine.

'Capital, this!' declared a red-faced man on Flora's right – just as the whole procession ground to a halt a few hundred yards from where they'd begun.

'Wagon off the rails!' shouted a host of voices, and the onlookers surged happily forward to manhandle the toppled wagon into place again, delighted to have their own part to play in the excitement.

There were several further stops before Locomotion pulled them into Darlington; indeed, as Ralph Newsome pointed out after a glance at his watch, by then they'd spent almost as much time stationary as they had moving along the rails. But their arrival was no less of a sensation for all that, and Flora had long since lost her nervousness to the exhilaration of the moment. By the time the locomotive had shown off its marvellous shunting ability and they'd loaded a brass band for the rest of the way to Stockton, Flora's face was alight with pleasure.

'The triumph of science,' Newsome declared when they stopped for water at Goosepool. 'That should suit your philosophy, Miss St Serf. The triumph of science over the elements? Humankind the creators of their own world?'

'It certainly seems like it,' Flora shouted back happily, only dimly aware amid the hissing steam of what had been said to her. 'And if this is possible – who knows what may be done in the future? Perhaps one day there'll be a locomotive which can reach the Moon, and apples growing in the deserts, and cows giving birth to lambs . . .'

'Oh – indeed,' murmured the explorer of wildernesses under his breath. 'You can't wait to stand the world on its head, and do the devil's work for him . . . You're an extraordinary creature, Miss St Serf,' he concluded aloud. 'A striking young woman, certainly – and yet, the moment I heard you deny the divinity of mankind I realized—'

'I beg your pardon?' Uncomprehending, Flora cupped her hand to her ear, since Locomotion had huffed and clanked into movement once more, and a new storm of cheering had broken out.

For some minutes afterwards, Ralph Newsome's lips continued

to form words and his face to register some strong emotion, but Flora understood none of it. Then at Whiteley Springs he was forced to give up the struggle altogether when a swarm of farm-carts on the road alongside the line decided to make a race of it, and the thunder of hooves and the hallooing of their drivers almost drowned out the answering catcalls from the wagons.

Flora, with her eyes tightly shut, was flying. This was how a bird must feel, a winged dart splitting the air, dividing it into smooth, rippling caresses like the fluttering of a thousand banners.

'Godless – and yet unrepentant.' She heard Newsome's voice in her ear, the words scattered at once in the wind. 'Are you never afraid?'

'Afraid? What is there to be afraid of?' Flora was soaring free, far above the fields and the hedges, far above Sophie and Darius Elder and Ralph Newsome, looping and diving with a heart as light as one of her own shining feathers. 'Afraid? Never!'

'Pagan—' she heard him say – or perhaps it was the voice of the breeze.

Pagan as a bird . . . Pagan as a cloud . . . Without opening her eyes, Flora gave up her soul to the cool skimming of the wind, while the future rumbled and clanked over the iron rails beneath her.

It was after half-past three when at last Locomotion reached the outskirts of Stockton. If Ralph Newsome had intended to bring his conversation with Flora to some kind of conclusion, he was utterly defeated by the welcome which surrounded them on their route to the docks. Here the crowds pressed right up to the rails on either side, yelling and whooping; the air was thick with the victorious pealing of church bells and the blare of 'God Save the King' from an assortment of bands, and – louder than all the rest – the blast of seven large cannon drawn up on Stockton Quay.

By the time Locomotion ground at last to a standstill, the passengers in the wagons were on their feet, eager to share their opinions with acquaintances on the quayside. Sophie and Darius Elder were already looking in Flora's direction. In another few minutes any chance of privacy would be gone.

All of a sudden the explorer cried out, clapped a hand to his eye, and sank down abruptly in his seat. Flora turned to him at once, full of concern.

'It's nothing,' he insisted. 'Merely a spark from the engine.' Yet he allowed her gently to prise his fingers away, searching for any sign of damage.

From a distance of six inches the affected eye regarded her keenly; Flora was close enough to feel Newsome's breath like the touch of velvet on her naked hand. Around them, the wagon was emptying fast, its extra passengers pouring haphazardly over the sides, shouting their bravery to the doubters among the crowd.

'I can't see any cinder there.' Leaning close to Ralph Newsome and peering cautiously into his face, Flora suddenly found her hands captured firmly in his.

'No – don't pull away from me . . . I may never have another chance to speak to you alone.' Newsome's lips pressed together for a moment as he swallowed. 'Miss St Serf – Flora – I believe you and I were fated to meet. You are . . . unique. I never suspected such a woman might exist – a woman who could be my saviour, who could deliver me from my darkest hours.

'No – let me speak.' He shook his head, a spasm of movement which caused a black lock of hair to uncoil over his brow. 'I know there's a difference in age between us, but that means nothing. You were put on this earth for me, Flora – and I must have you, I realize that now. Marry me. Tell me here and now you'll be my wife.' He raised his head sharply, shivering the black coil on his brow.

'Oh, my goodness—' Vainly, Flora tried to snatch her hands away.

'Marry me, Flora.' His black eyes seemed to draw her into their lustreless depths. 'Marry me, my wild Berber beauty – my white-skinned savage.' He was pressing her fingers in his own, so hard that the stone of her little gold ring cut into her flesh.

Flora gaped at him in shock. It was no more than Lydia had forecast, yet now that the moment had come she found herself as tongue-tied as a schoolgirl, bewildered by the fierce intensity of this man who held her hands trapped in his own, and who was staring into her face as if he'd stride through flames to make sure of her.

The bird that was Flora's heart had hardly settled back to earth: in her mind she was still borne along in her chariot of smoking fire, deafened by the blare of bands and a heart-stopping cascade of bells. Helpless, she stared at the man at her side. Incredibly, this sorcerer of the desert wanted her for his wife. He'd already shown her that day how the impossible could be made to happen: nothing was absolute in the world any more, nothing inviolate . . .

'Your sister – Miss Newsome . . . You said yourself, she wouldn't approve of me. I couldn't—'

'This doesn't concern Hester. If you become my wife I'll no longer need a housekeeper, and Hester will live elsewhere.'

'You must give me time to think . . .'

'How long?' Impatiently, he squeezed her fingers again.

'A week – only seven days . . .'

'Oh, Flora!' trilled Sophie's voice in her ear. 'For a moment there I thought we'd lost you! Wasn't that the most amazing thing you've ever known? Wasn't it utterly splendid?'

Ralph Newsome released her hands at once, and Flora turned in time to see Darius Elder standing at his wife's shoulder, his face rigid with anger.

4

If anything, the journey south was even more silent than the outward journey had been. The previous night's celebratory banquet had turned into an awkward affair – their little corner of one of the long tables entirely absorbed in its own tensions and suspicions while pompous city fathers and railway officials droned their self-congratulation against a clatter of knives and forks.

Darius Elder's fury was powerful enough to be touched, yet across the table, Ralph Newsome seemed unaware of it, while Sophie, with her head lowered over her plate, stole glances at the other three.

'Did I see you with something in your eye, Mr Newsome?' she asked at last in a strange, little-girl voice. 'Just as we arrived at the quayside . . . a cinder, perhaps, was it?'

The explorer looked up. 'It was nothing, thank you.'

Sophie's eyes roamed over her sister's face, searching for any sign of unease, any hint that Ralph Newsome might have moved matters in the direction she'd hoped. She glanced at her husband's face: Darius was angry – angrier, perhaps, than she'd ever seen him, though once or twice lately there had been occasions when she'd goaded him to a very satisfactory helpless rage. Darius would never use violence against her – she was sure of that: her eyes flicked across to Ralph Newsome's brooding countenance, and the small, tight smile she'd inherited from her mother drew up the corners of her lips.

The dinner ended very late that night, leaving no time for

confidences, and by the next morning the excitement of the outing had given way to simmering resentment and the sullen silence of too little sleep.

Sophie was now so listless and dull-eyed that Flora suspected she and Darius must have quarrelled during the night. Ralph Newsome sat half-turned in a corner to catch the light of the window on a book, only raising his eyes from it to direct meaningful glances at Flora. And not one of those glances, she knew, was lost on Darius Elder, sitting opposite her, his thoughts gathered as ominously around him as the folds of his grey travelling-coat.

Pressed into her jolting corner, Flora longed to be in London once more, where Ralph Newsome's compelling presence could no longer throw her thoughts into chaos. Even silent over his book, his dark energy dominated the confined space of the carriage, until Flora began to understand the force which could drive him obsessively through desert and mountain. *You are unique*, he'd told her – *marry me. I must have you.*

Lydia had begged her to do it: and Lydia had seen so much more of life than she had herself. Flora leaned her forehead against the window-pane, relishing the coolness of the glass on her skin. From the far side of the carriage, Darius Elder watched the movement; and Flora hoped devoutly that he couldn't read the thoughts which had led to it.

Seven days – then six, then five: such a short space to make the choice of a lifetime.

As the journey dragged on, the tension in the chaise became almost unbearable. Whenever they stopped at an inn, all four clambered down from the carriage and set off stiffly in different directions. Meals were bolted without a word, and were followed by a general scramble back into place as if all that mattered was the first sight of the city of London.

Next morning at breakfast in Montagu Square, Flora tried to answer her mother's questions as well as she could, but her mind was elsewhere, and for once Constance's nagging failed to irritate her.

Perhaps Lydia was right: what lay ahead for Flora, if she didn't accept Ralph Newsome's proposal? All at once she could see nothing but withered years in her mother's house, wasting her life on a vanished dream – and after her mother's death, a grim existence as

Sophie's pensioner, a faded, invisible sister, not quite a servant but not quite a mistress either.

A maid appeared in the doorway, breaking into her thoughts.

'Mr Elder, madam.'

'At this hour?' Instinctively, Constance's hand rose to her cotton morning-cap. 'I knew I should have put on my blonde lace with the moss-roses. If I hadn't been so anxious to hear about—'

'I showed him into the morning-room, madam.' The maid jerked her head to illustrate the point.

Constance rose to her feet, clutching her Bavarian robe to her stayless bosom.

'You must find out what he wants, Flora, while I make myself fit to be seen. Hurry along, now,' she urged, seeing Flora hesitate. 'Hurry along! Tell him I shall be down directly. And Flora – I know Darius is only your brother-in-law, but for once try to make yourself agreeable!'

Darius turned quickly from the window as Flora came into the room, and glanced beyond her for her mother. As Flora closed the door, shutting them in alone together, she saw his expression harden.

'Mamma will be down in a moment,' she told him. 'She's just changing her cap.'

'So much the better. It's you I came to see.'

'Oh?' Avoiding his eye, Flora busied herself with picking up the books which lay haphazardly on the table. 'I can't imagine what you might have to say to me.'

'Oh, I think you can.' In two strides Darius Elder reached the table and with a swift movement took the volumes from her hands. 'I want to know what you and Newsome were whispering about in that railway wagon at Stockton.'

Flora snatched back one of the books and slammed it down firmly on the polished mahogany. His brusqueness was almost a relief, strengthening her resolve to be independent of him.

'In the first place, Darius, we weren't whispering – and in the second, it's none of your business what I say to anyone.'

'Perhaps it isn't, but I still want to know.'

'And I've no intention of telling you.'

He laid his hand on her pile of books, frustrating her attempts to appear occupied. 'Flora, if you won't tell me, I shall ask Newsome

167

himself.' The expression on his face confirmed that it was no idle threat.

'Then if you must know, Mr Newsome got a cinder in his eye as we came into Stockton, and I was concerned for him. That's all there was to it.'

'Rubbish!'

'It isn't rubbish.'

'Dammit, he was holding your hands! I saw him.'

'I suppose it may have looked like that to a suspicious mind, but—'

Abruptly Flora broke off, and they both stared up towards the ceiling, where the sound of Constance's hard-heeled shoes could be heard marching across the naked boards of the room above.

Instinctively, they'd moved closer, bound together in guilty conspiracy while the footfalls paused, took a single step, and then crossed the room again towards the window.

'She'll be here in a moment,' breathed Flora.

Darius Elder's eyes swept down towards her, darkening as they met her own. He began to speak with a new urgency.

'Newsome's asked you to marry him, hasn't he?'

Flora's chin lifted defiantly. 'What if he has?'

'So he did ask you! And what answer did you give him?'

'No answer at all – yet.'

'Thank God for that!' For an instant, he closed his eyes in relief. 'But you should have refused him straight away. You must tell him as soon as possible that you've no intention of marrying him.'

Darius had moved nearer still, and now Flora found herself disturbingly aware of the rhythm of his breathing, of the tiny movements of his lips, of the texture of his skin and the faint sandalwood smell of his body. He looked tired, she thought, her annoyance forgotten for a moment in the discovery of thread-like lines of weariness at the corners of his eyes.

'Are you listening to me, Flora?' he demanded impatiently. 'I said you must write to Newsome at once, making it plain you won't have him. Fetch paper and a pen, and I'll tell you what to say.'

Instantly, Flora's determination returned.

'I'll do nothing of the kind.' She stepped back at once, breaking out of that treacherous closeness. 'What gives you the right to tell me what to do? I'll make up my own mind, and give him my answer as I promised.'

To her surprise, her voice seemed amazingly clear and resolute, and the sound of it gave her courage. Ralph Newsome had called her fearless: it must be her independence he prized, her determination to go her own way.

'You aren't seriously thinking of marrying the man?' Darius Elder was gazing at her in dismay. 'Please, Flora, put the idea out of your mind. Take my word for it—'

'Why should I? Did you take any notice of my feelings about your marriage to Sophie?'

'That was different—'

'Because Sophie is an heiress, and I'm not?' The tension of the moment made her reckless.

Darius's face clouded with anger, yet in spite of it he tried again. 'I beg of you, Flora . . .' He held out his hands awkwardly, unaccustomed to pleading. 'Don't do it! Don't marry this man. It isn't the answer to anything, believe me.'

For an instant, Flora hesitated, searching his face for a subtler meaning.

'Not the answer?' she whispered. 'Not the answer . . . to what? Darius – you and Sophie—'

In the room above a small object clattered to the floor, and they both glanced up guiltily. There was scuffling overhead, and then footsteps beating out a slow tour of the bare boards, counting away the seconds of that precious, unexpected intimacy.

Quite unaware of the consequences of her actions, Constance St Serf walked too far, and too slowly. By the time she was safely back at her dressing-table, the moment for honesty had passed.

'Sophia and I are perfectly content.' Darius addressed the words to the opposite wall. 'My only wish is to see you as content, one day in the future. But not with Ralph Newsome.'

'Just because you don't like him?' Flora drew herself up, disappointment stinging her to defiance. 'But then, it isn't necessary for you to like him. He's different from you. He has *passion*, a passion which lifts him above ordinary people, and gives him greatness. I can see that, even if you can't.'

'This is Sophie's doing.' His voice was hardly more than a whisper. 'Sophie has encouraged Newsome from the start.'

'Then I'm grateful to Sophie for thinking of my happiness.'

Deep inside her, a small voice begged her to take care, but it sounded too much like Darius Elder's for her to pay it any heed.

Perhaps if Darius himself had said more – if unspoken thoughts had burst out to fill the silences . . . But the relentless footsteps overhead had crushed out any chance of that.

'It's too late, then? You won't listen to me?'

'I have listened, Darius. And yes, it's too late.'

'Flora – please—'

She waited, not even daring to breathe: but the words which could have touched her remained unsaid.

'Please—'

'No more! I can't bear it.' Pressing her hands together in despair, Flora turned away towards the window, determined not to weep in his presence. 'You've no right to interfere in my life, Darius – no right at all. In future, I'll thank you not to meddle in what doesn't concern you.'

Without another word, he left the room. The front door banged behind him just as Constance St Serf came into the morning-room wearing her social smile and a coy, many-ruffled lace cap.

'Where is he, then?' she demanded indignantly. 'Don't tell me that was Darius I heard leaving just now?'

'He decided not to wait.' Flora bit her lip. 'For some reason.'

CHAPTER ELEVEN

I

Flora and Ralph Newsome were married in November, on a day of wind and rain which threw up wet leaves in little copper-coloured explosions and ruffled the fur of the squirrel mantlet which was the groom's gift to his bride.

Even in church Ralph Newsome was in high good humour, as he had been for the whole of the preceding month, from the moment Flora gave him her answer. For her part, Flora knew she should consider herself the most fortunate woman in London – one young lady was rumoured to have retired to a convent when the explorer's engagement was made public.

She'd broken the momentous news to Lydia almost at once.

'Have you told Dédalon yet?' Lydia wanted to know. 'The old devil will be most amused, I should think, to hear his little pupil is marrying a great explorer. He'll expect Bird of Paradise feathers or tiger-claws brought back to him, at the very least!'

'Perhaps,' agreed Flora and quietly changed the subject. The truth was that she hadn't said a word to the automaton-maker, and every passing day made her feel guiltier and more cowardly for not having done so.

She could have gone now, unaccompanied, to Shoe Lane. As an engaged woman she was already half-way free of her mother's authority but not quite under a husband's, and a hackney-carriage would have taken her there in twenty minutes. On several occasions she tied on her bonnet with every intention of calling on him – yet each time, a haunting sense of betrayal turned her back to her mother's door.

For Dédalon had called her *my daughter*, given in place of the dead child he'd adored. And *between fathers and daughters, there's always possession and power.*

The echo of his words made Flora uneasy. The automaton-maker had been unfailingly kind without ever asking for reward, yet in that very kindness he'd bound Flora to him with subtle bonds of duty. She knew in her heart he'd take her marriage for desertion – worse, for treachery – and she could already feel his cold, ominous displeasure like a chill at her spine.

Friendship demanded that she tell him in person: anything less was inexcusable. But, try as she might, she couldn't rid herself of the memory of his crabbed fingers stroking her cheek while he vowed to watch over her. The thought of Dédalon hovering for ever in the shadows of her life, watching and judging, was enough to keep Flora from going anywhere near his workshop in Shoe Lane.

Instead she sent off a small note on the eve of her wedding, and resolved to walk down the aisle in striped, dove-grey barège and an Austrian hat, to begin her new life entirely her own woman.

That walk – no more than fifty feet from porch to altar-rail – was to be the last test of her independence.

'Naturally, Darius Elder shall give you away,' Constance had decreed as soon as the engagement was announced.

Flora stared at her mother, horrified. 'Oh no, Mamma. That isn't possible.'

'Who else would you have? The General's too ill to go anywhere now, and he'd die before obliging us, anyway. No – Darius Elder is your nearest male relative, and Darius it must be.'

But Darius Elder had refused point-blank, and continued to refuse while Sophie sobbed bitterly and her mother cajoled. He might never have appeared at the wedding at all, had Flora not written a dignified little note, begging him to put aside his prejudices and be at her side when he was needed.

'You look . . . beautiful,' he told her in a low voice as she took his arm. Darius Elder – her brother-in-law, 'one flesh' with her sister, as the church would have it – a brother, and therefore forbidden.

Ahead of them, through the stone arch of the doorway, the paved aisle led to the altar, and to the future. Flora could see Ralph Newsome standing at the end of it, his hands clasped behind his back, rocking impatiently on the balls of his feet as he waited for his bride to arrive. Next to him stood his groomsman, and in the pew behind, the pinched blue back of his sister, the nape of her neck showing ashen below her bonnet as she bent forward over her prayerbook.

'Don't do it, Flora.' They'd started walking, and Darius Elder placed his left hand over hers as she clung to his arm. 'It isn't too late. There's still time to change your mind.'

Flora shook her head, mentally counting off the distance to the altar. Forty feet . . . thirty-five . . .

'Blame me, if you want to. Tell them I persuaded you.'

Twenty-five . . . fifteen . . . and now Ralph Newsome had turned to watch her come – and Mr Wesley, elevated to 'family friend' – and Sophie, with her secret little smile – and Constance, astutely watching every step, a posy like a corn-sheaf held up to her nose, concealing the expression of her mouth . . .

'Dearly beloved—'

Stony-faced, Darius Elder disengaged his arm and stood aside.

2

They were to live in the house in Russell Square from which, Flora understood, Hester Newsome would have removed herself by the day of the wedding.

Summoned to its drawing-room with her mother just after the engagement was announced, Flora had gazed uneasily round the olive-green walls with their load of pictures, wondering how soon she'd be able to have them redecorated. There was a shadowy melancholy about the room which had nothing to do with its lowered window-blinds: even the furniture had the dispiriting oddness of a museum – towering mahogany bookcases guarding the fireplace, an ebony table inlaid with bone plaques in the centre of the room, and alongside it, crouching like a cockroach, a sofa on black, outlandish, ebonized legs.

The room was full of the spoils of its owner's expeditions. On one wall a Damascus screen spread its midnight lace from cornice-rail to dado; opposite the fireplace, a huge cast-bronze cauldron squatted between a pair of life-size Egyptian figures, and even the table-tops were loaded with stone scarabs and incense-burners, and silver boxes of every size and shape.

Now Flora understood why Ralph Newsome needed such an army of porters. That room could have been the tomb of a plundering warrior king – or an explorer with a keen eye for antiquities.

Hester Newsome sent for cups of watery chocolate and two almond biscuits on a plate, and watched Flora sip with scientific intentness. She watched again throughout the wedding breakfast at Montagu Square, as if Flora were a curiosity about to be added to the bronze cauldron and the Damascus screen. Then she vanished suddenly while the floating islands were being served, before Flora could ask where she'd chosen to make her new home.

'Goodbye, Flora dear,' whispered Sophie when the newlyweds' carriage was announced. 'It's such a pity you didn't marry someone Darius approved of – then we'd all have seen so much more of one another. But I'm sure you'll be very, very, happy, in spite of that.'

'Let him get you with child as soon as he can,' muttered Constance in her daughter's ear as she pressed a cold cheek against Flora's. 'That way you'll be sure of him.' She held her daughter at arm's length and shook her head. 'You've fallen on your feet and no mistake.'

'At last.' Newsome settled himself on the morocco upholstery as the carriage moved off towards Russell Square. He tugged down the front of his dress-coat and brushed a few grains of rice from his shoulder, the faintest of smiles tightening his lips under the black moustache. 'At last . . .'

He swung his head suddenly to consider Flora, picking rice from her hat on the seat next to him. The carriage was a small enough space for a cascade of striped barège, and Newsome had spread his legs, allowing the movement of the carriage to rub his thigh against hers.

'Well, now . . .'

Something in the tone of his voice caused Flora to release the brim of her hat and look up. In truth, her mind hadn't been on the hat at all, but on certain other matters she'd managed to push aside until the moment she found herself abruptly and incurably alone with her husband. It had been more reassuring to think these thoughts with the curve of the hat-brim between them.

'Well, now . . .' he repeated, and laughed.

It was the laugh which paralysed her; it seemed to pour out from some molten inner core of the man like the roll of a victory drum.

'There was a moment when I thought that prig of an Elder would keep you away from me, even on your way to the altar – but no . . . You're a dog that knows its master.'

For a moment there was something like approval in his eyes; then he slid forward on the shiny morocco of the seat, pulled down the window-blind at his own side, and reached across to do the same for hers, plunging the little carriage into dimness.

'Mr Newsome . . . Ralph—'

'Shh . . .' He laid the fleshy tips of two fingers on her lips, filling her nostrils with the smell of stale cigar tobacco. 'Don't . . . speak . . .'

Flora's lips writhed, trying to say *But* – and the fingers increased their pressure, crushing the word into silence. When he was satisfied she'd say nothing, his hand slid down over her jaw and down the curve of her throat, pushing her back against the buttoned leather. His hand was hot, and rasped where it passed; Flora glanced down at it, lodged in the stitched neckline of her dress, crushing her gauze neckerchief like a bull among clover-flowers. It was a powerful hand, furred with black hair which rippled as its muscles, meeting resistance, suddenly flexed determinedly, pushing Flora back and down until the Austrian hat tipped forward over her eyes and her own hands flew up to rescue it.

He was wrenching at the striped barège now, dragging it up around her thighs in a crumpled cloud while his weight forced her legs apart. But the carriage was small, and her petticoats were tangled, and though he tore at them in violent haste, the layers of muslin and cambric, piped and tucked and scalloped, seemed to go on for ever . . .

'Ralph – oh, please—'

'Keep . . . that . . . mouth . . . SHUT . . .'

His weight was squashing her down, squeezing the breath from her lungs in great jerks as he prodded, hard, between her legs . . . But she'd put on drawers that day – 'You can't make your vows before the Lord,' Constance had shrieked, 'with your backside bare as a baby's!' – and though the legs only joined at the waist there was so much material in them, so much in the way of his furious need . . .

All at once the spasms stopped, and Flora heard him grunt and go rigid on top of her; then he rolled aside, leaving her gasping and shocked in a foam of damp cambric, half-way on the low seat and half-way on the floor, a wreckage of dove-grey barège and a ruined Austrian hat.

'For heaven's sake, sit up.' He'd already rolled up the blind on his own side, and was tugging down his waistcoat as if nothing whatever had happened. 'We're almost there.'

'Wait – stop the carriage – I want to get out—'

Struggling upright on the seat, Flora fumbled for the check-string, suddenly convulsed with fear of the future she'd brought upon herself.

'Take me back to Montagu Square at once – I must go back—'

His hand caught hers, and dragged it down.

'Don't be a fool! Where do you think you can go?'

'I want to go home . . .' Flora gulped hard, trying to stem the tears which were welling in her eyes.

'You're my wife now. Your home is with me. Your home is wherever I say it is.'

'Oh, please . . . let me go . . .'

He ignored her entreaty, but indicated her ravaged skirts, from which one knee still protruded, virginal in its white stocking.

'Tidy yourself up before we arrive.'

Yet the knee seemed to fascinate him, and before Flora could move, he reached out to grip it with his great black-furred paw. When she pushed him angrily away, his teeth flashed in the shadow of his moustache, revealing pointed incisors.

'You're my wife now,' he reminded her. 'Don't ever forget it.'

A few moments later, the carriage came to a halt and Ralph Newsome jumped down, ignoring the steps which the groom had unfolded for him. Without even glancing round, he held out a brusque hand to help his wife descend, and Flora did so, trying to shake out her crumpled skirts and smooth her dishevelled hat and hair as she came.

She was still trembling, and the hand that had laid itself in Newsome's was immediately snatched back. From the pavement, she glanced up at the house – larger and grander than Montagu Square, but with the same bland, all-concealing façade.

Perhaps now he'd leave her to herself for a while. What she wanted most of all was a quiet place in which to think, to make sense of the sudden, unimaginable dreads which beset her. *Please . . . oh please*, an hour's tranquillity in a room of her own, with the trunks sent round that morning from Montagu Square solidly and reassuringly full of her own possessions.

The front door of the house swung open, and Flora tried to draw satisfaction from her first step into a home of her very own as a married woman.

A few paces beyond the threshold, a thin, upright figure was waiting for her, pale hands knotted righteously at the waist of her grape-blue gown.

'Welcome to our home, Flora.' Hester Newsome's face twisted in an attempted smile.

Bewildered, Flora turned to her husband of three hours. 'But I thought . . . you said—'

Irritably, Newsome waved the hovering servant aside, and turned back to Flora.

'You didn't really expect me to turn my sister out of house and home, did you? For a young woman who's never directed a household of her own before? I certainly never suggested anything of the sort.'

'Never,' echoed his sister immediately.

'But you did! You said—'

'Hester will continue to direct the affairs of this house.' Ralph Newsome thrust his hands decisively into his coat pockets. 'She knows exactly how and where I like everything to be. That's something you have yet to learn.' Removing one hand from its pocket, he held it out stiffly. 'Now – shall we go upstairs?'

3

There was more of his 'collection' on the wall of the staircase: hawk-headed Tibetan ritual daggers, horn-shaped Balkan knives, silver swords from Ceylon, sabres, rapiers, Indian khanjars, Siamese ivory-hilted smallswords, Balinese kris, and where the steps turned under a small half-landing, pieces of ancient lacquered Japanese armour dangling like the shell of some long-hatched dinosaur.

There were bars on the window of her room.

'I believe it was used as a nursery by a previous owner.' Ralph Newsome raised one yellow blind to its fullest extent, letting the daylight fall in miserly strips across the floor.

At least there were no knives on the walls here, and no cauldrons in the corners. It was a high, plain room with walls of a cold buttermilk colour and curtains of the same shade which had been lengthened by an inset band of green a few inches from the hem.

The chimneypiece was marble, and the dust on the smooth grate-bars testified that no fire had burned behind them for a decade of winters. At least the bed was modern and curtainless, though it was spread, to Flora's dismay, with an odd coverlet of some close-cropped fur – no doubt another of the trophies from the 'collection'. Apart from that, there was a wardrobe, a small chest of drawers, a dressing-table, and a low chair with its loose cover held on by tapes; all of it

177

had the same sale-room desolation as the drawing-room on the floor below, and the sweet, thick, stale smell of closed doors and never-opened windows, the dull scent of shadows.

Ralph Newsome had crossed the room to a second door beyond the wardrobe.

'This dressing-room is mine.' He went inside, and his voice echoed back from the doorway. 'I have a bed of my own in here, so that room will be yours, to all intents and purposes. I suppose you'll want a place of your own.'

'Thank you.'

He emerged again from the dressing-room.

'Hester has engaged a woman to act as your maid. You'll find she has already put your belongings away in their proper places, but ring if you need her. Polly Marks is her name.'

At the bedroom door he stopped, and glanced back.

'Dinner is at five sharp. Please don't keep Hester waiting, will you?'

For several seconds after the door had closed behind him, Flora gazed at its dumb panels in disbelief. She turned to the dressing-table, and peered at herself in the mirror, almost hoping that the face which stared back should be the face of a complete stranger – as if she'd strayed by mischance into someone else's dream.

For two hours Flora remained alone in her room. At half-past four a housemaid knocked at her door and brought in the raw materials of a fire which she proceeded to set and light.

'Excuse me, Mrs Newsome, ma'am. That's your fire, Mrs Newsome, if it please you, ma'am.'

Flora rang for Polly Marks, who helped her out of the crumpled grey barège and into a sepia-coloured gown so plain that even Hester Newsome must approve of it.

'Will that be all, Mrs Newsome?'

The maid withdrew, and Flora examined herself once more in the mirror. *Mrs Newsome*. The most fortunate woman in London – the wife of the recipient of sonnets and locks of hair, of honours and memorial inkstands and carved Damascus screens.

Mrs Ralph Newsome. Flora regarded herself levelly in the glass and told herself not to be a silly goose. The episode in the carriage had simply been the ardour of a new husband – no more than thoughtless over-eagerness – and, fortunately, after Lydia's forthright warnings Flora was no ignorant innocent, horrified by her husband's intentions. Besides – thanks to her mother's views on decency in church she was as *intacta* now as she'd ever been, and no doubt Ralph would proceed with more consideration next time. Of course he would.

And if he'd appeared to promise that his sister would quit the house in Russell Square as soon as they were married . . . Well, perhaps Flora had misunderstood precisely what had been said. After all, Hester was Ralph's unmarried sister, and no doubt it was hard for him to reconcile the interests of a loyal sister and a new wife, and he'd sincerely intended it all for the best . . .

It must be so, because Ralph Newsome was Flora's husband now, for better and for worse, and there was no going back.

Taking a deep breath, Flora went downstairs.

At half-past ten that night, she sat on the edge of her bed, a shawl over her cotton nightgown, listening to the sound of her husband's footsteps in the dressing-room next door. At last the door opened and he came in, wearing an India silk dressing-gown over his shirt and trousers, and carrying a tortoiseshell box, which he laid on a small table by the bed.

'Amazing,' he muttered, frowning.

'Whatever's the matter?'

'Sitting there, all in white with your hair braided – you look almost virtuous.'

'But I am virtuous. At least, I was . . . I mean – I suppose I still am.' Flora was vaguely conscious of being a disappointment without understanding why. 'Isn't this how I'm supposed to look . . . Ralph?' she finished tentatively. His frown had deepened. 'Shouldn't I call you Ralph now?'

'When we're alone.' Suddenly finding something amiss with the fire, he picked up the poker and stabbed it vigorously into the grate, sending showers of sparks up the chimney.

'Is something the matter?' It had been a long, tense day, and in spite of her determination to please Flora was beginning to wish that whatever was going to happen next could be over and done with before too long.

'If you hadn't condemned yourself out of your own mouth . . .' Newsome stabbed the fire again. '*Dreamers that defile the flesh, despise dominion, and speak evil of dignities . . .*' He reached out to the branched candlestick on the chest of drawers, and snuffed out its three parallel flames, pinching them between his strong fingers. *'Wandering stars, to whom is reserved the blackness of darkness for ever.'*

'What are you talking about?' Uneasily, Flora drew her shawl up to her throat. 'What dreamers? What wandering stars?'

'What dreamers?' Newsome turned slowly to regard her, the firelight flickering on the red silk of his India robe. 'Why – godless creatures such as yourself, my dear. Pagans . . . savages . . . Though *you* – you don't even have the excuse of ignorance to explain your corruption—'

With a single jerk of his wrist he wrenched away her shawl.

'Loosen your hair, and take off that damned nightgown. You look like a novice nun, or somebody's governess. Get on with it!'

Shaking, Flora began obediently to struggle out of the voluminous white cotton. Without its shrouding comfort she felt very small and cold, and utterly defenceless; instinctively she drew her legs up underneath her on the fur coverlet, and crossed her arms over her breasts.

Newsome studied his naked wife in silence for a few moments, his eyes lost in the heavy shadow of his brows. Eventually, he nodded.

'Yes – now I begin to see you again, my little Berber savage. There was a time when I wondered . . . but no – I always knew what you really were.' Kneeling on the bed, he tilted Flora's face up to his own, cupping it between his hands. 'You're hardly a woman at all, are you? Just a ripe, soft, trembling little animal . . . as you told me yourself.'

He reached out to open the tortoiseshell box.

'Hold out your hand.' With a swift movement, he slid a heavy ivory armlet almost to her shoulder. 'Now the other.' This time there were two armlets of chased silver, a thick silver collar and several long, heavy necklaces of silver and amber beads. The beads were looped several times around and between her naked breasts, and dangled cold against her skin; thoroughly alarmed, Flora tried to collect up the longest necklaces, which trailed uncomfortably down over her belly and between her legs.

'Leave them.'

'But why must I—'

'Be silent!' Newsome snapped the box shut and rocked back on his knees to admire his handiwork. He smiled, his teeth flashing gold in the firelight. 'Oh yes,' he murmured. 'Now I have you . . .' He trailed a finger over her naked shoulder, the nail biting a thin furrow in her flesh.

'How your skin shines!' he whispered. 'Brown as resin – brown, and waiting . . .' The finger sliced down towards the tip of a breast. 'The Somali women have stars tattooed here . . . and here . . . It makes them almost beautiful, when you think of the pain they've endured. We'll arrange that for you, too. Just *here*, I think—'

He pinched her nipple, hard. 'And here.' He pinched her again, and laughed when she flinched. 'You're a little afraid of me now, aren't you? No doubt you'd run away if I let you – you'd run like the little animal you are.' His eyes grew suddenly hard. 'You worthless pagan thing . . . Don't resist me—' For Flora had tried to slide away from him over the fur coverlet. 'Defy me, and I'll break you as I'd break a mare, without a second's regret.' He worked his hand into the hair at the nape of Flora's neck and pulled her sharply towards him. 'Without regret – without guilt . . . Oh, without any guilt at all . . .'

'Let me go!' The words were no more than a gasp of fear; her hands had flown up to tear at his fingers. 'I don't know what you want – I don't understand . . .'

'Of course you understand—' He was holding her painfully against him by the mass of her hair, exploring her body with greedy possessiveness. 'A woman with no soul – no claim on decency . . .'

'No—'

'Why else do you think I chose you from the others? *One more animal among the rest* – that's what you said, and straight away, I knew . . .' His strong fingers were biting into her flesh now, probing and plundering. 'At that moment I knew I could do anything with you . . . that there was nothing too squalid . . . An Englishwoman – with the mind and appetites of a Berber slave.

'There was a Habashi girl, once—' His breath was coming in bursts at Flora's ear. 'So slender and beautiful . . . sinuous as a cat . . . I paid forty pounds for her and never grudged a penny of it. All I wanted was to have that perfect body between my hands . . .' Newsome's fingers trembled as they went about their work of despoilation.

'But she came to me with a cross round her neck!' His voice grated harshly. 'A cross! She was a convert, damn her! My very soul was crying out for the taste of her flesh, and I couldn't *force* myself to take her.

'But you—' He gripped Flora painfully by the jaw. 'You have no claim at all on humanity. Lie back!'

'No – wait—'

'Lie back, or I'll teach you to do as you're told.'

Consumed with misery, Flora lay back; the heavy beads slithered pathetically into her hair, and spilled and rattled over her naked skin. Huge tears welled up in her eyes and brimmed over to run away into the soft fur on which she lay.

'Oh, please – not like this . . .'

'Don't worry, I'll make a thorough job of it this time. Lift your knees, dammit!'

'But you're hurting me!'

'Lie still, damn you.'

'Oh, God help me . . . You're tearing me apart . . .'

'Excellent!' It was a cry of raw triumph. Enraged by that dark, brooding power which drove him relentlessly over desert and mountain, Ralph Newsome drove on into Flora until his victory was complete. Then at last he left her, aching and wretched as a ravaged wilderness, and stalked off to his dressing-room to sleep.

4

Next morning he rose as cheerful as the sun, and sauntered through to Flora's room.

'Breakfast is at eight.'

Painfully, Flora hauled herself up against her pillows to confront him. 'I don't want any breakfast. I want you to have the carriage brought round and my trunks packed, ready to go back to Montagu Square.'

'Nonsense! You're hysterical. You don't know what you're saying.' The explorer, splendid in a brown dress-coat with a velvet collar, examined his moustache in the mirror.

'I am not hysterical! And don't try to tell me I imagined what happened to me last night. How could you?' she burst out. 'How could you say all those terrible things to me?'

'Now, don't be a martyr, Flora – we both know you don't qualify for that distinction. Women like Hester – good, pious women – are entitled to be martyrs, but not godless little savages like you.'

Newsome folded the skirts of his tea-coloured coat around him, and sat down solemnly on the edge of the bed.

'There are pure, delicate, sainted Englishwomen in the world, of course – women who only live to be the mothers of heroes. But not you, my dear.' He leaned forward, thrusting his face into hers. 'Under the silk and the lace, you are as immoral as a beast of the field.'

'That isn't true!'

'As soon as I heard you speak, I knew you'd been created for me.' He reached out and caught her cheek by a fold of skin. 'How can one corrupt the damned? I shall do with you whatever I please, and no one can condemn me.'

He released her cheek and leaned away.

'Breakfast, as I said, is at eight.'

'Order the carriage. I'm going back to Montagu Square.'

'Don't be a fool! For a little savage, you'll do very well here with us. You'll have everything you need; if it's clothes you want, Hester will go with you into town and pay for whatever takes your fancy. If you want to drive in the park, Hester or I will take you out.'

'I don't want to buy clothes, and I don't want to drive in the park. I want to go home!'

Newsome rose calmly to his feet.

'Since this is your first morning here, if you don't want to go down to breakfast, I'll have something sent up to you.' At the door, he turned back briefly into the room. 'I shall be at the London Institution until dinner-time, but I'll see you then.'

And with that he was gone.

You may look for me at dinner, but you won't find me. Flora bathed quickly in the copper tub her maid had filled before the bedroom fire, letting the warmth of the water seek out the soreness of her body and strengthen her resolve. *Brutes*, Lydia had told her. *Only brutes do it like that, and I'd never allow it.* Yet it was all very well for Lydia to talk – Lydia was a mistress, while Flora was only a wife, bound to please her husband in any way he might choose.

Yet, try as she might, Flora couldn't imagine how she'd deserved the horrors that had overtaken her. What had she said? What had she done, to provoke the savagery of her husband's assault?

'You never can tell, with men,' Lydia had warned her once. 'Look at that great lump, Lord Fettlewell, who's all teeth and horses. Who'd ever expect to find him parading about in Agar Street, squeezed into petticoats and a divorce corset? Yet they say he comes there of an evening about once a month, and pretends to ply for trade with the girls.'

'Isn't there a Lady Fettlewell?' Flora had wanted to know.

'Indeed there is. And a squad of little Fettlewells, too.'

'But how can she bear it?' Flora was horrified on behalf of the unhappy countess. 'Everybody must know.'

'She married him, didn't she?' Lydia shrugged extravagantly.

No! Flora even spoke the word aloud, and the copper bathtub echoed the sound. She would not be there when Ralph Newsome returned from the Royal Institution. She would leave Russell Square and her husband of one night, and go home.

Without waiting for her breakfast tray to arrive, she dressed with deliberate haste, dismissed her maid, and packed some of her most treasured possessions into a hatbox. With the box over her arm and her bonnet tied firmly under her chin, she set off downstairs to the front door.

Hester was crossing the hall, and glanced up in surprise.

'Flora! Where are you going?'

'Home.' Flora barely gave her sister-in-law a glance.

'Has Ralph given his permission?'

'I don't need his permission.' Flora swung the door open. 'I'm going home.' The door slammed shut before Hester could say any more.

Flora had crossed the square and was beginning to look hopefully for a hackney-carriage, when she heard the sound of hurrying feet behind her.

'Flora – stop!'

The sound of Ralph Newsome's voice put new urgency into her step. Damn! She'd left the house too soon: he'd still been at breakfast when Hester had discovered her flight.

A few yards away, an elderly gentleman emerged from a doorway, gathering a shawl round the shoulders of his greatcoat.

'Flora – I insist you stop.' Newsome was almost within reach of her now, and for a moment Flora considered running to the elderly man and begging him to protect her.

'Now, my dear . . .' Breathing hard, Newsome captured Flora's arm, forcing her to halt. Suddenly aware that the elderly gentleman was staring curiously in their direction, he raised his hat. 'My wife,' he explained apologetically. 'A little difference of opinion.'

'Ah.' The old gentleman nodded, turned away, and shuffled off along the street.

'Now then, Flora.'

'Let go of me.' Flora tried to shake off Newsome's hand, but he was holding her too tightly. Deftly, he spun her round to face the direction in which she'd come.

'If you wished to take a walk, my dear, you should have told me. Hester would have gone with you – she likes to walk. Or your maid, at least. It's most unwise to go out alone.'

'I was going back to Montagu Square. I want to go home!' Once more, Flora tried to pull away.

'You were going to call on your mother?' Ralph Newsome's voice was bland. 'So soon?' With her arm trapped in his, he forced her to walk at his side.

'I won't stay with you, Ralph, and you can't make me. You know perfectly well why.'

'Oh, but I can make you stay.' The momentum of his stride was carrying her relentlessly along. 'Even if you'd gone to your mother's, I'd have come to fetch you back. You are my wife, after all.'

'Don't you think I know that?'

'My wife in the legal sense, I mean. My responsibility. According to law, I have complete control of you, body and soul. If you persist in running away, I can lock you up in my house and punish you as I see fit.'

'You wouldn't dare! If Mamma knew how you'd behaved—'

'What could she do? By your own free will, you're my wife now – *mine* – and I've no intention of letting you get away from me. Oh, no . . .' He tightened his grip on her arm. 'I need you too much for that.'

'My sister's married to an influential man—'

'My dear Flora, all your sister wants is to have you safely out of the way. I don't believe she trusts you with that husband of hers. No, my little pagan—' Newsome halted at last in front of his own house, and turned Flora's face up towards his own. 'You've been abandoned by them all. Even God Almighty doesn't care what happens to you – so I warn you, don't try to defy me again.'

Flora could feel him watching her as she slowly climbed the stairs, past the knives and the Japanese armour to the bleak bedchamber she'd hoped never to see again. In her heart, she recognized that Newsome had spoken nothing but the truth. In the eyes of the law a wife was as good as her husband's prisoner unless she had a fortune of her own or a powerful family. That was the price of her wedding ring.

Sophie and her mother could do nothing for her now, even if they cared to – and even if she were prepared to humiliate herself by confessing what she'd had to endure. And *that*, she knew, she could never bring herself to whisper to anyone. Constance would tell Sophie, and Sophie would assuredly tell Darius – Darius, who'd warned her, and pleaded with her not to become Ralph Newsome's wife.

Whatever happened, Darius Elder must never know how Flora had been trapped by her own pride, by the iron bars which portioned the sky beyond her window, and by the law, which had left her with no remedy at all for her mistake.

5

Almost at once, the pattern of Flora's new life established itself. Every morning, her husband went out to the Royal Society or to Gresham College, or whichever learned body had chosen to lionize him that day, and Flora remained in Russell Square, reading or sewing in the dark and ominous drawing-room with its ringing bronze cauldron and black Damascus screen. She might be Mrs Newsome, but Hester was mistress of the house, charged by her brother with ensuring that nothing in it changed by so much as a hair. Whenever Flora ventured to raise the window-blinds, even by an inch, she'd find them lowered again as soon as her back was turned.

She wasn't entirely a prisoner. She could go shopping – accompanied by Hester in the smart carriage with its powdered coachman and blue morocco upholstery. She could choose whatever she wanted to buy – though Hester was the one who paid the bill, and Hester had her own way of signifying when the purchase didn't meet with her approval. But otherwise, whenever Flora thought of leaving the house on her own, she'd find Hester in the hallway, politely enquiring where she was bound and then insisting on coming too.

Whenever Constance St Serf called, Hester was there, presiding over the conversation. When Sophie visited, Hester plumped herself down on the black-legged sofa, her head bent over a piece of shellwork, but close enough to hear whatever was said.

On her first visit, Sophie gazed round the drawing-room and wrinkled her nose in distaste.

'If I were you, I'd make Ralph let me redecorate this place

completely. Who on earth are those horrible fellows in the funny hats?' She pointed to the Egyptian figures. 'I wouldn't let Darius bring ugly things like that into my house.'

Just beyond her sister's shoulder, Flora noticed that Hester Newsome's hands had gone rigid, though her head remained bent like a wooden doll's.

'They're part of Ralph's collection,' she told Sophie quietly.

'Oh, well.' Sophie's shoulders twitched in a fleeting shrug. 'As long as you're happy with them, I suppose.' She considered Flora with eyes like chips of flint. 'You are happy, aren't you, Flora dear? Only Darius said I ought to make sure.'

'Of course I'm happy.' At the other side of the room, Flora saw Hester Newsome resume her task of sorting shells. 'What a curious thing for Darius to ask!' Involuntarily, her hand smoothed the skirts which hid from her sister's eyes the bruises her husband had inflicted on her the previous night.

By now she'd learned to read his mood, and wait in fear for the spasms of violence which seemed to give him release.

One day he announced brusquely that she was to go with him to the exhibition of a giant landscape panorama in the city. Rain was falling, but Ralph Newsome was expected to attend, with his wife at his side, and there was to be no escape.

All the way to the hall and back, Flora was conscious of being watched with a wolfish expression which made her heart sink. After a brief initial glance, Newsome completely ignored the giant picture they'd come to see, unable to drag his eyes from the spectacle of his wife's pale throat and rosy ear-lobes brushed by the midnight softness of her hair.

That night the tortoiseshell box was brought out again, and in spite of her desperate pleading Flora was dressed once more in all her barbaric finery – a counterfeit savage, miserably sacrificed to her husband's fantasy. Nowadays she forced herself to remain silent, as passive as a corpse while he crushed her limbs and pounded into her body. Frustrated, he grew maliciously inventive, finding new, exquisite ways of humiliating her and forcing her to cry out, to surrender her will entirely to his.

And when at last, bruised and revolted, she did gasp aloud in anguish, he laughed outright and told her she had the soul of a slave, as unfeeling as a goat or a sheep, and that her body was no more than a dumb vessel for the various pleasures of a Christian gentleman.

Next morning, as genial as Flora had ever seen him, he strode off to take coffee at his club among the other Christian gentlemen.

Once, and once only, Flora tried to appeal to his better nature, confronting him at the door of his dressing-room, she on her side of the threshold, he on his.

'I'm your wife, I acknowledge that,' she began, keeping the door ajar. 'And of course that gives you certain rights over my body. But – must we have it this way, Ralph? I'd be a proper wife to you, if you let me. Can't we ever lie together like husband and wife . . . and perhaps you could kiss me, and be more gentle? You've never once kissed me,' she added unhappily. 'Never at all.'

He turned his head away, and Flora saw his fingers tighten on the handle. When he looked at her once more, there was fierce disgust in his face.

'What would be the use of that? Ladies . . . white women . . . are of no interest to me. The sight of a blonde braid on the pillow is enough to make me vomit.' He glanced away again. 'Yet out in the desert, with some filthy camp-follower . . .'

'But—'

'Enough!' he roared, and slammed the dressing-room door.

Would lawyers have called it cruelty? Not without broken bones or the marks of the lash; yet to Flora the torment of her spirit was even harder to bear than the bruises her husband inflicted on her. In the darkness of her violated bed, she began to wonder how many other wives in the land had been tricked into delivering up their self-respect in return for an outwardly blessed hearth and home.

She became haunted by a vision of the ultimate escape, by the route poor Madeleine had taken into the cold waters of oblivion. But she refused to consider it: in her mind, the voice of her pride cried *You must survive it! You will survive it!*

It was early in May when Newsome hit her for the first time.

Dinner had been over for more than two hours, and tea had just been served on a silver tray in the drawing-room.

'Flora shall pour,' ordered her husband, seeing Hester reach out automatically for the spirit-kettle.

In silence, Flora poured boiling water into the pot, stirred the leaves, left the tea to brew for the correct length of time, and finally

188

poured it into the cups, leaving precisely the proper margin of bone-china rim showing above the liquid.

Ralph Newsome tasted his cup in silence. Coldly, he held it out to her.

'There's no sugar in this tea. You know I take one and a half spoonfuls of sugar in tea.'

Contemptuously, he set the cup down in front of her, and gestured towards the sugar bowl. Without a word, Flora measured out the correct amount of sugar . . . and then added another spoonful, and another, and another, until the cup was full of slopping, pale-brown sludge and the saucer and the silver tray were awash with tea.

'Come upstairs.'

The blow drew blood along Flora's cheekbone and spread a smudge of blue like coal dust under her eye.

'I warned you not to defy me!'

Determinedly, Flora came down to breakfast the next morning, certain he'd expect her to keep to her room, or to use cream and powder to hide the worst of the damage. Instead she took her place at the table in all her crimson and purple glory – only to find that she might have been invisible, for all anyone cared. Ralph Newsome munched his toast in total unconcern, and then left for his club. Hester's stony stare passed right through her, while the servants hurried about their tasks with lowered eyes. Bewildered, Flora rushed to a mirror as soon as breakfast was over to convince herself the marks were really there, like a fantastic blossom on her cheek.

'Hester—' she persisted. 'Look at me! This is your brother's work!'

Hester kept her gaze stubbornly averted. '"Thy bondmaids shall be of the heathen that are round about you,"' she recited. '"They shall be your possession."' All at once her eyes swept up to meet Flora's, ablaze with jealousy. 'You should be grateful to be allowed to sit at the feet of a man of such genius! Yet you contradict him and irritate him until he's obliged to correct you!'

Flora's hand flew to her ravaged cheek. Could it be true? Had some inherent wickedness of her own provoked this strength-sapping, mind-numbing violence in a decent man?

She began to wonder if she was going mad. But how do you measure your own madness, unless in the eyes of those who know and love you? Constance hardly ever called any more, put off by Hester Newsome's chilly piety and her watery chocolate; Sophie was too absorbed in her own unhappiness to bother with Russell Square, and Ralph Newsome wouldn't allow Flora to go to New Road; and as for Lydia – Lydia would have guessed the shameful truth at once, and Flora couldn't even bring herself to try to slip away for an hour or two to Park Street.

In the privacy of her room, she wept until a lifetime's tears were spent, and marvelled that this was the same Flora who'd flung Darius Elder's five pounds in his face, and had cut off her hair for the sake of a flame-coloured gown.

Yes . . . possibly she was going mad – or would go mad, before long.

Sometimes, when Newsome insisted she accompany him to a lecture, she'd notice other women gazing at her in envy or gliding up to her husband with enticement in their faces. She'd watch him take their hands with the same insistent pressure he'd once applied to hers, and let his eyes hold theirs caressingly, as he'd once held Flora's. And she'd smile at those ambitious women, and they'd smile back a little strangely, wondering at her confidence, amazed that she didn't guess their motives and the secret conquest they'd just made of her husband . . .

'Come, Flora,' he instructed one evening, holding out her mantle. 'We're off to the Haymarket.' And without any further explanation he swept her off to the Gothic Hall, a gaunt, crenellated building whose romantic vaults had been designed to suggest mailed knights and courtly revels, but which were more appropriate to dungeons and bones.

The hall was principally a museum, let out from time to time for exhibitions. But immediately Flora caught sight of the sign at the door, she refused to move from the carriage.

'I don't want to see it.'

'Don't be childish.' Newsome read out the inscription. '*The Great Automaton Exhibition*. Collard from the Royal Society's arranged it, and I'm told it's excellent. Far better than the pygmies at the Reading Rooms.' He stepped down himself, and held out his hand. 'In any case, we've been invited most particularly, and we're obliged to go.'

At that late hour the hall was even gloomier than usual, any sunlight which remained beyond its leaded windows screened by years of London soot. Round the walls, giant swords and shields glittered from their glass cases like the face of a besieging army; in a window recess, gaslight fizzed over the statue of an Asian horseman, gilding his harness and deepending the scowl under his pointed helmet.

With revulsion rising in the pit of her stomach, Flora gazed round the assembled automata. They'd been waiting for her, these reminders of her life *before*, these wary, secret people who watched her from behind blancmange-pink masks of cartonnage and wax. Dédalon had not forgotten her, after all; she could hear the rustle of his invisible eyes among the Gothic rafters of the hall.

Impatiently, Ralph Newsome fastened Flora's hand firmly in the crook of his elbow, and commandeered the services of a small man in rusty black who was waiting to conduct visitors round the exhibits. The guide doubled himself in a hairpin bow and led them at once to a tulle-skirted tightrope-walker on the far side of the chamber.

'Please note the absence of strings or visible rods.' His hand described a circle above the tightrope-walker's head to prove his point. 'The figure is not a marionette, but is fully automatic in every respect.'

He fumbled at the automaton's back for the weighted lever which would set her dancing on her wire, and as he did so it seemed to Flora that the little acrobat wore a look of numb resignation, as if a thousand men in shabby suits had fingered her spine before.

The guide led them to another exhibit, the almost life-sized figure of a young boy seated on a stool at a mahogany table with a quill in his hand and paper and an inkwell before him.

'This automaton, dear Sir and Madame, is more than fifty years old, and has been seen in every royal court of Europe. It was made by the famous Monsieur Jaquet-Droz and his colleague Leschot . . . Behold!'

The guide touched the mechanism, and at once the boy lifted his head, gazed about him, and reached out to dip his quill in the inkwell. A moment later, he'd begun to cover his paper in bold, flowing strokes, word after word and line after line, until at last, having filled three-quarters of the page, he added a final full stop, briefly scanned his own work, and leaned back, satisfied.

'What has he written?' The effect was so eerily magical that Flora was suddenly afraid to look.

'The boy writes in German,' said the guide apologetically. 'Poetry mostly, so they tell me.' He detached the page, and held it up. 'A pretty fine hand, though, isn't it?'

'Amazing . . .' Ralph Newsome leaned forward intently to examine the painstaking script. 'Now you must show us how it's done. Show us the mechanism inside.'

'I regret . . .' The guide assumed an ingratiating smile and polished the breast of his suit with one hand. 'I regret . . . but looking inside is against the rules. The *illusion*'s what matters, I promise you, sir. Much better to deceive ourselves the little fellow's real, than be disappointed by his insides.'

The guide led them on to a table of jewelled insects which scuttled and writhed in a most lifelike manner, and then to a platform holding a half-size chamber organ and its seated player.

'Now, this one, Sir and Madame, is considered the most remarkable piece in the entire collection.'

Even in that ghastly light, the little golden-haired organist made an exquisite picture, perched on her stool with her skirts spread out daintily and her hands extended towards the organ keys as if she only waited to be told which piece her audience had chosen.

'There's no pretence, your honour,' declared the guide. 'She really plays the instrument, pressing each key at the proper time, though it's hard to believe it. See for yourself.'

The little man wound the mechanism with a concealed key. After a moment the girl's bosom began to rise and fall, her gaze swept over her instrument as if seeing it for the first time, and her hands made a trial pass above the keys in the manner of a concert performer. Her sleeves, Flora noticed, ended in deep lace cuffs which covered all but the last joint of her fingers, and as she leaned forward over her keys those delicate fingers began to press them down in turn, moving from note to note as the arms dictated, the right hand always more active than the left.

In the unearthly glow of the gaslight, the illusion was almost perfect. It was well nigh impossible to believe that the gracefully swaying figure wasn't entirely human – impossible to accept that the charming head with its studiously lowered eyes wouldn't turn in gentle surprise to smile at a compliment. The maker of that automaton had surely mastered the secrets of life and near-life: here was a miracle to match Vaucanson's Duck, which had drunk its water and digested its grain, and had dazzled its maker with dreams of a godless creation.

It was only then that Flora realized the organist was playing Dédalon's country dance tune, the melody of the music-box which had been her tragic birthday gift.

'Who made this automaton?' she demanded in sudden alarm.

'Achille Dédalon, Madame. A Frenchman who's worked in London for some time. I believe it's taken him two years to perfect this piece.' The guide swept back an oily strand of hair which had fallen over his brow and gazed longingly at the musician. 'Did you notice how her breathing changed, Madame, as she rested after the minuet? Isn't she glorious? Isn't she perfect? Do you know, Madame, the first time she looked up at me like that, so shy and so modest, I swear I fell in love with her straight off.'

He simpered disgustingly, and reached out to finger a shining blonde curl.

'But I comfort myself she's no more than bellows and pin-barrels at the end of the day, in spite of her pretty outside and her fancy manners. That's why I say to you, the illusion's the best part. You don't want to look too closely at the rest.'

At that moment the automaton lowered her hands for the last time, stood up at her keyboard, raised her eyes demurely and dropped an elegant curtsey.

'Oh, you're a fine one, you are,' scoffed the guide, scratching his ear with a dirty fingernail. '*Now* you come up all friendly, because you want me to wind you up again. But I know what's hidden under those dainty ruffles – and it ain't a heart. I'll wind you if it suits me, my pretty, and if it don't suit, you may sit there in silence till doomsday. That's what I think of your winning ways.' He squinted over his shoulder. 'Shall I wind the little monster up again, Madame?'

'No, thank you,' said Flora with a shudder. 'I've seen enough.'

6

And then, in August, Flora discovered she was pregnant.

'No,' said Newsome flatly when she told him. *No* – as if the mere fact of his displeasure was enough to scour the offending cells from her womb. 'No – it isn't possible.'

'The doctor has confirmed it.'

'No. I won't have you pregnant.'

'I am pregnant – though I wish to heaven I weren't. The last thing I want is a child conceived in such a way.'

'How long?'

'Do you mean when will the baby be born? At the beginning of March, so the doctor says.'

'No.'

'Don't keep on saying *no*! It's too late for either of us to do anything about it.'

'Of course it isn't. You could have the thing taken away. Plenty of other women do.'

'Never!' Flora's refusal was so swift and decisive that an expression of genuine surprise came into his eyes. 'Not my baby! Oh, I know what I said about not wanting your child, but it's there now, and it's alive – and I won't do away with it, not for you or anyone else.'

'Get rid of it!'

'No! And if you try to make me, I'll do something desperate – I'll set fire to the house. I will!'

He was already gazing at her neat waist with an expression of horror.

'You'll swell up. For months,' he added with loathing. 'You'll be useless for months! Bloated – ugly – maternal . . . like a great sow about to explode with a litter.'

'Yes, I suppose I shall.' For the first time, Flora caught the faint scent of the power that might be hers. 'How unfortunate for you! I don't suppose a wife with a belly like a pork-barrel will seem much like a savage ready to be "broken" as you charmingly put it. Not even in your sick, fevered imagination, oh "Newsome of Nubia."'

And, with a glance of contempt, Flora turned on her heel and swept out of the room before he could say another word.

For three weeks after that he left her strictly alone, meeting her only for silent, sullen meals, during which his black eyes remained fixed on her across the table, lustreless and resentful.

The respite gave her courage. Daily, she inspected the miracle of her body, marvelling at the ease with which it had transformed itself from a worthless shell into a ripening pod of new life. She drew strength from it: she was no longer abject, but powerfully fertile – no longer a victim, but gloriously, robustly, sensually triumphant. She smiled serenely in response to Hester's glances of loathing and her brother's unforgiving scowls; soon her condition would make itself outrageously obvious – and then, one day at the beginning of March, she would no longer be alone.

After three weeks of this, just as Flora had begun to take her new-found invulnerability for granted, Newsome came into her room one night after the household had gone to bed, locked the door, and put the key in his dressing-gown pocket.

'No—' Half asleep, she pulled herself up against her pillows and struggled to relight the candle by her bedside. 'No – I won't. Not again . . . not now. Give me back the key, and get out of my room.'

'Be silent!' He lashed out with a hand, catching Flora heavily on the side of the head and sending the candlestick flying. 'Keep your mouth shut!' Dragging her out of bed, he hit her again, knocking her to her knees on the floor.

'Leave me alone!' With desperate strength, she tried to scramble away, one arm held across the precious nest of her abdomen, but he was too fast for her. Stepping on the hem of her nightgown, he sent her sprawling, and began to tear at the embroidered cotton.

'Don't! Oh, don't – not again!'

'I said, be silent!' He slammed his knee into her ribs, doubling her up, sending her rolling, naked, on the carpet. 'It's time you learned to keep your mouth shut and do as you're told, like the filthy degenerate you are.' As he pulled the last of her nightgown from round her legs, Flora set off crawling towards the dressing-room door and her single, slender chance of freedom. But in a couple of strides he'd caught up with her and kicked her sprawling again.

Trembling uncontrollably, she curled herself into a corner of the doorway, her hands over her head, foetal and helpless while his fists and feet battered the unprotected flesh at her back.

'Well?' he snarled at her between gasps. 'Not so clever now, are you? You pitiful dross!' His knuckles rained like stones on her head – once – twice – she lost count as her vision swam, filled with a multitude of crimson stars which seemed to roar and rattle in her ears. He began to kick her again – to kick her everywhere, until her limbs lost their ability to resist and her brain refused to accommodate anything but agony, agony . . . Then, when even her breathing seemed to have ceased, he threw himself on her, there on the bare boards in the dressing-room doorway, and violently took his pleasure of her unresisting body.

It was pitch dark by the time Flora became aware of the hardness of the floor on which she lay, the icy coldness of her limbs, and the violent shaking which racked them. Somewhere nearby, she could smell vomit, but she could see nothing, and she began to wonder if Newsome had blinded her in his frenzy. Then gradually, as the sight returned to her eyes, she identified a dim black line in the greater blackness which proved to be the gap between two floorboards, running under her shoulder. The fire in the grate had burned itself out; it must be the early hours of the morning.

Cautiously, she tensed an arm. At once she was repaid with a sharp pain and a deeper ache in her ribs where he'd kicked her. Slowly, over an eternity, she tested each limb, sliding it gradually away from her body, trusting it with a little weight, until she judged that nothing was broken. That in itself was a miracle: there had been a moment during his furious assault when she'd believed only murder could have slaked his rage, the ultimate climax of his sated senses.

Retching with pain, she dragged her body towards the bed, but the effort of climbing on to it was too much for her. It was all she could do to claw down the hated fur coverlet to hide her nakedness before she fell, aching and bloody, into a nightmarish sleep.

Some time later she woke in panic – minutes or hours later, she had no way of knowing – convulsed by a spasm of agony in the region of her pelvis. After a few moments the pain subsided, only to grip her again with redoubled force. Vivid waves of red and silver split the darkness as she rocked to and fro, clutching her abdomen. Why hadn't he killed her, if that was what he wanted?

As the pain subsided again to a dull ache she reached out a hand, groping for anything with which to summon help. Her fingers met the leg of the table by the bed, and with the last of her strength she jerked it away from the wall. The table toppled over with a crash, sending books, candle and candlestick clattering away into the darkness.

Endless minutes passed, and then, in the midst of another dreadful spasm, she heard a knock on the door; she could do no more than moan, but it was enough to bring Polly Marks to her side, yawning under her cotton night-cap and holding a candle aloft.

'Oh, my heaven!' the girl cried, suddenly fully awake. 'Oh, Mrs Syme! Oh, help, come quick!' Abruptly, she vanished from sight. 'The mistress is all blood, an' crying out. I think she's dying, Mrs Syme!'

Somewhere in the distance, Flora heard her husband's voice, angrily demanding to know what the devil the disturbance was about. Then the pain intensified, as if her belly were a crucible of fire; merciful blackness overwhelmed her again, and she knew nothing more.

CHAPTER TWELVE

I

In another existence, it seemed, the mists cleared enough to show Flora a strange female face very close to her own in the starched cap of a nurse – and her husband's face hovering just behind it wearing an expression of pious concern.

'Can she hear me, do you think?' His voice seemed to echo from a great distance, as if in a dream. 'Is she conscious now?'

'It's hard to say, sir.' The nurse peered closer at the fluttering eyelids, and stroked Flora's hand with professional detachment. 'But the doctor did say to let her sleep for a bit. Best not to tell her about the baby until she's properly rested. It'll come as enough of a shock even then, I should think.'

'Oh, the doctor knows what's right, I'm sure.' Flora was dimly aware of her husband turning away from the bed. 'We must only do what's best for my wife.' And then the mists rolled in once more, and she slept.

They wakened her for the doctor's next visit.

'It's a sad day indeed, Mrs Newsome.' The doctor sucked in a whistling breath. 'To lose a baby like that . . . so sad, so sad . . . And yet we must comfort ourselves that you're still alive at all. To have fallen down such a flight of stairs – you were lucky to survive it, in my opinion, let alone without any broken bones. If you'll allow me—'

The doctor inserted the wide mouth of his stethoscope delicately between the buttons of her nightgown and bent down to apply his ear to the cupped end.

'But when—' began Flora hoarsely, and then stopped when the doctor held up a hand for silence.

'I congratulate you, Mrs Newsome,' he continued after a moment. 'Your heart is strong. Alas, ladies in your condition – in your *recent* condition, I mean – such ladies often find their sense of balance adversely affected. No doubt that was how you came to fall in the first place.'

'But I don't remember any fall!'

'I expect you fainted, then.' The doctor's face had suddenly become expressionless; briskly, he restored his stethoscope to its leather case.

'You fainted, and as a consequence of that, you fell.' The diagnosis was conclusive. If there was any other explanation, the doctor had no wish to know it. 'It isn't uncommon, I assure you,' he added magnanimously. 'No blame attaches to you at all.'

'Don't you remember, my dear?' Ralph Newsome stepped forward into Flora's field of vision, and she realized he must have been standing by the hearth, listening to all that went on. 'Polly Marks found you here in your room in a dreadful state, and came to call me. Goodness knows how you'd managed to crawl upstairs again without help. Perhaps you hit your head on a step,' he added coolly, 'and didn't realize what had happened.'

'Oh, I assure you, my memory's perfectly clear.' In truth, Flora's head ached like the devil, but she managed to meet his stare with contempt.

'Much better forgotten, I should say.' The doctor assumed the brisk, jovial tone of a man about to be released from an unpleasant situation. 'You must concentrate on getting well again, Mrs Newsome, and that means a great deal of rest. I'll call again in two days' time, and you must keep to your bed until then.'

He swooped down briefly to press the pale hand which lay on the pristine whitework bedcover. 'Take heart, Mrs Newsome – there's no medical reason why you shouldn't have as many beautiful babies in the future as you could possibly wish. You must lie there and think of that!'

'And who invented the story of my fall downstairs?' Flora demanded as soon as the doctor had left the room. 'Was it you who thought of it – or was it Hester?'

'It seemed the most obvious explanation.' Ralph Newsome stood a short distance from the bed and surveyed his wife without emotion. 'I told the doctor I assumed you'd fallen, and naturally he accepted my account.'

'Oh, naturally he did!'

'It isn't usual to question the word of a gentleman.'

'How you can call yourself a gentleman, after what you did to me—'

'Come, come, Flora. You deserved to be punished – you know that perfectly well. I warned you what would come of defiance, but you didn't believe me. Well, now you know I mean what I say.'

The explorer inspected the nails of his left hand with casual interest. 'Not that it matters any more. The pregnancy's over, thank heavens, and in future I shall make sure there's no chance of it happening again. I suppose I should have known a little animal like you would breed like a rat in a sewer.' With one hand on the door handle, he glanced back towards her. 'You must get well soon, Flora. Life won't be the same without you.'

2

Sophie called with her mother the next day. Constance and her daughter were given chairs on one side of the bed, while Hester Newsome sat squarely on the other like a gaoler permitting a short family visit.

Sophie sat woodenly in her chair, Flora noticed, and her sympathy had the curious, distant quality of the almost asleep.

'We're cursed to be barren, we two,' she murmured, staring down at her hands and rubbing vaguely at one palm. 'Goodness knows what we've done to deserve it.'

From the far side of the bed, Hester Newsome studied Sophie, narrow-eyed.

'I've done everything I could think of,' Sophie went on in the same dreamy tone. 'Blood tonics – spa-water . . . I've slept with the windows wide open in the middle of winter – I've tried soft beds and hard beds, and beds with the foot propped up on bricks. I bathed in a filthy green well because a saint had blessed it, and everyone said it was bound to help . . . But it didn't.' She twisted her gloves between her fingers, handling them a little clumsily, like an infant. 'I'd make such a good mother . . . And the nursery's so pretty now. Ismene-Maria looks a perfect picture in the cradle.'

'Who is Ismene-Maria?' demanded Hester suddenly. 'I wasn't aware you had a child in the house.'

Sophie glanced up, the pupils of her eyes pinpoints of confusion. 'Ismene-Maria is . . .'

'Sophie's old doll,' snapped Constance, finding her voice at last. 'Sophie was very attached to her as a small child.'

'And still is, it seems.' Hester stiffened her spine. 'I've always believed there comes a time when a girl must put away such childish things and accept the burdens of wifehood.'

'I dare say that's true,' conceded Constance, and then added maliciously, '. . . for some.'

Wearily, Flora closed her eyes. Even if Hester Newsome had not been there, standing guard over her sister-in-law's tongue – what could she have said to her mother and to Sophie that would have given them the least insight into the misery she felt at that moment? How could they have helped, even if they had understood?

Lydia had fallen pregnant at fifteen, and had once tried to explain how it had felt to have a baby 'taken away'.

'It isn't so much what I lost, you see, but what it might have been. Not just a poor little scrap of flesh and blood, but perhaps a great beauty – or a great scholar, even – or just a loving-natured little thing, except that I had to let it go . . . Do you understand, sweetness? For ever after, it's the little mite who never put his hands to your breast, never laughed in your face, never felt his mother's breath on his brow . . . but carried away a piece of you, when he went.'

Flora's lost mite had been conceived out of hatred, not out of love. Yet it had been there, inside her – *hers* – the companion of her loneliness; and now she was left with nothing but the hollowness of an unfinished circle – of a breast aching to give, and of a soft, empty niche between cheek and shoulder, the exact size of a baby's head.

'But to fall downstairs!' Constance returned to the subject in hand. 'My first grandchild, and you had to take such a foolish risk! What in the world were you doing, I'd like to know, wandering about the house in the middle of the night in your condition?'

'Sleep-walking,' said Hester Newsome quickly. 'It isn't unusual, the doctor said.'

'Did he?' asked Flora rebelliously. 'I didn't hear him say it.'

Constance was too absorbed in self-pity to hear the ring of desperation in her daughter's voice.

'Most women of my age have three or four grandchildren round their knees by now. What am I supposed to say to Sybil Ivory when she tells me *this* grandson's learning to ride, or *that* one has written to her in Latin verse, or a granddaughter's working a sampler of the Sermon on the Mount?'

'Say whatever you please!' snapped Flora, her nerves as taut as harp-strings. Beyond doubt, there was no salvation to be had in that quarter. Even if she blurted out the truth at last, Hester Newsome would insist it was only the ravings of nervous exhaustion, and her mother and sister, each for her own reasons, would accept that explanation and slip quietly away.

Then Flora's nurse would be summoned to give a numbing opiate which would silence her cries and make her easy to manage. Under cover of night she'd be hustled away to an asylum and shut up alongside the raving and the pitiful until she, too, took refuge in blessed madness from the reality of her plight.

At the side of the bed, Sophie was now weeping indiscriminately for all children unborn.

'I want to go home, Mamma . . .'

With marytred dignity, Constance rose to leave.

'For your own sake,' she told Flora, 'get yourself with child again as soon as possible. And this time, see that you're carried downstairs.'

3

Flora was alone once more. Yet the silence of her isolation allowed her to think, and to consider her own situation with a new, uncompromising clarity.

In the first hours of consciousness following that dreadful night, she'd tried to convince herself that the baby which had died had been a hated child, for being *his*. How was it possible for any life which *he* had generated to come into the world pure and blameless, with nothing to mark it the issue of its mother's misery? Surely she'd lost a cursed thing rather than a blessed one.

Yet no matter what reason might say, Flora's heart told her otherwise. Ralph Newsome was the murderer of her longed-for child, a man who had killed: and what he'd done once in his blind rage, he could do again. A voice in Flora's head became unrelenting: she must not let Ralph Newsome kill her, even if she had to destroy him to be safe.

For two weeks she lay quiet, gathering her strength. On the fifteenth day after her 'accident' the doctor declared her well enough to go downstairs to lie on a sofa in the drawing-room, and she rose from her bed and allowed Polly Marks to hook her into her plain, sepia-coloured, unexceptional gown.

Even without a corset, her sides still ached where the boning of her dress cut into them, a constant reminder of Ralph Newsome's violence in case her resolution should waver.

Later that day, sent to rest in her room, Flora brought out the paper and ink she'd taken from her husband's study, hidden under her shawl. Sitting at her dressing-table, she filled several pages with bold, emphatic script, folded and sealed them with green wax, and then enclosed the packet within another letter addressed to 'Darius Elder Esquire, Elder's Bank, Fleet Street, London.'

Darius, God willing, would never know her secret; but he was the one man in London whom she trusted to keep it safe.

Three more days passed before she had an opportunity to smuggle her letter out of the house. Newsome went to Oxford – canvassing, no doubt, for an honorary degree – and for three more days Flora languished on her sofa, the all-important letter hidden under a fold of her skirt. Then, on the evening of the third day, Dr Daniel Hildenhall, the eminent phrenologist, called with a monograph on a particular characteristic of the Somali head – and Flora seized her chance.

As soon as she heard Hester accompany Dr Hildenhall to the front door, she limped from the drawing-room to join them.

'Oh, Dr Hildenhall – if you'd be so kind – I forgot to mention this earlier.' Avoiding Hester's eye, she held out her packet to the tall, angular scientist. 'The servant who usually takes our letters is ill, and I did so wish this to go tonight. Could you – would you mind—'

'Of course, Mrs Newsome.' Dr Hildenhall accepted the letter, glanced at the superscription, and stowed it away in the pocket of his greatcoat. 'I'll make a point of delivering it myself as I pass along Fleet Street tonight.'

Hester Newsome opened her mouth to object, and then closed it again in furious silence.

'You've done me a great service,' Flora told the doctor, and meant it.

When Ralph Newsome returned from Oxford, Flora was waiting for him in the chair by her bedroom fireside, still frail but bleakly determined. In the last light of the day, her skin had all the bloodless tranparency of a saint on a glass window, but the calm which sustained her was not a holy peace.

She'd left word for her husband to come upstairs as soon as he returned, but she knew he'd wait until it suited him to see her. Voices drifted up to her room, blended to a murmur by the echoes of the stairwell. Newsome was glancing at his letters, she guessed, or giving instructions on the care of his riding-boots, or complaining to the housemaid about specks of rust on the fire-grate in his study. At last she heard his footsteps in the corridor beyond her bedroom door.

He threw open the door as usual, then stopped and stared round like a dog which senses that something indefinable has changed.

'I will not be sent for like a servant.' Yet his voice was less confident than usual. He ran his tongue quickly over his lips, then thrust his hands into his coat pockets.

'Close the door, Ralph.' Flora's voice was steady. 'There's something I wish to say to you in private.'

'Is there, indeed?' Abruptly he kicked the door shut, and the bang seemed to please him. He stalked across the room and twitched at the unfamiliar sprigged muslin curtains. 'Where did you get these? What have you done with the others?'

'I had the others taken up to the garret,' Flora told him calmly. 'I found these in the linen closet, and Polly Marks hung them up for me.'

'Then she can just take them down again. What's Hester thinking of?'

With a furious jerk, Newsome wrenched the first curtain from its hooks. It cascaded down over his arm, and he shook it off angrily. 'In future you'll leave things as they are.'

'No, Ralph. In future things are going to be different.' Flora's voice was as clear and sharp as glass. Taken aback, Newsome examined her warily from the window.

'Oh? And why should they be different?'

'Because three weeks ago you killed our unborn child. And one day, if things go on as they are, I've no doubt you'll kill me.'

'Rubbish.' Newsome stood his ground, feet apart, his hands deep in his coat pockets. 'The miscarriage could have occurred at any time. You women are always losing babies.'

'I don't intend to argue with you – simply to tell you what I've decided to do about our marriage.'

'*You've* decided?' Newsome lifted his chin belligerently. 'It isn't your place to decide anything.'

Strangely enough, Flora felt no fear, only the coldness of the void inside her; and the chill of it passed out into her voice, where her husband heard it uneasily.

'For almost a year now, I've let you treat me like a whore –

someone you could torment for your own perverted pleasure. I bore it, because it seemed to me that I'd brought it on myself by marrying you. But now, by doing nothing, I've let you murder an innocent child.'

Flora stood up, steadying herself with a hand on the chimney-piece, and the icy marble sustained her.

'It's over, Ralph. I can't bring back that lost child – but I'll save myself if I have to ruin you to do it.'

'You're raving.' Newsome turned his back, squared his shoulders with a contemptuous swagger, and stared out of the window. 'Losing that child has unhinged you.'

'I've decided,' Flora continued with dreadful precision, 'that from today, Ralph Newsome, you will never touch me again – not in lust, nor in love, nor in hatred. *Never.*'

'You're my wife. I'll do as I please.'

He swung round to face her again, his hands deep in his pockets, his legs spread and his chin thrust out aggressively. 'Whatever I please – whenever I please.'

'No, you won't.' Flora's stare was unflinching. 'You won't touch me, because if you do – if there's ever the slightest possibility of it – I'll make sure everyone in London knows how Newsome of Nubia beat his wife into a miscarriage—'

'The fantasies of a hysterical woman!'

'And that their heroic explorer can't function as a man without the fantasy of brown skin and slave-chains.'

'They'd never believe you!'

'I think they will – when I tell them what happens on these expeditions of yours, the parts you never describe in your precious journals. Just fancy – Ralph Newsome impotent in an Englishwoman's bed! Gelded by the slaves of the bazaars—' she added mercilessly. 'They'll believe *that*, I'm sure!'

'You wouldn't dare!' Newsome's face was suddenly as drained of colour as the buttermilk walls.

'Do you really imagine your scientific committees will pay for your expeditions once your "research" among the savages becomes public? Because I very much doubt it. What they'll overlook in private is one thing, but once it's common knowledge . . . there'll be no honorary degrees, no knighthood . . . nothing.'

Newsome watched her with eyes as black and unreadable as a rat's, but his hands were no longer in his pockets, and his chin no longer thrust arrogantly forward.

Flora studied his discomfiture with stony calm, wondering how the infliction of pain could have given him such pleasure. She was beyond revenge: she hadn't dared to raise her hopes above survival. But her voice was steady, her future now mortgaged beyond recall.

'I've written out a complete account of our marriage – complete in every loathsome detail – and I've sent it to a safe place, with instructions that it's to be opened if for any reason my own voice has been silenced. So I warn you, Ralph – if you kill me or send me to a madhouse, that document will be examined, and the whole squalid story will come out.'

'You've done *what*?' This time Newsome gaped at her, appalled. 'You've written it all down, for anyone to read?' His eyes darted round the room, as if the damning paper had to be contained in it somewhere. 'I'll find that letter, wherever it is, and I'll destroy it. I'm your husband – I have a right to anything you've written.'

'They won't give it to you.'

'Oh, I think they will, whoever "they" are. I'll find that paper and see it burned.'

Flora shook her head. 'I may as well tell you, I sent it to Darius Elder, at Elder's Bank. The Elders may be your bankers, but I don't believe Darius will give up that document.'

'Oh, he will – never fear. And then we'll see who's in a position to make conditions!' Ralph Newsome strode to the door. 'For the present, you can stay in your room.' He stalked out, slamming the door.

Only then did Flora dare to let go of the chimneypiece and slump, shaking, into her chair. The whole business was so wretched – so futile. Why not let him kill her, and have done with it? Why struggle to save a sterile future, bound to a man whom she loathed?

Next morning, as Flora had expected, Newsome went straight to Elder's Bank, where he tried to extract from Felix the document Flora had entrusted to his brother. Sullenly, Felix referred him to Darius, and after a short and unpleasant interview the explorer was forced to retreat, having won no more than the certain knowledge that Flora's damning package actually existed.

This time he came straight upstairs to her room.

'Tell me – since you've decided to turn your back on your marriage vows – do you expect to go on living in this house in future?'

Newsome had stationed himself in the centre of the room, his legs

205

apart, his hands clasped behind his back, rocking to and fro on the balls of his feet as if only this regular rhythm kept him from exploding. 'Do you expect to hold this pistol to my head, yet still be treated as my wife?'

'That depends entirely on you.' Flora sat calmly on the edge of her bed, her hands folded in her lap. 'If you wish it, I shall leave your house, and you may divorce me for desertion.'

'What?' The rocking stopped abruptly. 'Have you any idea what it costs to arrange a parliamentary divorce? The lawyers would live off me for months!'

'Not to mention the scandal, of course.'

'Naturally, there would be a scandal.'

'And, naturally, you wish to avoid that.'

'I cannot afford . . .' With a great effort, Newsome succeeded in keeping his temper. 'I cannot afford to become known as a man whose wife ran away after less than a year of marriage. People would ask questions. It could ruin me.'

'Well, then—' Flora took a deep breath. 'If you insist on keeping up appearances, I shall continue to live here and be your wife in every way but one. I'll share the household duties with Hester, I'll stand at your side in public and pretend everything is as it should be – and I'll undertake any other normal duty you may think of.

'But I will have a new lock put on the door of my room, and I will not let you use my body for your sordid games.' Flora meshed her fingers in her lap. 'For those you may go wherever you please and do whatever you want. Take a mistress if you can find one, or trawl the streets for some woman who'll give you what I've refused. I no longer care.'

She met his eye levelly.

'Provided you keep your part of the bargain, I give you my word never to mention it outside this house, nor the way you've treated me since we were married. Newsome of Nubia will still be a public hero, since it's so important to you.'

Beyond the window a watery sun had broken through the clouds, striping her new whitework bedcover with the shadows of the iron bars.

'You must understand,' Flora repeated, 'that you will never, ever, touch me again as my husband. That is over and done with between us. Dead, and buried.'

As dead, she repeated silently to herself, *as I am. Like the little automaton organist, I have no more inside me than springs and clock-escapements. I have learned a bitter lesson: Dédalon would be proud.*

4

From that moment, Flora's position changed within the house in Russell Square. Outwardly nothing was different, but the subtle shift of influence in the household was quite plain to the servants who inhabited it.

Flora never learned how Newsome explained the change to his sister. Perhaps Hester already felt guilty for having allowed the damning letter to leave the house at all – or perhaps she never knew of Flora's blackmail, and assumed that some mysterious alliance had formed in the marital bed to undermine her authority. At any rate, she said nothing, though the loathing in her eyes betrayed her anger at having to divide her power with Flora, where she'd been used to absolute command.

Within days the sinister Japanese armour had been taken down from its place above the stairs, and the drawing-room blinds rolled up at last to their fullest extent, letting in blessed sunlight to strike warmth from the bronzes and the ebony. Yet the house remained a battleground, where the three of them circled one another like dogs in a yard, hackles raised, silently establishing territories.

Not long after this, Sophie called to see her sister.

'I'll speak with Sophie alone,' Flora told Hester firmly, and ignoring the scowl with which her sister-in-law left the room, she led Sophie to a chair well away from the keyhole.

'I don't like it here.' Sophie glanced round almost fearfully, like a child abandoned in a strange place.

'You'd get used to it, if you lived here.'

'Yes?' Sophie's eyes swept back towards her sister, wide and a little unfocused. Once more Flora noticed that Sophie's pupils were no more than dots in the grey discs of her irises.

'Darius made me come,' Sophie confessed. 'He said you'd sent him something to keep for you at the bank, and he thought you might be in trouble of some kind. I told him he was imagining things,' she added helpfully.

Flora hesitated. 'I'm not in trouble of any kind.'

'Oh, well, then.' Sophie looked relieved. 'That's what I told Darius. "Of course Flora's happy. Who wouldn't be – married to a man like Ralph Newsome?"' She managed a strange little trill of a laugh. 'Who'd have guessed, if they'd seen us in that poky house in Gough Square? And yet now . . .' She glanced round again, as if the Egyptian figures unnerved her. 'Do you really not mind all these horrible statues?'

'I don't notice them any more.'

'They say you can get used to anything,' remarked Sophie bleakly. 'But I don't think it's true.'

She extended a hand to trace the pattern of bone plaques on the table, then suddenly glanced up as if an idea had occurred to her.

'I dare say Ralph will bring home even more when he comes back from this new expedition of his.'

Startled, Flora's voice became sharp. 'What expedition?'

'To the Pole, I think.' Sophie frowned. 'Or perhaps to this Northwest Passage everyone's talking about. Didn't you know?'

'Oh . . . I dare say Ralph mentioned it in passing.'

'Darius never tells me anything.' Sophie frowned again, and rubbed her brow vaguely with her gloved hand. 'At least . . . I don't think he does.'

5

Flora found her husband in his study, seated at a desk spread with charts and maps from which he was copying information into a small black notebook.

'Why didn't you tell me you were planning to go away again?'

'I didn't think you had the slightest interest in anything I might do.' Newsome closed the notebook, leaving his pencil between the pages to mark his place. 'Though I imagine you'll be delighted to see me go.'

'I told you I was prepared to be your wife in every way except one. That includes taking an interest in your work.'

'Enough of an interest to threaten to ruin a lifetime's achievement.' Newsome surveyed her sulkily from his chair.

'I had no other choice.' Flora turned to leave the room. Her hand was already on the door handle when she heard his voice again, harshly interrogative.

'Tell me what you know about this fellow Franklin.'

'Franklin?' Flora frowned over the name. 'Captain John Franklin, do you mean – the man whose poor wife died just after he went off to the Polar Sea last year?'

'Trust a woman to remember that!' Newsome tossed his notebook on to the desk in disgust. 'But do you know where he is now? Do you know why he went abroad in the first place?'

'I suppose he's still in the Arctic, since I haven't heard of him coming back.'

'He's wintering on the Great Bear Lake, so they tell me, a couple of hundred miles from the Polar Sea.' Abruptly, Newsome swept his notebooks and compasses from a map of the extremity of the North American continent, and stabbed at its open spaces with a finger. 'He's somewhere round here. Come and look at the map, dammit! I won't bite you.'

Flora stood at his shoulder, trying to make sense of the spidery black lines which marked rivers and lakes in what seemed a great deal of blank nothingness. At the top of the map the creeping track of the coastline dwindled to a trail of dots and dashes, and finally died out altogether as if it had lost itself in a frozen mist. In places Newsome had supplied it firmly in pencil.

'Where does it go between *here* and *here*?' Flora indicated the two unjoined ends of the wriggling line, the two loose threads which had been left to tie off a continent.

'Where, indeed!' Newsome frowned at the map. 'Though for good, logical reasons those lines must meet somewhere below the Pole. There must be a sea-route from the Atlantic to the Pacific, though no one's been able to prove it exists.'

'The Northwest Passage.'

'You've heard of it, then.'

'I should think everyone's heard of it. And I'm pleased to hear Captain Franklin's safe, since he sounds like a brave man. It must be a dangerous place to explore.'

'It's no more dangerous than the desert,' retorted Newsome at once.

'I never said it was. No one's making light of what you've done in the past, Ralph. You've no need to be jealous of Captain Franklin.'

'I'm not jealous! I'm just tired of hearing nothing but *Franklin, Franklin*, wherever I go.' Newsome's scowl deepened. 'Apparently he's sent back word through the Hudson's Bay Company to say he's charted a good way westward from the mouth of the Mackenzie, though the ice beat him before he could join up with Beechey coming the other way in the *Blossom*. Thank heaven for that,' he added sourly.

'Perhaps he'll try again in spring.'

'No, he's coming home as soon as the rivers are clear to travel. And no wonder!' added Newsome crossly. 'They say he'll be *Sir John* before the end of next year, and *Dr Franklin*, and I don't know all what. Those fellows at the Royal Society can't stop babbling about his cleverness.'

'Ah – I see. Newsome of Nubia is temporarily forgotten.'

'You may sneer, Flora, but travel happens to be my profession. Books – lectures – that's where the money comes from.'

'Oh, I'm sure Africa will come back into fashion once the subject of the Arctic has gone stale.'

Newsome slapped his hand down on the map.

'Not until this Northwest Passage is proved to exist, all the way from the Atlantic to the Pacific. People are wild about the idea. It's "the last great adventure", according to the newspapers. The public won't rest until the question's settled – and Franklin certainly won't rest, I assure you.'

'Then I should leave the hard work to him.'

'Why?' Newsome stared at her belligerently. 'I'm every bit as good a geographer as Franklin. Why should I let him finish the route and grab all the glory?'

'But all your experience has been in hot countries! This is polar exploration, isn't it?'

Newsome thrust out his chin. 'The principle's exactly the same, no matter what climate you're dealing with.' He drummed his fingers on the desk-top. 'Franklin won't be ready to go back to the Polar Sea for at least three years. Now, if I can prove there's open water from the Boothia Peninsula westward as far as his last survey point . . . that would complete the final link in the chain. Newsome will have discovered the Northwest Passage.'

He spread his hands like a conjuror. '*The Newsome Passage* . . . No – *The Newsome Strait*. That has a certain ring to it.'

'But if the Government is paying for Franklin to chart the sea-route, why should they put up the money to send you to the Polar Sea?'

'I don't need the Government.' Newsome rolled up his map with decision. 'Private investment's the answer. The societies will give me some of what I need, but I'll find the rest in the City.'

'In the middle of a banking crisis? Didn't you tell me yesterday that banks were collapsing all over the country?'

Newsome leaned back in his chair. The clouds of resentment had cleared at last from his brow, and he smiled for the first time that day.

'Not Elder's Bank. In fact, the Elders seem to have come through this spot of trouble pretty well. And I think I've already convinced Felix that a little investment in the Northwest Passage would pay him a handsome return.'

CHAPTER THIRTEEN

I

'This is all your doing!' Quick as a cobra, Hester Newsome cornered Flora by the foot of the stairs. 'You've sent him away again – driven him out of his own home.'

'It's none of my doing, I promise you.'

'Isn't it?' Hester's round little eyes glittered, trembling their papery lids. 'You – whom he raised from nowhere to be his wife . . . How have you repaid him?' In the gloom of the stairwell she slid closer. 'By sending him out to consort with lewd women! Oh, I know where he goes, don't worry.'

The lowest part of the balustrade rose between them, interposing its iron bars. Hester Newsome leaned on the mahogany newel, winding her hands possessively round its polished smoothness.

'What was a little pain, when you could have saved a man's soul by your suffering?'

'You don't know what you're saying!' Flora began to climb towards her room.

'He'll go to Hell because of you!' Hester called after her.

'Nonsense!' snapped Flora from the turn of the stairs. 'He's going to Hudson's Bay.'

Having set his sights on the Northwest Passage, Ralph Newsome lost no time in forming a committee of distinguished men to support his scheme. Geographers and men of science lent their names to the cause, and proclaimed their support in *The Times*: Mr Ralph Newsome's latest expedition was to be solely for the object of science, to determine the existence of the Northwest Passage beyond all possible doubt, to chart the last portion of unexplored coastline, and to make such observations on the general physics, meteorology and natural history of the region as might seem appropriate.

Having hoisted their colours, the members of the committee were pleased to find subscriptions pouring in from all over the country. The sonnet-writers sent in their guineas and two-guineas, while parish councils raised ten apiece and the senders of curls of hair contributed their promises of prayers. Dr Hildenhall was co-opted to the committee, bringing with him the blessing of the Phrenology Society and a volume on the *Measurement of the Eskimo Head*. The Society for the Dissemination of Christian Knowledge begged to be included, and offered Dr Theodore Breen, a small, globular man whose head and shoulders were all of a piece and whose clothes seemed to fit him like enamel.

The summer of 1827 was fixed for their departure from London, and a ship chartered for Hudson's Bay. The Hudson's Bay Company, prompted by their substantial shareholders, the Elders, had reluctantly agreed to let the party winter at their Northern District headquarters, York Factory – the location of their Chief Factor. From there, in the spring, Ralph Newsome planned to sail north in patent folding tarpaulin boats as far as Wager Inlet, where he'd march across country, dragging his collapsible craft, to search the coastline westward from the Boothia Peninsula.

Far too often now for Flora's liking, Felix Elder arrived at their door in Russell Square, his little chin lost in the folds of the highest, stiffest neckcloth she'd ever set eyes on, and an artful cluster of kiss-curls nodding on his bull's forehead.

'Hey-ho – capital!' And Felix would swagger through the hallway, tossing his hat and cane to the footman, to shut himself in the explorer's study with the latest lists of provisions and equipment, and as much claret as he could drink before his coachman came to help him home.

'Hey-ho—'

'Good day, Mr Elder.'

'And to you, Mrs Newsome.' Felix never paused in his strutting progress across the hall. 'A pleasure – a delight, as always . . .' His voice would float contemptuously back to her, and Flora would remember the submarine banking-hall with its mould-green walls, and the mortification she'd suffered there.

The expense of the expedition seemed fearful. Flora was never admitted to its inner mysteries, but occasionally lists of equipment were left where she could find them, and she read them through with astonishment. Almanacs, artificial horizons, thermometers, telescopes, compasses and protractors were all apparently vital, together with their stands, clips, clamps, tripods, station-pointers and object-glasses, not to mention portable bedsteads, tents, bolts of canvas and oilcloth, axes, knives, pruning-hooks, spirits-of-wine stoves and their kegs of fuel, lamps, lamp-oil, candles, pots, cauldrons, kettles, siphons, fishing-tackle, lead shot, gunpowder, a staggering quantity of brandy, ink, gum, paste, pencils, enough books to stock a library of moderate size, and a heap of water-bags.

'Water-bags?' Flora looked up from the list in surprise. 'Why must you take water-bags?'

Newsome scowled at her idiocy. 'For fresh water, woman! Why else? The most important part of any expedition is its water supply.'

'But aren't there lakes and rivers everywhere in that part of the world – and snow and ice, where the ground is frozen? Why must you carry more water with you?'

Exasperated, the veteran of deserts opened his mouth to retort, and then hastily closed it again.

'It's too complicated to explain,' he muttered quickly. 'Give me the list.' Next day, however, Flora noticed that the water-bags had been crossed off.

There were other entries on the equipment list which caused Flora's eyebrows to rise.

'Why', she asked one afternoon, bringing Madeira and fruit-cake to a gathering of committee men, 'do you need a silver teapot at the Polar Sea?' Not noticing the glances of amusement exchanged among the gentlemen, she pursued the point. 'And silver knives and forks – and a salt-cellar – and a chafing-dish . . .'

'My dear,' said her husband with heavy irony, 'a gentleman doesn't abandon the obligations of his position, simply by virtue of being many thousands of miles from home. Quite the reverse, in fact. To lead men, a commander must show that he's worthy of that leadership.'

'By taking tea from a silver teapot?'

'By maintaining the habits of his class, Mrs Newsome,' put in one of the committee members.

'A regular regime indicates firmness and resolution.' Newsome nodded his agreement. 'The instant you let standards fall off, the moral fibre of the men collapses entirely and they begin to question their orders like some barrack-room committee. A good leader insists on three meals a day plus afternoon and mid-morning tea, and Sunday services with a proper, portable organ. With a regime like that, a man can survive in the harshest places.'

'The Eskimos seem to survive there perfectly well,' Flora objected. 'They must know all about Arctic conditions, and yet I've never heard of them drinking tea.'

'But of course, dear lady—' One of the gentlemen smiled at her naïvety. 'The Eskimos understand perfectly how to keep an *Eskimo* alive.' A ripple of supercilious amusement ran round the company. 'But what will do for a wild Eskimo is hardly sufficient for a civilized English gentleman. Would you have us eat seal-fat like the natives, and build snow houses for our shelter?'

And the gentlemen of science rumbled with amusement once more.

As the preparations gathered pace, Flora's mind turned at last to her own situation. What was she to do when Ralph Newsome set off for the Polar Sea, and she was left alone in the house with Hester?

The bustle of recent weeks – and the stream of callers, even if they were no more exciting than Felix Elder and the angular, lugubrious Dr Hildenhall – had contrived to bring Flora back into the world again, a little disbelieving, like a child awakening from a vivid nightmare.

She'd refused to lower her guard: Newsome's step on the stairs at night or his savage look in her direction were still enough to make her heart pound and her skin dampen with alarm. Moreover, the desolate inner numbness which had been her only refuge from his violence remained with her still, and probably always would. Yet now at last she could believe that somewhere outside that house there was laughter, and singing, and the smell of the lavender which had bordered the paths at Richmond . . . And as spring succeeded winter she began to feel restless – not yet alive, but restless . . . until the thought of spending another month under the same roof as Hester Newsome was more than she could bear.

Travel was on everyone's lips. Hudson's Bay . . . Rupert's Land . . . the Polar Sea . . . As the preparations intensified, Newsome himself became steadier, as if the rage inside him was assuaged by the sight of an open door and the prospect of escape. Motion was everything. Travel, journeying, movement . . . until Flora herself caught the infection, and felt an overwhelming need to fly far away and be transformed by her flight.

She recognized now that the bargain she'd made with Ralph Newsome could only ever be a temporary solution. In two years' time he'd return from the Northwest Passage, the nation's darling once more, no longer prepared to tolerate a wife who'd blackmailed him with his own secrets. More than ever, Flora was seized by a need to break with the past, and to mark that break with a cleansing, symbolic release.

'I want to come with you as far as Hudson's Bay,' she told Newsome one day. 'Once you've all gone ashore, I'll sail back to London with the ship.'

'You're mad!' Newsome looked up in astonishment from a schedule of stores. 'Sail to Hudson's Bay? It's out of the question.'

'Why is it out of the question? There's more room aboard the *Nebula* than you need – you said so yourself. You've offered a place to Dr Breen, so that he can look for his precious lost tribes in Rupert's Land. Why shouldn't I come?'

'Why should I do anything to oblige you? A woman who could hold her husband to ransom in the most contemptible way . . . Why the devil should I want your company a moment longer than I'm forced to endure it?'

'Because . . . if you let me come as far as Hudson's Bay, I promise you'll be quit of me for good. It's all I want from you Ralph – no money, no roof over my head – nothing. When you come back from finding your Northwest Passage, I'll be gone from this house and from your life. You may divorce me if you please, and I won't contest it.'

Newsome was watching her with narrowed eyes.

'And the paper at the bank?'

'I'll destroy it. The secret of our marriage will die with me. No one will ever know you were anything but a perfect husband. Let people assume the separation was too much for us.'

Thoughtfully, Newsome chewed the ends of his black moustache, while Flora waited on tenterhooks.

'I'll swear it, if you want me to.'

'But not on the Bible, I imagine.' His lips twitched in a sneer.

'I mean it, Ralph. I'll keep my promise.'

'Better than you've kept your marriage vows, I suppose?'

'Better than you've kept yours!'

For a few moments he returned to chewing his moustache.

'All I want is to be free,' she pleaded, seeing him hesitate. 'I want to be finished with all this – to put the past behind me, and set out for . . . oh, for the future, I suppose. To run – to fly – to sail, even . . . Do you remember the railway, when we rode into Stockton – I closed my eyes then, and it was almost like being a bird, as free as the breeze . . .'

Her voice trailed away, leaving Newsome to consider her in silence.

'I suppose I can understand that,' he conceded at last.

'And you'll let me come?'

'To Hudson's Bay, and no further. If it means the burning of that damned paper and your silence afterwards, then I dare say it's worth the price.'

2

Four months later, in the dawn coolness of the wharf at Wapping, Flora stood by her husband's side, watching the bare spars of the barque *Nebula* emerge from the mid-river mist. Even in late July there was a stillness to that last grey hour before sunrise, a soft melancholy which touched each member of the small group waiting on the quayside, damping voices to a murmur.

Only Felix Elder seemed unaffected by the general mood, though a series of lion-like yawns indicated that for him this wasn't so much the start of a day as the end of the previous evening. Flora examined him with distaste from a distance of a few paces, and concluded it was a miracle Felix had come at all to see the expedition on its way. Only jealous concern for the Elders' investment could have diverted him at that hour from seeking his bed – or someone else's.

Even at this late hour, Flora didn't fully understand why the Elders had agreed to charter a ship and outfit Newsome's attempt on the Northwest Passage. Even assuming the expedition returned successful, they could hardly expect to make much of a profit on their investment: the twenty thousand pound reward, unclaimed for almost a century, would soon be eaten up in repaying the costs of the trip.

Flora's eye travelled on from the yawning Felix to his brother Darius, standing alone a short distance beyond, and her expression darkened. Darius had no business at all to be there: Flora had said so – both to Ralph and to Sophie – but it had made no difference. Now she glanced away from him with a small hiss of impatience. He'd no right to be there, no right at all.

Sophie, in contrast, had never considered coming to the quayside. Two months earlier, old General St Serf had died, and Sophie had immediately become obsessively concerned for her own health, refusing to stir out of doors for fear of dirt and infection.

For a long time now, she'd dosed herself against imaginary ills. On the rare occasions when they met, Flora had found her more distant than ever, speaking in disconnected phrases and with a peculiar absence of rhythm which made Flora suspect she'd been drinking.

'No, thank God,' Constance had reassured her. 'The last thing we need is a dipsomaniac in the family. She takes far too much opium, that's all.'

Now the mysteries made sense – Sophie's pinpoint pupils, her cold, slightly damp skin and the constant air of lethargy which had puzzled Flora so much in the past. She'd started with a sleeping draught, reported her mother, and then gone on to the opium-and-liquorice comfort of Dover's Powder, and finally to regular doses of laudanum itself, added in drops to distilled water.

'And what about Darius?' asked Flora. 'What does he think of all this?'

'It stops her hysterical fits, I dare say,' observed Constance blandly. 'Most men would be pleased to have a silent wife. And at least she isn't drinking.'

Sophie hardly seemed to have noticed that since the General's death Chillbourne was now held in trust for her. The income from the estate made her a rich woman in her own right, although in point of law it was effectively her husband's. And though Darius Elder had swiftly assured Constance that her house and her allowance would continue as before, the fact that it had been his 'generosity' and not Sophie's had been enough to make Flora angry all over again.

'Goodish land, Chillbourne,' Felix remarked casually during his next call at Russell Square. 'Rode over it with brother Darius last week, just to see what changes were needed. Been left to rot a bit, unfortunately, but we'll bring it to heel before long.'

His arrogance left Flora fuming. To think of the Elders as masters of Chillbourne, graciously extending its bounty to the very people whose rightful place they'd taken . . .

Flora scowled at the black spars of the *Nebula*, still stark against the sky like picked bones. Yet now at last she could distinguish tiny, insect-like figures creeping among the yards, casting loose the harbour stow and making ready to go down-river on the noon tide. As she watched, a long shadow detached itself from the ship's hull and began to creep slowly towards the group waiting on the wharf. On either side, a regular splash of oars counted off their last minutes ashore.

Flora allowed herself a final glance along the line of waiting passengers. Beyond Newsome stood the two doctors – Dr Theodore

Breen, his face polished pink with the excitement of his search for the Lost Tribes of Israel, and Dr Hildenhall, bound for the Polar Sea to study Eskimo heads. Whether the Eskimos would meekly submit to his measuring callipers was, as Newsome muttered privately, Hildenhall's problem and not his.

Beyond the two scientists, Flora's roaming eye flicked over the faces of the other members of the expedition. Some of them were clearly glory-hunters – half-pay naval lieutenants who'd run out of wars, army veterans hoping for plunder – but there were also one or two others whom Flora suspected were only a step or two ahead of the law, and a scattering of bored idlers looking for excitement. None of them would see Britain again inside two years, while with favourable winds, Flora and Polly Marks would be home in a matter of three-and-a-half months.

Once more, her gaze came to rest on Darius Elder, silently contemplating the fretted surface of the river. No one could deny he'd acted honourably in the matter of her sealed letter, and Flora had been grateful; but when he'd tried to find out what lay behind it, she'd cut him off sharply. And now he was here, watching the *Nebula*'s boat approach the quay. For the second time Flora frowned and looked away.

A week earlier, when everything had still seemed perfectly straightforward, Flora had put on her bonnet and mantle, and left Russell Square in a hackney-carriage to call on Lydia in Park Street.

It was the first time she'd seen Lydia since her marriage, and the visit had given rise to a good deal of heart-searching. For almost a year she'd been a virtual prisoner in Russell Square, and afterwards, in her new-found freedom, the separation had seemed almost too great to overcome: how could she explain what had kept her in seclusion for so many months? But now at last the coming sea voyage seemed to offer an excuse for calling – something exciting to discuss, forestalling awkward questions about the past.

The spout above the oil-shop still dripped as before, and the pork-butcher's doorway gave out the same dry tang of blood and sawdust. If Lydia had been offended by the long separation she didn't show it, but welcomed Flora to her home with delight. Her little parlour was as full of striped silk as ever; apparently Colonel West was still paying the rent and the wages of the pork-butcher's daughter.

'You look tired, sweetness.' Lydia put her shining head on one side and considered her friend carefully. She reached out to gather Flora's hands in her own.

'Ah . . .' she murmured, her eyes softly sad. 'You've had a hard time of it, my dear. Sometimes it isn't easy, I know.'

That was all; and yet, to her great relief, Flora suddenly found herself able to chatter about the coming expedition, and Dr Hildenhall the bump-reader, and Dr Breen and his lost tribes, as if the missing months had never come between them.

'You're mad,' Lydia told her flatly when Flora announced her intention of sailing as far as Hudson's Bay. 'It's all snow and ice there, isn't it? Nothing but swamp and crawling things that bite. No place for a woman like you.'

'I must go, Lydia. It's like a compulsion, this longing to fly away from everything here.' Before Lydia could ask from *what* precisely, she added quickly, 'Sir Humphry Davy took his wife all over Europe for two years on his scientific journeys. One of the gentlemen from the Royal Society told me.'

Lydia gazed complacently round her comfortable parlour. 'Well, as far as I'm concerned, my dear, you can keep your sailing ship, and the storms and gales that go with it. Just see you remember always to be sick on the leeward side, and to take out your hairpins if there's lightning.'

Lydia frowned, and a velvety groove appeared between her brows, giving her an air of amiable petulance.

'You aren't listening to me, Flora.'

'Tell me—' Flora asked suddenly, 'do you ever see Dédalon these days?'

'Oh, certainly! He comes here sometimes, and we gossip just as we used to. "Semiramis," he says, "you remind me of old times." He always asks about you, but for so long I've had nothing to tell him.'

'Then tell him—'

'Speak to him yourself, why don't you?'

'No . . . Please, Lydia – tell him . . . Tell him I beg his pardon.'

'But whatever for, my love?'

'Just tell him, please. He'll understand.'

Dédalon had been right, from the very beginning. Behind the Arab robe and the hero's smile, behind the harlequin's coat or the organ-player's lace, men – and women, too – were unfeeling mechanisms, driven solely by the most basic of instincts. Love, tenderness, charity, everything else was an illusion, in which Flora no longer believed.

As the *Nebula*'s boat butted at last against the foot of King James's Stairs, Flora glanced at her husband: surely at such a moment even he must feel humbled by the great journey which lay ahead. What she saw was Newsome of Nubia, his eyes alight at the prospect of conquest and his face already turned to the west, where the virgin Northwest Passage awaited the first sight of her ravisher.

It was Darius Elder who held out a hand to her at the foot of the slippery steps leading down to the boat. She took it grudgingly, for steadiness alone, and slithering to the very edge of the weed-encrusted stone, leaped down into the arms of the burly Coxswain amidships.

Darius had no right to be there, waiting to board the *Nebula* with the other expeditionaries. Why on earth should a banker want to trudge to the Polar Sea – and at the side of a man he despised, into the bargain? And yet, Newsome had told her, Darius had immediately claimed a place on the expedition as the price of his family's support.

Spying, Newsome had muttered. Why else should an Elder insist on coming, unless to safeguard his bank's investment?

'Don't you care at all?' Flora had demanded of Sophie, her fingers itching to shake her sister like the wooden-headed Ismene-Maria.

Sophie shrugged, and made a face. 'Why shouldn't Darius go? I hardly see him these days, anyway, so he might as well be at the North Pole, or wherever he's going.'

'This isn't a stroll in the park, Sophie! He'll be away for two years.'

For a moment, Sophie stared at Flora, and then her eyes slid away.

'Bella's had puppies, did I tell you?' Her glance strayed abstractedly round the room. 'Six of them – all pink and wriggling, like little rats. They're ever so pretty.' Her eyes swung back to meet Flora's, and her lower lip bulged defiantly. 'Darius doesn't like my dogs, you know. I should think they'll be quite happy when he's gone.'

Sophie didn't care. Provided she had her dogs, and her house, and her laudanum, Darius could do as he pleased – and at that particular moment, he was determined to sail for Hudson's Bay.

Well, then, let him come, if he must. Flora drew a bleak satisfaction from the certainty that Darius Elder's power over her was broken. There was no softness in her now for any man, and no trust: Ralph Newsome had destroyed that part of her for ever, and she couldn't even bring herself to mourn its passing.

3

Stripped of her mist-wraiths, the *Nebula* turned out to be a stout, kettle-bottomed barque borrowed for the occasion from the general carrying trade and hastily fitted with accommodation for a dozen or so passengers and their mountain of baggage. If she'd seemed substantial from an open boat alongside, the illusion vanished as soon as Flora and the rest of her passengers set eyes on the cramped, cupboard-like cabins which were to be their homes for the next six weeks. For a promenade there was the open deck, and for a drawing-room, dining-room, card and reading-room, the single saloon which linked the cabins, almost filled by a long mahogany table and an iron stove standing in a great quantity of ash at one end.

The table, Flora noticed uneasily, was bolted to the deck – as was every item of furniture in her cabin, from the tiny wash-stand with its chamberpot below and spotted mirror above to the two narrow bunks placed one over the other, and the sofa opposite which was no more than a leather-covered shelf against the wall.

Over all the accommodation hung an indefinable smell, a mingling of salt and stale water, of old varnish and tar, and of whatever the steward had been mixing in his pantry as they passed. Out in the saloon, Flora saw Dr Hildenhall and Dr Breen exchange glances of dismay.

Yet what was a little discomfort, compared with the hardships of the Polar Sea? Dismay was quickly pushed aside, and everyone turned out for a dinner of pig's brawn, baked potatoes and pickles which appeared on thick china dishes at three o'clock, with the vessel still in the calm waters of the river. The food – and the brandy-and-water which went with it – had a most encouraging effect, and before long the various members of the expedition were beaming at one another across the saloon table and speculating on the day they'd return, crowned with honour, to those self-same waters.

What Captain Machin thought of his charter wasn't recorded, but fortunately his opinion of the collapsible boats stowed in his hold didn't filter back from the forecastle until the vessel was well out at sea.

Nebula, he'd growled to the Mate, might be a blowsy old scow with the sailing manners of a sea-cook's cat, but nothing on this earth or above it would get Captain John Machin afloat in one of those tarpaulin wash-basins – not if the ocean boiled and Neptune himself guaranteed a safe passage. And jamming his salt-stained hat more firmly over his eyes, the captain had stamped below to study his charts of the North Atlantic.

The feeling of well-being lasted for almost a week while the *Nebula* battled down the Channel in the teeth of a stiff breeze and passed out at last into the long grey swells of the Atlantic Ocean. By then the ship's saloon had taken on the character of a gentlemen's club, crowded with jolly good fellows who were mightily pleased with themselves. Flora and her maid had begun to feel like intruders, and she noticed that Darius Elder seemed to prefer the open deck and the company of the crew to that of the expeditionaries. On the rare occasions when he and Flora met, he passed her by with distant courtesy, as if he accepted she'd no desire for more.

Then came a night when the prevailing westerlies began to freshen, and the *Nebula* laboured in a rising sea, clambering ponderously up the face of each wave only to slide with a sideways hitch of her stern into the trough of the next. Gamely, she thrust her nose into each watery wall, shaking the deluge from her shoulders with a rolling shrug before plunging determinedly on her way.

At breakfast-time there was a sudden absence of expeditionaries at the saloon table. Flora, surprised to find herself unaffected by the ship's motion, worked her way forward as soon as she'd dressed, hand over hand past the steward's pantry, for a brief glimpse of the *Nebula*'s canting deck.

So this was the ocean! All at once it occurred to her that she'd entrusted her safety to a very small, fragile, floating object amid a fearsome waste of water. Overnight, the *Nebula* had shrunk to the size and substance of a leaf, adrift on a restless immensity which tossed up their lives as casually as dice on a board.

All the stories Flora had ever heard of ships foundering or capsizing rushed back into her mind, yet the very danger of her situation offered comfort of a kind. *So be it*, she thought: *let the sea decide. So be it*, she repeated aloud – and wondered if this was really why she'd come.

One by one, the missing members of the Newsome Expedition emerged from their cabins for brief spells during the day, their faces wan and apprehensive. The saloon skylight had been covered for safety, and the only recreation was a book or a game of cards by the light of the wildly swinging lamp. By afternoon the confidence of the first few days had begun to give way to squabbles and irritability. There was no more eager discussion of the enterprise to come; instead, most of Newsome's volunteers crawled back to their berths to count off the hours to Hudson Bay and curse the foolhardiness which had brought them.

For several days the *Nebula* alternately stood on her head or her tail, varying her rhythm with a playful wriggle from side to side which set the glasses clinking in their racks and shoes tumbling willy-nilly across cabin floors. Lying miserably in their narrow bunks, her passengers found themselves one minute pressed flat into their thin mattresses and the next almost floating off them as the ship's stern rose and fell. When the vessel rolled, it was all they could do to avoid being folded into a heap at one end.

All round them, every plank in the ship seemed to be squealing and groaning in protest. Day and night, feet thundered overhead, trunks rumbled to and fro beneath the lower bunks, and huge seas crashed against the hull only inches from their sleepless, anxious heads.

To his fury, Ralph Newsome succumbed with the rest. When Flora went to call on him in his cabin, she found him crouched in his bunk, horribly ill, hugging a rose-painted chamberpot to his chest and muttering savagely that he'd never encountered such seas in the Mediterranean.

His putty-coloured face made Flora smugly conscious of her own good health. It was hard not to gloat when she felt so amazingly well, better than at any time during the long, dark months in Russell Square. Shipboard life fascinated her, and she was content to spend hours at a time, wedged on the long sofa beneath the *Nebula*'s stern windows, watching the tangled skein of the vessel's wake unreel itself across the swell.

On the third afternoon of the gale, Flora was lying on her sofa under the stern windows, warmed by several glasses of brandy-and-water brought to her by the kindly steward, when she began to feel restless. The thought occurred to her that if spectacular things were happening on deck, she ought to be there to see them.

Leaning for support on the panelled wall – the *bulkhead*, she corrected herself – Flora made her way carefully to her cabin, where Polly Marks peered out silently from the lower bunk with the drowned eyes of a dead fish. It was a matter of precise judgement to snatch her broadcloth cloak from its hook as it swung within reach, but a few minutes later Flora was dressed and out in the saloon once more, handing herself through it to the short passage by the steward's pantry which led to the open deck.

Cautiously unfastening the outer door, she put her eye to a six-inch gap. With the impact of a fist, a blast of wind suddenly punched through the crack, wrenched the knob from her grasp and hurled the door back on its hinges. Flora now had a perfect view of the soaking deck, criss-crossed with lifelines; but lifelines meant nothing to Flora, and the idea of returning to her stifling cabin never occurred to her for a moment.

Dodging the crazily swinging door, she darted across the nearest patch of wet and slippery deck to the main shrouds, the sturdy web of rigging which supported the mainmast. There she clung, gazing out into the broad Atlantic, her fingers fastened to the tarry, iron-hard hemp while the wind tore at her heavy cloak, whipping its skirts above her knees.

This was what she'd come to see! The *Nebula* was moving among grey-green mountains whose snowy ridges soared cleanly against a sky of wonderful ferocity. Even as Flora reached the ship's side, one of the emerald hills, as sheer as a slice of green glass and veiled in hissing spume, was bearing down upon the vessel with sublime slowness. At that moment it seemed as if there had never been anything so translucently beautiful, so ravishingly sinister as that great mass of tumbling water. Flora watched it, mesmerized, quite unable to tear her eyes from its perfect glass wall, now with a toppling crest of spindrift.

The explosion of its impact shook the *Nebula* from truck to keel, and a long shudder ran through her. Her masts swung in a wide arc across the sky, setting the yards roaring in their parrels while below, poop and forecastle had become two islands separated by the white water which boiled in the well between them, confined and furious.

As the wave struck, Flora felt her fingers plucked from the rigging by an immense force which drove the air from her lungs and swept her from her feet, crushing her in its inexhaustible embrace. *So this is what it's like to drown*, she thought, curiously unafraid.

All at once an almighty blow on her back hurled her forward until her cheek burned against the roughness of tarred rope and the solid edge of the ship's rail pressed into her chest. No longer mesmerized, she began to fight urgently for breath, her wet fingers scrabbling for a grip on the rigging and her feet kicking out amid the surging whirlpools all around. As the water sucked away she filled her lungs at last, coughing and retching. Even now the sea still dragged round her thighs, tugging at her sodden cloak as if reluctant to give her up, challenging the firm pressure which kept her bound to the shrouds and safely out of its grasp.

Flora tried to blink away the film of sea-water and tears which blinded her. Her head was still twisted to one side against the unyielding hemp of the rigging, but now, just beyond her right shoulder, she could make out a lean brown hand, the fingers clamped securely round the nearest stay. She guessed that its partner was anchored to the rigging at her left shoulder, and that some alert seaman had seen her plight and had saved her from being swept away by catching hold of the rigging on either side of her helpless body and pulling them both hard against this support.

Lesser waves still lashed the *Nebula*'s sides, and the deck still plunged as before, but the immediate danger was past. Evidently, Flora's rescuer thought so too, as he relaxed his hold on the shrouds, supporting her with an arm about her waist while she gasped for breath. With no strength of her own, Flora laid her head thankfully against her saviour's chest and closed her eyes.

To be held so . . . as she'd given up hoping to be held, in the disastrous marriage she'd made . . .

Long after she could have stood alone, she remained, unmoving, shocked by her own shamelessness. All the months of learning to withdraw inside herself – of learning to survive without the least touch or caress, yet not to regret her loneliness . . . In a second all of it had been washed away by that traitorous wave, leaving her clinging like a drowning soul to the body of her rescuer, savouring each moment of closeness to another human being.

'I don't expect you'll thank me for this,' observed a bitter voice above her head. 'You're never grateful for my help, Flora – even when you need it.'

Instantly, Flora drew back her head, her eyes wide with alarm. But Darius Elder didn't return her gaze, too absorbed in watching the procession of waves which advanced on the ship and choosing his moment to leave the safety of the shrouds for a swift dash across the open deck. Rivulets of water still trickled from his dark curls into the corners of his eyes and the creases at his mouth. His eyes were no longer pale; for a moment Flora fancied she could see in them some of the shifting shadows of the sea, the same overwhelming force which had so nearly swept her away.

'Now!'

Suddenly they were in motion, running haphazardly for the door to the accommodation, Flora's feet slipping and scuffling on the wet planking as she was forced to keep up. Ahead of them, the door gaped open as she'd left it, but now several inches of sea-water swirled in the passage beyond. Gripping the lintel with one hand, Darius thrust her into the damp shadows.

'Can you stand alone?'

'I think so.'

'Good.'

At once he turned away to the fore-hatch, where half-a-dozen seamen were trying to salvage the hen-coop, torn from its lashings in a welter of broken spars and wet feathers. Taken aback by his abruptness, Flora watched him skid away across the wildly sloping deck, the damp bulk of his travelling-coat grey-black, his boots soaked and dull. Swallowing her pride, she'd been about to thank him humbly for saving her.

Behind her, she heard a discreet cough from the passageway, and turned to find Dr Breen, ankle-deep in water, clinging to a coat-hook to keep himself upright.

'My goodness!' he squeaked. 'How fortunate Mr Elder was there, to save you from going over the side! Mr Newsome owes him a great debt – a great debt, indeed.'

With a little cry of frustration, Flora gathered her sodden skirts and splashed past the doctor towards the saloon.

CHAPTER FOURTEEN

I

On the fifth day after it had started the storm blew itself out, though for some time afterwards the *Nebula* continued to labour through the high seas it had created. While the vessel continued to roll, Flora spent her waking hours in the saloon, though not out of any respect for Captain Machin's lecture, sternly delivered after her reckless adventure at the ship's side.

Now, if she knew Darius Elder was on deck, Flora stayed below. If he came into the saloon when she was there alone, she immediately made an excuse for retreating to her cabin. Polly Marks, almost recovered from her seasickness, found herself hauled ruthlessly from her berth to keep her mistress company wherever she went – and all so that Flora shouldn't find herself alone again with Darius Elder.

It wasn't her head but her body which had rebelled: she was sure of that, but the fact didn't make her surrender any less shocking. She'd set sail from England a hard, tight nutshell of a woman, the woman she'd made herself by scouring her mind of the daydreams allowed to other wives. Yet in a second the sorcerer sea had overturned it all by sending death itself to lick her with salty tongues. Oh, how weak is our flesh, quickened by fear and a hunger for the meanest caress! Better, perhaps, to have let the wave take her after all, carrying her treacherous body beyond the consequences of its own frailty.

In future, she would put herself beyond temptation.

For Ralph Newsome's benefit, she made light of the incident, as if she'd suffered no more than a thorough wetting.

'Stupid woman,' he growled from his bunk. 'Captain Machin said you might easily have gone over the side, if that precious spying brother-in-law of yours hadn't caught you.'

'The Captain's making the most of his story, I think!' Flora forced an airy laugh. 'Darius simply kept me from falling down into all the water that came on deck.'

'Did he, now?'

Uncomfortably aware of Newsome's scrutiny, Flora fussed with the fresh bread she'd brought from the steward's pantry.

'Even spies can be useful sometimes,' she said lightly.

Newsome grunted, broke a crust from the loaf, and nibbled it with suspicion.

'I wonder if Felix sent him to watch me, or if it was his own idea . . .' He chewed for a few moments in silence. 'No – I expect Darius thought of it himself. Felix says that sister of yours has given her husband no end of trouble, so no doubt he was itching to be clear of the woman. But that's no surprise to us, is it?' His lip curled, revealing the milky points of his incisors.

'No—' he went on, 'Felix is the man for investment, not Darius. Persuade Felix he's sniffed out a good thing, and he's only too pleased to convince the other directors he can make them rich by laying out a pound or two here and there.' He waved the crust of his loaf. 'The trouble is, his brother Darius doesn't trust me.'

'And so you think he's spying on you?' echoed Flora, puzzled. 'But what is there to spy on, if Felix has simply agreed to pay for the expedition?'

'Nothing at all,' mumbled Newsome airily, his mouth full. 'Nothing at all, I'm sure.'

2

The passing of the storm brought a full attendance at meal-times, and a general coming-and-going through the saloon, which to Flora's relief meant she was never again obliged to be alone in Darius Elder's company. Now that they were approaching colder latitudes, the members of the expedition were usually to be found round the black stove in the saloon, by common consent the warmest place on the vessel after the cook's galley.

As the weather grew bleaker, Flora hunted out the thicker clothes she'd been advised to bring, until she spent most days in a plain woollen gown over a flannel petticoat and stout wool stockings, with a heavy shawl thrown on top of it all. Perversely, she discovered a kind of comfort in her new shapelessness, as if the layers of wool which transformed her into a walking cushion could smother the longings of her body as thoroughly as they disguised its womanly form.

If she went out on deck now, it was always in the staid company of Dr Breen or Dr Hildenhall. Both of the doctors regarded 'taking the sea air' as a bracing part of their daily routine, though what else they imagined blew into the saloon through the ventilators and the gaping cracks in the door-frames was a mystery to Flora.

'The salt air agrees with you, Mrs Newsome,' Dr Breen assured her. 'Ah – it's a fine thing to be a young person, and facing adventure . . . Look at Mr Elder, now! When he came aboard I'd have put him down for a city banker to his fingertips, with his well-cut coats and his skin pale from passing all his time with his ledgers. Yet look at him today!'

Reluctantly, Flora looked.

'Isn't it wonderful,' continued the doctor, 'what a few weeks' sea air can achieve?'

It was true: sea air, or perhaps the same transforming power which had affected Flora herself, had worked a visible magic on Darius Elder. He seemed to have become subtly taller and broader; his gestures were more generous, and his movements more relaxed and spontaneous than she remembered. As she watched, he set his weight to the main topsail brace with half-a-dozen seamen, simply for the pleasure of action – and then grinned as they scoffed at his rope-burned palms, rubbing them carelessly on the breast of his greatcoat.

Some sixth sense caused him to glance across to where Flora stood, her arm in Dr Breen's. He made a slight gesture of greeting and then continued to watch her with an appraising curiosity which made her uneasy.

'If you please, Dr Breen – I think I'd like to go back to the saloon now.' Without looking again in Darius Elder's direction, she went below.

With two weeks still to go before the *Nebula* could hope to anchor in Hudson's Bay, her passengers at last set eyes on the ice.

At first it could only be glimpsed through Captain Machin's telescope as a necklace of pearls strung out on the horizon. However, a day's sailing brought them as close to a large berg as the Captain cared to go, near enough to reckon it as tall as the *Nebula*'s mainmast, and its mass underwater – so the Mate declared – many times greater than the part they could see.

That part was impressive enough. Dazzling in the sunlight, the iceberg was a bright, drifting mountain, pure white except for a cobalt-blue hollow in its side like the col under an Alpine ridge. Far below, where the berg's waterline lifted and dipped in the swell, a tattered fringe of weed had clung; above it ran a frieze of colour where the shot-silk of the berg overhung the waves – streaks of watery vermilion, aqueous green and the palest of blues – as if the skirts of maidenly white concealed a petticoat of harlequin colours.

As the *Nebula* drew nearer to the entrance to the Hudson Strait itself, the ship passed into a region of mists and silence, an eerie overworld of ice. Sometimes the floes were as smooth as tables, broken fragments of a great frozen sheet which had cracked apart to allow the *Nebula* to pass; here and there the whiteness had clustered into fantastic pinnacles, as if a city of glass were forever grindingly at war with itself, splitting and colliding over a black, black sea.

In the mist-smoked open water all was silence except for the splashing of the ship's forefoot in the swell; yet down in the cabins, sleep was continuously disturbed by the bumping and scraping of ice-floes against the *Nebula*'s hull. Even the smallest slabs groaned sullenly along her flanks before giving way, and the uproar continued day and night, until the only peace to be had was on the freezing deck amid the foggy, swirling breath of the northern bays.

The mists thinned briefly to allow a glimpse of Resolution Island, and then closed in once more as Captain Machin groped his cautious way through the Strait, standing for hours at the steersman's shoulder, his beard spangled with droplets condensed from the raw air.

From time to time, a wheeling seabird would remind them they were not entirely alone, and one day a white bear appeared on the ice not far from the vessel, swung his great head for a moment to sift their stench of tar and spoiled rations, and then loped away with an unhurried, rocking gait.

On a day of light winds, when the ship seemed to make no progress at all through the water, a native family paddled out to them – 'Eskimo,' confirmed Dr Hildenhall excitedly – the women in a large sealskin boat laden with children and household baggage, and the men paddling alongside in slender single-handed canoes. Leaning over the ship's rail, Flora felt a pang of envy for the close-knit little group, bound tightly together by the precariousness of their existence. Then the wind freshened, their Eskimo escort fell away, and a gradual thinning of the ice round the ship indicated they were crossing the bay itself.

A new sense of purpose began to invade the vessel. Charts were spread out on the saloon table, and the portable barometer was taken to pieces and reassembled; meals were disrupted by arguments over the correct method for dissecting the crops of birds, and a great many unscientific bets were made on the date of their arrival at York Factory.

Flora knew the length of her stay ashore would depend on the number of days it took to unload the expedition's stores: the fort itself lay on the bank of the Hayes River, some miles upstream from the bay and from Five Fathom Hole, which was as near as any ship of size could go. As soon as their vessel was seen from the fort's lookout beacon, a schooner would come out to pick up the cabin passengers and their personal baggage, and any mail they might have brought with them.

As the *Nebula* drew nearer to her destination, Flora found herself infected by the growing excitement on board. Somewhere to the west, now only a handful of days away, lay a monstrous wilderness, boundless as thought, dwarfing the human creatures which clung to its surface. Lines from all the books she'd read kept returning to her: descriptions of sheer precipices whose tops were lost in veils of cloud, meteor showers in skies of indigo, cataracts and rapids of feathery fury . . . How could humankind look on such wonders, and imagine itself master? In such a place, what purpose could silver teapots and starched shirts possibly serve, except to show up the relentless vanity of the invaders?

'What can you see?' Flora leaped instantly to her feet when Newsome returned to the saloon to report that land was at last in sight. 'Are there many mountains? Are the cliffs high? Can you see any forests or glaciers?'

'No . . .' For a moment, Newsome's voice faded and his brow creased in a frown. 'It's completely flat,' he announced. 'Flat – and empty. There seems to be nothing there at all.'

3

York Factory, when they reached it, was far from nothing; but it stood, undeniably, amid a great deal of nothingness. When Flora climbed unsteadily up the boarded walkway to the top of the river-bank, she found a flat and swampy land stretching out in all directions apparently endlessly, and studded with lichenous boulders and scrubby clumps of dwarf willow. She halted on the walkway, shocked at the sheer desolation of the place; it was utterly empty, and ominous in its emptiness. From the foreground to the sparse trees on the horizon there was only one object of note, and that was York Factory itself, stronghold of the Hudson's Bay Company and their principal depot in the Northern Department of Rupert's Land, confronting its bleak domain from behind a wind-flayed palisade.

The palisade and the buildings behind it were built of white-painted wood scraped almost bare by the weather, with the remains of a little green paint here and there in a brave attempt at gaiety. The buildings were arranged in the shape of an 'H' – plain, no-nonsense constructions, some a single storey high and some two, solid as country loaves and pierced with the smallest windows consistent with letting light in and keeping the winter out.

To Flora's sea-softened eye, the place was a monument to right angles and straight lines, as if a curved wall or a meandering path would have been a dangerous concession to the disorder of nature beyond the gates. As she walked with the others towards the buildings along the bar of the 'H', she noticed that even the wooden platform under their feet led up from the river with the straightness of an arrow-flight. Behind her, she heard Ralph Newsome murmur approvingly: here were gentlemen who knew the value of keeping a strict regime in the wilderness – of brandishing the pocket-pistol along with the company flag.

Chief Factor John McTavish welcomed them cordially enough, while making it plain he wished their Honours in London had chosen some other post for the distinction. Explorers in these northern territories were clearly a confounded nuisance, an awkward distraction from the single-minded business of gathering furs. Moreover, churchmen and bump-readers anxious for Eskimo heads were as good as powder-kegs in that carefully handled region.

Nevertheless, their Honours' instructions were holy writ. Those of the *Nebula*'s passengers who seemed to be gentlemen would be lodged in the gentlemen's guest-house, and the rest could live with the post servants until the expedition set off for the Polar Sea the following spring.

For the few days she was to remain ashore, Flora was given a small, wooden-walled room hardly bigger than her cabin on the *Nebula*, with a bare planked floor, a rudimentary wooden bedstead, a wash-stand, a wooden chair, and a low ceiling which had once been white but which was now ale-brown with the smoke of a hundred clay pipes. The walls must once have been white too; now they bore a curious random pattern of black stars, which turned out on closer inspection to be the bodies of a legion of mosquitoes and bulldog-flies, squashed to death by whoever had lived in that room during the short, insect-ridden summer months.

Mr McTavish, gaunt and whiskered, waited in the hall to be told his arrangements were perfect, and Flora duly did so.

'You'll join us for meals, I hope, Mrs Newsome. We're a rough crew in a rough place, but we try to keep ourselves comfortable all the same. I'm persuaded you'll find we keep a respectable table here.'

'It's ill-luck,' he observed at dinner, 'that you've missed Governor Simpson by about six weeks. He's gone to spend the winter in Montreal.'

Flora, at McTavish's side, tried to look disappointed by the news, but failed. She'd heard enough of George Simpson in London to be sure she'd dislike him on sight: the Governor might be the absolute ruler of Rupert's Land, answerable only to the Hudson's Bay Company's London Committee, but even those who praised his efficient management of company affairs also felt obliged to mention his arrogance and tyrannical ways.

Flora glanced across to where Ralph Newsome was lecturing the post doctor on the causes of tropical malaria. There was no room for two sultans in that small oasis in the wilderness. It was probably just as well Governor Simpson had left for Montreal.

At that moment the explorer turned his attention to his host.

'I don't suppose you get many visitors, McTavish, in such an unhallowed spot as this.'

'It's a wee bit on the bleak side, I grant you,' conceded McTavish. 'But you're bound for somewhere a good deal worse, Mr Newsome. I'll wager York Factory will seem like heaven to you after a few days on the march.'

'I'm not unaccustomed to hardship,' remarked Newsome stiffly.

'In hot countries, though, so I hear.'

'Hardship is hardship,' snapped the explorer, but the Chief Factor merely smiled.

'Dr Breen!' he called out, with the casual assurance of a man whose word is law in his own dominion.

'Sir?'

'Dr Breen, I'm told you believe some of our Indians to be a Lost Tribe of Israel. Now, I'm no theologian, but they must surely be very badly lost, to have wandered so far from home.'

A ripple of laughter ran round the table.

'Ah, but you see, it may be the others who have wandered.' Undeterred, Dr Breen pushed his spectacles higher on his nose. 'You see, I firmly believe that the early events described in the Bible actually took place on this continent, and not in Mesopotamia as most people imagine. Now, you may find that notion far-fetched, but the flood myths of many North American tribes, their languages and their habit of levirate marriage—'

'*What* kind of marriage?' interposed McTavish with a broad wink which set off another outbreak of laughter.

'Marriage', Dr Breen persevered, 'to a brother's widow – which, as you know, is barred by our Christian church, along with marriage to a dead wife's sister, and so forth, as being an incestuous union—'

Of their own accord, Flora's eyes sought out Darius Elder on the far side of the table, only to see him glance up, suddenly and mysteriously drawn to her at the same moment. At once, Flora switched her attention back to the roly-poly doctor.

'Dr Breen,' McTavish interrupted him, 'have you ever *met* an Indian?'

'No, sir, I have not.'

'Or even set eyes on one?'

'No, sir,' admitted the unfortunate doctor, and then added rashly, 'My home town of Banbury is not well endowed with foreign persons.'

'Tomorrow, doctor,' promised McTavish, laughing, 'I'll take you to meet some of your Lost Tribesmen. I'll be most interested to witness a moment so important to science.'

'May I—' Dr Hildenhall's voice rang out from the far end of the table. 'May I come with you tomorrow to see the Indians?'

'Ah – Dr Hildenhall, our phrenologist . . .' The Chief Factor turned his attention to the new target. 'Yes – by all means come with us tomorrow. We'll call on the natives at the Plantation yonder, and you may see if there are any ripe heads you'd like to collect.'

McTavish's smile was wide and inoffensive, but it was evident that he found Hildenhall as much of a trespasser in his swampy fiefdom as Dr Breen.

'I *measure* heads,' Dr Hildenhall corrected him with dignity, 'according to Combe's system of phrenology.' Unconsciously, Hildenhall slid into academic mode. He fastened his thumbs into his lapels, and his voice rose in pitch as if the assembled company were a hall full of students.

'I have dedicated my life to seeking out the factors which have rendered the native races incapable of advancing themselves as we in Europe have advanced . . . Defects of character – a disharmony of personality . . .' His eyes swept up to the ceiling as he expanded his theme. 'For instance, some months ago I was privileged to examine a skull reputed to be that of a Choctaw Indian male – and I noted that an area known as the seat of *self-esteem* was remarkably over-developed—'

'And where would that be, Dr Hildenhall?' The Sloopmaster's almond-shaped black eyes flashed with annoyance under his crow-black brows.

'The seat of self-love? Oh . . .' The doctor's hand flew up and alighted on a spot a little behind the crown of his head. 'Just here. In the vain and arrogant you can feel it quite easily with the fingers . . .' His voice died away in dismay at the sight of McTavish's scowl.

Precisely in the spot Dr Hildenhall had indicated, the Chief Factor's head was innocent of hair, and as domed and shiny as one of his own silver dishcovers.

4

If McTavish had no option but to shelter the expeditionaries at York Factory over the winter, he was anxious that the *Nebula*, at least, should leave as soon as possible to be sure of clearing the ice which annually closed up the bay. Yet, in spite of the fact that it was already late September, the work of unloading her was slowed to a snail's pace by the mass of small items packed into her hull and Ralph Newsome's insistence on having everything checked off on his interminable lists.

'He'll never drag all yon clutter to the coast with him.' Dourly, the Chief Factor watched a stack of camp-beds and spirit-stoves being landed from the schooner. 'He should take a lesson from the Cree and the Chipewyan, and live off the land. All he needs is a skin coat, a few blankets, a rifle to shoot game, and a kettle to cook it in.'

'Perhaps you should talk to him,' suggested Flora. 'As someone who knows the country.'

'No, no.' McTavish waved the idea aside. 'Let the man have his way. I doubt I'd only be wasting my breath!'

Then, on the evening of the 23rd, while the 'gentlemen' dined once more round the Chief Factor's table and a large part of the *Nebula*'s crew were being entertained ashore, a short, vicious storm boiled up out of nowhere at all and swept across the bay with startling ferocity.

While Captain Machin fumed impotently on the York Factory landing-stage, the *Nebula* dragged her anchors; and before the handful of men left aboard could do anything to prevent it, she'd grounded, heeled and filled, and lay on her beam-ends at the mercy of the gale.

The morning of the 24th brought a dawn as pinkish-grey as a pigeon's wing, with no trace of the *Nebula* but a great raft of splintered timbers piled up against the shore of the bay. Amongst the wreckage were pathetic reminders of the vessel's mission – lengths of tattered canvas, a broken telescope stand, part of a smashed sledge, and a sodden pink bonnet which Flora's maid had left in her cabin for the voyage home.

'Worst of all, we've lost the collapsible boats!' Outraged, Ralph Newsome stamped into the Chief Factor's office to join the dismal conference already in progress. 'I always said we should have unloaded the boats first of all – and now we'll have to manage without them.'

'Never mind your blessed boats!' shouted Captain Machin, his grey whiskers stiff with indignation. 'What about my ship? Five good men drowned and gone, thanks to your insistence on coming to this godforsaken spot – and all you can think of are your damned toy boats. They'd never have carried you out of the river, man! Though better *you* drowned than five of my men!'

'I'll report you to your employers for that, Captain Machin.' Newsome's face had coloured with anger. 'That – and your incompetence, which has cost me half-a-dozen good boats.'

'Report away, sir, if we ever manage to get home from this place.' Captain Machin returned the explorer's glare with interest. 'In my opinion there never was such a hare-brained scheme as this expedition of yours. No doubt that's why the good Lord saw fit to put an end to it.'

'*An end to it?*' Newsome drew himself up, his eyes glittering. 'By no means, Captain Machin. By no means at all. We press on!'

'Impossible, Mr Newsome.' Chief Factor McTavish, who'd been listening sourly to the exchange, now pulled himself upright in his chair. 'It's a scunner, I dare say, to have come so far only to fail at the last ditch. But even you must see that without these boats of yours, you've no longer any chance of reaching the Polar Sea. Put the notion out of your mind, man, and set off southward by river before winter sets in.'

Ralph Newsome surveyed the Chief Factor scornfully.

'Give up my expedition?' He snorted in disbelief. 'I should think not! No – since this fellow here—' he indicated the glowering captain '—has lost my boats, I'll simply go north overland instead. I'll have less time to search westward from Boothia, certainly, but I'm confident I'll still reach my goal. The more obstacles you put in an English gentleman's path,' he informed McTavish loftily, 'the more determined he becomes to surmount them.'

'You forget you're here on sufferance, sir!' snapped the Chief Factor. 'I'll thank you to remember I didn't ask for your company over the winter. The London Committee, for reasons of their own, informed me I must put up with you and give you such help as you needed. Well – now that your expedition's out of the question, I intend to clear your entire party out of York Factory as soon as you can get your bags together.'

'I'm delighted to hear it,' agreed Captain Machin sourly, 'but we've no ship to go home in, and I don't imagine another vessel will call here before summer. Though I've no wish to be stranded in these parts, I assure you.'

'And I've no wish to feed an entire ship's crew, along with Mr Newsome and his people,' McTavish informed them. 'Rations are short enough as it is. However, there's still enough time to send you south by river. It's a rough journey, especially for a lady—' He glanced apologetically at Flora, sitting mutely in the corner. 'But if you leave immediately you should reach Red River, at least, before winter sets in, and possibly even Lachine.'

He turned to Darius Elder, leaning against the wall nearby.

'What do you say, Mr Elder? Will that arrangement suit you?'

'Perfectly, if it's acceptable to the others.'

'It's acceptable to me,' Captain Machin put in at once.

Newsome flicked his hand contemptuously. 'Mr Elder and the Captain can go if they please, but I've no intention of leaving.' To emphasize his point, he plumped himself down in the nearest chair.

'Oh, I shall go, never fear, and take my crew with me,' growled

Captain Machin. He rose and moved to the door. 'Tell me when we're wanted, Mr McTavish, and my men will be ready for you.'

'A good seaman,' remarked the Chief Factor as the door closed on the *Nebula*'s master.

'So good, he managed to lose his ship,' retorted Newsome scornfully. 'Good riddance to him, I say. And good riddance,' he added, looking directly at Darius Elder, 'to any spineless cravens that want to go with him.'

Coldly, Darius Elder met his gaze. 'If you stay, I'll stay.'

'Neither of you will stay!' snapped the Chief Factor. 'And you, Mr Newsome – think of your wife! If you don't go south she'll have to remain here along with you. I can't possibly send a lady alone among a party of seamen and boat's crews. Not at this time of year.'

'I'd have my maid with me,' Flora reminded him quickly.

'Even so.' McTavish frowned. 'No – it would never do. Your husband must take you.'

The explorer's eyes swept coldly over Flora.

'Mrs Newsome won't mind staying. She has a taste for adventure – haven't you, my dear?'

'I'd rather leave, all the same.'

'And I have no intention of leaving.' Newsome grew suddenly angry, and turned on McTavish. 'Do you take me for a coward, sir, to retreat at the first difficulty?'

'I take you for a fool, sir!' McTavish banged his fist on the desk. 'A fool who's determined to risk his own life and the lives of his men – not to mention causing great hardship to a decent woman.'

'You seem extraordinarily concerned for my wife, all of a sudden. Mrs Newsome can quite easily travel south in the spring, after I've left for the Polar Sea.'

'You'd keep her here all winter – among forty men, with her maid as the only other white woman for hundreds of miles?' The Chief Factor stared at Newsome incredulously. 'Take her south, man, while you still can!'

'I will *not* leave.' The explorer folded his arms.

'You forget, sir, that in the Governor's absence *I* say what happens in this part of the world.' The Chief Factor scowled across his desk. 'And my decision is that you leave York Factory as soon as boats can be made ready.'

'Turn me out of this fort,' warned Newsome, 'and be assured that your London Committee – and my friends in the Government – will hear how you prevented me from mapping the last stretch of the

Northwest Passage for the glory of His Majesty. Oh, I know why you want rid of me, you and your masters in London. It's well known that the Hudson's Bay Company would much prefer to keep these territories remote and unexplored, except by their fur traders.'

He rose to his feet. 'You seem to have forgotten, McTavish, that the search for a passage to the Pacific is written into the charter by which your company holds this land. You're bound to help me, and I intend to hold you to your instructions.' Newsome stared down his nose at the Chief Factor, his black brows twisted arrogantly, confident he'd made an unanswerable point.

'Well, Mr Elder?' demanded McTavish. 'Your bank is one of the company's largest shareholders, after all. What do you advise me to do?'

For a moment, Darius Elder regarded the explorer in silence from his post at the wall. Then his gaze shifted to Flora, a lonely, valiant figure among that crowd of angry men. After a few seconds, he seemed to make up his mind.

'It seems to me, Mr McTavish,' he concluded slowly, 'you'll have to chain this man hand and foot, if you want him out of here – and that could be awkward for their Honours in London, whatever the circumstances. So if he won't leave of his own free will, you may have to let him stay.'

'Hah!' exclaimed Newsome triumphantly.

'Though if Ralph Newsome stays here until spring,' Darius added in the same impassive tone, 'as I said – I'll stay too.'

The Chief Factor got to his feet, pushing his chair back so abruptly that its legs squealed on the wooden floor.

'See to the canoes,' he instructed his clerk, 'and take the name of every man who wishes to leave. Tell them', he added with another glower in Newsome's direction, 'that no one's bound to risk his life on this daft expedition, no matter what paper he's signed. I want every man-jack out of here who's prepared to go.'

His glance fell once more on Flora, and he shook his head. 'This is a sad day, Mrs Newsome, and that's the truth. I could wish your husband was more concerned for his wife's welfare – and I suspect you may wish it too before we're finished. But there it is. I've done my best for you, and I can do no more.'

The door banged behind him, and he was gone.

CHAPTER FIFTEEN

I

By evening, six of Newsome's expeditionaries had chosen to make the journey south, disheartened by the barrenness of the land and the sleet squalls which had begun to rattle on the roofs of the York Factory buildings. None of them were among the 'gentlemen' of the party, a fact which their commander recorded with satisfaction in his journal.

Dr Hildenhall had elected to stay, still set on his study of Eskimo heads. Dr Breen, too, decided to stay, but only after a moment of deep self-doubt following his visit to the Indians at the Plantation. He'd tried to question them in Hebrew, but was disappointed to find them bemused, if hospitable. Through an interpreter, he enquired about a great flood in times past, and was overjoyed when they nodded and agreed that yes, there had been a fearful flood – only a year earlier, at the Red River Settlement, when men had paddled from house to house in canoes, and one of the white traders' forts had been swept away.

Despairing, the doctor stared from one brown face to the next, searching for the features of the Israelites carried off by Sargon's Assyrians two and a half thousand years earlier. What he saw were the work-stained blue *capotes* of the men, the all-enveloping blankets of the women, and the babies wadded with moss in their cradle-boards. And all the time the Indians gazed impassively back at him, wondering what this strange, hesitant white man could want with them, and why he was regarding them with such comic dismay.

'But I haven't given up my theories,' Dr Breen assured Flora later. 'I still hope to identify the site of the Garden of Eden.'

'Then I wish you'd been with me this morning,' Flora told him, 'when I watched a young native girl walk down to the river with that strange long Indian stride, and it occurred to me that she could easily have been an Eve for your Eden. Her movements were so graceful, as if she'd never carried a burden or dragged a load. Though I suppose she'll age as quickly as the others in a year or two. Their women seem to lead such dreadfully hard lives.'

'An Indian Eve?' Dr Breen's eyes grew as round as the thick lenses of his spectacles, and Flora realized that while the doctor's Adam might have been made of the dust of the North American continent, his face had been as white as the doctor's own, and soap and water had been readily to hand. 'A *native* Eve . . .' murmured the doctor again, struggling with the concept. 'Oh, I don't think so. I don't think you'll find it anywhere in scripture.'

On the morning set for the departure of the boats for the Red River Settlement, the little doctor cornered Flora in the doorway of the Gentlemen's Guest-house, clutched her by the wrist, and cried, 'There are women here!'

'Of course there are.' Gently, Flora disengaged his grip. 'The Cree Indian women from the Plantation manage the laundry, and make moccasins and snowshoes for the men at the fort.'

'No, no—' Dr Breen shook his head, while his dumpy body heaved with the effort of struggling for breath. 'Besides those! I've just learned that the Governor and the Chief Factor keep women of their own here – and most of the other officers besides. Not Indian women, but *half-breeds*—'

His eyes bulged with the enormity of his discovery.

'They're the daughters of Company employees and native females. Oh, they call themselves "Mrs Simpson" and "Mrs McTavish", but it's only for custom's sake. They are concubines, Mrs Newsome, nothing more! These men keep harems as shamelessly as any Turk!'

'Are you sure of all this, Dr Breen? I must confess, I haven't set eyes on any of these ladies.'

'Nor will you, I trust.' He leaned closer to Flora, the better to breathe the damning words in her ear. 'I'm told that when they tire of these paramours, they simply pass the women on to one of their employees, together with any children the wretched creatures may have borne.'

He fished out his watch and consulted it. 'They tell me I'll find McTavish in his office at nine, and it's almost nine now. I really cannot, in all conscience, let such wrong-doing pass without protest.' And little Dr Breen drew himself up like a miniature avenging angel, wedged his spectacles more firmly on his nose, and stalked off to confront the Chief Factor with his discovery.

Less than an hour later Flora saw the doctor standing miserably on the landing-stage, his portmanteau at his feet, preparing to board one of the waiting boats. Unlike Ralph Newsome, Dr Breen had no influential backers in London, and the Chief Factor had turned him out to search for his Eden among the respectable settlers of Red River.

2

Wait! Take me with you! Take me back to a place I know, to a wilderness of soot-blackened brick, to stinking streets and scented pastrycooks' shops, to uproar and gaslight, and the leather smell of the booksellers' in Paternoster Row . . .

From the landing-stage, Flora followed the procession of boats with her eyes until the last craft had dwindled to a speck among the shallows and sandbars of the river. The spruce-laden wind whirled her silent prayer far out over the nothingness of sedge and willow; and with a sigh, she turned back up the long walkway which ran like an arrow-flight to the heart of York Factory.

By the next day, Newsome, still smarting from his run-in with the Chief Factor, had set up a rival court in the Gentlemen's Guest-house, where his silver tableware was unpacked and his own mess set up in the hall. Like some visiting emperor, he strode round the fort on periodic tours of inspection, casting an eye over the blacksmith's forge or the boatbuilder's yard, and throwing a word of approval to the tradesmen with lofty condescension.

It became impossible to remain on good terms with both sides at once. As far as Ralph Newsome was concerned, McTavish and the other officers of the fort had revealed themselves as enemies, secretly working to frustrate the Great Discovery. Dr Hildenhall, after his *faux pas* over the bump of self-esteem, was deemed to be Newsome's, along with the other gentlemen explorers. Darius Elder . . . was seldom to be seen. While apparently still lodging in the guest-house with the others, he roamed York Factory and its neighbourhood on affairs of his own, turning up unexpectedly among the clerks in Bachelors' Hall, or down in the oil-store, or leaning on the wall of the cooper's shop, listening to the cooper's gossip and watching truss hoops being hammered over the hot, wet staves in a clamorous cloud of steam.

As for Flora, even John McTavish, though he treated her with his customary gallantry whenever they met, clearly assumed her loyalties must lie in the rival camp, and restricted his conversation to gloomy observations on the weather.

For a couple of weeks at the beginning of October, the skies remained clear enough to reveal a bleak beauty, even in that comfortless spot. Overnight, the first frosts reddened the sedges, and one morning Flora woke to a landscape as splendid as an oriental carpet, rich in crimson and indigo, and black and ochre-yellow where lichens patterned the blue-grey boulders.

But winter was approaching; and winter in those latitudes, Flora had learned, was an imprisonment, a combined siege by landscape and weather. She had no fear of physical confinement – she'd endured far worse in Russell Square – but she was afraid of the gathering spectre of loneliness. To Ralph Newsome she was of no more significance than a barometer-case stamped with his initials; the 'gentlemen' followed his lead, and though an occasional fresh-faced junior clerk stopped by to show her a carving he'd made or a model built of fish-bones, Flora knew it was only because she was a white female creature, and they remembered mothers and sisters at home.

Reason told her to welcome the isolation, to use the solitude to nourish her self-sufficiency; but the few seconds of disastrous weakness which had come with the giant wave had shaken her resolve, and made her doubt whether she could survive the winter without at least a little human companionship.

Dr Breen had revealed there were other women in York Factory – women who might speak English and provide some fellowship during the long months of winter. For some time Flora waited, hoping that Mrs Simpson or Mrs McTavish might call on her out of sisterly concern, even if their menfolk had fallen out. But two weeks passed and nothing happened, though Polly Marks, Flora's maid, seemed to encounter the women almost every day.

'The officers' ladies? Sure – I see them when I go to the laundry, or out to fetch water. Some of them have a little English, though mostly they rattle away in some jabber of their own.' Gripping the edge of one of Flora's sheets between her teeth, Polly stretched out to fold it, and for a moment there was silence.

'I must say,' she confided at last, 'they're very curious about *you*, the York Factory ladies. They're always pestering me to know what you eat, and whether you take your food up on your knife, and what you wear under your gowns. So I had to show them, didn't I? And your nightgowns too, and the pins for putting up your hair.'

'I hope they traded something about themselves in exchange for all of that,' said Flora enviously.

'Oh, bless you, yes. For a start, I can tell you the Governor's wife – inasmuch as they call her "Mrs Simpson" here – is the Sloopmaster's sister.' To Flora's irritation, Polly fastened her strong little teeth on to a second sheet, breaking off her tale. At last she went on, 'Their father was an English sea-captain and their mother a native woman, and they seem as much a part of the Company as that flagpole yonder.'

'And Mrs McTavish?' Flora prompted again.

'Nancy McKenzie – the daughter of an old Hudson's Bay man. They say most of the older men stick with one woman through thick and thin, but the Governor, being new to the country, thinks it's a fine chance to run several at a time.' Polly wrinkled her nose in disapproval, and patted her piled sheets into a respectable cube.

'It seems to me, it's all very well to say *needs must* when there's no clergyman for a thousand miles, but there ought to be decency, even in the jungle. You'd think the Governor ought to set the poor Indian folks a good example, instead of taking advantage of their innocence.'

Polly shook her muslin cap in disapproval, then took a step closer to Flora and lowered her voice in awe.

'They do say the Indians here are so benighted they trade their women to and fro like so many cattle.'

'Why shouldn't they, since we do it in England?' retorted Flora angrily, thinking of Sophie. '"Money marries money",' she recited. 'How else does an heiress buy herself a husband? Yet I suppose Dr Breen would think it a good Christian union, provided the contract was sealed by a priest and a ring.'

Day by day, as the weather worsened, Flora found her world narrowing down even more to the two boggy quadrangles inside the York Factory palisade. In the creeks, boats were being hauled up out of reach of the spring surge of ice; buildings were made tight against the cold, and a final supply of geese salted down for the winter cooking-pots.

Confined indoors by snowfalls and hailstorms, Flora read every book she could lay her hands on, from the doctor's volumes on public health to *Rules For Improvement in Conversation* borrowed from one of the clerks. Several times when the weather was clear, she thought of taking matters into her own hands and going to seek out the invisible Mrs McTavish for herself. Nancy McKenzie, as Polly had described her, sounded the most approachable of the fort's ladies; yet somehow Flora's courage always failed her before the resolutely closed door of the Chief Factor's quarters, and her mission became an aimless promenade along the raised wooden platforms between the buildings of the fort.

Then one day, wrapped to her ears in shawls and coats, Flora was wandering between McTavish's house and the tinsmith's workshop when she saw a female figure approaching on the planks of the walkway, too late to avoid a meeting.

The woman was of middle height and strongly made, from her broad-boned face to the wide feet which carried her firmly on her way. Her step seemed neither the tripping pace of a European woman, nor the long, springy native stride; and Flora could hardly resist staring as the stranger drew closer, revealing eyes and hair of profound blackness against a skin of warm Mediterranean olive. Her plain woollen gown was hung about with necklaces and half-covered by a blanket such as the Indian women wore, but she bore her head like a queen in her own dominions, and carried her long clay pipe in the crook of her arm like a sceptre of office.

As the distance between them diminished the woman stared unblinkingly into Flora's eyes. For a moment she slowed her pace as if to speak, but instead let her gaze travel slowly from the top of Flora's head to the toes of her boots. Then, with a faint sound which might have meant either approval or contempt, she swept on her way, her skirts brushing Flora's on the narrow platform and her quill-embroidered moccasins padding over the boards as she went.

There was no mistaking her message. While Mrs Newsome might wish to introduce herself to Nancy McKenzie, Nancy McKenzie had no wish to make Mrs Newsome's acquaintance; and in York Factory Flora was on alien ground.

'All I wanted was someone to talk to,' she mourned later, coming across Darius Elder down by the landing-stage, watching a crow make a meal of a fish cast up on a frozen sandbar. 'I didn't mean her any harm. I'm not Dr Breen – I don't care who she is, or what she does.'

'It isn't what you mean that matters.' Darius Elder continued to watch the crow. 'It's what you *are* that's important to Nancy McKenzie. A white woman. A threat.'

'But a woman, all the same – just as she is. If you flayed us both, who could tell which of us was which?' she added, recalling the automaton-maker's words.

'Hildenhall would find an extra bump or two, I dare say. And Dr

Breen would do his best to see a difference, since it's so important to him.'

'But if I don't care, why should Nancy McKenzie mind so much?'

'Because your future doesn't depend on a minor difference in pigmentation,' he said sharply. 'Hers does.'

He leaned back on one elbow, stretching out his long legs on the planks of the wharf as if this act of relaxation eased an old and time-hallowed ache. When he spoke again, the sharpness had dissolved from his voice.

'I saw the start of all this in India, when I worked for the East India Company.' The fingers of one hand traced a line on the weathered boards, and uneasily, Flora remembered the story Lydia had told her of the imprisoned princess.

'As soon as the officers began to bring their wives out from England,' Darius continued, 'the native women became natives first and women a poor second.' He glanced towards Flora. 'Haven't you noticed the way the clerks stare out of the counting-house windows as you pass? In an outpost like this, you're every man's domestic angel – his dream of home – Dr Breen's white Eve. The mixed-blood women like Nancy McKenzie and her friends are afraid that one day their menfolk will throw them over for white angels of their own. They'll copy your manners quickly enough, but they won't make a friend of you.'

Flora flung up her hands in frustration.

'Why is it that wherever we go, we seem to take the worst of ourselves with us? I came here, hoping for so much – for innocence, for peace . . . And yet I can't see anything but the narrow, crushing footprints of bigots and hypocrites . . . Why must we do it? Why must we spoil whatever we find?'

Darius swivelled on his elbow to examine her with an expression of guarded curiosity.

'Do you care so much?'

'Of course I care!' Her voice rang bitterly on the breeze. 'All this talk of discovery and exploration – it's no more than common rape.'

'Well, now . . .' His eyes searched her face minutely. 'I didn't expect that from the wife of Ralph Newsome.'

Flora stood up at once, dismayingly aware of having given away more than she'd intended. He tilted his head to look up at her – speculatively, as if whatever she'd just revealed required careful consideration – and his silence agitated her further.

'I'm sorry, Darius. As you say, as Ralph Newsome's wife I ought to keep such thoughts to myself.'

'That isn't what I said.'

'It's true, all the same. Domestic angels must learn to know their place. Good day to you, brother-in-law – I'll leave you to your crows.'

Without giving him a chance to respond, Flora hurried back to the safety of the fort.

3

October became November; the snow showers increased, the thermometer plunged well below freezing-point, and winter on the shores of Hudson Bay became an ordeal to be endured. Every evening, Flora went to sleep in the stifling, tallow-smelling, stove-heated guesthouse, and every morning she woke to a double window-pane frosted with her night-time breath, and to the realization that another day stretched ahead in lonely emptiness.

She had less to occupy her than any of the expeditionaries, though they did little more than sit by the stove, picking over old scandals and grievances. The nothingness beyond the palisade lay over the fort itself like a blanket of monotony, made maddening by the raw polar winds that moaned round the wooden buildings.

The gentlemen explorers in the guest-house had long since overhauled all of their equipment which had survived the wreck, and had turned to less scientific diversions. Evenings were given over to card-playing and a determined assault on the expedition's large supply of brandy. Before long, drink and boredom reminded the 'gentlemen' of the existence of Indian women near the fort, and soon the low, liquid sound of Cree voices could be heard throughout the building as the expeditionaries pursued their researches.

'You're paying them in brandy!' Flora protested. 'It's contemptible! You know John McTavish has forbidden it.'

'McTavish can forbid what he likes,' snorted Newsome. 'I'm not one of his cringing servants, to be told what I can or can't do. Besides – the Chief Factor and his officers have made sure their own comforts are looked after. Why should the rest of us go without?'

He stretched and yawned, and then turned to survey Flora with contempt. 'And when it comes to the point, it's none of your business.

You told me I could take whatever women I pleased, provided I left my over-fastitious wife alone.'

Before Flora could escape he reached out, grasped her left breast through the woollen material of her dress, and gave it a painful squeeze.

'In future, madam, keep your prudish nose out of matters that don't concern you.' He leaned back and yawned again, lazily content. 'In fact, why don't you keep out of my sight altogether?'

4

From the very first, Flora had been lonely: now the men of the fort had conspired to deny her even a shred of humanity. Flora was a curiosity in their midst – an oddity – offensive to the mixed-blood women, an object of veneration to the clerks, and a priggish inconvenience to her husband and his fellow 'gentlemen'. As a woman she'd ceased to exist. Even Polly Marks had plunged into a heady romance with the cooper, and Flora would happily have changed places with her for the chance of a single affectionate word.

Yet to allow herself such feelings was to invite pain, and she'd vowed never to risk that again. In order to survive Ralph Newsome, she'd made herself her own prisoner; and her shameful weakness after the passing of the giant wave had shown her the prisoner could never again be trusted with liberty.

But as one empty day succeeded another, Flora began to feel as if she was staring into the abyss of madness. Then, one windless afternoon, returning to the guest-house from one of her brief outings along the frozen walkways, she was startled by a movement in the shadows by the door; two figures sprang apart and emerged sheepishly from the gloom – Polly Marks and her cooper, pulling at caps and smoothing dishevelled hair to cover their embarrassment. Polly's face was flushed, and her eyes sparkled; her lips hung a little apart, rosy and swollen from recent kisses, curved into a smile by the memory of her lover's endearments.

Flora could hardly bear to look: if she walked out into the snowy wilderness one unbearable day, who would notice? Who would care? In desperation, she turned to the one person in York Factory in whose eyes she might recognize her own existence.

She found him in the trading-room, diagonally across the rear quadrangle from the back of the guest-house and known in Hudson Bay slang as the 'Indian shop', where knives and kettles and blankets and coils of tobacco were exchanged for pelts through a window in an outer wall. The wood round the handle was scarred by years of locking and unlocking, but at that moment the shop was open, and heated to furnace-point while the Chief Trader and a pair of his clerks took an inventory for their Honours far away in London.

Next to the counter stood giant iron scales for weighing out sugar or tobacco in quantity; beyond them, on the point of leaving with a knife he'd just bought, stood Darius Elder.

'Ah . . . Flora.' He seemed about to move past her when she reached out to touch him lightly on the arm.

'Will you wait while I buy a few yards of flannel, and walk back with me to the guest-house?'

He glanced down at the hand which still rested on his arm, and then his eyes rose curiously to her face.

'If you wish.'

'It should only take a moment.'

He waited in silence until the transaction was complete, then held open the door for her.

'You're limping.' Outside, using the narrowness of the walkway as an excuse, she pressed as close to him as she dared, the skirt of her gown, full over her hips, continually brushing his thigh. 'Whatever happened to your leg?'

'I twisted my ankle, shooting partridge down at Point of Marsh. But it's mending.'

'Perhaps I should poultice it for you.'

He glanced at her quickly, frowning. 'Thank you, but that isn't necessary.'

'I've nothing else to do.'

This time she lifted her face to his, allowed her eyes to linger in his blue ones a moment too long, and gently collided with him as they walked.

'If you've nothing to do, I suggest you find something to read.' He fixed his gaze on the guest-house looming ahead, and Flora's heart beat with wild mischief. Brother-in-law – *brother*, as Sophie had made him – Flora was safe from him, as physically forbidden as one of his own sisters, yet he was not secure from her. That stern determination to avoid her gaze had told her all she needed to know, and she

250

hoarded its memory like the most precious words of love. He wanted her – she was alive: alive, but safe from him.

At the guest-house door he turned to leave, but Flora dawdled, leaning against the doorpost, her spine arched and her hands cradling the parcel of flannel behind her back.

She saw him frown and hesitate. 'Is something the matter?'

'No . . . Nothing.' She arched her back still further, tilting her hips towards him, springy and inviting where they swelled below her neat waist.

'If you're sure . . .'

'I'm certain.' She let her lips fall open a little.

'Well, then, I'll leave you.'

He started to turn away again: and in that instant a devil blew out of the nothingness to possess Flora's heart, a desperate, malicious, lonely devil, frantic for attention. As Darius twisted away from her, Flora stretched out to rake the hard edge of her boot quite deliberately across his swollen ankle. Heart thumping, she waited for him to cry out in pain.

He didn't make a sound. He simply gave her a hard stare, the tiny muscles round his eyes drawn into white arrows of agony. A moment later he'd limped on his way, without a word, along the wooden platform.

After that Flora's nights became a misery of sleeplessness. The hungry demons reawakened inside her refused to let her rest, and kept the lines of print dancing before her eyes if she tried to read. During the day, the wild little devil whispered in her ear, tempting her, goading her, throwing the object of her torment constantly before her eyes until her existence seemed to contain nothing else.

In the small hours of the morning, listening to the scurrying of female feet and the murmur of voices beyond the wooden walls of her room, Flora assured herself that the place itself was to blame – an alien presence in a resentful land where walls of snow and ice shut in the human soul to brood on its own longings. She was as much at the mercy of its mood as the most junior apprentice.

Driven to mischief, one evening she lay in wait on the upper floor of the guest-house, a loose wrapper thrown over the light ribboned corset which thrust up her breasts into soft white spheres. At last she heard Darius Elder come upstairs, the slight unevenness of his gait ringing like a tocsin in her ears. She saw surprise and then desire in his face, before his eyes rose slowly, wintry as sleet, to challenge hers.

For a moment Flora felt the old fear rise in her throat; then he turned away to his own room, leaving her with a crazy impulse to run after him, calling *You want me – admit it – tell me so and give me peace . . .*

'What has he said to you? Darius Elder—' Newsome put his arm across the bottom of the staircase after breakfast the next morning, blocking Flora's path. 'He's said something, hasn't he? He's been asking questions, trying to get information out of you.'

'He's said nothing at all,' Flora replied with perfect truthfulness.

'Don't lie to me! I saw the two of you exchanging glances across the table.'

'You're imagining things, Ralph. I've no interest in anything Darius may have to say.' This time she avoided Newsome's eye, conscious of lying. 'Besides – what information could he want from me?'

'He's spying – I told you.' Agitation or the heat of the stove had produced a fine glaze on Newsome's forehead. 'He suspects I got money from Felix under false pretences.'

'And did you?'

Newsome blinked, several times, rapidly. 'Not entirely.'

'So he's quite right to be suspicious.'

'Keep your voice down!' Newsome peered up the wooden staircase, then lowered his voice to an urgent mutter. 'If he asks you if you know anything about gold found near the Polar Sea, you're to say *yes*, do you hear me? Tell him McTavish has often talked about it.'

'But is there any gold?'

'There are plenty of rumours. Old Indian tales from the Coppermine River area, talking about yellow metal in the rocks nearby.'

'No more than rumours?'

'Oh, I admit I dressed it up a little for Felix's benefit. How else could I make him give me the money I needed?' Newsome shrugged, unabashed. 'Darius was against it from the start, but fortunately he was out-voted by the other directors. Now he's come here to spy on me, to destroy my reputation if he can.' Leaning on the hand-rail, Newsome gnawed at the knuckle of his thumb. 'He's always been against me – just like the others. McTavish hates me, and he's turned his officers against me too. Oh, I've seen Hargrave and Miles watching me, when I go out to check our stores – don't worry. I know their little game.'

A new thought struck him. 'And I warn you, my lady – take care what you do. You may be my wife in name alone, but by God, you'll remember where your loyalties lie, or I'll make you remember. Betray me to that spy Darius Elder, and you'll regret it.'

To brighten the dark days between Christmas and New Year, the clerks were allowed to hold dances in their quarters, to which all the mixed-blood women of the fort were invited, and a number of Indian matrons from the Plantation. The 'gentlemen' might attend if they wished, but it was made tactfully clear to Flora that by reason of her 'position' her presence would put a damper on the fun.

From her window in the guest-house she listened wistfully to the scraping of fiddles and tried to imagine the cheerful company gossiping, drinking, nursing their babies and capering the night away between the smoke-yellowed walls of Bachelor's Hall. In London it might have passed for a rout in the Coal Hole, but by its own standards it was a decorous entertainment – so that when a quarrel broke out between an apprentice clerk and a drunken explorer over a pretty Cree girl, the Chief Factor at last decided enough was enough.

At first light next morning, Ralph Newsome was informed that his entire party were to move out beyond the fort's palisade to a large building at nearby Sloop Creek which had formerly been used as a boat store. Carpenters had already been dispatched to divide up the new quarters and to install the iron stoves which would make it endurable; from now on the expeditionaries were to keep contact with the fort to a minimum.

Dr Hildenhall and Mr Elder had not been among the authors of the trouble; they could, if they wished, remain in the guest-house. As for Mrs Newsome—

'She'll come with me.' Newsome gripped Flora possessively by the elbow. 'Her place is with her husband, naturally.'

Darius Elder had been leaning on the wall of the Chief Factor's office, his eyes half-closed as if the conversation wearied him. When he spoke, Newsome wheeled round in surprise.

'You can hardly expect a lady to live in that cabin at the creek.'

Newsome's grip tightened on Flora's arm.

'I warn you, Elder – keep your nose out of my affairs, or I'll teach you some manners myself.'

'Mr Elder's right,' put in McTavish quickly. 'Sloop Creek's no place for a lady. And certainly not with that rabble you've brought with you. I wonder she isn't disgusted by the whole jing-bang of them. Their behaviour would shame a farmyard.'

Newsome let go of Flora, and leaned ominously on the Chief Factor's desk.

'Have a care, McTavish! I won't be told my business by a bog-Scotch docket-scribbler, even if he has the whole Hudson's Bay Company to back him!'

'Mr Newsome!' McTavish was on his feet at once, his greying hair and whiskers standing out as if an electric charge had galvanized them. 'I'll thank you to get out of my office before I have you thrown out.'

'You'll apologize for that, Newsome.' Darius Elder was no longer leaning on the wall, but standing free of it, his feet a little apart, as if balancing himself for some physical assault.

'Gentlemen . . .' Flora inserted herself between her husband and the furious Chief Factor. 'Since I seem to be the cause of this argument—' It was a lie, but it offered a means of saving face. 'Since I'm the cause of the argument, may I tell you now that I'm quite prepared to move out to Sloop Creek whenever our quarters are ready.'

She risked a glance at Darius Elder's face. The two white spots she remembered of old were blazing on his cheekbones.

'I'm sure if I survived the *Nebula*, I'll find the house at the creek quite adequate.'

As she left the office, for an instant she found herself next to Darius in the doorway.

'Flora – why, in heaven's name—'

'It's better that I go with him. Believe me . . . it's better for all of us.'

CHAPTER SIXTEEN

I

Their new home at Sloop Creek was a prison in all but name, and Polly Marks complained loud and long at being parted from her cooper and thrown into such spartan surroundings. Ralph Newsome, deprived for months now of the illusion of motion which had assuaged his restlessness, soon became savage in confinement, and his dangerous mood infected the men sharing his exile. Bored to death and free from the constraints of the fort, the 'gentlemen explorers' spent their days in drinking and daredevil target-shooting by the creek, in gambling, and in any other mischief tedium could invent. Taking their cue from their leader, they made no concession to Flora's presence in the house, and ended each day in such a riot that she had to stuff pieces of cotton in her ears to sleep at all.

Beyond the long walls of the building the cold was now intense enough to make the expedition's mercury thermometer useless, but the wind had died away entirely, leaving a frozen calm of amazing stillness. Snow covered the landscape quite deeply, and without the boarded walkways of the fort it was impossible to go far, unless on snowshoes. It was as much as Flora could do to slither to the edge of the ice-bound creek, wrapped in a heavy cloak, a merino gown lined with Bath coating from the company store, thick woollen drawers, mittens, and moccasins lined with three pairs of flannel socks over her stockings.

'Where have you been?' Scowling, Newsome watched her one day as she returned from her improvised outing.

'I've been down to the creek.'

'Why?'

'*Why?* To get some air, that's why. The house is so stifling, I can hardly breathe.'

Newsome regarded her narrowly. 'I don't trust you, Flora. You've changed in the last few weeks. Before we left the fort, I'd begun to wonder if you hadn't taken up with one of the clerks. Or someone closer to home,' he added significantly.

'What nonsense!' Flora forced herself to meet his stare. 'Who do you imagine would look at me, tied up like a bag of laundry?' She held her arms clear of her well-padded sides.

'All the same – at least down here I can keep a watch on you, and make sure you aren't tempted to carry tales to the others.' He pointed across the snowy landscape towards the palisade of the fort. 'McTavish is determined to protect his trade with the Indians, and I'm pretty sure he's turned Hildenhall against me. But these fellows here – they'll stick with me. And you'll stick with me, until I say you can go.'

'You're insane!' whispered Flora. 'You're obsessed by this wretched sea-route.'

At once, he gripped her arms so tightly that she gasped in pain, and glared down into her face, furious at such profanity.

'Do you think you can measure a Newsome by the standards of the McTavishes of this world?' He gave her a shake. 'Well – do you? Because, I warn you, anyone who's not *for* me is against me. Remember that, my dear, righteous, stupid wife.'

She was close enough now to smell the brandy on his breath, and didn't dare to provoke him further. Satisfied, he released her to seek the sanctuary of her wooden-walled cell.

In a strange, self-lacerating way, Flora had almost welcomed her imprisonment by the creek, and little by little, left alone with her thoughts, she felt her sanity begin to return. In the isolation of her room she could convince herself that she needed no one, and could trust no one – and that her shameless behaviour to Darius Elder had been solely due to the isolation of the place; she would never give in to such madness again. At least at Sloop Creek she was free of all temptation: Darius never came near the house, no doubt relieved to be clear of his irrational sister-in-law.

In any case, she'd soon be gone from Hudson's Bay, bound for London and whatever the future might hold – neither Ralph Newsome, if fate was kind, nor Darius Elder . . .

2

It was on the creek bank that Flora met Darius again, one morning in March when a lull in the snow showers had left the landscape unexpectedly clear and bright. He was carrying a gun over his shoulder and a bundle of lifeless fur at his belt, but he wasn't alone. At his side walked a small, wiry figure with faintly bowed legs, wearing a weather-worn blue coat pulled in at the waist by a bright scarlet sash, and a blue woollen hat ornamented by a jaunty tuft of feathers.

'Good day to you, Crébiche. You look a great deal better than the last time I saw you.'

The mixed-blood *voyageur* came from the Red River Settlement, but he'd been forced to winter at York Factory after falling ill with influenza brought in on the company's ship.

'Back from the dead!' Crébiche crossed his arms over his chest with an expression of the most ridiculous solemnity, wagging the plumes in his hat like the feelers of the crustacean which had given him his name.

How different York Factory must be, Flora reflected, in the height of its brief summer, when the river was laced with the craft of the inland canoe brigades delivering their packs of furs and loading up with trade goods! Instead of wintry silence, the air would be thick with the mixture of French, English and Indian tongues that passed for the patois of Rupert's Land; and for a few short weeks there would be colour, and laughter, and activity. Then all too soon the company ship would sail for England and the canoes would melt away into the vast hinterland, leaving the fort to its long winter sleep.

Poor Crébiche hadn't been expected to see the spring, left to die far from home, consigned to the care of the post's lugubrious and long-nosed doctor. Only sheer perversity and the stringy toughness of a five-year-old steer, said the doctor, had contrived to carry him through.

'When will you go home, Crébiche?'

'Soon as I can. Soon as the ice breaks on the rivers.' He pointed to a small white bird with a grey-brown back hopping nearby. 'Snowbird thinks it won't be too long. Maskisees from the Indian village wants to go south with me – and he says it won't be so long now.' Crébiche grinned, a sudden explosion of white teeth against the deep tan of his skin. 'Maybe you want to come too? I don't think you take up very much room in the canoe.'

Flora smiled, and let a small sigh escape from her; too late, she realized that Darius Elder had heard the tiny, plaintive sound. Lowering the butt of his gun to the hard-packed snow, he glanced grimly towards the building from which she'd come.

'Leave this rats' nest, Flora, and come back to the fort until spring. Tell Newsome this is no fit place for a woman like you.'

Flora shook her head. 'He'd never let me go. As it is, he'll be furious if he sees us talking together. He thinks . . .' She stopped suddenly, biting her lip.

'Thinks what?'

'Nothing. It doesn't matter.' She avoided his eye. 'Ralph doesn't seem to know what's real and what's fantasy any more.'

He was watching her intently. 'I'm not sure I can always tell the difference myself.'

For several seconds Flora studied the hem of her dress, convinced Crébiche must think her the most awful fool.

'I don't believe it's safe for you here,' Darius said at last.

Flora looked up, and managed a valiant smile. 'Thank you for caring, but it isn't as bad as you think.'

He pitied her: as she stumbled back to the sturdy shed which served as her prison, she almost laughed aloud at the irony of her situation. Goodness only knew what she must look like – nothing remotely seductive, at any rate, after months in that wilderness. A glimpse in her tiny hand-mirror had already revealed slaty shadows under her eyes and the wings of her cheekbones, and skin of almost churchyard transparency covering the veins of her hand when she raised it to brush away what she'd taken for a smudge of dirt.

A few days later Darius Elder returned alone.

'You shouldn't have come here,' she told him. 'Ralph has me watched whenever I go out.'

'I didn't intend to come, but . . . I was concerned about you.'

'If we walk up the creek a little, we'll be hidden behind the bank.'

It was strange how instantly those few words created a sense of conspiracy, drawing them together as the sound of her mother's footsteps had once done in the house in Montagu Square.

'Tell Newsome you're sick,' Darius suggested. 'Tell him the doctor says you must stay in the fort for the sake of your health. You look frail enough, goodness knows.'

'He'd never believe me. It would only cause trouble, and winter's so nearly over. Only a few more weeks and I can go home, like Crébiche.'

'Your husband's already caused enough trouble for a regiment. I suppose you know McTavish's clerks have been sneaking down here at night to drink and play hazard? Some of them have gambled away a year's wages, in spite of being threatened with dismissal if they were caught. McTavish is breathing fire. He'd put the whole expedition in irons if he thought he'd get away with it.'

'If the clerks are suffering, then I'm sorry.' Flora stared sadly out over the snowy hollow of the frozen creek. 'I'll try to make Ralph stop them from coming here.'

'Young Rigby, the apprentice, was stabbed in the arm a couple of days ago.'

'I heard about that – poor child. He's only fifteen, you know, and they filled him with brandy to see what he'd do. He was sick, and they laughed – and he pulled out a knife.' Flora shook her head. 'It was only a penknife, a silly little thing.'

'He'll recover, I dare say. But that's what I mean when I say it's dangerous here.' He caught Flora by the arm, and turned her to face him. 'Dangerous for you, too.'

'Please don't.' Firmly, Flora pulled her arm from his grasp. 'I promise you, it's much better if I stay where I am. Perhaps I can stop things from getting out of hand altogether here.' She set off carefully along the creek, holding up her heavy skirts, stepping where the snow was packed hardest, and after a moment she heard him follow.

'You mustn't come here again.' She'd halted to catch her breath in the shelter of some snow-bound willows, the brush of her cloak drawing a little avalanche from the overloaded branches. 'You're right - it's dangerous for us to meet.'

He considered this in silence for a moment. 'But, then, it always was.'

That night, as she lay in bed, Flora renewed her vow: she'd let nothing touch her again – nothing that might disturb her hard-won peace of mind. Let Polly Marks build pretty fantasies around her cooper; Flora had learned the truth in a hard school, and would never suffer again. Darius Elder could come to the creek if he liked, but he certainly wouldn't find Flora waiting for him.

Two days later Darius did come back to the creek – and, by a strange chance, Flora was there, and having met him felt obliged to stay and talk for a while out of sheer politeness. A couple of days after that, Darius came once more, and again shortly afterwards, until, gradually, as the remaining weeks of winter dragged by, Flora found herself cherishing his visits, brief and hazardous though they were. Almost always they met at the creek-side and walked a little, or if a watery sun had driven the worst of the chill from the air, rested for a while on a stack of wood left by the boatbuilders against the return of spring.

There was no harm in talk, no harm at all – and there was precious little even of that. It seemed enough for them both to be in one another's company, wrapped in a silence thick with unspoken thoughts.

There was nothing for any passer-by to see, though if Newsome and his men had risen from their beds by noon, it was usually only to slump for the rest of the day round the iron stove, filling the house with tobacco smoke and boasting about their previous night's adventures.

Yet recently Flora had become aware of a new note in the voices which rumbled round the black iron hearth. She heard the words 'river' and 'thaw', and guessed that the meltwater flood from higher streams was rupturing the ice beyond the fort, piling up its frozen debris in great slabs and shattered columns down-river. In the house at Sloop Creek it seemed that the march to the Polar Sea was at last being planned in some detail.

'Crébiche says the ice at the river-mouth will give way at any moment.' Darius Elder pointed towards the broad expanse of the Hayes, swollen almost to the top of its banks under its load of broken ice. There was still snow on the ground, but there were blackbirds among the willows now, and as soon as the ice-dam had broken, allowing the flooded river to burst into the bay, the route to Red River would be clear for navigation.

'McTavish will send you away as soon as it's safe,' he reminded her. 'That's a blessing, at least.'

'And Ralph will be off to the Polar Sea.' Flora hesitated, the remaining hours of Darius's company suddenly precious to her. 'Do you still mean to go with him?'

Darius Elder shrugged. 'That's why I came here.'

'To spy on him? To see whether there really is gold in the north?'

'There isn't any gold. There never was.'

Flora turned to stare. 'You know that?'

'Felix may not be able to tell when a man like Newsome is lying, but I can. Newsome made up the story to raise money for his expedition, and Felix fell for it, as they say in these parts.' Darius Elder picked up a handful of snow, and threw it at a nearby clump of sedge. 'He's an unscrupulous rogue, your husband. How you ever imagined you loved him—'

'Love?' Flora gazed out grimly over the flooded creek. 'Love's nothing but an illusion, as my friend the automaton-maker used to say. Lust – desire – oh, certainly, or the race would die out. But that's a hard reality for the moralists to swallow, so for delicacy's sake we dress it up as something finer, and call it *love*.'

She flung back her head, exposing the whiteness of her throat.

'Oh, I used to believe in a magical, preordained, inescapable kind of love – until I learned better. And as you told me yourself—' She rolled her head until she could look at him. 'As you told me yourself, "affairs of the heart are hardly the way to decide the destiny of families". Isn't that what you said?'

'It sounds priggish enough for me to have said it.'

'But you were right.' Flora buried her chin in the collar of her coat. 'Do you know how the automaton-maker used to describe love between a man and woman? *Two monkeys coming together to make a third monkey*.' She laughed softly. 'All the rest is illusion and self-deception.'

'Not always.'

'You're a fine one to talk! You'd never have married Sophie if she hadn't been an heiress – you said so yourself, though I grant you, you never pretended to love her.'

'I should never have married Sophie,' he said softly.

Flora glanced up in surprise. 'You can say that?'

'I admit that I never loved Sophie. I married her precisely because . . . because I didn't love her. But that doesn't mean that I can't love at all, or that you can't—'

'There is no love. There's only lust and self-deceit. Nothing more.'

'You're wrong! You are the living, breathing proof that there's more.'

And before Flora could protest, he'd swung her into his arms and his lips were hard on hers, and inside the shapeless bundle of her clothes her body was singing like a harp-string, filled again with a sharp desire which split her to the core . . . for Darius Elder, her sister's husband.

'No!'

She pulled away from him, and, lifting her heavy skirts, began to run back along the creek bank, her boots sliding on the snow, the hem of her cloak falling under her feet and making her stumble.

That place was to blame – that prison of wind clinging to the edge of infinity, stripping away everything but the basest of instincts. Nothing was sacred, nothing inviolate in that harsh wilderness. In such a place bishops became monkeys, English ladies became whores, and men died with as little ceremony as a bulldog-fly squashed under the thumb.

Safe within the four wooden walls of her room, Flora waited for calm to return to her. Beyond the window, dusk was falling over a mottled landscape where snow still lay in deep drifts in the hollows, but where blackish boulders and tufts of willow had begun to wear untidy holes in the thinnest parts of the covering.

The wind had dropped, leaving a hollow silence broken only by the ringing of the bell which marked the end of York Factory's working day, and the answering howl of the kennelled sled-dogs. Winter was retreating – there was no doubt of it – and Flora felt her heart lift with relief.

Without any warning, the door of her room crashed open, and Newsome stood framed in the doorway, his face flushed the colour of port wine, and his dishevelled hair falling lankly over his brow.

'Whore!' he shouted at her, his voice thickened by a day's drinking. 'Trollop!' He slammed the door violently behind him, and set his back against it. 'Don't gape at me like that, as if you're as innocent as the day. You were seen.'

At last Flora found her voice; to her dismay, it emerged as a croak.

'Seen? Seen where?'

'Seen with *him*. Seen with your lover – kissing him, down by the creek.' Newsome crossed the room in two heavy, vengeful strides and gave Flora a vicious push which sent her sprawling across the bed, her left arm suddenly numb from the shoulder.

'You couldn't wait, could you? You couldn't wait until you were out of my sight to crawl into another man's bed.' He bent over Flora, and wound his fingers painfully into her hair, dragging her up into a sitting position. 'Or perhaps your sister was right,' he sneered, 'and you and Elder have been lovers from the start.'

'You must think I'm a fool—' Newsome shook her fiercely by the hair. 'You and those blockheads at the fort. Well, you're wrong. I know you're all conspiring behind my back – more than conspiring, in your case.' He shook Flora again, jarring her teeth. 'I should have guessed a little savage like you would go looking for a new master.'

Drawing back his free arm, he hit her – explosively, on the cheekbone, in a red-hot burst of fire which seemed to weld flesh and bone in searing pain. A soft warmth trickled down her cheek and

262

over her lips, and drops of bright crimson stained the bodice of her gown.

The sight of blood seemed to please him. For a moment he swayed over her, his lips slack with satisfaction. Then, wiping his knuckles on the bedcover, he turned away unsteadily to the door.

'I warned you not to betray me,' he told her thickly, 'but you didn't listen. You thought that damned paper of yours was your insurance. Well, it won't save you – and it won't save Darius Elder, when I settle with him in the morning. I'll teach him what happens to men who try to take what's mine.' And Newsome slouched out, slamming the door behind him.

3

For hours afterwards Flora lay on her bed, waiting for the clamour of the house to fade into the hush of drunken stupor. She'd staunched the blood and wiped the tear-stains from her face with water from the pitcher, but her head still throbbed with a dull, steady beat and her face was swollen and aching where Newsome's blow had landed. Yet, through it all, her mind clung to a single thought. She must warn Darius: she must escape from Sloop Creek and make her way to the fort.

At last, in the small hours of the morning the house finally grew silent. Cautiously, Flora opened the door of her cubbyhole a fraction and peered out; it was quite possible that one of the 'gentlemen' had fallen asleep by the stove where brandy had overwhelmed him.

Mercifully, the room was deserted – though Flora could hardly believe, as she made her way softly through it, that the whole house wasn't roused by the thunderous beating of her heart.

By moonlight the fort seemed a great way off across the snow, its palisade and huddled roofs a greyish smudge against the whiteness; in spite of the thaw, the drifts round Sloop Creek were still deep, and she realized that to reach the fort on foot was going to take as much strength as she possessed.

Thrust upright into the trodden snow by the doorway was a row of snowshoes, long, curved, canoe-shaped wooden frames criss-crossed with narrow strips of hide. As quickly as her chilled fingers would allow, Flora seized a pair and slipped the unfamiliar fastening over her boots, encouraged by their lightness. She soon discovered that walking in them wasn't so easy; time and time again she crossed the long points, pinning one under its fellow and tripping herself up. In the first few yards she fell several times, and each time, as she struggled to rise and realign her shoes, she stared back at the house, afraid that by chance someone might have noticed her dark shape moving against the brightness all around.

The frozen air sought out the wound on her cheek, pinching it to a thousand needle-points, but she struggled on determinedly, slipping the snowshoes from her feet whenever her boots could find a grip on the sparse grass. By good luck the night was clear and the snow in the deep drifts frosty and firm; as she lifted her feet it fell like dust through the net of the snowshoes instead of clogging them to a dead weight. Shuffling and plodding, she kept on towards the palisade of the fort, willing herself to keep her feet parallel and to avoid the scrubby willows in her path.

From somewhere in the distance she heard a great grinding and roaring, and guessed that the river-ice was moving at last. But the thought was gone as soon as it occurred to her, pushed aside in the relentless need to press on without pausing for rest. Every so often she peered up towards the fort to check her direction, but tried to ration her stops: the wide stretch of snow seemed to diminish so slowly, and her strength to ebb so fast.

It was the watchman at the gate who half-carried, half-dragged her into the fort, bawling for assistance. Exhausted, she was hardly aware of being undressed and helped into a bed where her hands and feet were rubbed to warmth and hot bricks wrapped in towels placed round her; a female face – the elusive Mrs McTavish, she suspected – hovered over her for a while, and a low, blessed voice urged her to drink the scalding broth whose steam filled her nostrils.

'Tell him . . .' she murmured through swollen lips. 'Tell Darius Elder . . .'

'Hush now, and sleep.'

'But he's coming . . .'

'Hush . . .'

And though she struggled against it, sleep claimed her at last, her warning unheeded on her lips.

Flora woke early next morning, and stared for several seconds at the stained white ceiling overhead before remembering she was back in the guest-house at the fort. She turned her head – and at once the pain of her scarred cheek brought back vivid memories of the previous evening and her flight through the snow. Goodness only knew what the Chief Factor had been told . . . or Darius Elder, for that matter.

Darius. She must find him at once.

Stiffly, she climbed out of bed, and began to struggle into the clothes which had been laid across a chair the night before. Fumbling in her haste, Flora fastened the final buttons, threw a shawl round her shoulders, and left the room to set off on her search.

A knock at Darius's door produced no answer, so Flora opened it and looked inside. Nothing but impersonal neatness greeted her eye – yet his gun was missing, and Flora guessed he'd gone out early to shoot.

There was no one else in the guest-house. Perhaps Dr Hildenhall took his breakfast with the post's officers these days. Wondering what to do for the best, she went out into the brightness of the morning, lingering on the walkway for a moment to gaze round at the reassuring, homely faces of the fort's buildings and the giant red ensign challenging the breeze overhead.

A sudden commotion at the gate attracted her attention: a wood detail returning from one of the saw-camps, perhaps. Then a familiar figure emerged at the head of the little group advancing along the central platform, and Flora was unable to stifle a gasp of dismay. In a moment, Ralph Newsome had spotted her across the quadrangle and pointed her out to the others. His pace quickened to a run with his men at his heels, until the whole group was clattering towards her along the wooden walkway.

Flora's first instinct was to bolt back into the guest-house and haul a heavy table against the door. But to do so would be to admit guilt of some kind, and she'd done nothing wrong. Besides, she was safe in the fort. If she could only find McTavish or the Chief Trader and put herself under his protection, she couldn't believe even Ralph Newsome would be allowed to drag his wife away by main force.

Before Newsome and his men could reach her, she ducked round the corner of the guest-house and hurried towards the rear quadrangle where the tradesmen had their workshops and the Chief Factor had his own lodging. The door of the trading room was open, and she walked quickly towards it, hearing her husband's voice call unpleasantly behind her.

'So you ran off to the fort, did you? All the way to the fort, in the dark and the snow! You could have saved yourself a great deal of trouble, you know. You're just going to have to walk all the way back.'

Flora reached the door of the Indian shop just as Newsome caught up with her, breathing heavily from his run. The smell of the previous night's liquor still hung about him, and his eyes were clouded with an angry redness. The other 'gentlemen' had halted a little way off to watch the outcome of the meeting.

'I'm staying here,' Flora said quietly.

'By heaven, you're not! You're still my wife – and the law says you go where I go, unless I decide otherwise.' He glanced round, calculating the wisdom of laying hands on her, suddenly aware that a handful of clerks on their way to the depot building had begun to hover curiously at a little distance.

'I'm not your wife any longer,' declared Flora, ignoring the onlookers. 'Not after last night.' With a fingertip, she traced the ugly scar on her cheek. 'From now on, I'll do as I please.'

Out of the corner of her eye, she saw a group of labourers lay down their snow shovels and drift inquisitively towards the crowd on the walkway; but it was too late to worry about appearances.

'I should have said this a long time ago,' she announced in a loud voice, 'instead of keeping up a ridiculous pretence. You're a monster, Ralph Newsome – a cruel, disgusting monster. And from now on, you *have* no wife. Certainly not this one.'

'You impertinent trollop!'

Losing his temper altogether, Newsome made a lunge at her, and Flora stepped backwards into the store.

'Not my wife, are you?' he shouted from the doorway. His eyes flicked round the dim interior of the trading room, taking in the gun-screws and fish-hooks and stacks of blankets and tin kettles. 'Well, then, let's see if anyone else wants you. Over there!' In a stride Newsome caught up with Flora and pushed her towards the iron scales. 'Down! Down where you belong, with the rest of the trade goods.'

Grasping Flora's shoulders, he forced her down until she sprawled across the flat iron plate of the scales. The boldest of the crowd had pressed into the room behind them, faces jammed the doorway, twisting back to relay each new development to their friends outside. No one dared to interfere, or to rescue the domestic angel who'd fallen so far from grace.

'Here she is – this woman who declares she's no longer my wife.' Newsome turned towards his audience. 'I hereby put her up for sale to whoever wants her. Who's going to make me an offer?'

'Ralph – for God's sake!' Flora tried to slip sideways from the scales, but he was holding her too firmly.

'No one seems to want you,' he sneered. 'I wonder why? What a pity your lover isn't here to give me a price – unless he's too mean to buy what he can steal.' Raising his voice again, he called out, 'The best offer buys Mrs Newsome outright, and I wash my hands of her. Do as you please with the woman.'

'A dozen made-beaver!' shouted a wag at the back.

'Well said there.' Newsome turned towards the sound, his eyes glittering. 'Now, who'll make it two dozen? Someone must have a use for a bed-warmer, in this place.'

The crowd sniggered uncertainly, and for an instant Flora felt the grip of his fingers on her shoulders relax. Seizing her chance, she squirmed from his grasp and scrambled from the iron scales towards the door. The crowd drew aside as she reached them, those in front pressing back against their friends behind. Like an eel, Flora slipped through, tripped on the walkway, and found herself floundering hopelessly in the snow beyond.

A tall figure was striding across the quadrangle, attracted by the commotion. It was Darius Elder, his gun over his shoulder.

He glanced curiously at the knot of onlookers, and then in growing disbelief at Flora's bruised cheek.

'Flora – what in the world—'

'Now, isn't this fortunate?' Newsome's voice rang out from the trading-room doorway. 'Here's one man who might give me a good price for my slut of a wife. He should know what she's worth, if anyone does.'

The words were lazy with insult. Immediately, the crowd fell silent, watching the two men face one another across the snow of the quadrangle. No one laughed any more. In a second, a grotesque comedy had turned into something altogether more deadly.

Darius Elder's voice was icy. 'Take back that remark, and apologize to your wife.'

'I will not. You're a treacherous worm, Elder. You deserve one another – you and that lying bitch of a woman.'

'Hold the gun.' Without taking his eyes from the trading-room doorway, Darius Elder passed the weapon to Flora. He began to walk forward, stripping off his coat as he went.

'I don't brawl in the snow with barrow-men.' Newsome leaned against the doorpost, offensively unconcerned. 'I'll deal with you in my own good time.'

'Pistols, then. As soon as you please.' Darius halted his advance.

'Pistols,' agreed Newsome coolly. 'And by nightfall you'll be a dead man.'

'No!' cried a voice from behind Darius's shoulder. Almost at once there was a sharp explosion and the crash of shot blasting the wall by the trading-room door, leaving a riddled half-circle. Very slowly, Newsome slid down the doorpost to his knees, his face contorted with pain and one bloody hand pressed to his tattered coat-sleeve.

Knee-deep in the snow of the quadrangle, Flora continued to hold Darius Elder's gun to her shoulder, while its heavy, smoking barrel wobbled erratically towards the trading-room doorway. She was staring, mesmerized, at the result of her shot.

'Is he dying?'

'Twelve inches to the left might have done it.' Darius took the gun from her hands before it fell into the snow. 'How did you know this was loaded?'

'It had to be.' Flora stared, quite unable to tear her eyes away from the sight of Newsome's men scrambling to help their chief. 'If there's any justice in the world, the gun had to be loaded.'

'We must go.' This time it was Darius who took her arm. 'McTavish will want explanations, and things might get awkward for you. The Hudson's Bay Company have scant sympathy for women who shoot their husbands.'

'But where can we go?' Flora was still transfixed by the group round the trading-room doorway. 'I've no fear of prison – not after this place.'

'The ice on the river broke up last night, though I don't suppose you heard it. Crébiche reckons it's low enough now to risk the trip south. He suggested I go with him, instead of going on to the Polar Sea, but I wouldn't leave until I'd seen you safely away from here.

'Now we can both go. *Now*, Flora—' he repeated sharply, trying to shock her out of her trance. 'Before that madman gets the bird-shot out of his arm and accuses you of trying to murder him.'

PART THREE
May 1828

CHAPTER SEVENTEEN

I

To Crébiche's eternal credit, he accepted his extra passengers without hesitation as soon as Darius Elder had explained the cause of their sudden departure from York Factory.

'*Mon Dieu* . . .' Crébiche's eyebrows rose in an expression of solemn amazement, followed almost immediately by the return of his habitual grin. 'Is good Maskisees' *canot* is a big one—' He jerked his head in the direction of the river-bank where a long, vermilion-painted canoe had been pulled up on the ice alongside a modest heap of belongings. 'Though even a big Indian *canot* is a little boat.' He grinned again, and shrugged. 'Still – Maskisees and the lady are small, and I am not so large myself. If we overturn, it will be thanks to you, my tall friend. You will have to sit straight as a jack pine and not move so much as a hair.'

In a matter of minutes the pile of baggage had disappeared into the bow and stern of the canoe, and with great care – the skin being of fragile birchbark – the narrow craft was made ready for boarding. Flora's boots slipped in all directions as she struggled over a small mountain range of stranded ice-floes towards it.

'Go in please—' Crébiche extended a supportive hand. 'But step on the wood only, with care. And sit here, exactly, to keep the balance.'

A lone Indian boy sat on the landing-stage to watch them leave, dangling his skinny legs over the newly liberated river. There was no one at all at the mouth of Sloop Creek when they called to pick up a few precious possessions of Flora's – 'notting big, notting heavy,' Crébiche had warned as they scrambled up the ice-piled bank towards the converted boat store. The building itself was deserted: Polly Marks, the cooks and the labourers must all have hurried to the fort after their employer, leaving their greasy kettles by the waterside and the hall stove smothered in its own ash.

Flora's hands trembled as she gathered her small bundle together, her mind still too numb to make a sensible choice. Stockings – a chemise – her silver hairbrush and mirror – a bracelet and earrings,

271

and a tortoiseshell comb Lydia had given her – a decent chintz gown, wadded small, her scissors and needles – and over her arm, a pair of blankets.

'Hurry, Flora.'

It seemed shockingly little to show for the ruin of a marriage, and Flora was grateful for the solidity of Darius Elder's arm as she made her way quickly back to the canoe. With bewildering haste her bundle was stowed away under an oilcloth cover, and hands reached out to pluck her from dry land. Yet the sun continued to shine with baffling indifference to her flight, and a crow mocked from the nearby willows. Disconcerted, she hesitated for a moment on the creek bank.

'I shot him, didn't I?' Shading her eyes, she gazed back towards the distant palisade of the fort. 'I fired the gun – and I hit him.'

'You wounded him, that's all. And I dare say you dented his pride.'

'I should have killed him!' exclaimed Flora bitterly. And, turning her back for the last time on York Factory, she climbed into the waiting canoe.

It seemed almost incredible that such a frail Indian craft, light as a leaf and dipping no more than six inches below the surface of the river, could carry them safely over the hundreds of miles of turbulent water which lay ahead. Even the Hayes River, normally broad and matronly where it passed the fort, was swollen with meltwater; out in mid-stream, the debris of winter churned in the current, slate-coloured slabs of waterlogged ice which rolled like seals to display undersides shaggy with silt.

Now Flora began to understand the raw power of the spring melt. On either hand the bank was piled higher than a man's head with river-ice torn up by the flood and folded over its own thick crust; beyond it the snow had become threadbare, holed by tufts of scraggy grass, and even among the broomstick trees, dun patches of soil had begun to break the uniform white.

They could hardly expect pursuit, though Flora couldn't stop herself from glancing back at least once in the direction of the fort – awkwardly, to avoid tipping the canoe. To her surprise, York Factory had already diminished to a strip of white palisade surmounted by the flickering red beacon of the Company flag. As she watched, the flag swelled out like the scarlet stains which had appeared on Ralph Newsome's coat-sleeve: were they searching for her now, hunting down the domestic angel who'd so forgotten her duty? Her gaze met that of Darius Elder, sitting behind her in the canoe.

'It's what lies ahead that matters.' He smiled suddenly, and the sunlight thrown back from the ice struck blue sparks from his eyes.

'I believe you're actually enjoying this! Here I am, a runaway wife and a criminal – and you sit there grinning, as if the whole thing was a wonderful adventure.'

'So it is! But keep looking ahead, or you might turn into a pillar of ice.' He pointed to where the river seethed with soiled white shards among islands already overloaded with the glittering debris of the flood.

Spring, enchanted with her success of the past few days, had evidently set to work with a will to drive out the last traces of winter. Already the piled ice-masses had been quarried by the river, gnawed into fantastic, green-stalked mushrooms with bulbous tops which glistened wetly in the sun. Diamond-clear rills trickled from folds in icy cushions; steep clefts grew into valleys, spread into bowls, and then dwindled to mere dimples as the sun rose higher, smoothing the sharp ridges to a white blandness all around.

Crébiche, accustomed to such wonders, knelt intently in the bow of the canoe, his paddle cleaving the black water, and for a while Flora studied the regular twisting of his back, marvelling that a series of movements which from the river-bank had seemed so fluid should in fact be so minutely complex. Reach forward, arching asymmetrically – plunge – draw back, shoulder muscles flexing into a furrow over the spine – and then a contemptuous flourish and lift of the paddle as it was carried forward once more in a flying arc of brilliants. Reach – plunge – draw – and lift . . . endlessly, tirelessly as the hours passed, every stroke duplicated by Maskisees in the stern of the canoe.

To the clerks at the fort, Maskisees was Bent Leg, the Cree who walked with a dragging foot. On water, however, a crippled limb was no handicap at all, though Flora was amazed that such a slight young man could propel a boat with such power. Crébiche, on the other hand, short and wiry, gave an impression of sinewy strength whenever he rose on his knees to check their course among the icy islets.

If it was Crébiche who knew the river, it was Maskisees who'd built the canoe, a floating miracle achieved with no more than an axe, a knife and an awl, a sliver of a boat made of birchbark and thin, flexible timbers, sewn with pine fibres and caulked with spruce-gum. After the massive frames of the *Nebula*, it was a continuing wonder that a craft which two men could carry with ease should float at all: yet all that day it skimmed the flood, responding to each stroke of the paddle with an almost prescient willingness.

The canoe was alive, and the river was a live thing beneath it: no animate creature could have remained unaware of their supple, joyful harmony. Release was in the air, biting the nostrils like the wild green smell of new spruce. Where winter rules for eight months out of twelve, spring does not come gently, but plunges headlong into regeneration, budding, shooting, unfurling and begetting in an explosion of life impossible to ignore. Little by little on that urgent river, Flora's heart began to lift to the beat of the paddles, as a sweet, sharp breath whispered in her ear of new beginnings which laughed at wintry carefulness. Caution was never part of spring's design.

2

All that day the river became narrower and its banks steeper, shaved here and there by fresh landslides where frost and then meltwater streams had undermined the soft clay, freeing clumps of trees to slither down like skittles on the piled ice below.

They camped that night at a point where the bluffs were low and a patch of mossy ground lay clear of snow and sheltered from the wind by the fringe of the forest. Now that the sun had gone it had begun to get cold again, and Flora was glad to spread out her hands to the blaze which Maskisees conjured out of the dry branches of a nearby fallen tree.

The men worked swiftly, without discussion, following a routine which they must have practised a thousand times before. Flora was surprised to see Darius Elder do his share, and be accepted by the other two without question.

'What do you know about making camp in a forest?' she asked, watching him deftly strip the branches from a dead trunk with a few strokes of an axe.

'Enough.'

Puzzled, she continued to watch, fascinated by the purposeful economy of his movements in those alien surroundings. In a shooting-coat and corduroy trousers stuffed into stout leather boots, he looked more like an employee of the Hudson's Bay Company than one of its shareholders. With his winter-weathered skin and the firelight glinting on his dark curls he might have been a *voyageur* himself, had it not been for the strip of fine cambric shirt which showed whenever his coat swung open. He glanced up unexpectedly, and caught her staring.

'Is something the matter?'

'No – nothing at all. It's just that . . . you look so different, all of a sudden. Not at all the same man I saw with Felix at the coronation, or shut up in the bank.'

'Not at all the same man.' The axe bit fiercely into the dry sinews of the tree.

'Madame Newsome—' Crébiche's voice interrupted from the neighbourhood of the fire. 'You like pemmican? Tonight, supper is pemmican boil with flour.' He spread his hands apologetically. 'Not very elegant, but maybe tomorrow we find you a duck or a hare.'

Flora had once sampled pemmican at the fort – a mixture of pounded dried buffalo meat and fat, sewn up in skin *taureau* bags as portable rations for travellers. At the time she'd thought it greasy and strong-tasting, and generously larded with curls of buffalo hair; but now, camped in the blue shadows of the forest-edge, her appetite sharpened by the evening chill, she found herself looking forward to the meaty porridge with anticipation.

The men dug into the communal kettle, but Crébiche gallantly served Flora's portion in the tin pan kept for baling the canoe, and followed it with a beaker of tea. Flora received it bubbling hot, and when, unthinkingly, she touched it to her lips, the steaming liquid seared a painful path over the still-swollen skin, producing a sharp intake of breath which caused Darius to glance towards her in concern.

Twenty-four hours – hardly a single day had passed since Ralph Newsome had branded her face with the marks of his fury in the house at Sloop Creek – no more than twelve hours since Flora had fired the gun.

The scenes remained in her mind – vivid, but already unreal in the very brightness of their detail. Some other deranged wife had attempted to kill her husband in a strange and distant land – not Flora, not the unremarkable woman who sat with her back against a stump, devouring pemmican with unwashed hands as if she'd never seen a table-napkin or a finger-bowl in her life.

The meal disposed of, Maskisees and Crébiche stretched themselves out for the serious business of smoking their pipes, and a companionable silence settled over the circle of firelight, leaving the river and the fire to take up the burden of gossip in sighs and whispers and the fizzing snap of burning logs.

Flora's eyes were beginning to close, borne down by a delightful lassitude, when from the forest behind them came a sudden thrashing followed almost at once by the stifled screech of something small and despairing. Maskisees removed the pipe from his lips, made a face, and murmured a word to his neighbour.

'Do you know about *Wetigo*, Madame Newsome?' Crébiche indicated the black wall of trees with his pipe-stem. 'Maskisees reckons maybe that noise just now was Wetigo, riding through the forest on the wind, looking for 'yumans to eat for his supper.'

'Wetigo?' Flora opened her eyes wide in alarm. So much had been new and different that day; who knew what monsters might exist in that wilderness of trees?

'Wetigo has ice for his insides, and black hair all over – shaggy, like a bear. He hides under the river-ice, waiting for 'yumans to come, and then he jumps out—' Crébiche threw up his hands. 'And grabs the 'yumans, and eats them.'

Maskisees had watched the performance with grave attention. Now he removed his pipe and spoke again.

'Maskisees says Wetigo will eat his own gran'mother if there's no one else,' Crébiche interpreted, 'and his wife and little ones too. Only the strongest man can go out and fight him.' Crébiche tapped his chest. 'Strong here, in the heart, and in the head too. If he falters even once, the scream of Wetigo will freeze him where he stands, and he will become Wetigo's supper.'

'That is . . . only a story, isn't it?' Flora stared from Crébiche to Maskisees, seeking reassurance. 'There's no such creature as a Wetigo, surely.'

'Who knows?' Sombrely Crébiche knocked the embers out of his pipe against a nearby boulder. 'Sometimes people do terrible things to one another with no explanation, except they have Wetigo inside them, and they're driven a little mad. Who's going to say the Indians haven't hit on the right way of it?'

Through the last, transparent, shivering smoke of the fire, Crébiche's gaze rested steadily on Flora. Then he sighed, stretched, rolled himself fully dressed into his blanket and fell asleep with the promptness of a man who has nothing to fear from evil spirits. In another moment, Maskisees had done the same, pausing only to tie his skin cap more firmly on to his head and place his pipe carefully where his hand would find it first thing on wakening.

The fire was flameless now, reduced to a coronet of incandescent branches between the encircling stones, the final crimson glory before ashes. The tang of woodsmoke mingled in the air with the sugary, amber scent of pine resin and the blue coolness of the forest which lay like a vigilant mother, exhaling a cradling peace around the life within it.

Darius Elder had been lying on his side, thoughtfully watching the branches burn themselves to whiteness in the heart of the fire. Soon Flora was alerted by a faint prickling of her skin to the fact that he was examining her with an expression of thoughtful concern. Defensively, her hand flew to her ravaged cheek.

'You're free of him now. Free for ever.'

Flora shook her head, closing her eyes against the tears which threatened to engulf her. 'I'll never be free of him. He's like . . . like a Wetigo . . . he's inside me. Ice. Deadness.'

Gently, Darius reached out to touch her swollen cheek.

'Not true.'

She shook her head again, dislodging his fingers. 'The scar will fade, and there'll be no sign of him on the outside – and I dare say there'll be other moments of peace like this. But he's left me nothing of myself. I realized that last night. Nothing at all.'

'There was a time when I believed much the same.'

'About me?'

'No, about myself. When I came back from India. When I was *sent* back from India,' he repeated with defiant precision.

'You fought a duel. I heard the story in London.'

'The duel didn't matter.' His hand, straying through the grass-stems, encountered a thin, whippy branch, and he began to poke with it amongst the ashes. 'It was what came before it that mattered.'

He continued to stir the ash, cutting furrows and trails in it, drawing it out in bleached sunrays, breaking it ever finer.

'There was a girl . . .' he said at last, 'the daughter of one of the native princes, who happened to find herself stranded a long way from home . . . and I was able to give her some assistance, otherwise I don't suppose I'd ever have set eyes on her. And – well – it's a long story – but one way or another, I fell in love with her.'

He glanced up suddenly, challengingly; but Flora's eyes held nothing except a distant fear.

'Call it what you will,' he continued, 'love, infatuation – *illusion* if you insist – but it was more than a physical need, far more than sheer lust for a smooth skin and a willing body. I've known enough of that to recognize the difference.' He glanced at Flora again, but her expression remained unchanged.

'This was . . . oh, a desperate desire to cherish and to shelter . . . to possess her, yes, but to be possessed, too, and to see the sunrise reflected again and again from her face, like a constant miracle I could never quite believe.

'And simply because of that,' he finished, 'because I loved her – she died. And afterwards I came to believe, like you, that there was nothing left for me in the world. That love had died with her.'

'Her father locked her up because she tried to run away with you.' Flora hugged her knees, resisting the urge to reach out to him, taking refuge in unshakable fact. 'That wasn't your fault. What could you have done?'

'It was my idea for us to run off together. Did they tell you that, those gossips in London? *Foolish* – that's what my employers called me. By which they meant I'd stirred up a scandal, and put them on bad terms with her father, the prince.' The stick drew savage parallel lines in the ash. 'The plain fact was that poor Madhu died because I loved her, and because, having made her defy her father, I could do nothing to rescue her. If we'd never met, she'd still be alive today.'

'She must have . . . loved you a great deal, to take such a risk.' Flora was ashamed to find herself envious, and drew back from the tragic ghost. 'And so you came home.'

'No – not immediately. The East India Company packed me off with a company of irregulars to Assam, to hunt out the camps of the Burmese dacoits who were raiding the company elephant-hunters. I had to spend months wandering in the hills, living off the land as best I could. I imagine the Company meant it as a punishment, but they could have sent me to Hell, for all I cared.'

'I always thought you'd been shut up in a counting-house somewhere, or behind a desk in a shipping agency.'

'Good heavens, no.' He smiled fleetingly. 'Not until after that stupid duel, when I was sent back from India and the family forced me to take a hand in the bank.'

Across the river, an owl hooted mournfully in the trees, and Darius glanced briefly towards the source of the sound.

'All my life, it's been *the bank, the bank* . . .' The stick moved again, tracing a pattern of interlocking whorls which began to spiral out extravagantly from a central point. 'Felix is the one who enjoys the family business. It excites him to have a finger in every pie in the

City – to know all the scandal, and whose estates are mortgaged to the ears, and whose family diamonds are only paste.'

He threw the charred stick entirely into the fire, raising a halo of sparks. 'Unfortunately, the family don't trust Felix not to make a botch of things. They wanted a sober, sensible, dull young man to take up a partnership – someone who'd make an irreproachable marriage and spend the rest of his tedious life shut up in the bank, piling up profits for the rest of the family to spend.'

'And you agreed to be the one?'

'Not in so many words. I just didn't disagree. I suppose I felt it was all I deserved, after what I'd done.'

'You said to me . . .' Flora struggled with a memory. 'You told me you'd married Sophie *particularly* because you didn't love her.'

'Marriage to Sophie meant safety. I suppose I was afraid of the pain of loving again.' He leaned back on his elbows to consider the frigid stars above. 'I should never have done it.'

'Because of Sophie?'

'Because of you!' Abruptly, he swung back to stare at her. 'Because even having you as an enemy was better than nothing at all. You hate magnificently, Flora. Oh, I loved you for it.'

'No—' Flora covered her face with her hands, blotting out his vehemence. 'Love is—'

'An illusion – yes, yes, I know. But even if it is—' He reached out to draw her hands clear. 'Even if it is only an illusion . . . By heaven, it's worth the risk! Damn the bank! Damn Felix, and damn the Northwest Passage, too!' A loud snore from the other side of the fire reminded him of the two sleepers, and he lowered his voice. 'All I care about is you.'

'Please don't say that.'

'It has to be said. I want to wake you out of this . . . this trance you seem to be in.'

'And Sophie?' demanded Flora suddenly. 'What about Sophie?'

He released her hands as abruptly as if she'd slapped him.

'What about Sophie?'

'You're my sister's husband,' Flora reminded him brutally, rebuilding her defences.

'You know how little that means to her. You've seen how she is. She couldn't wait for me to go off on this expedition.'

'She's still your wife.'

'Tell me, then – if there was no Sophie – if we'd never married . . .'

279

'How can you ask me that, when you *are* married to her?' Flora made a sweeping movement of her hands, as if that question settled the matter beyond argument. 'Please, Darius—'

'Very well.' He hesitated for a moment, and then seemed to come to a decision.

'Sleep now. You've been through a great deal today.'

Carefully, he drew Flora's blankets over her where she lay on the oilcloth square which served as a groundsheet, and then rolled himself into his own alongside.

For several minutes there was silence except for the soft bickering of the river among its rocks and a faint, regular snoring from beyond the dying fire. Then another spasm of rustling broke out among the black trees behind them, and Flora had a sudden vision of the insatiable Wetigo setting out in search of new victims to devour.

'Darius—' she whispered.

'Yes.'

'Is it possible . . . I mean – do you think there could really be such a thing as a Wetigo?'

He took so long to answer that she began to wonder if he'd fallen asleep. Then at last she heard his voice in the darkness.

'I believe you can fight your own Wetigo and win, if that answers your question.'

Flora's hand moved out, searching for his. He made no move to withdraw it; gently, her fingers folded themselves into its warmth, and in an instant she was asleep.

3

Crébiche and Maskisees were awake even before the rim of the sun had broken the horizon, and were immediately ready to travel. Under normal circumstances they'd have kicked their companions into wakefulness with shouts of '*Lève! Lève!*': but normally there were no ladies present, and so instead Crébiche contented himself with clattering kettles briskly together as he dismantled their simple camp.

Flora woke in a rush to find herself woefully stiff after a night on the hard ground, and rumpled and sticky in her layers of thick clothing. Beside her, Darius Elder's place was empty, and she raised herself on one elbow to gaze in surprise at the scene of activity. Evidently, they were about to leave at any moment, though the day was still cold and her hair must look like a bird's nest. She sat up immediately, one hand flying to her head while the other groped in her bundle of belongings for her silver-backed brush. A few feet away, Darius paused in the act of rolling up his blankets to survey her.

'Sleep well?'

'Yes – I slept very well,' she admitted, 'But I must look a perfect fright.'

'Different,' he conceded with a smile. 'Yesterday you seemed . . . fragile, as if the slightest touch would have shattered you. This morning – well, you look quite different.'

It was true: Flora felt indecently well. She was still only twenty-five years of age, not old enough to be beyond the excitement of waking up with her nose in the grass and the smell of pine-needles clinging to her fingers. Even the roughness of the blanket under her chin, and its damp warmth where her sleeping breath had fallen – even that was vaguely thrilling, as if a single night in the open had been enough to sharpen senses dulled by long confinement.

Darius was kneeling less than a step away, and her heightened awareness brought her the deep honey-gold scent of his skin as he breathed. He wanted her – he'd said as much the night before, though she'd known since that evening at the guest-house door – and the knowledge no longer filled her with bitter satisfaction, but with joyfulness, a sweet, intoxicating joyfulness quite shocking in a woman who'd just tried to murder her lawful husband.

'I still have to wash, and brush out my hair.' Anxiously, she disentangled the blankets from her skirt. 'And my boots are all mud. Surely Crébiche can wait for half an hour—'

Darius glanced over his shoulder as Maskisees passed on his way to the canoe, the iron kettle over one arm and the *taureau* of pemmican under the other.

'Flora, my dear tousled friend – by the time we reach Red River, I promise you'll have given up caring how dirty your boots are, if you still have any boots left to worry about.' He retrieved the clay-caked boots and set them down at her side.

'So far, you've seen the easy part of the journey. It'll become a good deal harder before we're done, by all accounts, and there are no carriage-rugs or parasols where we're going. Don't look so horrified! You'll struggle through, or I wouldn't have brought you – but don't expect to look elegant at the other end. Now, up you get. Crébiche says we've a fair stretch of river to cover today.'

'Did I even miss breakfast?' Flora gazed round in amazement as the camp vanished about her. An honest emptiness had begun to assail her, the hunger of a healthy young animal.

'We'll stop for something to eat in two or three hours. Come on.' Darius held out a hand to help her to her feet, kicking the blankets aside.

'But you must wait for a moment! At least let me . . .' Embarrassed, she indicated the nearest trees. 'You know.'

'Don't go far, then. It's easier than you think to get lost in the forest.' He bent to pick up the roll of blankets. 'I'll wait for you at the canoe.'

In spite of her dishevelled state, as the canoe slid like a fish into the fast-flowing current, Flora stared round in fascination at the surroundings she'd only glimpsed in the dusk of the previous evening, and became aware of a curious fluttering of the heart. What did muddy boots and a rumpled dress matter when the first clear, infinitely precious sunlight of the day was making colours ring with such luminous vigour? Overhanging the water's edge, the first new leaves spattered the bare branches with apple-green glass; citrines and diamonds glittered in the stream, dappling rocks tufted with sulphur yellow against the deep shade of the forest.

All at once it seemed to Flora that they must be travelling into the heart of spring. The rush of green to the branches was surely accelerating as they passed by on a river which ran swifter with every mile, and the excitement of it sang in her heart.

Darius had taken a paddle that day: she could hear the splash of it behind her as she finally brushed out her hair, hoarding the pins safely in a fold of her skirt.

Different, he'd said – and it certainly was different, brushing one's hair in the soft breeze of a spring morning, twisting to collect it over one shoulder, teasing the tangles down to the very ends while a capful of wind lifted the lightest strands like the touch of a lover . . .

Out of vanity and pure mischief she flung the entire shining, rippling mass behind her, where it flew about like a wild thing in the sunshine, a dark cloud sparking copper stars from its depths.

Then, meekly bowing her head so that he should see the defenceless white nape of her neck, she captured her hair in a shining sheaf and trapped it modestly with pins.

'I remember when you had it all cut off.' Behind her, Darius

Elder's voice was distorted by the exertion of paddling. 'You sold it to buy a gown.'

'A gown to impress you, if the truth were told.' She smiled back at him over her shoulder.

'It was a wasted sacrifice, then. Your hair has life and strength in it, like the river. Don't cut it again.'

Flora was about to retort that she'd do as she pleased with her own head – and then thought better of it, and reflected that perhaps she, like Samson, stored the essence of herself in her hair.

It was after midday when they reached the place where the rapid stream of the Steel River met the slower flood of the Hayes. Even the three men, paddling strongly, found progress up this new watercourse almost impossible, and though for a while Crébiche and Maskisees managed to propel the craft along with poles, there was soon nothing for it but to 'track' the canoe by sending a man ashore with a line to pull it yard by yard up the rushing current, scrambling over rocks and the steep, slippery clay of the river-bank.

As the sun rose higher Flora exchanged her cloak for a shawl fringed with a pattern of palms. The hours passed, but not tediously: there was endless delight to be found in watching the water curl past on either side or fly from the guiding paddles in a scatter of liquid light.

That night they camped on the river-bank once more, Flora and Darius lying companionably close, exchanging drowsy confidences long after the other two had slid into sleep.

'Why should firelight make blue eyes so green?' Flora reached out to trail a lazy finger along the line of his cheekbone. 'Greener than tide-pools when the sun strikes the sand at the bottom – little seas full of circling, fluttering secrets . . . trapped there, until the ocean returns.'

Her finger traced a delicate path past his ear and on, down, across the warm hollow of his throat until it came to rest in the white cleft of his shirt, faintly entwined with a thread of dark hair.

There he captured it and kissed her palm, his lips moving against her skin with the suppleness of water. Between forefinger and thumb, his eyes glinted greenly in the darkness.

'I'm almost afraid of you, when you look at me like that.' Disturbed, Flora pulled her hand away.

'You weren't afraid of me that night at the fort, when you waited at the top of the stairs.'

'I was afraid – oh, yes, even then – but I thought I was quite safe from you.' She turned her head away. 'It was a shabby game. I should never have done it.'

He reached out, gently drawing her face towards his own. 'And now we have our two chaperons.' He glanced towards the embers of the fire and the two sleeping forms beyond it. 'So you're quite safe here, too. And if I tell you I love you—'

'No!' She put her hands over her ears. 'Not that. Tell me anything you please – tell me you want my body – you want to possess me – anything, but not lies about love.'

For a long time afterwards he lay in silence on his side, regarding her with tender frustration.

'Oh, my darling Flora,' he murmured at last. 'How did we come to make such a mess of our lives?'

4

By noon the next day they'd reached the mouth of Hill River, a flying torrent which tumbled along between steep banks as if pressing business awaited it somewhere below. In places the banks rose up in massive bluffs, bare of vegetation; in others, where the slopes were gentler, spring had already showered creamy yellow over the mats of willow-scrub which clung determinedly to the clay, knotted into a shoulder-high tangle of stems.

Paddling was impossible here, and even tracking was difficult on the steep, inhospitable shore. Flora insisted on going ashore herself wherever possible to lighten the load, her thin black kid boots skidding hopelessly across the steep slopes and sliding into clefts in the rocks until her toes were skinned and aching.

Most of the time she went hand over hand, catching at woody stems to keep her balance or scrabbling for fingerholds: yet the sheer physical effort of it all – the bursting lungs and torn, blackened fingernails – was a welcome release of the forces which struggled, frustrated, inside her.

That night, exhausted, she fell asleep before either Crébiche or Maskisees had knocked the ashes out of his pipe, and never felt the kiss which brushed the pale skin at her ear, or the hands which drew the blankets gently up around her.

The next day was no easier, but Flora flung herself into the hardships of the passage as though her sanity depended on it. For the first time she discovered the art of portage, when Crébiche and Maskisees suddenly picked their craft out of the water at the foot of a small cataract and Crébiche upended it on his head, staggering off with it across the flat rocks alongside the fall like an exotic, elongated mushroom.

'Let me carry something.' Looping her skirt up under her belt, Flora moved towards the piled baggage.

'Impossible!'

'But you must, Crébiche! I can't watch you all work so hard, and do nothing to help.'

Crébiche hesitated, the canoe over his head, torn between gallantry and the impulse to accommodate a lady's whim.

'Take the cooking-pot, then.'

Flora snatched it up. 'And?'

'That's plenty.' His voice echoed hollowly under the birchbark.

'Certainly not.' Swooping on the pile, Flora gathered up the tin kettle, rolls of oilcloth and a blanket or two as well as her own small bundle of belongings. Hugging her burden to her chest, she slithered off in the wake of the bobbing canoe.

Late that evening, camped at the foot of yet another waterfall, Flora surveyed the mud which caked her skirts, and smiled to think of her mother, so perfectly *comme il faut* on her ridiculous Egyptian throne. A few hours earlier, perspiring from her labours and hopelessly hobbled by too many clothes, Flora had slipped behind an outcrop of rock to tear off the flannel petticoat and drawers which had kept her warm at the fort. After a moment's deliberation – the men having lain down in the grass to smoke and rest – she marched out, begged a loan of Crébiche's long hunting-knife, and retreated once more behind her rock to unbutton the bodice of her dress and slit the knotted laces of her corset.

Liberated from its whalebone torment, she emerged from hiding. The flannel petticoat and drawers could remain in the bushes for the amusement of the local beavers, but some things were too precious for a lady to lose, and the ravaged corset was smuggled back to the canoe, modestly wrapped in the folds of her shawl.

She was hardly *comme il faut* any more, but far too elated to care. Even the bruising on her face had begun to fade, hidden by dirt and the assault of the sun. What did it matter if she hadn't undressed or washed properly for days, and her hands were hacked and her knees scraped where she'd stumbled on the rocks? Every morning she continued to brush out her hair in lazy, luxuriant splendour – because she knew *he* would watch her do it, and his demons be roused along with her own.

Even Maskisees smiled at her now in a kind of grim approval; she'd made herself useful, and therefore acceptable in his sight. There were so many portages on this part of the route that as soon as one was over, another waited just ahead. And between the portages there were rapids to be run, where sharp rocks combed the racing current into skeins before plaiting it again in a mass of foaming curls.

Here the poles came out again, steadying the canoe for an instant where the flood slackened behind a buttress of stone, then hurling it forward into a bucking, toiling cascade of water until with a sideways leap it gained the slack of another eddy and rested again. Crébiche, in the bow, would rise up on his knees to look ahead, choosing his route and pointing it out to Maskisees in the stern; in a moment the canoe would be off on its surging, twisting, breathtaking way to the tail of the next eddy and another few seconds' respite.

Mile after mile was passed in this way, until Flora lost all track of how far they'd come. But already the landscape around them was beginning to change from one of narrow defiles to a region where a black saw-edge of trees fringed the sky in all directions, and the river spread out to embrace small tufted islands as if haste were the last thing on its mind.

By now the weather was warm enough to bring clouds of biting insects to colonize the shore; but as the canoe cleared Swampy Lake the sun disappeared behind a veil of cloud which continued to thicken for some hours. Knee Lake, when they reached it, had become a grey waste compressed by a leaden sky which seemed to bulge with more ominous, angry power by the minute.

Crébiche squinted upwards, his lips pursed in thought, and then went off for a conference with Maskisees. In spite of the threatening sky not a drop of rain had fallen, and a traverse of the open water offered a tempting alternative to a slow crawl along the shore.

As a result, the canoe was still some distance from dry land when the storm broke. With alarming swiftness the surface of the lake became ridged with choppy wavelets which slapped the birchbark sides in sullen warning of larger things to come. The rain fell with the suddenness of a tipping vat, changing from the first few exploratory drops to a deluge in a matter of seconds, spattering the wavelets and bouncing in tiny jets from the oilcloth-covered packages between the thwarts of the canoe. The men were hauling grimly for the shore now, carving great bites out of the lake with each stroke of their paddles while the rain rattled on the shoulders of their sodden coats.

Crébiche's sharp eyes had spotted a place where overhanging trees guarded a sickle of green; there the rushes were less dense, and a man need only wade a short distance to pull the canoe to shore. But long before they reached this refuge, each one of them was wet through; Flora's shawl sagged in dripping folds over her head, and her dress was so sodden that when Darius moved to lift her ashore, she wouldn't allow it, scrambling into the black shallows with the others and gathering her soaking skirts about her thighs in order to splash out on to the grass.

Fortunately, enough wood had stayed dry among the trees to make a large fire, larger than was needed to cook the two ducks they'd shot earlier in the day, but comforting in its warmth. Sitting in the wet pool of her dress, Flora hunted out the pins from her hair and combed it loose where the heat of the fire could dry it. It was small consolation to realize that beyond the dripping branches of the pines, the downpour had at last died away, leaving a lake of molten copper in the red-gold light of evening.

An hour later, Crébiche, thoughtfully rooting with a twig among his teeth, wandered down to the shore, where Maskisees was staring intently at something in the middle distance.

'Indian canoes on the lake,' Crébiche announced after a few moments. 'Over by the point.' He waved a hand in the direction the canoes had taken. 'Maskisees reckons they're his people. He wants to go over and visit for a bit. Do you want to come, or will you stay here?'

'I think this lady's had enough of canoes for today.' Darius Elder squinted into the dusk, where a pinpoint of light indicated that a fire had been lit on the nearest promontory.

'I'd rather stay here and keep warm,' agreed Flora, 'if I won't be missed.'

On the point of leaving, Crébiche turned to Flora with a frown.

'Better you take off your wet things and dry them properly. Don' sleep in them.'

'What about you? You were out in the rain, too.'

'Don' matter for me. Besides—' Crébiche shrugged. 'I'm like a beaver. One good shake and the wet's gone.' It was true: between the heat of the fire and his own vigorous, muscular body, Crébiche had begun to dry out. Amazed, Flora watched the canoe glide away into the twilight at the head of an arrow of fiery ripples: only then did she realize that she and Darius Elder were now alone on the darkening grass.

'Crébiche was right.' Darius was feeding the fire, his face hidden. 'You shouldn't sleep in those wet clothes.'

'No. I suppose not.' After a moment's hesitation, Flora fetched a couple of sticks and made a great business of spreading her shawl out to dry. She could feel Darius's scrutiny like the touch of a feather on bare skin; defensively, she twitched at the shawl, trying to make each movement officiously brisk, smoothing the light woollen folds over the sticks like a washerwoman of fifty summers. But when nothing remained to be done she had to turn back to him, awkwardly, in her wet dress, her breath coming a little faster than before.

'You should dry your shooting-coat.' She pointed to it, for want of anything else.

'That's true.' He bent to retrieve the coat, and spread it on a forked branch next to her shawl. A faint miasma of steam began to enfold both coat and shawl, like the raising of a filmy white veil against the blackness of the trees.

'And your boots,' he said. 'Here – let me help.'

In silence Flora held out her foot, and he went down on one knee to loosen the laces and ease the soft leather round her heel, tossing each boot down near the fire while she placed a hand on his shoulder to balance herself. The second boot lay on its side in the grass, but he kept her instep in the warmth of his palm.

'Your stockings are damp.'

'I know.'

The green sea-pools confronted her, full of circling mysteries; the heat of his hand carried itself upwards, rousing another warmth deep inside her like a strange, melting ache.

Setting her foot on his knee, she raised the hem of her dress and petticoat with calculated slowness as far as her thigh. Sliding the second finger of each hand into the top of her white silk stocking, she slipped garter and all down to her toes.

'A gentleman would turn his back,' she told him when it was gone.

'I suppose he might.'

Once more she drew up her skirt, enjoying the movement of his eyes, and slid the second stocking softly downward, ruffling it over the sheen of her naked skin, amber in the firelight. The coolness of

288

the grass stems between her toes exhilarated her, and the brush of petticoats on her bare legs.

'Your shirt is wet.'

Without a word, he crossed his arms to pull it over his head, revealing a flat, taut stomach and the dark-shadowed muscles of his chest.

Flora's hands had already moved to the buttons of her bodice, forcing each damp little disc through its hole with a soft pop of release. Her fingers unfastened her belt with the sureness of habit, letting the waterlogged wool of her dress peel away like a dark shell into the grass at her feet.

He was already naked – long-boned, broad in the shoulder and over the smooth, darkly dusted planes of his chest, narrow-hipped as a thoroughbred, waiting with a kind of wild grace in the firelight.

Flora reached to the hollow of her back to pull out the strings of her petticoat, then drew the delicate embroidery forward over her breasts, rolling her hips like a sloughing snake to rid herself of its wetness.

She stepped out of its crumpled ring, naked now except for her damp chemise – yet more than naked, since it clung to her limbs like a second skin, revealing more than the first in its sinuous folds.

Darius pulled her against him, drawing the thin fabric over her body and her shoulders, spilling her hair over his chest; she lifted her arms to let it pass, extending herself against him, revelling in the electrifying strangeness of flesh on flesh.

His hands slid down, his fingers skimming the cleft of her spine and spreading, imprisoning her against him, crushing his desire against her softness.

All of a sudden, the stark reality of his need for her made Flora afraid. She began to draw into herself, shuddering uncontrollably, the lashes of her closed eyes fluttering against the tight whorls of hair on his chest. Not understanding, he held her closer, as if his strength could somehow quench her jarring dread, but her panic simply increased.

'My darling, don't—' His hands moved up into her hair and filled themselves with it, as if there at least they could possess her, and not be repulsed.

In despair she leaned her brow against him, cupping it in trembling fingers, agonized and bewildered at the same time.

'If you don't want this—' he murmured into her hair.

'But I do . . . I want you so badly every part of me is aching with it. I want to take you into me – to hold you until we're one and the same . . . but I can't, I'm too afraid.' Another long, anguished shiver passed through her. 'Oh, I knew it was true – he'll never let go of me, he's still laughing—'

In silence, Darius swung her into his arms and carried her away from the fire, lying down with her in the grass under the deep shelter of the trees. With a sob of despair Flora turned away from him on to her side and drew up her knees, her face and breasts pressed towards the all-forgiving earth.

'Flora.' In the pine-scented darkness, she heard his voice. 'Flora, my darling – can't you look at me, at least?'

Reluctantly, she raised her head, and turned it. He was lying stretched out with one knee raised, impassive as marble in the cool dusk: away from the fire, the shadows were softer, a purple obscurity among the whispering grass-stems.

'Come closer.'

'I can't.' At once the panic renewed itself, and she began to shiver again.

'Yes, you can. Come close enough to lie touching. Against my side – here, where I can feel you warm on my skin. I won't lay a finger on you, I swear it. Not until you tell me. Not unless you tell me.'

'Oh, my love, I can't . . .'

'You can, because I love you. And because I won't give you up – no matter how long I have to wait.'

When she continued to hesitate, he repeated 'Come', and this time Flora slid towards him, a little surprised to find how readily her body fitted against his, and her shoulder into his, while her knee curled against his thigh. He kept his word, only moving the arm whose shoulder supported her cheek, curving it like a shield at her back.

'You must despair of me,' she whispered. 'I'm such a fool.'

'No . . . I'm the fool. In spite of all we've said, I didn't understand.'

Among the reeds, a frog struck up a serenade with its high whistling call, and was joined in a fluting duet by another nearby.

Experimentally, Flora reached out to brush Darius's ribs with her fingertips, feeling his skin slide with the sleekness of the lake under her own. More confidently, she let her hand glide up over his chest to the hollow between neck and shoulder where his collar-bone made a delicate span; then fluttering like a bird over his throat and down the shallow dip of the breastbone to the fine concavity of his stomach, taking pleasure now in the warm firmness of the flesh passing below her palm, tingling a little like salts on the tongue. His hip-bone filled her hand, then her fingers lifted and separated, moulding the long muscles of his thigh.

Searching higher, they encountered dense, springy hair, and she withdrew her hand. Gently, he captured it and guided it back, until she felt him swell against her fingers.

'Now do you see the power you have over me?'

Faintly, cautiously, she began to believe.

'Close your eyes,' she said, 'and let me kiss you.'

His mouth was soft and pliant, and tasted faintly of Lydia's port wine. After a while she drew back, but remained lying against him, her breasts soft against his side, considering the cinnamon-coloured blur of the lips she'd just relinquished. Now the old hollowness began to rise again inside her, an emptiness pierced by a hot coil of longing which rolled and pulsed, demanding deliverance.

She touched him again, and bent over to kiss his closed, defence-less eyelids.

'Now . . . perhaps. I don't know . . .'

Slowly, he raised a hand to cradle her naked shoulder as if it were the most fugitive thing in the world.

'You lead, I'll follow.'

He followed faithfully, though Flora was not even sure where she expected to lead, except to some plateau of peace where their joining would exorcise the demon of want which possessed her. Yet, even at the end, when he finally lost himself within her, a deep sadness remained, like the ache of a need imperfectly expressed.

He leaned over to kiss her, the shadow of his dark head no longer fearful, and she freely surrendered her lips. The scent of bruised grass-stems rose about them as they lay entwined.

'Do you remember when you kissed me at the creek?' Slowly, Flora traced a pattern of interlocking loops over Darius's skin. 'It was only the second time in my life.' And then, afraid he was going to utter the hated name, she added quickly, 'No. He never did. Not once.'

'Only your second kiss? Then who gave you the first?'

'The orange-seller at the corner of Fetter Lane. I let him kiss me once, because I wanted to know what it felt like. But I kept my lips closed all the time.'

'And what did it feel like?' She could hear the smile in his voice.

'I can't remember.' Embarrassed, Flora hid her face against him, relishing the faint, sharp smell of his body and its coolness against her lips.

'Well, I'm relieved you've forgotten. I wouldn't like to think you'd leave me for the first fruit-seller we come across.'

The silliness of it made her laugh: there was such comforting permanence in the word *leave*, as if a deeper union had been created than the brief fusion of two bodies.

'My dear, sweet innocent,' he said.

'I wish I was, for you.'

'But you are an innocent – not in the ways of loving, perhaps, but in the pleasures of it all.'

'There's more?'

'Oh, much, much more. But you must trust me first.'

'I do trust you.'

'No . . . not entirely, I think.' He lifted a strand of her hair and curled it thoughtfully round a finger. 'There's part of you that still hides from me, keeping its distance like a deer in the forest. I see it sometimes, watching me through your eyes.'

'I don't mean to be like that. I do want to trust you – truly, I do.'

'That's enough for a beginning. Perhaps I can earn the rest, when you let yourself believe I love you.'

Gently, he stroked the dark disc in the centre of her breast with the curled wisp of hair, watching it harden and stand proud. His hand swept across, brushing it with the firmness of his palm before his fingers enfolded it, teasing and manipulating. With a long sigh, Flora arched her back, letting her arms fall above her head so that the delicious, tingling lassitude could run like a clear spring over her body.

'I like to hear you sigh like that.' His lips found her breast, and then its pair, creating little empty voids into which her nipples were drawn in delightful discovery.

The lassitude became a languor, a drowsy dream in which the seat of consciousness seemed to have deserted her brain and moved to a point deep in her belly which hummed and throbbed with a rhythm entirely its own. As his lips and hands moved over her skin, she sighed again, and the sigh became a groan in her throat as her hips began to move of their own accord, circling against him.

'Oh, wait . . .' It was hardly more than a breath.

'Enough?'

'No . . . no . . .' Reassured, she surrendered again to the dream which was opening her, exploring, sending delicate tongues of fire to flicker through her body in little exquisite rushes, until the rushes combined in an irresistible torrent like a meteor shower; she let out her breath in a long, ebbing hiss, quite unaware she'd been holding it.

'Oh, glory . . .' She turned her face aside, seeking out the rough reality of grass on her cheek, but he was moving against her now, moving into her, searching for the core of awareness which had wakened like a live thing inside her. Her mind no longer controlled her body: it responded to him instinctively, meeting him, holding him, rising to a returning tide of blissful, molten ripples.

The wave broke in a roar of sensation that exploded and popped inside her, leaving her to float, rootless, clinging to him while it receded in all its multiple eddies. Later, he held her close as he'd done once before – safe, and drowsy, and complete.

And when the first of the dawn found them still alone on the shore, and picked out a line like a narrow satin ribbon on Flora's cheek, he softly traced it with a fingertip and promised, 'You'll never have anything to fear from me. You know that, Flora, don't you? I'd give up my heart's blood sooner than harm you.'

CHAPTER EIGHTEEN

I

The sun had cleared the horizon by the time Crébiche and Maskisees returned the next day, but the wind which continued to roughen the surface of the lake had done away with any need for haste. It had been hard enough to make the short crossing from the promontory where the Indian band had camped; the wind would have to moderate a good deal before it was safe to go on.

Maskisees went off to search for gulls' eggs along the shore, and, seeing Crébiche lie down by the fire to sleep, Darius volunteered to go into the trees with his gun in search of game for the pot. Flora, reluctant to let him out of her sight, went with him.

After the windy shore there was a green quietude among the spruce and milky stemmed birch, where sunlight trickled through the branches to bleach the cushions of ghostly reindeer moss underfoot. Further from the lake and its ruffled fringe of willow and aspen, the ground rose a little and the trees became stern, close-growing conifers, their stems criss-crossed by snapped poles, grey and matted like sodden feathers as they sank into the soft litter.

Footsteps fell lightly on the spongy floor, but in that soft silence they were still enough to startle the crossbills out of their liquid piping, and bring a watchman whisky-jack skipping down a ladder of twigs to inspect the newcomers.

'There's no reason to hurry.' Leaning his gun against a stump, Darius stretched himself out on the moss of a small clearing. Flora lay down in the crook of his arm and closed her eyes to think; in that green and ancient eternity, it was hard not to imagine a future.

'When we were little, Sophie and I,' she murmured, 'we used to play a game called "What if" . . . For instance, if our governess made us wear our sun-hats, we'd say to one another, "What if a giant crow came down, and flew off with Miss Woodhead?" Our garden in Richmond was such a strange, magical place . . . You could almost believe the "what ifs" might come true.'

'Like "What if you and I had never met?"' He stroked her cheek with the thumb of the hand which held her, but didn't open his eyes.

'No . . . I mean what if you'd never married Sophie, and I'd never married Ralph? What if there'd been no expedition, and no York Factory, and I'd never shot my husband . . . or . . .' She took a breath. 'What if we never went home at all . . . ?'

'And stayed here for ever?'

'Just here, out in the forest – on the edge of a lake somewhere, or on a river-bank with beavers nearby and spruce hens in the woods . . . We could build a cabin, and live on wild rice and whatever you could shoot, and swear Crébiche and Maskisees to secrecy. No one would ever know where we'd gone. We'd just disappear from sight.'

'You'd be lonely with no one to talk to.'

'You'd be there. You're all I need.'

'There'd be no shops, and no fancy gowns to buy.'

'And no temptation to cut off my hair again.'

A sigh of wind rustled the branches overhead, and white sunlight flickered on his smile. Afraid he wasn't taking her seriously, Flora rolled over to lie between his legs, her head on his chest.

'Why shouldn't we do it?'

'It's a fine dream, certainly.'

'It needn't be a dream. Not if you meant what you said last night.'

'My darling, all I want in the world is for us to be together. You know that.'

'We could be together here! No one in Rupert's Land seems to care about legal marriages, or who has a wife or a husband already – you saw how it was at the fort.'

'That's true.' He paused, testing her vision of a way ahead. 'I don't suppose Ralph Newsome would care if he never saw you again. Crébiche could tell everyone I'd drowned crossing a lake, or died of some disease.'

'And Sophie would be left a rich widow.' A sobering thought struck her. 'But it would mean starting again – with nothing at all. You'd give up a great deal.'

'The bank? The family? I'd gladly give up a hundred times as much.'

There was silence for a moment, and then he spoke again.

'Perhaps it would be possible to stay here after all. I doubt if Sophie would miss me for more than a day or two. She might even be glad to be rid of me.'

Flora's eyes flew open in hope. 'Do you really think so?'

'You've seen how she is. I only came on this crazy expedition because I realized Sophie cared less about me than one of her pet dogs. I'm sure she'd have preferred me to be a greyhound.'

'Mamma said Sophie was taking too much laudanum.'

'Laudanum, paregoric, poppy capsules . . .' Darius lifted a hand in frustration. 'I'd no sooner destroyed the stuff than she got hold of more. The only time she ever smiled at me was when she was half dazed with opium. And somehow I always had the feeling it was my fault – that I'd failed her in some way, and she had to blot out my existence to be able to go on.

'Oh, I know she wanted a child,' he added, 'and by ill-luck that seems to be the one thing I can't give her. But I'd have done anything else within my power – given her anything else she wanted. Yet she flew into a screaming rage whenever I tried to talk to her, and I felt as if I were being punished for something I didn't understand.'

'Sophie was never easy to live with,' Flora admitted.

'Nor am I, I dare say.' Darius stared upwards to where the supple treetops nodded their windy heads in agreement. 'But I was never unfair to her. Not until now – now that I'm planning to leave her for another woman.'

'What if . . .' whispered Flora wistfully, 'what if, at this very moment, Sophie's lying in the arms of a lover of her own? What if she could hardly wait for you to go, before running out to seduce the handsome young footman who rides on the back of her carriage – or one of Felix's rakish friends from St James's Street . . . Isn't that possible?'

She felt him pulling up her skirts until the hot, dappled sunshine warmed the backs of her thighs, and his hands cupped themselves over her naked buttocks.

'I hope she is,' he murmured.

'Mmm?'

'Sophie. I hope she's taken a lover – two lovers, or a dozen if she has the energy for it. Then I needn't feel guilty about having you.'

'Do you really feel guilty?'

'A little. But I love you so much, there's no room for guilt. I love you, and I want you.' Gently, his fingers explored the cleft between her thighs. 'You only have to come near me, and the wanting begins.'

'Suppose Crébiche comes to look for us?'

'You won't shock Crébiche.'

'Mmm . . .' She slid down between his legs, and began to unbutton his trousers. 'We could try . . .' she said, applying her lips

296

and tongue, and then, as she heard his breathing become raspingly uneven, nibbling faintly with her teeth.

He groaned, raising himself on his elbows and rolling his head back, his eyes tightly closed.

'Enough?'

'No . . . Heaven help me. . .never . . .'

Flora had known pain, and had learned pleasure; now, subtly, she blended the two until he suddenly climaxed violently, gasping and surrendering himself to a long, agonized shudder which seemed to convulse his entire body.

'Oh, my stars . . . Where did you . . .' He shook his head, helpless. 'I mean – I never guessed . . .'

'There are some things I understand,' she reminded him softly. 'Though . . . it's quite different, doing it out of love.'

'Out of love?' A little blearily, he opened his eyes to regard her. 'Do you mean that?'

'I don't know what else to call it.' She lay languidly in the hollow of his side, in the space that had become hers. 'This is no illusion, and yet – what is it, when you feel wings beating inside you, when you want to sing and whirl into the air, and gaze and gaze at someone without ever filling your eyes to overflowing?'

'I hope it's love, because I feel exactly the same.' He reached out to smooth her hair where the breeze had plucked it from its pins. 'I can't give you up now, and that's the truth. It would be impossible.'

'And we can stay here in secret like two outlaws, and never go back?'

'Why not?' He glanced round at the airy mystery of the forest, smiled, and then bent to kiss her lightly on the lips. 'Why not, indeed.'

She pulled him down to her, and he kissed her again, moving on in leisurely contentment from the warmth of her lips to her throat and then the chestnut-pink tips of her breasts nestling inside her unfastened bodice.

'Will you . . .' she asked shyly, 'will you do what you did to me last night?'

'The very same?'

'Oh – please . . .'

And soon Sophie and her lovers flitted away through the trees like the whisky-jack, carrying the forest and the lake, and the canoe, and eventually time itself along with them.

*

Two hours later the hunters returned to the shore with a lone duck to show for their efforts, their hands intertwined, and sheepish, secret smiles on their faces. Crébiche scrutinized them gravely as they came.

'The sooner I'm back at Red River the better, before my wife starts to smile at some other fellow like that.' He stared out across the quietening lake and nodded. 'We go now, I think, while the wind is looking elsewhere for us.'

For the rest of that day, the lake put on its most splendid face for them, stretching out, limpid and cool, until every island sailed freely on its own reflection, a fleet of emerald ships adrift on an aquamarine sky. When they skirted the shore, individual trees detached themselves from the mass: tapering larches, frivolous in fringes of spring-green and tiny tufts of crimson flowers; the purple twigs of a dogwood; and, at the very top of a gaunt, bare fir, a fish eagle, surveying the intruders in his domain with stiff distaste.

'Perhaps this is Dr Breen's Eden, after all.' Dreamily, Flora trailed her fingertips in the still water. 'An endless wilderness garden . . . and we are such small parts of it. It's like being an ant among countless millions of grass-stems . . . Who would notice us two, among all this?'

Near a marshy point, a bull moose waded out, chest-deep, from the willows, and raised his dripping muzzle to watch them pass.

'Can we stay here, Darius – oh, can we stay, do you think?'

She said nothing during the rapids and portages of Trout River, where clouds of biting insects flew into ears and open mouths, and crept into crevices to raise their maddening weals. But on the blue stillness of Oxford Lake, Flora whispered again, 'Can we stay here – oh, can we stay, do you think?'

But the canoe flew swiftly on into a maze of channels where black pools sprouted dead, contorted branches like sparse hair and charred poles showed where fire had seared the forest.

At Sea Portage they met a north-canoe manned by eight noisy, genial *voyageurs*. Crébiche vanished into a back-slapping, shoulder-punching mêlée and returned with an invitation to supper; but already Flora felt uneasy. Eden had been made for two, and here were almost a dozen, the vanguard of a multitude beyond.

The next morning she watched the north-canoe speed on its boisterous way, listening to the strains of 'Rose Blanche' receding on the breeze, unhappily aware that a serpent had entered her garden.

As they swept towards Norway House, the trading post on the threshold of the great inland sea of Lake Winnipeg, Flora was even more disconcerted to see an enormous, high-prowed, brightly painted canoe drawn up on the foreshore, and a dozen or so dark-skinned men lounging around it, smoking.

Crébiche flung a remark over his shoulder to Maskisees in the stern. 'Simpson,' he added for Flora's benefit. 'The Governor's express *canot*. Those men are Iroquois, from Lachine. Very quick,' he confirmed, and as if determined to make a stylish arrival before these titans of the water, increased his stroke until their own canoe fairly flew towards the bank.

Flora's heart sank as they reached it. Norway House was disconcertingly like York Factory in miniature, with its walkway and regimented buildings, and its flag flying from an outcrop of pinkish rock nearby.

Chief Trader John MacLeod greeted them with unconcealed interest – Captain Machin and the *Nebula*'s crew had passed that way in October, and Dr Breen had been loud in his warnings of the trouble in store at York Factory. But the Chief Trader was clearly a man under strain. Governor Simpson had arrived not long before: and no sooner had he detailed an assistant to show Mrs Newsome and Mr Elder where they might spend the night, than he hurried away to dance attendance on his superior.

Flora disliked the Governor on sight. For one thing, he resembled pictures of Napoleon Bonaparte closely enough to make her wonder if the late Emperor had mysteriously resurrected himself, dyed his hair red, and sailed off to carve out a new empire in North America. It wasn't so much that Simpson was small and strutting – though he was – or that his easy smile never seemed to rise above his prow of a nose to register in his eyes: what disgusted her most was that in spite of his oily charm, the anxious fawning of his inferiors proclaimed a different Simpson, as faithfully as wax holds the shape of an invisible key.

At dinner, all eyes followed him nervously, his employees awaiting his orders with the unthinking obedience of dogs, and greeting his smallest sally with a roar of undeserved mirth.

With great ceremony, he placed Flora next to him at the table, and if her sun-peeled nose and dishevelled clothes made him suspect the circumstances of her journey, he set about investigating them in the most oblique manner possible, in the lulls of Piper Fraser's playing.

Had she left her husband in good health? Hadn't she found the winter at York Factory harsh and tedious? Why – by a strange coincidence – Captain Franklin himself had passed through Norway House only a few months earlier, on his way home from the Polar Sea . . . She must be anxious for the day when Mr Newsome, too, would return a hero to the bosom of his wife . . .

Flora answered as well as she could, hoping devoutly that if George Simpson noticed her shudder and look away, he would put it down to the rigours of the journey she'd just endured.

'I can't bear all the questions and the lying,' she mourned later, sitting with Darius on a slab of smooth, fissured rock at the nearby river-mouth. The rock, she noticed, had a disconcerting resemblance to raw flesh when it was wet.

'I hate having to smile and pretend everything's just as it should be. Sooner or later, the real story will come out.'

'I doubt it.' Darius tossed a pebble among the reeds and watched the ripples spread. 'Oh, I suppose McTavish will tell the Governor about the shooting when he reaches York Factory, but Ralph Newsome will be far away by then, and Simpson will hardly be anxious to make an issue of something that makes company discipline look slack. Besides – what's a handful of bird-shot in the arm of a famous explorer? Even if the story does get out, it'll be a nine days' wonder, no more.'

'Do you really think so?'

'By the end of summer no one will remember it happening.'

'Except Ralph. He'll remember,' Flora objected bleakly.

'I'm sure he will. And I'm sure he's in no doubt that your marriage is over, for all practical purposes. But what can he do about it? He'll come swaggering back to London, the hero of the Northwest Passage, and the whole nation will throw itself at his feet. Why should he want to rake up an old scandal that makes him look a fool and a blackguard?'

'That's true.' Flora's face began to brighten. 'He may not care at all where I've gone.'

John MacLeod sent them south in a stout, double-ended York boat, with its gaff-rigged sail and crew of oarsmen. After the regimented routine of Norway House it was a relief to be travelling again, and for

300

four and a half days the low, marshy shore of the lake was once more the only limit to the glorious future Flora and Darius planned together. Even the breeze which filled their single sail promised them unfettered happiness in the honesty of their love.

For four and a half days they sailed the lake, smiling idiotically over their secret, and on four blissful evenings they lay together among the granite knolls of the lakeside, exploring the pleasures of guiltless desire.

And then, at Red River Settlement, they found propriety waiting for them among the neat little houses, in the shape of Mr William Cockran, the Church of England missionary and self-appointed conscience of the colony. Under Mr Cockran's grim eye the rough-and-ready arrangements of the traders were an outrage to the sanctity of hearth and home. To promote the good Christian ideal, his wife had opened a boarding school for mixed-blood girls in which cooking, sewing, cleanliness and chastity were the cardinal points of the universe, with chastity, above all, as Magnetic North. There would be no pipe-smoking or casual liaisons at Red River, if the Cockrans had anything to do with it.

Flora was received politely into this earthly paradise, but with a certain amount of suspicion – Dr Breen having already passed that way. She was offered a room in the Cockrans' home for the length of her stay; Mr Elder was firmly lodged elsewhere.

Within a day Flora had brought out the crumpled chintz gown which she'd reserved for 'best', and had re-laced her corset.

'It must be so *painful*', Mrs Cockran remarked over dinner the first evening, 'to be parted from Mr Newsome when he faces such danger . . .' She glanced slyly at Flora, noting the signs of hasty flight and trying to determine how matters stood. 'Such a *gallant* man. Such an *adornment* to his country.'

'You're very kind,' murmured Flora, the words sticking in her throat like the pieces of Mrs Cockran's boiling fowl. Only that morning, she'd rediscovered the gold bracelet and earrings she'd brought with her from the house at Sloop Creek, and had gazed at them, suddenly cold with horror. They'd been an engagement present from her husband: now they reminded her that she was still his in point of law, no matter how far she might have escaped from him in spirit.

It only took a few minutes to seek out her companions of the journey. With a hearty embrace, Crébiche accepted the bracelet as a gift for his wife, while Maskisees gravely took the earrings, and limped off with the explorer's elegant gold hoops swinging among his smoky tresses.

Mrs Cockran persisted with her interrogation.

'I'm astonished Mr Newsome should think of sending his wife all that way by canoe – even in the care of a gentleman like Mr Elder . . .' Mrs Cockran peered at Flora closely. 'But then, being accustomed to great hardships himself, I dare say he didn't realize how the rigours of such a journey might affect the delicate sensibility of a woman.'

'I didn't mind,' declared Flora incautiously. 'I'd do it again, if I had to.'

'Indeed?'

'There are places where the landscape is quite glorious – more romantic than I'd have believed possible.' Flora glanced up, caught Mrs Cockran's bulbous eye, blushed, and glanced away again.

'Ah . . .' Mrs Cockran leaned back in her chair, her lips pursed and her head on one side, as if the outcome of her investigation had been exactly as she'd expected.

'A Stoic, I see,' she observed acidly, leaving Flora in no doubt that what she really meant was *abandoned wretch* . . .

'We can't stay here!' cried Flora miserably to Darius. 'There must be somewhere else we can go.'

'There is. In a week or so, there's a boat going east as far as Lachine, and I think we ought to go with it. Red River's no place for people like us.'

Flora gazed at him, taken aback. 'But . . . Lachine's half-way to England, surely.'

'It's Montreal, more or less.'

'You think we should stay in Canada, then,' she ventured uncertainly. 'Is that what you mean? Make a new life for ourselves in Montreal – or perhaps go on to America?' She glanced round to be sure they were unobserved, then wound herself round his arm with a sigh. 'Oh, well – I suppose anywhere at all will do, as long as we can hide away together.'

'As long as we're together.' He hesitated for a second, and then repeated, 'As long as we're together, nothing else matters.'

It took them almost a month to reach Montreal, and then less than an hour for Darius to find a banking-house with whom Elder's Bank was accustomed to doing business, and who declared themselves honoured to provide Monsieur Elder *soi-même* with all the credit he could possibly require while he chose to dignify their city with his presence. Dismayed, Flora watched her lover slip back into the habits of another existence. By evening, in spite of her protests, they were installed in the most sumptuous hotel money could command, and the principal *vendeuse* of the most exclusive retail establishment in the city had been instructed to bring a selection of wearing apparel for Mrs Newsome's inspection.

'I don't call this hiding ourselves away,' she murmured that evening, splendid in amber silk with a French bustle and a perfume-bottle dangling from a gold chain round her neck. 'When the bills of exchange reach London, Felix, for one, will know we've been here.'

'I want you to have the best.' Darius avoided her eye, staring instead round the commotion of the hotel dining-room. 'By the way, I've asked them to find a maid for you while you're here.'

'But it's all so extravagant! You shouldn't let me get accustomed to such luxury, you know,' she added teasingly. 'We shan't have anything of the kind in future.'

Without answering, he refilled their glasses with champagne. By the time he set down the bottle, his face wore a sombre expression which made her heart flutter like a caged bird.

'You're right – we ought to discuss what to do next.'

Across the table she laid her hand on his. 'As long as we're together, my darling. Nothing else matters.'

'Nothing at all.' The faint popping of bubbles reminded him of the waiting wine, and he raised his glass to his lips.

'To us—' persisted Flora bravely.

'To us,' he murmured. 'And no regrets.'

After so many nights spent on hard ground, it was pure, unadulterated heaven to lie in Darius's arms on a feather mattress between slippery linen sheets which skimmed the skin with the coolness of lake water. Yet Darius made love to her that night with an intensity which alarmed her, not because she sensed any diminution in his need of her, but rather the opposite, a desperate attempt to immerse himself completely in her, shutting out the world and all its clamorous demands.

Later, as they lay sated and heavy with tenderness, his head damply against her cheek, Flora made a desperate attempt to lighten his mood.

'Do you know – we haven't said a cross word since York Factory?' Her voice sounded unnaturally clear in the hot, velvet dimness of their room. 'We used never to be able to speak without quarrelling. Isn't that odd?'

With an impatient exhalation of breath, he turned on his back, and stared up at the shadowy ceiling.

'It's no use. Simply no use.' Defeated, he swept a stray curl from his brow. 'I've tried to believe we could do it – heaven knows how often I've told myself no one would miss us, and Sophie would be better off without me. But I suppose I knew all the time that sooner or later I'd have to go back to London, to make everything square. *Then* we can do whatever we want – I swear it, Flora.'

'Back to London?' Panic reduced her voice to a croak. 'You want to go back to England – back to Sophie?'

'No, not back to Sophie, of course not. But I do know this, my love – I'll never be happy with you on the basis of a lie. I must go back to London and let Sophie divorce me, or whatever's necessary. I don't care how much the lawyers take for seeing a bill through Parliament, but it must be done, honestly and above board.'

'But why should it matter?' Flora rose, dismayed on one elbow. 'Even if I were to divorce Ralph, we couldn't ever be married, you and I – not legally. You heard Dr Breen yourself at McTavish's table, saying a wife's sister is as good as a sister in blood, and marrying her is impossible. That means you're my brother in the eyes of the church, and all we've done for the past two months is commit incest, over and over again.'

The tremulous pinpoints of light in his eyes flickered dangerously towards her.

'And again, and again . . . And I can't believe there's anything more wonderful, in this world or the next.' He reached out to touch her cheek. 'But you aren't entirely right about English law.'

'And how do you know that?'

'Because one day last year – just on a whim, I suppose – I made it my business to find out. And the fact of the matter is that at present – and I don't say it may not be changed in the future, if the churchmen have their way – but at present the law would allow us to marry, if Sophie and I were divorced. It isn't illegal, though a church court can dissolve such a marriage at any moment if it sees fit. Still – I'm sure we could avoid any difficulties of that kind.'

Gently, he tried to pull her down to rest her head on his shoulder, but Flora would have none of it.

'So you want me to divorce Ralph – dragging every sordid detail out in public for people to laugh at – and you actually propose to tell Sophie she must divorce you, so you can go off with her sister . . . And then you say we *might* be able to marry, if you can bribe enough bishops . . . Oh, Darius, why can't we just stay here in our comfortable sin, and leave them all to forget us?'

'Because that would be the coward's way. I can't believe we'd be happy, Flora – not piling lie upon lie, and wondering when we'd be found out.'

'But how am I to divorce Ralph?' Flora wanted to know. 'Who would stand witness for me? His sister, do you imagine? And anyway,' she added miserably, 'I promised I'd never say anything of our life together. That was my price for coming to Hudson's Bay.'

'Then let him divorce you for running off with me.' Darius pulled her closer. 'Does it matter? The lawyers will find a way out – what else are they for? And if it's a question of money—'

'I thought it was all going to be so simple. Out there in the forest we were as free as foxes or . . . What do they call those impudent little birds?'

'Whisky-jacks.'

'Yes – we were as free as whisky-jacks. Like little birds, lost among the trees. And now it has all become so complicated . . .'

For a long moment there was silence, then Flora asked in a doom-laden tone, 'Do you really believe Sophie will have taken a lover?'

'No.' His voice came wearily out of the darkness. 'I wish I did.'

For two weeks they stayed in Montreal, and every day Darius tried to shower Flora with expensive gifts, as if attempting to make amends for what was to come.

On the fourteenth day he said, 'I think we should go on to New York now, and arrange a passage to England.'

'You once said you'd give up your heart's blood for me, if I ever needed it,' she reminded him accusingly.

'My heart's blood – without a thought, I promise you.' He gazed at her sadly. 'My heart's blood, Flora – but not my conscience.'

3

On 7th September 1828, the full-rigged *Swift* delivered them from New York to a London quayside – and from the future into the past. As each sea-mile slid in a curl of foam under the vessel's forefoot, Flora could feel the bands of *comme il faut* and *à la mode* tightening round her wrists, just as they'd dropped away on the outward journey.

The bunks aboard the *Swift* were narrow, never designed for two people who dreaded in their hearts what lay ahead, and felt they must prove while it was still possible how deeply and tenderly and inexorably they were part of one another. By now there was hardly a thought, or a touch, or a breath without its precious meaning; foreboding heightened every response, until each lived only in the other – sad together, hopeful together, leaning on the ship's rail, wrapped in one another's arms, counting the minutes from the New World to the Old.

On their last night aboard, as the *Swift* battled up the Channel, Flora strove with lips and hands and every part of her to make him absolutely hers. She surrendered her body, as she'd been forced to deliver it up to Ralph Newsome – and saw tears come into his eyes. She invented sweet tyrannies and took outrageous liberties, and cried out in his arms, rendered helpless and formless, clinging to him with the passion of the drowning for implacable rock. Nothing was sacred, nothing inviolate which could yield itself in the name of love and become a memory between them.

At last they rested, and waited sombrely for the grey London dawn.

A hackney-carriage carried them from the docks to Montagu Square. Maggie – unchanging, reassuring Maggie – was crossing the hall with her arms full of bedsheets when the footman opened the door, and she threw them down at the foot of the stairs to run out, flinging her arms round Flora's neck.

'Ooh, Miss Flora,' she crooned. 'Oh, my wee lamb! And looking so brown and thin! You've surely not fed yourself in these outlandish places you've been.' For a moment she held Flora at arm's length and studied her closely. 'Ah, but your mother will be so glad to see you! She's had such a time with Miss Sophie lately – ye canna imagine all that's happened—'

Behind Flora in the doorway she caught sight of Darius Elder, and gave a great shriek.

'Oh, Mister Elder, it's yourself! Well, there's a mercy, to be sure – we didn't expect you for a year yet.'

Before Darius could utter a word, she'd flown at him, spun him about and was pushing him back in the direction of the waiting carriage.

'Get you away home to Miss Sophie, sir! The mistress is at New Road this very minute, just as she's been every day these past two months. Ach, it was a bad day when you took it into your head to go away for so long—'

'What's happened to my wife?' Darius stood his ground. 'Is she ill?'

'Ill? Who can say? Best go and find out for yourself, man, before the poor lassie comes to more harm.'

'Darius—' Flora called after him as he swung himself into the carriage. But there was time for no more than a single shared glance of despair before he was whirled away to New Road and Sophie. Flora did her best to bury her anguish in sisterly concern.

'Maggie, what's the matter with Sophie?'

Maggie wiped her hands vigorously on her apron, as though she'd rather be rid of the whole affair.

'Well, now, dearie, who's to say? One day it's this – next day it's another . . .'

'Another *what*, for goodness' sake?'

The old woman glanced round the hallway to make sure none of the servants were within earshot, and lowered her voice.

'Two months ago, Mr Elder came here in a fair old upset – the other Mr Elder, Mr Felix, you understand. He came to say to your mother that he thought Miss Sophie was behaving very strangely, and what did Mrs St Serf think they ought to do about her. He also said some hard things about Mr Darius, I may tell you, for going off and leaving his wife in his brother's care.' Maggie drew in her chin and primly folded her hands.

'And what did Mamma say?' Flora prompted her guiltily.

'Well – you know what Miss Sophie's always been like. You'd never call her a peaceable soul at the best of times.' Maggie tugged at the lobe of an ear. 'Why, I can still remember, when you two were both wee lasses, how she used to screech like Satan's imp whenever she was cross, and throw her toys at my head until I ran. And what about her terrible sulks when things weren't just exactly the way she wanted them?'

'It's true. She'd go quiet for days, and nothing would bring her out of it.'

'Well, at first your mother thought matters were no worse than usual, and it was just Miss Sophie having one of her little turns. Then it seemed she'd taken to wandering about the house all day like a sleepwalker—' Maggie mimed the blank expression of a dreamer, 'or lying in bed with that old doll of hers, weeping for no reason at all. Your mother always reckoned it was because there were no . . .' she mouthed the word, '*bairns* . . . Though I was never so sure of that myself. I still think there's a sickness at the root of it.

'At any rate, one day the knife-boy from New Road came flying round here pell-mell in Miss Sophie's carriage. He'd a note in his hand from the housekeeper to say Miss Sophie had filled herself with laudanum, and been found blue and sweating on her bedroom floor. They were trying to walk it out of her just at that moment, but the housekeeper wasn't sure if they'd keep her from falling into a stupor, and would Mrs St Serf please come as quick as she could . . .'

Maggie shook her head and sucked her blackened teeth in disapproval.

'They managed to save her life, poor lass, but afterwards the doctor left a nurse to keep watch, and took all the medicines out of the house. Then, two weeks later, what didn't Miss Sophie do, but give her nurse the slip? They found her down in the kitchens, cutting her wrists with the boning knife and bleeding all over the flags.

'After that we were terrified at what she might do next, I promise you. Two of her maids walked out, saying they were afraid for their lives, though I can't believe there was much spirit in them, to be scared of a wee woman like Miss Sophie. Still – maybe now her guidman's at home she'll take a think to herself and settle down to be a decent wife to him.'

'Maggie . . . does that mean . . .' Flora tried to keep her voice steady. 'Do you believe Sophie's trouble was caused by Darius – Mr Elder – being away for so long?'

Maggie frowned for a moment. 'If it was any other woman I'd say yes, Miss Flora. But I've known you two girls since you were born, and I've never yet seen Miss Sophie more concerned about another human creature than she is about her own affairs. No, as I told you – I reckon there's a sickness of some kind at the root of it. If Miss Sophie disnae care to live any more, then I'm persuaded it's for her own sake, and not for her husband's.'

She regarded Flora for a moment with a bright, quizzical eye, and then reached out to gather her into a vast hug.

'Ah, lassie,' she murmured. 'Don't go blaming yourself, now. This business is between Miss Sophie and her Maker. You and Mr Elder aren't the cause of it.' And as she felt Flora stiffen in her arms, she whispered, 'Never fear, I won't say a word. But I saw the way he looked at you.'

It was fortunate that Constance St Serf didn't share Maggie's insight. At six that evening she returned to Montagu Square and embraced her daughter with a restrained smile.

'You're well enough, after all your travelling?'

'Yes, Mamma.'

'And your husband, Mr Newsome – how is he?'

'It's four and a half months since I left him, Mamma. But I dare say he's well, and no doubt somewhere at the Polar Sea.'

'It's a pity your brother-in-law couldn't tear himself away from the wilds a bit sooner.' Mrs St Serf's nose twitched resentfully. 'Men!' she complained. 'They can't resist an adventure – completely forgetting the poor women they've left at home. Your father was just the same. Still,' she added, 'now Darius's back, he can take some responsibility for his wife. I suppose Maggie's told you about the goings-on at New Road?'

Flora nodded. 'Maggie thinks Sophie's ill in some way. Do you think . . . Is it possible she's going the same way as Papa?'

Mrs St Serf scowled at her daughter. 'It was Bonaparte who did for your father, my girl. The price of bravery – that was your father's trouble.' She paused, silently daring Flora to disagree. 'No, all Sophie needs is a change of air. All her doctors say so.'

The next day saw a conference at New Road between Darius, his brother Felix, Constance St Serf and two eminent doctors. From Mrs St Serf's account later, it seemed that Felix had begun by roundly abusing his brother for leaving a demented woman in his care, and Darius had promptly threatened to throw him out of the house, until the doctors intervened. The medical men had talked in vague terms about fluxes and humours and – with an uneasy glance at Major St Serf's widow – *inherited melancholia*, before agreeing there was no prospect of an easy cure.

But one thing was clear: Mrs Elder needed a change of scene, and more of the bracing mineral waters which had helped her before in

Bath. The doctors' opinion was that she must go abroad at once for the sake of her health, and naturally her husband must take her.

Flora had gone with her mother to New Road, and waited in the morning-room until the conference was over. She was gazing, white-faced, out of the window when the door opened softly, and Darius came in.

'Have they told you?' he asked as Flora flew into his arms.

'Told me what?' Afraid of the worst, she buried her eyes in the breast of his coat.

'Sophie's ill – ill in her mind. They say the only treatment for her is to go abroad.'

Flora raised her face, dismal as a rain-drenched flower. 'And you? Must you be the one to take her?'

He nodded silently.

'But *why*?' Flora's cry of despair was wrenched from the heart. 'Why you, when we had such plans—'

'What else can I do? Do you want me to abandon her, and let her destroy herself? Am I supposed to have Sophie on my conscience for the rest of my life?'

'Don't you understand? She's only doing it to get you back – to make a prisoner of you – to keep you away from me!'

'That's unfair of you, Flora – and unworthy of you. Do you really believe a grown woman who talks to no one but an old wooden doll is sane?'

'But what about me?' Filled with nameless fear, Flora pounded with her fists on his chest. 'What am I to do, while you're running all over the Continent with Sophie? I've lost you already – oh, I knew this would happen if we came back to London!'

'Flora – my darling—' He pulled her closer, trapping her rebellious fists. 'This makes no difference to what I feel for you. As soon as Sophie's better there'll be a divorce, just as we planned, and after that—'

'After that we'll both be in our graves!' cried Flora bitterly, tears of betrayal springing into her eyes. 'So much for all your promises! So much for *trust*, and all your fine plans!'

'Flora – please – don't say that! What else can I do? A woman has already died because of me – because I could do nothing to help her. Poor Madhu will be on my conscience until my dying day. I can't abandon Sophie as well – not even for you.'

'But you don't love Sophie! You said so yourself!'

'I married her, and I swore to look after her. Flora, my love—'

He held her against him, as if trying to make a shelter of himself to enfold her. 'We'll have to be patient, that's all. One day this will all be settled – and until then we can still go on seeing one another—'

'And I could be your mistress, is that what you mean? A little charity for a poor, mistreated woman? Another five-pound note, like the one you once left in my purse?'

'It wouldn't be like that.'

'Of course it would! Oh – not again! Not again!' Flora pressed the heels of her hands into her eyes as all the fear and humiliation of her marriage returned to possess her. 'You promised!'

'But for heaven's sake – how could I have forseen this?'

'Oh, why did you say all those things to me? Why did you force me to hope, when I'd learned to live with nothing?'

'Flora – please! Everything will happen as we planned, I promise—'

'Don't promise!' Almost mad with despair, Flora tore herself free. 'Don't dare to promise me anything! Your promises are worthless – just as *his* were! Very well—' Flora swallowed down the tears which threatened to overwhelm her. 'Very well – run off to the Continent if you please. But if you go, I shall know you're a liar, just like all the rest, and I'll make *you* a promise – I shan't be here when you come back.'

In the sudden silence, Darius's knuckles cracked as he clenched his fists.

'Take care, Flora. You don't mean that.'

'I mean every word.' She was being unreasonable, no doubt: but pain had long since swept away reason, and she could bear no more. 'You asked me to trust you, and, heaven help me, I did. I trusted you – and I loved you as well as I knew how. If you leave me now, I swear I'll never trust you again.'

'I . . . cannot . . . abandon Sophie.'

'Very well.' Flora's voice rang out with the clear, fatal note of a funeral bell. 'Then you've abandoned me.'

He sent a note to Montagu Square the next morning.

If I call at two this afternoon, can you manage to be alone?

'There's no reply,' Flora told the waiting messenger, and stood in the hallway until his liveried coat-tails had disappeared from sight behind the front door.

PART FOUR

September 1828

CHAPTER NINETEEN

I

The next day at four, amid a hustle of lady's-maids, valets, nurses and grooms, Mr and Mrs Darius Elder's carriage, followed by a two-horse *fourgon* crammed with absolutely necessary baggage, boarded the Rotterdam steamer.

At five minutes past four, Flora sank down on an Egyptian chair in her mother's parlour and wept as if she would die; and Constance St Serf was astonished at the sight of such unexpected sisterly concern.

'I don't expect she'll be away for ever.' Constance stood before Flora, her hands folded over her stomach, a little at a loss. 'Come now, Flora – you'd be better occupied in thinking about your own future, it seems to me. I presume you'll be off home to Russell Square in another day or two.'

Without raising her face from her hands, Flora shook her head.

'What? Not going to Russell Square? And why not, may I ask?'

'You might as well know,' hiccuped Flora. 'I've left Ralph. For good,' she added.

'What nonsense!' Constance put her hands on her hips. 'Of course you haven't left him. Whoever heard of such a thing?'

'Ralph knows all about it,' murmured Flora miserably. 'He agreed I should go. It's best for both of us.' Red-eyed, she struggled to maintain some dignity. 'We made a bargain, and my part of it is to leave his home and his life for ever.'

Constance tumbled down quickly on the end of a Greek sofa as if her legs had suddenly lost the ability to support her.

'Oh, you wilful girl! How could you agree to something so disastrous? No matter what little squabbles you've had with your husband – he's still better than *no husband at all*.'

'I've left him, Mamma. The marriage is over.' Flora's complexion was almost blue-white in its pallor. She shook her head, dazed.

'Everything's over,' she whispered.

'And you tell me Ralph Newsome's agreed to this?'

Flora nodded silently.

'Well!' Constance drew in her neck like an affronted chicken. 'I shan't ask what's happened to cause this state of affairs – no, I shan't. No!' She held up a bony hand, though Flora had made no move to enlighten her. 'But does Mr Newsome propose to support you, now that you're apart? How do you expect to live?'

'I shall support myself,' murmured Flora uneasily.

'I suppose that means you mean you intend to live here, with me. I don't imagine you gave a moment's thought to the future, when you abandoned your marriage.'

This was true enough to keep Flora silent for a moment. Then determination reasserted itself, and she made an enormous effort to sound confident.

'I'll find a way of supporting myself, don't worry. I could . . . go out governessing – or become a teacher in a free school.'

'Which would pay you enough to keep a mouse,' her mother pointed out. 'Oh, Flora – how could you be so reckless? And just when—' Constance closed her mouth abruptly, with a little quiver which rustled the ribbons on her cap.

'What were you going to say?'

'Oh . . . just that . . . Mr Theodore Wesley – you remember Mr Wesley – has been most attentive to me recently, and I think . . . I think I may fairly say that *developments* are in the wind.' Constance smirked, and twisted her lips into a small cupid's bow.

'He's proposed!' Flora tried to wipe away her tear-stains with a finger.

'No – he hasn't proposed yet . . .' Constance wriggled her shoulders in anticipation, and then a new and gloomy thought struck her. 'Though I doubt if he will propose, with a grown-up, husbandless daughter haunting the house like a wet Sunday at Vauxhall.' She gave a sniff of self-pity. 'How can I tell Mr Wesley my daughter is a runaway wife, a helpless drain on his resources?'

'I'd have thought the resources were yours, surely,' objected Flora, 'your income from the Chillbourne estate. Unless Mr Wesley has come into some money of his own, of course.'

'If only he would!' Constance sniffed again. 'No, if Mr Wesley makes me his wife, I shall naturally pretend my income is his. It will be as good as his, in any case.' Constance searched in her sleeve for a handkerchief. 'I wish you'd spared a thought for me before you plunged, Flora – I really do.'

*

Ten minutes later Flora tied her hat firmly on her head and escaped to find the one person whom, at that moment, she needed most – Lydia Seaward. More than a year had passed since Lydia had wished her godspeed, and now Flora longed more than ever to hear the sound of Lydia's sensible, down-to-earth voice. Lydia would understand, if anyone could.

The pork-butcher's daughter answered the door in Park Street, peered at Flora, and exclaimed, 'Oh, it's you, ma'am! Well, she ain't here no more – not a bit of it. Removed, bag and baggage she has. Gone off to Mount Street now – and not the side next the burying ground, neither.'

'*Mount Street*? Are you sure?'

'Certain of it, ma'am, since she sent round for that great brass-mounted bed she said was definitely hers, and not Colonel West's. Oh, it's Mount Street, sure enough.' And the pork-butcher's daughter confidently supplied the number of the house.

Puzzled, Flora rang the bell at the door in Mount Street which was supposed to be Lydia's. Overhead, lacework balconies guarded the elegant windows instead of the oil-seller's dripping pipe, and she could hear the brisk clash of crockery from the basement by her feet. It was ten in the morning, a time when Lydia was habitually alone, but who could tell what transformation went with such a house?

A footman with a blue chin and a striped waistcoat answered her ring, invited her to step inside and jauntily carried off her name to Mrs Seaward.

'Mrs Seaward's taking a bath,' he announced when he returned.

'Oh, then tell her I'll call again tomorrow—'

'There's no need for that, ma'am. I'm instructed to have you taken to her at once. Stitch—' he signalled to a hovering maid, 'Stitch will show you the way. Excuse me, ma'am—' The footman detained her with a gesture. 'Mrs Seaward ain't alone. She suggested you might wish to lower your veil or borrow one of hers.'

Amazement temporarily overcoming her unhappiness, Flora climbed the stone staircase at the heels of the maid, pulling down a length of gauze hat-ribbon to hide the upper half of her face. The staircase led up to a corridor lit by a silver chandelier. Had Lydia come into a fortune, then, to have soared to such splendour?

The maid halted at a nearby door, and as she tapped on a panel Flora heard laughter and the typical sing-song of conversation intended to be devastatingly witty. There was a cry of 'Enter!' –

surely Lydia's voice – before the maid threw open the door on an extraordinary scene.

The room was a bedroom – the *maréchal's* bed stood imposingly at one side of it, its brocades and tassels and fine linen sheets disordered enough to indicate that someone had only recently got out of it. For the rest, it was simply a large and luxurious bedroom – with an unexpectedly huge bath set up in the centre of the floor, as long as a sarcophagus and plated in silver. Its shining sides reflected the rich colours of the carpet, and at each corner a rampant dragon's foot was buried to the knuckle in the sumptuous pile.

And there in the bath was Lydia, pink with the warmth of something rich and scented, her silver-blonde hair piled like a delightful blancmange on the top of her head and some of the rose petals from the water sticking to the curve of her bosom like the freckles on a lily.

As the footman had warned, Lydia was not enjoying her luxury alone. Two gilt chairs had been drawn up to the side of the bath, each one containing a man, sipping champagne but dressed as if for the most formal of levees. The ebony cane and dyed ginger hair, Flora realized, belonged to a Minister of State. His companion, whose white silk gloves smelled suffocatingly of Eau de Portugal, had made his fortune in the Indies and now drove out in a gold-appointed barouche known to fashionable London as the Sugar Bowl.

Both heads had turned to watch Flora enter the room, and two pairs of male eyes probed her veil with unabashed curiosity.

'Sweetness – you're back!' Lydia waved a cushiony arm from her wallow. 'Come in, come in! Stitch will bring you champagne and bonbons – Stitch—' She snapped dripping fingers at the maid, and immediately an exquisite cobweb of a glass appeared, accompanied by a silver bowl full of plump pink globes, dusty with sugar.

Lydia dispatched her visitors with playful tyranny.

'Off with you both! Back to your debates and your coffee-houses! My dear friend and I intend to gossip, and I won't have you eavesdropping on our secrets.'

She extended a languid hand to be kissed, the movement raising a creamy, pink-tipped breast from the drift of scented froth under each man's nose. Flexing their shoulders and exchanging knowing little smiles, Lydia's callers obediently took their leave.

'But it's so wonderful to have you back safely!' As the door finally closed, Lydia patted the nearest vacant chair. 'It's a relief, too, I can tell you. When the *Nebula* was reported missing I was almost beside myself, worrying about you – and then, of course, the ship's master came back, and I realized you'd been marooned in that place . . . But you're back, dear heart, and that husband of yours must be mercifully far away at the Polar Sea – with your dashing cavalier at his side, more's the pity.'

'Not . . . exactly.'

Now, when it came to the point, Flora felt suddenly helpless to put into words all that had happened to her since leaving London. To explain, she had to understand: and her emotions were still so confused, her mind still dazed with disaster – and yet that was precisely why she'd called.

'First tell me how in the world you came by all this,' she proposed. 'When I left, you were locked up with the butcher's daughter in Park Street, and now . . .' She indicated the splendour around them. 'Have you inherited a fortune, to pay for all this?'

An expression of infinite cunning spread over Lydia's beautiful features as she began to explain. No, there hadn't been any fortune – unless you counted the blissful harmony of face and figure which had inspired no less than three of London's wealthiest men to offer their protection.

'Do you remember young Rosangle, the Marquis of Highbury's nephew?'

Flora frowned. 'The poor boy with the stammer?'

'The *rich* boy with the stammer,' Lydia corrected her. 'Though you'd be surprised how little you notice a stammer when it says "f-five-and-twenty thousand a year".' Lydia curved her spine, rolling like a milky serpent, and a marble knee rose up through the rose petals. 'Colonel West introduced him, oddly enough . . . And that very evening the dear creature told me he'd positively *die* if I didn't leave the Colonel and put myself in his hands.'

Frederick Rosangle was nineteen years old, and built like an Adonis; Sir Edward Lashley, the Chancery judge, was equally rich, if less pleasing to look at, but as Lydia observed with practical good sense, 'I can always shut my eyes, can't I?'

'And there's dear Marcus Fitzhallow,' she added with satisfaction.

'Lord Fitzhallow?'

'Well, of course.' Lydia's eyes flew innocently wide. 'Oh, Flora, he's so perfectly sweet! He sends me oranges from his stove-house – sends them all the way in a tilbury, with a perfectly beautiful footman in livery and a feathered hat.'

319

Flora shook her head, amazed. 'And do you mean to tell me you're taking money from all three?'

'Presents, sweetness,' Lydia corrected her primly. 'And yes, I'm taking everything they give me, if you want to be sordid about it. This is a very expensive house, you know. Did you see the fellow at the door? Have you any idea what he costs me each week in stockings?'

Lydia wriggled righteously in her tub. 'Besides,' she added, 'I've discovered a good business principle. When a commodity is in demand, you should keep the price high and ask whatever the market will bear. Pass me my robe, sweetness, will you?'

A loose gauze wrapper overflowing with ribbons lay across the foot of the bed. By the time Flora had returned with it to the side of the bath, Lydia had already stepped out, glistening like an alabaster figure draped in garlands of foam. She gazed round the palatial bedroom, and trailed a finger along the edge of her silver bath.

'Yes,' she pronounced decisively. 'Yes, I'd say it's definitely true. Here I am – an independent woman, not waiting for the say-so of some ill-natured fellow. I can pick and choose among the lot of them!'

Trailing the damp wrapper and a line of tiny footsteps, she proceeded towards the bed

'And if you want a warning of what happens to a woman when she trusts herself entirely to one man, think of that little French miss – what was her name? Madeleine – the little creature who fell so in love with your father and found herself abandoned for her pains? *There*'s a lesson for us all.'

Enthroned on her bed, Lydia suddenly became aware of Flora's dismal silence and downcast eyes. As she watched, a large tear dripped from Flora's cheek to make a damp circle in her lap.

'Flora, my precious!' Deserting the bed, Lydia pattered to Flora's side, tripping over her trailing hem as she came. 'My dear, dear friend—' She cradled Flora's heaving shoulders in a soft, damp arm. 'Is it that husband of yours? What has he done now? Come on, tell me all about it, and we'll see what's to be done.'

Yet there was, as Lydia admitted once the story had been told, precious little to be done for the present. *Time*, she counselled: *everything straightens itself out in time*. Still – even to be able to share her misery made Flora feel a little better. Perhaps time would bring a miracle after all – or help her to learn to live without the man who was her sister's husband.

Mr Wesley called in the evening, flashed his ivory teeth at Flora as she passed him in the hall, and wheezed his delight at seeing her safely home again.

'Did he propose?' she asked her mother at supper.

'He did not.' Constance gazed unhappily at her plate. 'And I don't expect him to, under the circumstances.'

Flora pushed her plum-cake away untouched. 'I don't feel like eating.'

'Starving yourself won't help,' observed her mother. 'You hardly ate anything at all yesterday.'

'I'm not starving myself, Mamma. I just feel a little . . . peculiar. I dare say it's all the upset over Sophie,' she concluded, avoiding her mother's eye.

2

Next morning's dawn was her third without Darius.

Lying in the lonely dimness of her bed in Montagu Square, Flora found her thoughts drawn back inevitably to the source of her pain: had she been right to send Darius's messenger back to him empty-handed?

Yet who could doubt that Darius had abandoned her? He'd enticed her from her self-sufficiency like a wild dove, with gentleness and a few grains of hope in the palm of his hand; it had been the hardest flight of her life, that brief flutter from the safety of solitude. She'd given him all he'd demanded – even her last small reserve of indifference, the kernel of herself she'd meant to keep unassailable for ever – and having triumphed, he'd run off with his spoils, and gone back to Sophie.

Sophie . . . had been ill. Flora tried hard to dwell on sisterly thoughts – on their childhood together at Richmond and the giddy, intimate confidences only sisters share. Yet *what if* . . . What if Sophie had never made up her mind to acquire Darius Elder, and to flaunt him in Flora's face like a new hat that enchants for a week before familiarity dulls its gloss?

Darius came to her in dreams now, when she hadn't the power to

321

send him away. In the charmed darkness he possessed her totally once more, so startlingly distinct that tiny details she'd never noted before impressed themselves on her waking memory – the bluish tint of the skin at his hairline, the soft, indulgent lobe of an ear, his long, rippling sigh as he entered her . . .

Oh, sweet heaven . . . What else but love could engender such fierce tenderness, such raging, desperate longing? Yet even as she woke, feverish and dizzy, the knowledge of his betrayal rushed in to torment her all over again.

As the first of the sun struck her window, Flora felt the familiar queasiness return to the pit of her stomach. She sat up in bed and at once felt dizzier and odder still; it was as much as she could do to find her chamber-pot before being abruptly and violently sick.

Then it struck her that neither Sophie's illness nor Darius's desertion might be entirely to blame.

She pattered across to the door, locked it, stripped off her nightgown, and examined her naked body in her dressing-table mirror, balancing on tiptoe to view the smooth, creamy swell of her abdomen above the clutter of brushes and trinket-boxes. Experimentally, she trailed her fingers over her breasts, trying to decide how they must have felt to an exploring hand . . . They were firm and full, and ached slightly to the touch, strained like bursting fruit.

Different, definitely different.

There was no other obvious sign except a vague, creeping lushness – an extra covering, butter-thick, over her bones – a broadening and mellowing where before she'd been lithe and quick.

Flora stared at herself in the mirror, no longer in any doubt. A solemn, apprehensive Flora stared back – a Flora carrying Darius Elder's child.

'Do you really think it's possible?' As soon as she'd dressed, Flora hurried to Lydia's to share her fears. 'Tell me it isn't true, Lydia – please. Perhaps I'm only a little sick,' she finished hopefully.

Lounging in the chair next to Flora's, Lydia pulled a face.

'There's only one sort of sickness that produces those symptoms, and that's baby-disease. And since you're so sure it wasn't Ralph Newsome who popped it in there, there's only one other possibility. The dashing Mr Elder has left you something to remember him by.'

She leaned over to pat Flora on the hand. 'At least he's rich enough to support the child.'

'Oh, no!' Flora shook her head at once. 'He mustn't ever know. He went off and left me, Lydia – I won't ever beg from him.'

'But for goodness' sake – you're still in love with the fellow!'

'But I don't want to be!' Flora made an effort to sit bolt upright in her chair. 'You were right when you said it was madness for a woman to put all her trust in one man.' She swallowed hard, but couldn't suppress a cry from the heart. 'How could he treat me like that, Lydia?'

'It was bad of him.' Lydia shook her head sombrely. 'And I can understand how your poor pride's hurt, which is hard to bear when your husband's mistreated you, too. But whatever you may say – with a babe to look after, you're hardly an independent woman.'

'I was going to find work. I thought I would go out governessing or become a pupil-teacher,' confessed Flora miserably.

'Not with a child of your own, my dove. Not unless your mamma will take care of it for you.'

'Mamma? Oh, glory . . .' Flora turned to meet Lydia's gaze, her eyes round with dismay, while her hands moved protectively to her waist. 'What am I going to tell Mamma? The baby won't be born until early summer, and everyone will know it isn't Ralph's.'

'But you don't have to tell your mother whose baby it *is*, do you? Tell her it was some man you fell for in the Canadas. She'll be so busy scolding you for that, the real truth won't occur to her. Flora? Are you listening to me?'

'It's true.' Flora's voice was so low as to be almost inaudible. 'No one will take a governess with a child of her own. And Mamma's made it quite plain she wants me out of her house, so she can be sure of Mr Wesley . . . Oh, Lydia, what am I going to do?'

'You must pocket your pride, and send a message to Darius Elder.' Lydia hesitated for a fraction of a second. 'That is . . . if you're bent on keeping it.'

Flora stared at her. 'You mean—'

'There's a woman in Hog Lane who helps girls in your situation. Quite a clean woman, considering – or I wouldn't think of sending you. And she doesn't tell tales afterwards, or come back looking for more money, like some.'

'No – I could never do that!' Flora shook her head as if trying to rid herself of a temptation which buzzed like a persistent fly.

'Five minutes, dear heart, and it's done. Then it all comes away, and *pfft*!' Lydia waved a hand. 'No more baby. Just as if it never was.'

323

'Except that it isn't as if it never was,' objected Flora bitterly, torn by the memory of another lost child – another lost future, destroyed by Ralph Newsome's violence. Yet what kind of future awaited this new baby? If she was determined to go her own way, the child would be born in scandal and given no name but *bastard*; worse – it would be born to a mother who couldn't afford to raise it.

'Have you ever . . . been to the woman in Hog Lane?'

'Once – a long time ago, before I learned a few little ways of taking care.' Lydia examined a row of knuckles like pink seashells. 'I remember crying a great deal, because it was so painful, but I don't suppose it was as bad as childbed. And yes, I know you can die of it – but you can die of bearing a child, too, so I don't see that it makes much odds.'

'I wonder,' murmured Flora doubtfully. She clasped her face in her hands. 'I just don't know what to do. I must have some time to think.'

'Well, then . . . why don't you go and tell Dédalon all about it?' Lydia shrugged her shoulders. 'He sometimes talks a good deal of sense, for all he's tucked away in that workshop of his. And he does keep asking for news of you, though I've had precious little to give him.'

'Dédalon?' Flora stared at her in alarm, confronted by a sudden vision of the automaton-maker holding her hands in his, and gazing at her with a strange, absent fondness. 'But I haven't spoken to him for so long . . .'

'Then go and see him, why don't you? He cares for you like his own daughter, sweetness – he really does. It would be a great kindness to call on him.'

'He'll be angry with me, I know it, because I didn't tell him I was going to be married. I've made such a mess of everything, just as he warned me I would.'

'Nonsense,' insisted Lydia breezily. 'Dédalon's far too fond of you to be angry. At least let me tell him you're home again, and were asking after him.'

'But you mustn't tell him about the baby, Lydia! Oh, please don't say anything about that.'

'Not if you don't want me to, sweetness, I promise.' Lydia shook her head, and sighed. 'I just hate to see you in such trouble, that's all.' She regarded Flora sadly. 'Take some time to think about your future, of course. But don't leave it too late to decide, will you?'

Flora had gone to Lydia for practical good sense, and she had to admit that Lydia's advice had been clear and unequivocal; either ask Darius Elder to support his child, or do away with it. Oh, she'd offered it kindly enough, but in Lydia's new world a woman had to look out for herself, without letting sentiment get in her way.

Semiramis: Flora had heard one of Lydia's visitors murmur the name as he kissed the gold rings that knobbed her hand. *Goodbye, Semiramis* . . . Not *Lydia* – not any more.

And Semiramis, Flora discovered, was a focus of London gossip. Not satisfied with her three rich lovers, it was whispered, she'd had herself served up at a banquet for the Turkish Ambassador, naked on a silver platter, garnished with a single string of pearls. She was so rich, the ladies hissed behind their fans, that she threw away her white kid gloves as soon as they became soiled, and had her satin boots sewn smoothly over her feet every day. And everyone knew who'd hinted to her pet Minister of State that the Supervisor of Ports should be sacked: and sacked he was, the following day, and his horde of nephews with him.

Semiramis, it seemed, had become an independent woman.

The fact remained that Flora hadn't. Two weeks later, when for the third time she was forced to run from the breakfast table in order to be sick, her mother finally confronted her with an ultimatum: if Flora was ill, she must consult a doctor – if she wasn't, then . . .

The few sentences that followed brought a piercing shriek from Constance St Serf, and sent Maggie running for sal volatile and brandy-and-water. A baby on the way was bad enough when the mother and father were separated; but it didn't take a genius to realize that a baby expected in the middle of May could hardly have been conceived by a man who'd set out for the Polar Sea twelve months earlier.

Oh, certainly, Constance had been anxious to become a grand-mother – but not to such a child as Flora had chosen to bring into the world. How could she boast of the first lisped 'Grandmamma' of a blatant *by-blow*? Who would admire the perfect beauty of a *mistake*? And worse than all that – what would Mr Wesley say?

'I don't care what he says,' snapped Flora, her nerves at breaking-point. 'I'll find work, and somewhere to live where I won't be an embarrassment to anyone. I may not be able to earn a great deal, but at least it'll be an honest income, honestly earned.' She struggled to sound confident. 'I won't be a burden to you, Mamma – don't worry.'

However, as Lydia had pointed out, good intentions counted for very little when there was a baby to support, and there were times during the days that followed when Flora began to think seriously that a visit to Hog Lane might be her only salvation. Yet the baby was Darius Elder's – the only tiny part of him she'd been able to save from the ruins of her love. The child had been conceived in tenderness, unlike the poor, murdered scrap which Ralph Newsome had forced on her. If she'd mourned the death of that other, doomed baby . . . how could she possibly bring about the end of this one?

At that precise moment in her Cologne hotel room, Mrs Darius Elder picked up the bottle of saline waters her doctor had prescribed, and hurled it against the wall.

'I will *not* drink that filthy concoction!' She watched, her eyes bright with triumph, as the liquid streamed down in dark vertical lines to form a puddle among the glass shards on the floor.

Darius dismissed the terrified nurse with a gesture, and turned back to his wife.

'That was foolishness, Sophie. The doctor said it would do you good.'

Sophie's eyes glittered, and her hands clenched into fists at her sides. 'It was filthy, I tell you. It came from some dirty hole in the ground.'

'I'll send out for some more.'

'Don't bother! I'm not ill, so I don't need their medicine. Send out for some laudanum, if you must.'

'You aren't to have any more laudanum. You know that.'

'I'll have what I like.' Sophie stamped her foot. 'If you won't get it for me, then the porter will, or the chambermaid.'

'Sophie—' Darius surveyed her despairingly. 'You promised you'd try anything the doctors prescribed. Don't you want to be well again?'

'Why should you care?' Absently, Sophie rubbed her hands together, as if something sticky clung to her palm. 'Nobody cares about me,' she said plaintively. 'Nobody at all.' She glanced down at her hands in sudden distaste. 'They don't even bring me proper soap, and yet everything here is so dirty . . . Why is there never any soap in this place?'

In a couple of strides, Darius crossed the room and gripped her raw, roughened hands in his, halting their compulsive kneading.

'Sophie,' he told her urgently, 'you've got to get well again!'

'Why?' Her eyes met his, unblinking. 'Why should I do anything for you?'

Because until you are well, screamed a voice in Darius's head, *I cannot leave you. I'm trapped here, caring for you, while Flora believes I've betrayed her and makes herself wretched. Even if I thought she'd read any letter I wrote, what could I say? That she must wait – that I'm imprisoned here, unable to go to her, to hold her and make her understand?*

With a groan of frustration he released Sophie's hands.

'I'll send out for another bottle – and this time, you'll drink it.'

On the last day of October, resting before dinner in her room at Montagu Square, Flora heard the clatter of a carriage pulling up at the door, followed by a brisk, workmanlike knock. Her mother had gone out, she knew, having covered her face with so much powder to hide the ravages of her daughter's misdeeds that she looked like a floured bun with currants for eyes.

Flora listened while the hall filled with the uneasy growl of male voices; then the drawing-room door opened and shut – the callers would wait for Mrs Newsome to come down.

There had been something so muted and reverential in the tone of the voices that Flora's thoughts fled immediately to Cologne and to Darius Elder. Some accident had taken place – a steamer had sunk, he'd been thrown from his horse, shot by a madman . . . One after another, the dreadful possibilities chased one another through her mind, regardless of her determination not to care.

Throwing aside the rug which had covered her knees, Flora flew to the door, and was half-way downstairs by the time she met the maid who'd been sent to fetch her.

The callers were standing awkwardly on the drawing-room carpet, and refused her offer of chairs.

The more urbane of the two, a man with smooth hands and a great many seals on his watch, introduced himself as Richard Edgerton of the Hudson's Bay Company and his ruddy-faced companion as the master of the *Prince Rupert*, just back from York Factory.

'Aye,' agreed the captain, regarding Flora with a certain softness about his deeply seamed eyes which told her as clearly as any announcement that his news was bad.

327

'What's happened?' She glanced between the two men. 'Why have you come here?'

'Best sit down, ma'am, I should think,' Edgerton advised. 'It isn't an easy errand we've come on.'

Maggie, who'd been hovering by the door, came forward to put her hands on the rail of Flora's chair. Flora took a deep breath.

'It's Ralph, isn't it? You've come to tell me something's happened to him.'

The captain glanced towards Edgerton, who nodded. 'I'm afraid so, ma'am. It's my unhappy duty to tell you that Mr Ralph Newsome is dead.'

'*Dead?*'

'Aye,' confirmed the captain. 'Dead.'

Flora closed her eyes for a moment, and Edgerton took the gesture for a paroxysm of grief.

'I'm sorry, ma'am – I greatly regret having to be so blunt, but there was no other way—'

'That's quite all right, Mr Edgerton.' Flora recovered herself enough to wave her callers to chairs, and this time, gratefully, they sat down.

'Now – will you tell me exactly what happened?'

Edgerton's tale was brief, and was confirmed by a businesslike letter from Chief Factor McTavish, written on the Governor's instructions and conveying the deepest sympathy of all the officers and men at York Factory.

Very likely, thought Flora.

Mr Newsome, said McTavish, had gone north with his party in the middle of May – 'not long after you yourself left', he added tactfully.

The explorers had been transported in company boats along the rim of Hudson Bay as far as Chesterfield Inlet. There they'd been put ashore – no doubt with a sigh of relief, thought Flora – and left to trudge north towards the uncharted coast.

Navigating by sextant, they'd pressed on through snow-fields and half-frozen swamps, skirting pool after pool where the ice had become treacherous, stopping continually to take readings from their instruments or to collect samples of rocks and plants.

At least Mr Newsome had set eyes on the Polar Sea, reported McTavish, albeit from a distance. The explorers had caught a glimpse of it one morning from an outcrop of rock, and had immediately halted to make sketches of the landscape and of their leader pointing to the faint pencil line on the horizon. No one had noticed Dr Hildenhall wander off beyond the rocks, bent on some investigation of his own. Yet in a few seconds he reappeared, running as fast as his legs would carry him and followed by a huge female white bear and her cub whom he'd been unlucky enough to disturb.

Without a thought for his own safety, said McTavish, Mr Newsome had drawn a pistol and thrown himself in the path of the bear. But the pistol-ball had hardly caused the creature to falter. A moment later, her nine-foot bulk had reared above the explorer and crushed him to the ground: by the time the rest of the party had driven the animal off with the clatter of kettles and a charge of bird-shot, Newsome of Nubia lay dead at their feet.

Grimly, the little band of explorers had struggled back overland to York Factory with their leader's body wrapped in his country's flag. At York Factory they'd put what remained in a cask, and topped it up with rum for shipment—

'Stop!' cried Flora, clapping her hands over her ears. 'I don't want to hear any more.'

The *Prince Rupert*'s master glanced a little nervously at Richard Edgerton, then cleared his throat.

'I was going to ask you where you wanted us to put him.'

'*To put him*?'

'Now that we've brought him back, you see. At the moment he's in the company warehouse at Gravesend. In a puncheon,' he added helpfully, and seeing Flora's eyes widen in alarm, he went on, 'That's a little bigger than a hogshead, you understand—'

'Captain . . .' murmured Edgerton uneasily.

Flora stared at the men, appalled, as the full truth sank in. Ralph Newsome had returned from his glorious adventure in a wooden cask; for the present, he lay in a corner of a dusty warehouse, awaiting the instructions of his widow.

'Oh, well,' Constance remarked later, removing her hat in front of the drawing-room mirror and teasing out fetching little corkscrews of hair. 'Oh, well, that puts an entirely new complexion on things.'

'And why should it?' Flora wanted to know.

'Because you're a widow now.' In the mirror, Constance made a *moue*. '*His* widow – a hero's widow. You have all the advantages of the connection, without the inconvenience of the man himself. Oh, do stop that, Maggie!' For Maggie was snivelling steadily in the corner. 'There's no need to weep!'

'Puir man – it's only decent.' Maggie dabbed at her eyes with her apron.

Flora threw up her hands impatiently. 'None of this is of any interest to me.'

'But of course it is!' Constance spun round. 'This is the answer to all your troubles! We shall tell everyone the baby is Ralph Newsome's – and who can disagree?'

'But that's impossible. Ralph was killed in June, and the baby won't be born until next May. I'd have to be an elephant, to have carried it so long.'

'Who's to know the child wasn't born in February or March?' demanded Constance. 'Especially if you give up tight-lacing at once, and go off to the country immediately after Christmas for the lying-in. Then when you come back in the summer we can say the baby's been small and sickly ever since it was born, several months earlier. Under the circumstances, who could expect anything else?'

'Oh, indeed.' Flora was becoming angry. 'And I suppose you've solved the problem of who's to pay for this country jaunt, and where I'm to live after the baby's born.'

'Well, of course!' Constance stared at her daughter as if Flora had suddenly become half-witted. '*You* will pay for it all. You – the widowed Mrs Newsome. After all – you'll have a good deal of his money to do it with, won't you?'

CHAPTER TWENTY

I

'I want nothing more to do with him!' insisted Flora whenever Constance raised the subject of Ralph Newsome, his reputation, and his money. 'Let Hester have it all – she's the one who deserves it. All I want is to be allowed to forget him.'

But the British public thought otherwise, far more excited by the romantic appeal of a dead hero than a live one. By next morning Franklin had been forgotten and Newsome of Nubia's canonization had begun in earnest, with every newspaper carrying an account of his superhuman battle with the bear.

In their rectory parlours, the sonnet-writing ladies wept over his gallantry and snipped out the printed columns to lay under their pillows. In one account, the bear had grown to a staggering eighteen feet; in another there were two bears, murderous monsters with slavering jaws into which the explorer had rushed in defence of his men.

The *Clarion* had allowed him a last murmur of 'For my country . . .' before oblivion: and the people of Britain thrilled to his call, as they never had for Franklin. It was almost twenty-five years since Nelson had returned from Trafalgar, and four since Byron's body had been brought back from Greece. The nation was in the mood for a new dead hero, and Ralph Newsome – who'd expired on the threshold of the Northwest Passage – conquered the hearts of his countrymen instead.

To Flora's horror, letters of condolence began to arrive at Montagu Square from all kinds of people, sympathizing with Mrs Newsome in her great grief and proposing subscriptions and memorials and scientific foundations in her husband's name, on all of which they begged the widow's blessing.

'Tell them to ask Hester!' Flora protested. 'She's his real widow, not me. Tell them to go away and leave me alone.'

'Don't be silly, Flora.' Constance parted the curtains to peer into the street, where yet another carriage had drawn up at their door. 'They want his widow, not his sister! Oh—' Constance struck her temple with a finger. 'That reminds me . . . Two gentlemen from the Society called, to say you must leave the funeral entirely to them. They have all sorts of extravagant ideas for it, and a lying-in-state – just imagine!'

Mr Wesley went to the funeral in irreproachable black, but with a greenish cast to his coat and crape hat-band, and in such a gale of camphor that Constance felt obliged to open the drawing-room windows when he called to report on the proceedings.

'Forty-six carriages to the Uxbridge Road,' he wheezed, raising a hand in triumphant greeting as Flora entered the room. 'Thirty-seven of them as far as Hanover Square and St George's burial ground – all the institutions competing with hatchments and feathers – and a eulogy from the President of the Royal Society, no less. "Gave his life for the furtherance of knowledge . . . the world has lost a prince among pioneers." You know the sort of thing.'

He beamed with satisfaction, so broadly that his upper denture went into a tilt before pinging back on its springs.

'Plaguey teeth,' he remarked in passing. 'Trials of life, hey? Sad day for you, though, Mrs Newsome, left a young widow as you are. Still – as I said to your mamma when I heard the news, "He'll have left her comfortable. A man like that – he must have left her comfortable."'

'He's left a fair-sized house,' agreed Constance, tugging at her woolwork in the seat next to Mr Wesley's, 'even if it is in Russell Square. And the bronzes, and the carvings – they'll fetch a good deal, I should think.'

'Many relatives, had he?' asked Mr Wesley, reaching for his teacup. 'Dependent aunts? Unmarried sisters?'

'One sister – Hester, whom you saw at the wedding.' Constance's head drew nearer to Mr Wesley's ear. 'And a cousin married into a coalmine near Manchester, I understand.'

'Ah well, then.' Theodore Wesley smacked his lips. 'Childless widow takes half, Mrs St Serf. Point of law, as I've been at pains to establish. Many's the married lady I've cheered with the words "Widow takes half, if there's no will" – or a third, as the case may be. Yes, Mrs Newsome, he'll have left you comfortable, depend on it.'

Constance looked up from her woolwork to glare at Flora.

'Do you hear that, Flora?'

'I heard it all. And it doesn't make any difference.'

'Well, I don't know – I really don't.' Constance pulled her thread briskly through the canvas. 'Would you believe it, Mr Wesley – Flora's determined not to touch a penny of what's properly hers, all because of some foolish disagreement she had with her husband in Rupert's Land! She'd rather starve than do her duty as his widow – though I've told her over and over, the widows of famous men belong to the nation, and *ever* so many distinguished gentlemen have begged leave to call. And considering—' Constance closed her mouth suddenly over the extra fact she'd been about to consider – namely, Flora's *condition*, and the incalculable benefit of providing the child with both a father and an income at a single blow.

'I've made up my mind,' insisted Flora, and meant it.

She said precisely the same to Hester Newsome when she called, swathed in deepest black from head to toe, and veiled and gloved and shod in the same mournful colour. When Hester removed her veil, her face was grey; the only hint of colour in her entire appearance was the rim of red surrounding each tear-swollen eye.

'You can't desert him now!' Hester's thin black fingers trembled in her lap like the legs of a crushed spider. 'You are his widow, whether you like it or not. There mustn't be any scandal – please – I beg of you.'

'I promised Ralph I'd keep silent. That hasn't changed.'

'More than that – oh, Flora, I implore you . . .' Hester laid a pitiful black claw on her arm. 'I know we've had our differences in the past – and yes, perhaps my loyalty to Ralph has occasionally blinded me to his shortcomings . . . But he was a great man – everyone says so – and you must allow him a little latitude on account of that . . .'

A second black claw joined the first.

'Flora, I beg of you! If you want me to go down on my knees, I shall. Anything, sooner than have Ralph's name tarnished by any hint of scandal. And you'll have half of his money, remember. There was no will, but as his wife, you're entitled—'

'I don't want his money!' Flora repeated for the hundredth time. 'I don't want his name, and I don't want any part of this ridiculous business of turning him into a saint – because he was far from a saint, Hester, and you know it!'

*

On one point, however, Flora was determined to keep her word. The next day, dressed in the decent black weeds on which her mother had insisted, she made her way to the offices of Elder's Bank in Fleet Street.

'Mrs Ralph Newsome to see Mr Felix Elder, if you please.'

Oh, the rewards of fame – Flora was ushered immediately through the green dimness of decorously shoaling clerks, and on to the bank parlour to wait. Felix appeared amazingly swiftly, his face flushed with rapacious good living and a small, unpleasant smile twitching the corners of his mouth.

'I've come to fetch a certain document which was deposited here two years ago, in your brother's care.'

'Have you, indeed?' Felix seized a chair, spun it about, and sat down, straddling the seat, with his arms folded on the back rail. From there he considered Flora with insolent curiosity, the same unpleasant smile now hitching up his puffy jowls as if he were in possession of a singularly amusing secret.

Flora began to feel uneasy.

'Why don't you send someone to fetch it?'

'It's lost.' Felix's offensive smile deepened. He passed a fat finger round the inside of his enormous cravat, and Flora remembered hearing that he ran through a dozen of the stiffly starched monsters each morning before achieving a perfect knot.

'How can it be lost?' To her annoyance, she heard her voice rising a fraction in pitch.

Felix shrugged as far as his padded shoulders allowed.

'There are thousands upon thousands of documents in a bank like this.'

'But that's ridiculous! It was a perfectly ordinary packet, tied with tape and sealed with green wax—' All at once, Flora realized he was lying. 'I don't believe it's lost at all. What have you done with it?'

'If I say it's lost, it's lost.'

'That document was my property. I demand to have it back.'

'Oh, you *demand*, do you?' Felix stretched his chin clear of the starched cambric, and leaned foward, narrowing his eyes. 'Do you know she tried to kill me, that sister of yours?'

'I don't see what that has to do with—"

'Darius was away on his ridiculous jaunt, of course, when all the trouble boiled up at New Road. Always poking around when you don't want him, my brother – but thousands of miles away when his

334

wife goes off her head.' Felix snorted at the memory. 'I told her straight, she ought to be locked up – and what do you think she did? She threatened me with a paper knife!'

'If you'd said such a thing to me, I'd probably have done the same.'

'No doubt you would – but then, the St Serfs are all mad, in my opinion. Everyone knows your father, the gallant Major, went clean off his hooks – and I don't reckon the old General was much better. I told Darius as much when his sister suggested the marriage in the first place, but he didn't seem to care.'

'How dare you speak about my father like that! You were lucky to find a St Serf that would look twice at a family of money-lenders.'

'That's pretty rich, coming from a swindler!'

'*What* did you call me?'

'I called you what you are, Mrs Newsome of Nubia. You were a fine pair of swindlers, you and that late, much lamented husband of yours, for whom you're so decently in black. That man told me a pack of downright lies about his intentions in Hudson Bay!' The curls trembled on Felix's bull-like brow. 'I have it on the best authority that there's no gold at all at the Coppermine River, which is something I'm sure your husband knew perfectly well when he took my money to look for it.'

Flora shook her head. 'I know nothing whatever about it.'

'Oh, don't you? Well, I can tell you this – if Ralph Newsome hadn't come back to England in a barrel, I'd have made things pretty hot for him in London. So I won't be one of the fools subscribing for his tombstone, or any of this other nonsense.'

Flora brushed the matter aside. 'I came here for the document I left for safe-keeping, not for a lecture on Ralph Newsome's sins.'

'No . . .' Felix looked sly. 'Though you might say they're one and the same.'

'What do you mean by that?' Flora felt a chill slowly ascend her spine, as if her back were being immersed in freezing water.

'Come now, Flora – you know what I mean. The contents of the document in question – the little story you wrote . . . It was—' He kissed his fingertips in a gesture of perfection. 'It was quite fascinating.'

'You've *read* it?'

'Oh, several times. I didn't want to miss any of the . . . delicious details. Dear Ralph certainly learned a few tricks on his travels, didn't he?'

335

Felix was smiling again – the loose, libidinous smile Flora had seen on his face as he gazed at Lydia, a smile which curled his fat lips and flared his nostrils, and indicated exactly the nature of the ideas going through his mind. The thought of that fleshy, gossiping, dissolute ruin knowing every sordid particular of her life with Ralph Newsome made Flora almost physically sick.

'That document was placed here on trust!' she began. 'Darius promised me—'

'But Darius isn't here, is he? And I neither know nor care where he's got to.' Felix folded his arms belligerently across his chest. 'As far as I'm concerned, the longer he stays away, the better. The bank ran perfectly smoothly while he was gadding about the Canadas – so this time he can disappear for as long as he pleases.'

'He'd be furious if he knew what you'd done!'

'Pooh—' Felix shrugged again. 'The honourable Darius was the first to break the seals on your document, if you must know.'

'*Darius* read it?'

'Of course!' Felix avoided her eye and fiddled with his fingers on the chair rail. 'Darius couldn't wait to see what was in it. I remember his breaking the wax and cutting the tape with a penknife.' Felix stole a sideways glance at her. 'That surprised you, didn't it? Your upright, honourable brother-in-law—'

'Give it back to me at once.' Flora's voice was suddenly as cold and as hollow as the wind which had howled from the wilderness beyond York Factory. 'Just give me back my paper, before any more of your filthy cronies are invited to read it.'

'Tch, tch.' Felix wagged a finger. 'You are in a lather, Flora dear! Well, perhaps if you ask me nicely, I'll send someone off to search for it after all. Are you going to say *please*?'

Flora rose to her feet, shaking with a rage violent enough to burn the bank and the entire Elder family to a heap of despicable cinders.

'Send for it! Send for it, Felix, before I finish what Sophie began and cut your disgusting throat!'

Felix laughed – not entirely confidently – but went to the door nevertheless, bawling for a clerk.

'Fetch Mrs Newsome's box from the vault!'

He turned back to Flora, swinging his shoulders with deliberate nonchalance.

'You can have your paper. But don't think I've forgotten what's in it!' He leaned towards her. 'You see, I'm tired of hearing about the

336

high and mighty St Serfs, and how they're so far above us ordinary mortals. Well, in future you'd better look out for what a mere money-lender can do – Mrs Newsome.'

2

Darius had read the paper.

Flora could remember nothing at all of her homeward journey in the jolting, tobacco-smelling hackney-carriage, nor of Maggie's shocked face examining her own, nor of lying in bed during the days that followed, sleepless and reliving against her closed eyelids every moment of what she now knew to have been a cold-blooded and calculated betrayal.

She never wept, wounded too deeply for such easy release. Instead she lay in her curtained room, picturing his face – Darius's face – and searching it for signs of the contempt in which he must have held her. What could have been easier for him than to tempt a broken, disheartened woman with a few scraps of kindness? How he must have laughed at the suddenness of her surrender – at her pitiful, abject fears and her humble gratitude for his attentions!

I'd give up my heart's blood, sooner than harm you. She could still recall Darius's expression as he spoke the words, alight with sincerity. Could it really have been nothing but deception – nothing but illusion, another lesson learned in heartbreak?

Two monkeys, coming together to make a third monkey – that's how Dédalon would have described it – like a stallion with a mare, a male with a female, driven by no more than the seasonal twitchings of the organs inside them.

And what to do with the poor, hapless third monkey, the wretched result of Darius's deception? For a few bleak moments Flora considered going straight to the woman in Hog Lane: then she changed her mind. Lydia was right. A woman should make herself independent – should take, and manipulate, and cheat, and *use* to her own best advantage. Sometime in May her child would become all the companion, lover and confidant she could ever want – hers, entirely and completely hers.

All she needed, besides, was a means of supporting them both.

'Where are you going?' demanded her mother as she came downstairs.

Flora lowered her black veil, and secured it at her throat with a jet pin.

'I'm going to Russell Square,' she said firmly, and opened the door on her widowhood.

In the days that followed, shrouded in black, Flora spent her afternoons in state in the drawing-room at Russell Square, where a procession of eminent gentlemen came to press her hand and murmur condolences, while her heart ached for another death altogether.

'His name will be written in letters of fire in the annals of exploration . . .'

'A torch of enlightenment never extinguished . . .'

'You must be so proud . . . so proud . . .'

Dr Hildenhall called, clasped her hand with the frenzy of the drowning, stammered an apology for having been the unworthy cause of his leader's death, and followed it with a bizarre hymn of phrenological praise.

'I always noted that on Mr Newsome's head the area between Hope and Caution, identified by Spurzheim as *Conscientiousness*, was quite amazingly large. As one would expect, his actions were always motivated by a feeling of *natural obligation*, or *duty* . . .'

Across the room, Hester Newsome's eyes met Flora's unblinkingly.

'In addition, Benevolence was notably rounded, and Firmness rose like a walnut on the top of his head . . . In short, he was an exemplar, dear Lady Newsome, a model among men.'

'Precisely,' said Hester, looking directly at Flora. 'An exemplar. I'm sure you would not disagree, sister-in-law.'

'No indeed, Hester.' Flora clasped her hands over her secret consolation. 'But I see your name in all the newspapers, Dr Hildenhall. And there's talk of a medal.'

'From the Society of Ethnologists, I'm honoured to say. And the Fauna Institute has made me a Fellow, for identifying Hildenhall's Mouse.'

'Your reputation's made, then, Doctor. You'll be Sir Daniel before we know it.'

'I hope I shall deserve it, Mrs Newsome. Yet . . . reputations are fickle things, as I'm sure you understand. They can be made – but they can also be destroyed by the slightest slur.' Hildenhall's gaze slid round to rest on the fearsome figure of Hester Newsome. 'I should hate to see anything besmirch Mr Newsome's good name . . . or my own, for that matter.'

He paused, twiddling his fingers.

'That being so, I've taken some trouble to make sure that certain . . . trifling incidents . . . during our winter at York Factory have been forgotten by all concerned. It would be in no one's interest, I'm sure you'll agree, to tarnish the valour of your husband's last expedition.'

'Oh, I do agree, Dr Hildenhall.'

'*Tarnish*?' enquired Hester suspiciously.

'And fortunately Hudson's Bay is a great distance away from here,' continued Hildenhall with a smile. 'Things that happen there can be . . . forgotten.'

'I hope they can, Dr Hildenhall. I hope they can.'

Flora had planned a brief charade – and yet a month after the funeral, with the flood of condolences and memorials showing no sign of slackening, she began to feel as if the corpse of Ralph Newsome had been hung round her neck like Mr Coleridge's albatross. Did the country expect her to throw herself on his pyre as Indian widows were said to do?

On 5th December, Flora sat at breakfast in Montagu Square, reading the lines which, having had a month to think of them, a distinguished poet had contributed to *The Times*:

> *See his noble locks in gore bedaubed,*
> *A Polo or a Cortés thrown away!*
> *See the slavering monster pause, o'er-awed,*
> *To learn the fatal outcome of that day.*

'The post, Mrs St Serf.' Maggie came into the room with letters on a tray, and Constance pounced on them at once.

'Ah! Here's one from Darius Elder.' With precision, she slit the wafer, spread open the page, and scanned the lines in silence for a moment.

'They've been in Altenbaden, he says – but they're about to leave for Florence at any moment, so there's no forwarding address.'

Across the table, Flora stirred her coffee intently.

'Sophie seems better, he says, though she still has *bad days* – whatever that may mean.' Her mother scrutinized another few lines.

339

'She cannot be left alone, apparently . . . and there's something here about a straw hat which I can't make out. At least, I think it says "straw hat" . . . Now, what would he be wanting with a straw hat?' Constance held the page close to her spectacles.

'Oh, what does it matter?' Irritably, Flora tried to concentrate on an invitation from the Royal Scientific and Geographical Foundation to be guest of honour at the unveiling of its new portrait of her husband.

Her mother's eyes rose briefly from the page. 'He says he trusts you are well, by the way.'

'Trusts I'm well?' The tremor in Flora's voice would have told a more perceptive mother a great deal. 'Is that all he says about me?'

'What else did you expect? I don't imagine he'll have heard you're a widow yet. Not in Altenbaden.'

'No.' Flora gathered up her letters and rose from her seat. 'And I don't suppose he'll care.'

A few days later, a lonely figure in widow's weeds, she sat in the place of honour among the distinguished gentlemen of the Royal Foundation who'd gathered to see their new portrait unveiled. On the other side of the room, *Ralph Newsome at the Polar Sea* waited behind a black curtain between portraits of Halley and Wren, a telescope believed to have been owned by Captain Cook, and a lock of the hair of the Princess Pocahontas, tied with a faded ribbon.

The speeches were long, but Flora heard none of them. Pale-faced behind her veil, her thoughts drifted in the direction which drew them like a lodestone whenever her attention wandered. *He knew, all the time.* Ralph used me, and then Darius used me – though at least Ralph never pretended anything else. Darius Elder – hypocrite and liar – father of my child . . .

She glanced up, startled, when the curtain whisked open on Newsome's portrait. The artist had been instructed, the President explained, to place the explorer in heroic pose, brandishing his empty pistol at the furious white bear which towered over him, while members of his expedition – Dr Hildenhall would be delighted – cowered, aghast, nearby.

Murmuring their approval, the learned gentlemen went on to apply themselves to lamb cutlets and claret and several more speeches, until at last, the celebrated widow forgotten, they began to chat among themselves or slump in their chairs in after-dinner sleep.

No one noticed Flora slip from her place and leave the room. In the street outside, Hester's carriage waited to take her back to Montagu Square and her memories.

As she crossed the hallway, the bright new canvas, still swagged in its black curtain, caught her attention. Ralph Newsome, she thought, looked almost devil-may-care as he faced the prospect of death. Against the barren rock of Rupert's Land his coat was as elegantly cut as he could have wished, his cheeks newly shaven, and his boots buffed brightly enough to dazzle.

Yet it was the expression on his face which held Flora's gaze. It was strange how, from memory, the artist had exactly caught that look of cool, cruel arrogance, of a man who'd expect a silver teapot on his table in Hell.

Involuntarily, Flora's hand rose up behind her veil to trace the pale snail-trail of the scar which crossed her cheek. And that, she told herself bitterly, was the very least of the wounds he'd given her; the others might be invisible, but they gaped open still.

From habit, Flora still kept in her black velvet reticule the scissors she'd treasured during that weary winter at Hudson Bay. To her annoyance, she couldn't reach as high as she'd have liked: but with a raking lunge she buried one of the blades in the still-pliant canvas of the portrait, and jerked downwards with all her strength, surprised to see the fabric tear with no more sound than a sneeze.

Breathless and filled with an almost sexual exhaustion, she stood back to survey her handiwork – a gash which sagged open like an accusing mouth, all the way from Ralph Newsome's shoulder through his powerful, domineering body to the frozen ground at his feet.

3

The portrait was repaired, of course, and some unknown disgruntled Franklinite was blamed for its destruction. Yet for ever afterwards, the explorer's expression seemed a little less jaunty, as if for the first time in his life Ralph Newsome had caught a glimpse of a power more terrifying than his own.

On Boxing Day, now five months pregnant, Flora left London with Maggie on the Brighton coach. Brighton was safe; Brighton was secret. No one who was anyone, Constance had insisted, had bothered with the seaside town since the end of the Regency and King George's waning interest in his exotic Pavilion.

From Brighton they took the local fly to the village of Polney-by-Sea and put up at the Swan, where Maggie dropped a few remarks to the effect that Flora was her niece, a shipmaster's wife whose husband had recently sailed on a voyage to Shanghai. Before long they found a small house to rent and a local girl to act as maid-of-all-work. With tears and promises to return for the birth, Maggie went back to London.

After that there was nothing for Flora to do but walk the sea-front at Polney, wrapped in a thick cloak against the late winter storms, watching the open boats of the line-fishermen bob like gulls on the distant swell and the occasional brig shoulder her way up-Channel, short-canvassed against the growling sky.

In Polney they knew her as Mrs Newberry, though Flora hated the deception and was afraid of seamanlike questions on the tonnage and rig of her husband's vessel. But for the most part there was no one to speak to and nothing to do except walk and think, and resent the growing unwieldiness of her body and the solitary confinement she was forced to endure for its sake.

Walking on the sea-front, she thought a great deal about her father, and about Madeleine, the girl he'd loved briefly and then deserted. Had the affair been any more to him at the time than an adventure, entered into out of boredom and a sudden lust for an available young body?

It had been so much more to Madeleine – love, risk, trust, hope – everything. Illusion, illusion . . . See how we're deceived, again and again . . .

Flora stood on the great square stones of the harbour wall and stared out to sea. She had no intention of throwing herself and her baby into the water, though Darius Elder had discarded her as carelessly as Lydia might drop one of her soiled kid gloves. Nancy McKenzie at York Factory would have been amused to see an English lady join her in the white man's trap.

Darius and Sophie had spent the winter in Nice, Constance reported in a letter, where the mistral had blown for days at a time, whipping Sophie's nerves to breaking-point and driving her doctors to despair.

'Darius trusts you are well,' Constance's letter continued, 'which is kind of him, with Sophie to think of.'

Imprisoned in Polney, Flora began to wonder if the anger in her heart could print itself on the face of her unborn child.

*

Her mother's next letter, hard on the heels of her last, was splashed with patches of watery brown where tears had mingled with the ink.

Looking round for mischief, Felix Elder had spitefully announced that due to a falling-off in revenue from the Chillbourne estate, Constance's quarterly allowance had become too much of a drain on its income. In future he proposed to reduce it by half – out of which she could find the rent of the house in Montagu Square, or move to somewhere more suited to her means.

Constance had rushed to the bank, where Felix kept her waiting in the dimness of the Front Office until it suited him to see her. With Darius abroad, he told her loftily, he had full authority to administer Sophie's inheritance; the St Serfs were no longer in charge of the General's fortune.

And worse than all this – Mr Wesley had indicated, with the utmost regret, that under the circumstances he couldn't consider entering into a union with a lady of such restricted means as Mrs St Serf had become.

'I shall be a solitary widow for the rest of my life,' she mourned. 'A lonely pauper . . . Never again to know the touch of a husband's hand . . .'

Flora could imagine the weeping which had accompanied her mother's letter, great, raging drops which welled like lava from a volcano of outrage within. The Elders had struck again. Constance's world had been destroyed – her prospects of Mr Wesley had been destroyed – all for pride, and Felix's malice.

4

The first yellowish tufts of herb-Alexander were dotting the hedge-banks of Polney when Flora received the next letter from her mother. Constance had written in feverish hope: Darius had at last sent the address of a villa near Mentone where he expected to remain while Sophie consulted a professor specializing in the therapeutic effects of galvanism. Mentone was sheltered from the enervating north wind, and there were olive and citrus groves, and romantic castle ruins; but though Darius had tried to be optimistic, it was clear that Sophie's moods were as unpredictable as ever.

'Oh, he trusts you are well,' added Constance as an afterthought, before soaring on to matters closer to her heart.

'As you may imagine,' she reported, 'I sent off a reply at once, enclosing every single detail of Felix's high-handedness. Naturally Darius will write to London the moment he gets my letter, ordering Felix to put everything back as it was – *and perhaps even to increase my allowance by a little*, in order to make up for the suffering I've endured on his account. Mr Wesley,' she added in large, significant letters, 'is quite remarkably hopeful, and sends you his most respectful regards.'

Yet, in spite of Constance's optimism, the next month passed without a word from Felix or from Elder's Bank. At the beginning of May, Constance pinned her hat sternly on to her head and set out to interview Felix in his lair.

Her account of that meeting arrived in Polney blotched with more great, feathery tear-stains and a hatchwork of scorings-out where her pen had run away with her.

'If you could only have seen how impertinently Felix treated me – me, the mother of his brother's wife, even if my grey hairs didn't deserve better! He flatly denied getting any letter from Darius, and said that even if Darius *had* written, he'd have paid no attention to it, having full authority to do as he thinks best while his brother is abroad. "How should Darius know the facts of the matter?" he wanted to know – and oh, Flora, I fear Felix's word is now absolute law in the bank.

'Imagine,' added Constance woefully, 'Felix told me a lady should be able to live on far less than I've been used to, and said he remembered from the past that I've always been given to extravagance! The insolent creature! He would not have dared whisper such a thing, had your dear father been alive.'

Several furiously scored-out lines followed; perhaps Constance had had second thoughts. Then the letter continued plaintively, 'Why has Darius not written to Felix as I begged him? If he were here in London I would ask him directly, but as it seems that for Sophie's sake he will be abroad for a long while yet, I really do not know where to turn for money.

'Accordingly I have sent away Cook and one of the maids (Polly), and also James, which upset me greatly as I can't abide having the door opened by a woman, it is so vulgar, and I fear he will go directly to Mrs Bradshaw who tried to get him away last year. Yet I should rather have my door opened by the Devil himself than lose this house.

'Oh, Flora – why does Darius not help us? I cannot think of anything I have done to harm him. God bless you, my daughter, since

344

Fortune and Your Mother cannot. Mr Wesley sends you his best regards in the circumstances. Your desolate Mother, Constance St Serf.'

Flora was left with no time to reply. At three in the morning of the 15th May, her labour began. Maggie, who'd arrived for the lying-in sent for the midwife, and once the woman had inspected, clucked her teeth, and departed again, settled down with maternal calm to wait.

If she'd expected Flora to cry out in pain as the contractions took hold, she was wrong, for Flora's mind was fixed on matters far beyond the travail of giving birth. Like a finger continually straying to an aching wound, her thoughts kept returning to the events of the last six months. The Elders hadn't changed: an Elder was incapable of changing, Darius no less than the rest, and Flora should have had the sense to realize it.

The snapped seals on the document she'd entrusted to his care had finally cleared the scales from her eyes. He'd promised the world when it suited him – and broken his promises as casually as the fragile discs of green wax which had hidden the secret of her marriage.

Sophie and her fortune had passed to the Elders – and now, exiled in Polney, Flora was consumed by the birth-pangs of an Elder child.

When the midwife returned at ten, Flora was pacing to and fro across her bedroom, her arms wrapped round her distended body and an expression of grim determination on her face. At every contraction she stopped, swayed, supported herself on the wall, and after a moment set off again, forcing each foot in front of the other as if every step was a sign of the triumph of her will.

'Your child will be a wanderer like his father, Mrs Newberry, if you walk about so,' the midwife reproved her, and then fell silent when she saw the expression in Flora's eyes.

At last, unable to walk any further, Flora allowed herself to be helped on to the bed. She could no longer pace up and down, but she could push – heaven only knew how fiercely she could push! She saw Maggie and the midwife exchange glances above her head, but nothing in this life or the next would have deflected her purpose at that moment. Gasping, bracing her spine and making hard, furious fists of her hands, she hurled all her strength behind thrusting her child into the world.

The Elders: the Elders had brought her family nothing but pain and misery. Why did the Elders never suffer as she was suffering? And as her body strained in each wrenching, agonized convulsion, Flora focused the pain, like pinpoints of white heat, on the Elders and their malice.

CHAPTER TWENTY-ONE

I

The baby was a boy, with a calm, clear gaze which held no hint of his mother's bitterness.

'You and I . . .' murmured Flora, curving her body over him as he lay in her arms, holding him as if sheer, unadulterated love could absorb him into her once more. 'We have no one else, you and I. But who else do we need?'

At the end of June, she returned to London.

'He's a pleasing little creature, I suppose.' Reluctantly, Constance inclined her head to inspect her new grandson. 'Though they do say such babies generally are – the ones born of *affection* rather than duty.' From his nest of shawls the baby returned her stare with an expression of mild astonishment.

'He's a little lamb!' exclaimed Maggie indignantly, hugging the child to her bosom as she had done almost all the way from Polney. 'He's a grand wee fellow, Mrs St Serf – and no matter how awkwardly he came into the world, he's here now and I won't hear a word said against him.' Officiously, she adjusted the voluminous shawls. 'Heaven help us, he sleeps like an angel! And you should see him feed—'

Flora leaned over Maggie's arm to smile proudly at her son. 'He's perfect, Mamma. Even his fingernails are like seed-pearls when he catches hold of my thumb – so tiny you wouldn't believe.'

Constance condescended to bend a little closer.

'Fortunately, he seems destined to be dark. That's a mercy, at least, though his eyes are rather blue.'

'There's still time for them to change,' said Flora without much confidence. She'd already discovered that to look into her son's questioning gaze was disconcertingly like confronting his father.

'And you'll name him Ralph, as I told you?'

'No, Mamma.' The pride fled at once from Flora's face. 'Though

I dare say Hester Newsome will expect me to, when she hears. I thought I'd call him Edmund, after Papa.'

'Oh . . . Edmund. *Edmund Newsome*.' Constance rolled the syllables experimentally round her tongue. 'Edmund Newsome – poor Mrs Newsome's son. Poor, dear little Edmund.'

For another few seconds, she struggled with her conscience. Then, abruptly, she held out her arms.

'Give him to me for a bit, Maggie. You've had a long journey, all the way from Brighton.'

'He's no trouble at all.' Maggie hugged the infant more tightly against the billowing capes of her travelling-cloak.

'Nevertheless, I'll take him now. I've a nursery all prepared for him – for as long as we're permitted to stay in this house,' Constance added grimly.

'I'd best carry him up to it, then.' Maggie avoided her mistress's outstretched hands and set off down the hall. 'Who knows – you might drop him on the stair.'

Flora, about to follow, paused to glance round the hallway she'd last seen six months earlier, on the day of her journey to Brighton. Something was missing, and after a moment she realized what it was – the steady ticking of a mahogany-cased clock which had stood on a table against the wall. The table was empty now, and Flora guessed that her mother had sold the clock, no doubt for precious little, to pay for some 'necessity' she hadn't been able to bring herself to confess. The Elders: the Elders again.

There was no question of hardship. The money Flora had inherited as Ralph Newsome's widow was more than enough to cover the household expenses in Montagu Square and the rent of the house itself. Constance had quickly dropped any mention of wishing to have the place to herself – especially since her hopes of Mr Wesley had been dashed. Mr Wesley remained a good friend, but in recent weeks he'd taken to arriving in a violently waved snuff-coloured wig, and Constance was now dismally certain another woman had caught his eye.

Flora did her best to mend the situation. It wasn't as if Constance was entirely without support, she explained to Mr Wesley: she – Flora – was now well enough off to keep her mother in modest comfort. But Mr Wesley shook his head. Perched on the edge of a Grecian sofa, he gazed sadly at his boots, and tried to explain the delicate nature of the change which had taken place.

'A wife's income', he explained fastidiously, 'is rightfully her husband's, as you know, and therefore I should have no hesitation at all in spending it – but to be kept by a lady's daughter . . . Oh no, dear Mrs Newsome – no gentleman could contemplate that.'

One glance at Mr Wesley as he sat on the sofa revealed more than any words could have done. A few months earlier he'd have settled himself at his ease, already in his mind half-way to joint proprietorship of the house in Montagu Square. Now, thanks to Felix Elder's spite, he'd dwindled again to being an afternoon caller, his rosy future reduced to ashes round his much mended nine-shilling boots.

Mr Wesley sighed heavily for the hundredth time, and polished the knees of his trousers with the palms of his hands.

'I did think – perhaps – later on, a *cottage orné* in Denmark Hill . . . With Gothic windows and roses round the door . . . and a pony-gig for driving out on market days . . .' Mr Wesley sighed again. 'But no. Once more, the Elders have destroyed my prospect of happiness. They're scoundrels, ma'am – lice on the noble head of the City! Fleas, ma'am! Jiggers! Ticks! *Pimple mites*! Fit only to be squashed under the heels of gentlemen.'

His venom temporarily exhausted, Mr Wesley sank back into weary melancholy.

'"Invest!" they said. "Lay out your money where it's sure to make more." And then, once I'd wasted my fortune in all kinds of ridiculous ventures, they had the gall to lecture me for my imprudence!'

'Mamma told me all about it,' agreed Flora sympathetically.

Mr Wesley's lower lip bulged with resentment. 'It was old Mr Elder himself who urged me on. D'you know, he made me buy French fives when Napoleon was sent to Elba and the stock was at its highest, and then forced me to sell again when the fiend escaped, and you couldn't give the wretched things away! Said I'd held on too long, the old blackguard!' Mr Wesley slapped a knee in frustration. 'And when I asked what I should do next, d'you know what he said?'

Without waiting for an answer, Mr Wesley exploded, 'He told me to go and find an heiress with three stars to her name in the East India stockholders list, and marry her out of hand!' He threw his arms wide. 'I appeal to you, Mrs Newsome – do I look the kind of Casanova who'd deceive a lady in that way?'

'Not at all, Mr Wesley.' Pretending to cough, Flora stifled a smile behind her fingers.

'And now it's too late, I know exactly where I should put the money.' He leaned solemnly towards Flora. 'I've been up to Newcastle to see this new locomotive of the Stephensons'! It was a splendid sight, I can tell you – Rocket pulling her coal-wagons along like a thoroughbred, with her slide valves smacking to and fro—' Mr Wesley skidded to a sudden halt.

'It's the slide valves,' he explained helpfully, 'which distribute the steam to the cylinders.' He circled one hand and pumped with the other. 'They're connected to rods, you understand, which run from loose eccentrics on the driving axle—'

Smiling quite openly this time, Flora held up a hand in protest.

'I fear you've lost me already, Mr Wesley. I'd no idea you were such an expert on the work of the railway engineers.'

Mr Wesley's face assumed a wistful expression beneath his mousy bangs.

'Ah, Mrs Newsome, if only I had my fortune once again! I've been making such a close study of the subject that I could lay out every penny of my money in railways, and be worth a million in no time at all.'

He counted off the railway companies on his fingers. 'There's the Bolton & Leigh just opened, and the Dundee & Newtyle before that, and the Canterbury & Whitstable, and Cranford & High Peak. And, of course, there's the Liverpool & Manchester under way now – with Rocket I dare say – and the Leeds & Hull to come, and a link proposed between Manchester and Bolton— Oh, they're all at it, Mrs Newsome, I assure you. A quick stoking of capital and they're off, digging out cuttings and throwing up tunnels here, there and everywhere. If only I had my fortune again – *chuff* – *chuff* – *chuff*—' Once again Mr Wesley turned himself into a locomotive, his elbows flailing like connecting-rods.

Only a short distance down the track, however, he ran into the buffers of fate.

'The Elders are no better than robbers!' he declared, an unhappy middle-aged man once more. 'It isn't even as if I minded so much for myself, Mrs Newsome, but to be so cruel to your mother – the mildest and sweetest of women . . . Do you know – if I had it in my power, I swear I'd steal her money back from them! I would! Show me how it can be done, and I swear to you, I'd steal from Elder's Bank itself!'

Long after Mr Wesley had left, his words continued to ring in Flora's ears. He'd made a comical figure in his snuff-coloured wig, dreaming of steam locomotives and Gothic cottages in Denmark Hill – and yet even in the heart of a man who'd borne his own misfortunes with stoical resignation, there burned a flame of outrage on behalf of his friends. *Show me how it can be done, and I swear to you, I'd steal from Elder's Bank itself!*

Poor, loyal Mr Wesley. The Elders had stripped him of his dignity just as surely as they'd stripped Constance of her harmless vanity and Major Edmund St Serf of his last, fleeting peace of mind.

And as for Flora – Darius Elder had left her nothing except loneliness and pain and broken faith, and the shame of knowing how he and Felix had gloated over her secret testament of cruelty.

The blood drummed in her ears when she thought of it: she'd been helpless to retaliate, as Felix had known perfectly well. She was helpless now, yet she longed so much to strike back, even in the smallest way – to dent that insufferable arrogance, to prove that she was not, after all, powerless against them.

Show me how it can be done, and I'd steal from Elder's Bank itself.

Oh, if only it could be done! If only she could steal back even the pittance taken from her mother – how her heart would rejoice!

Flora smiled to think of Mr Wesley as a bank robber – or herself, for that matter, Newsome of Nubia's tragic widow, demure in black but dreaming wistfully of thieving.

The wickedness of stealing from a bank didn't occur to Flora for a moment. The automaton-maker had taught her to value justice and equality above anything else – and letting loose a monkey on Grandmamma St Serf's hat had taken far more courage.

Show me how it can be done . . .

It was impossible, of course.

Of course . . .

Long after the lamps had been put out that night, Flora sat up in bed, scribbling figures on a sheet of paper by the light of a single candle.

In his crib by the bed, Baby Edmund had fallen asleep at last with an absorbed expression on his face, as if some weighty matter was still revolving in his mind. Maggie had tried hard to keep him for herself at night; young mothers needed their sleep, she'd insisted, and she could easily bring Edmund down for his feed in the early hours. But Flora could only sleep with her baby by her side. Her need of him, born at the same instant as Edmund himself, had not diminished by so much as a thread: by day she was forced to share him with her mother and Maggie, but in the secret night hours she hung over him, marvelling, or wrapped him in her arms for the sheer bliss of holding his warm, milky body against her own.

Yet even then she was not wholly at peace. Part of her could not rest until a blow had been struck, a debt repaid. And so while Edmund slept, Flora applied herself to her arithmetic.

Felix Elder had deprived her mother of two hundred and fifty pounds per annum, which would go into the coffers of the Elders instead. Therefore, in all fairness, Felix should be made to give back two hundred and fifty pounds per annum, or its equivalent; here Flora scratched busily with her pen, and calculated that a capital sum of eight thousand, three hundred and thirty-three pounds, invested in Long Government Stocks at three per cent, would yield . . . precisely two hundred and fifty pounds per annum. *Quod erat demonstrandum* – Flora laid down her pen with satisfaction.

The only problem which remained was to steal eight thousand, three hundred and thirty-three pounds from Elder's Bank. And since Flora was neither a robber nor a house-breaker, Felix Elder must somehow be made to give it up to her.

It was Mr Wesley who'd shown her, quite innocently, how this might be managed. If men of vision were looking everywhere for railway companies to invest in, and if Felix Elder fancied himself a shrewd investor – why shouldn't Flora invent a railway company of her own, and sell him non-existent shares? The idea seemed so simple, she was amazed that the whole of London hadn't stumbled upon it.

On one point, however, she was absolutely firm: to take back what had been unfairly wrested from her mother would be justice, but to take anything more would be stealing, and Flora wasn't a thief. Dédalon would have applauded the distinction . . . and for a moment Flora was so pleased with her scheme that she seriously considered calling on the automaton-maker, and asking for his opinion.

Almost as soon as the idea occurred to her, she rejected it. Dédalon would question her about her marriage – scold her, no doubt, for not having consulted him – guess more, perhaps, than she wanted to reveal . . . He'd always had a way of penetrating her most secret thoughts, as if he could analyse them as easily as the workings of one of his ticking, bland-eyed manikins; and there were places in Flora's soul still too tender to be submitted to the automaton-maker's scalpel. She would call on Dédalon . . . another day, perhaps.

Instead, the next morning, leaving Maggie and her mother hovering jealously on either side of Edmund's crib, she dashed out to see Lydia.

To her annoyance it took almost half an hour to rouse Lydia out of her bed, and another fifteen minutes of soft bread rolls and cups of chocolate before she was capable of giving her full attention to anything.

'An imaginary railway company . . . hmm.' Lying full-length on a sofa, Lydia considered the idea with the narrowed eyes of a connoisseur. 'If you were a professional criminal, sweetness, I'd say "Why not, and good luck to you", but really . . . Anyone who believes it's possible to steal – how much is it you want—'

'Eight thousand, three hundred and thirty-three pounds.'

'Exactly! Anyone who thinks it's possible to steal precisely so much and not a penny more is clearly a dangerous amateur, and doesn't know enough about thieving to keep herself out of Newgate Jail. And how would that help your baby son, may I ask? His father doesn't know he's alive, and now you propose to deprive him of his mother into the bargain.'

'Oh.' Flora gazed miserably at her shoes. 'I thought it was quite a good plan.'

'But you haven't given it much thought at all,' Lydia told her. 'For one thing, Felix Elder knows you too well for disguise, so you'd need at least one other person to help. And who did you think would forge the stock certificates for this wonderful railway? Let me tell you, Flora, forgery is an *art*, otherwise every back-street housebreaker would be making banknotes.

'My pa was a coiner, you know,' Lydia recalled, 'when he bothered to do anything at all. But he was an artist, in his own way. He could make a shilling piece out of a lump of old cooking-pot that you'd swear had come straight from the Mint. Beautiful fakes, they were.'

A maid had appeared with two more chocolate cups on a tray, and Lydia raised herself on her elbow to sip the creamy froth.

'Ma used to say that with Pa's talent he ought to go on to half-sovereigns instead of wasting his time on small stuff, but he never

353

would. And yet, you know what they say – the bigger the swindle, the more likely it is to succeed. In other words, if you want to cheat a bank of its funds and get away scot-free – then the more you rob them of, the better.'

'All I want is Mamma's money,' Flora insisted at once. 'Anything more would be dishonest.'

'I thought you wanted to teach the Elders a lesson they wouldn't forget?'

'I'm not a thief, Lydia!' Flora gazed at her friend reproachfully. 'I don't want a penny more than I can prove they owe us.'

Lydia frowned, and stirred the chocolatey ooze at the bottom of her cup with a finger.

'Railway shares . . .' she murmured slowly. 'Railway shares . . .'

For a second or two she applied herself to sucking her finger, then popped it out of her mouth and waved it gravely in the air.

'What we want to do, it seems to me, is convince Friend Felix he's been clever enough to get his paws on something no one else has thought of. Then he'll be India-rubber in our hands.'

'In *our* hands, Lydia?'

'Well, of course! Do you imagine I'm going to be left out of all the fun?' A wicked smile lit Lydia's face for an instant, then her expression grew serious again. 'Now – who's going to make the share certificates for this wonderful railway of ours . . . Someone who draws like an angel, and can engrave, and print, and keep silent about what he's done . . .' She leaned over and slapped a hand on Flora's knee. 'Dédalon's our man! You must go and see him at once.'

'Oh, Lydia – not Dédalon . . .' Flora picked uneasily at her bonnet-strings, almost prepared to give up her scheme, sooner than visit that place of jewelled birds and monkey-bishops. 'Besides,' she added hopefully, 'Dédalon may not want to help us.'

'He'll help us, if you ask him.' Lydia waved away Flora's misgivings. 'You've no idea how he plagues me with questions every time I see him. Where are you, how are you – are you happy enough . . . Oh, there's no doubt that he'll help us – if *you* go and ask him.'

3

It was seven years since Flora had set foot in Gough Square, and she was startled to find how little it had changed. A single glance was enough to show her the same rows of grimy windows which had witnessed her comings and goings, the same tottering railings, and the younger brothers of the barefoot boys who'd sailed matchwood rafts in the gutters still squatting over their game.

The gaunt house where Dr Johnson was said to have compiled his *Dictionary* still stood by the archway leading out to Three-Leg Alley. The great man had been arrested for debt there, too – but then, the arrival of bailiffs was no novelty in Gough Square, where countless back doors and bolt-holes allowed the inhabitants to scamper away like rats under the noses of their creditors.

A rickety wooden staircase clung like creeper to the tenement directly opposite her old home, and for a moment Flora sheltered there, contemplating her past through its crooked wooden ribs.

So much had changed in her life, yet Gough Square, that sunless crevice in a busy city, had only shrunk a little with the passing years. High among the rooftops, crows still argued noisily over scraps of gristle from the pieman's floor, or flew down to stalk across the flags, dragging their ragged tails like the skirts of a pedagogue's coat. Half a furlong away, the bustle of Fleet Street funnelled through the alleyways in an endless growl, just as it had on that rainy day when Flora fled down Mrs Moss's steps, hugging her contraband silver, straight into Darius Elder's arms.

Even as she watched, a tall figure turned under the archway by Dr Johnson's door, and Flora's heart missed a beat. Then the stranger emerged from the shadows, red-haired and whiskered on each cheek. He glanced at her boldly as he passed, twisting his tawny tufts and scattering the sparrows with a swing of his cane.

Yet her mood persisted, sharpening the memory of that long-ago morning until it seemed as if only an hour had passed since her candlesticks lay in the churning gutter and the inkstand beside them, its taper-snuffer still dangling from the breast of Darius Elder's coat.

She remembered the bailiff's cart at their door, black and unmistakable, proclaiming as openly as any handbill that the inhabitants of that building could no longer pay their way. A century earlier Mrs Moss's house might have seemed impressive. Now the four pompous steps at its front door were merely a nonsense, their pride worn thin by the shuffling of commonplace feet. These days the house wore a hangdog look; every brick in its sooty face stood proud of the mortar, and the stone which garnished its windows had begun to fall away in ragged slices into a basement too dank even for weeds to flourish.

There were no curtains at the windows any more. Mrs Moss had sold up two years earlier, according to Mr Wesley, forcing him out to new lodgings with a clergyman's widow near Red Lion Square, but who'd bought the place, he couldn't say.

Now, thanks to Lydia, Flora knew.

The door of the house stood ajar, and from somewhere inside came the sound of a hammer beating on metal. Tentatively, she walked forwards across the square, and immediately became aware of the sweet smell of sawdust drifting out through the open door, mingled with another, sharper scent: after a moment she recognized it as the stink of boiling glue. With sudden decision, she climbed the steps and went inside.

The room immediately to the right of the door had been their landlady's sitting-room, a forbidden parlour of panelling, ancient damask curtains and hoarded candle-ends. Now it had evidently been given over to metalwork, almost filled by a clanking pedal-lathe and a forge sprouting tongs and pincers like coarse black bristles. Nearby, a man with a leather apron tied at the back of his neck stooped over an anvil, but he neither saw nor heard Flora pass amid the uproar of his hammering, and she went on unchallenged.

A swept-up pile of sawdust now marked the spot at the foot of the stairs from where she'd watched Sophie set off for a new life at Chillbourne. The stairs themselves were half-filled with stacked timber, and on the floor above, the first of the rooms which had been Mr Wesley's was littered with swatches of fabric, pots of buttons and curling hanks of hair; there was a glue-pot in the hearth now, and a leaking sack of cotton-wool on the trivet where he'd boiled his lonely kettle.

Across the little hallway, a drilling-machine occupied the bedroom which Flora had shared with her mother. The faded paper still bore the ghostly stain of Constance's wardrobe, but a workbench stood in the window now instead of a dressing-table, strewn with spools of thread and tallow horns of needles, and sparkling with drifts of gold and silver paper in place of the diamond studs Constance had held so dear.

The house was still familiar, but in the strangest way, as though two parts of Flora's life had become tangled, one image superimposed upon the other. Over them both hung an unforgettable smell – a distinctive brew of metal-parings and resin, of turpentine and lacquer, of oil and cheese and stale bread, and monkey, and man.

Disconcerted, Flora walked on towards the first-floor room which had been her mother's 'drawing-room', that precious symbol of the family's gentility, where Flora's father had died before the unheeding smile of the music-box dancer.

She could hear music now, the reedy piping of a serinette, a little clockwork organ designed to teach captive finches to sing. The trilling faltered as she stepped into the room, and a figure at the workbench glanced up, his pliers suspended over the entrails of the machine.

'Well, well – Flora, *ma petite*!' The automaton-maker laid down his pliers and came shuffling sideways from behind his bench, bent and bird-like himself, his hair rather greyer than she remembered, and drawn back like straggling feathers.

'My dear child!' He scuttled across the floor to take her hands, pulling them to his thin chest and peering up, curiously, into her face.

'My little Flora . . . and all in black. Black, black – the colour of the grave. Your husband's been dead a year already, hasn't he? Why must you go in black?'

'It's the custom, for another few months. And I suppose I've just got used to it.'

Dédalon extended a crooked finger to touch her cheek.

'You should never have married that man. If you'd asked me, I'd have said "*Don't* – he has the face of a tyrant".' Slowly, the finger traced her jaw. 'You should have asked me, Flora. I promised you once I'd take care of you like a father . . . And as you see – you've come back to me in the end.'

'How was I to know he had the face of a tyrant?' Flora turned her head uneasily. 'What was there to see, for goodness' sake?'

'Oh . . . a certain rigidity round the eyes . . . deep shadows at the turn of the nostrils – here—' Dédalon touched the base of his nose. 'A tightness under the lower lip, where the habit of selfishness develops the muscle . . .' He shrugged. 'By our fortieth year we wear the face we've made for ourselves.'

'How do you know all these things, Dédalon?'

'Because, my dear, I create faces. I create people.' With a sweep of his arm, he indicated the workshop. 'Tell me what you think of my sorcerer's castle! This house was for sale, and my workshop in Shoe Lane was too small. So . . .'

High summer lay over London, but it was excluded from that house, as if the automaton-maker carried twilight with him, the proper context for his magic. The window-panes were smeared with dust, and rain, and more dust, filling the room with a tobacco-coloured dimness in which the light of Dédalon's perpetual fire was the only bright element.

Half-built figures lay everywhere. Beyond the serinette, the bald pink head and forearms of another conjuror sprouted from a naked mechanism; a bird, part-feathered, lay on its side on the bench like a fowler's supper, while next to it a clown's face had been impaled on a rod to be painted, the firelight lacquering its skin with the sheen of old wax fruit.

'I like this room.' Dédalon tossed some wood shavings into the grate, and the flames crackled into life, drawing a startled scrabbling and rattling of chains from the corner by the workbench. A small, pale face popped into view, framed in cream-coloured fur.

'Hello, Solomon!' called Flora, and held out a hand.

The capuchin perched himself on a blanket-covered box where her mother's davenport desk had once stood. He whistled at her through bared teeth, and scratched his side vigorously.

'Solomon, my son, don't you recognize our dear friend Flora?'

Solomon whistled again, and hopped off his box to sweep a scatter of shavings into the air.

'*Méchant!*' exclaimed the automaton-maker. 'Where are your manners, *mon fils*? And just when I was about to show off our latest piece of cleverness. Move aside! Make way for the lady!'

Taking Flora's arm, he led her across the room to where a heavy, rust-coloured plush curtain cut off a section near the window.

'See!' With a flourish he drew back the curtain, laying bare a skeletal automaton, as large as a seated human figure but lacking any of the external signs of humanity, such as a head or hands. The creature was still only a mechanism in a frame of brass, but a mechanism more complex than any Flora had seen, as intricate as the workings of a dozen clocks in one. A battery of cylinders held cams against ruby-faced levers; a cat's cradle of chains clung to their fusees, waiting to regulate the springs and pawls and wheel-trains which controlled the stumps of the automaton's limbs.

'Did you ever set eyes on anything so miraculous?' Dédalon hung over his creation, entranced, stroking its parts like a lover. 'The music of the spheres . . . pure logic – elegant reason . . . My conjurors are toys beside this – even the little organist. This will be—' he drew in a long, sibilant, adoring breath, 'as near alive as anyone has seen.'

'As big as a real person?'

'Perfectly life-size. My *maître*, you know – the man who taught me as a boy at the château – he made two life-size figures during his time there. He was a disciple of Vaucanson.' Dédalon nodded reverently. 'He saw the Duck. He saw *inside* the Duck, and learned how it was controlled.'

'I thought no one was allowed to see the workings of an automaton.'

'Only one who can dissect what he sees.' Dédalon held up a sharp forefinger.

'My Maître Dutoit made two grand automata, a walking Moor and a flautist. Each one took more than two years to complete, and they were never put on exhibition. They were made solely for the amusement of the Comte and his friends.' Dédalon made a small, apologetic gesture with his hands. 'The mob destroyed the master-pieces when they stormed the château. They were simple country people, afraid of magic.'

He stared intently at the wall, as if summoning up the two lost figures before an inner eye.

'The flautist played each note with his fingers, so . . . and from his chest, with bellows and valves.' The automaton-maker's hands danced in the air. 'And he closed his eyes – so – and moved his head to and fro, as if the music carried him off . . . And the Moor – ah, the Moor was as tall as a tall man, with great feathers in his turban. He strode forward like an emperor, one step after another, swinging his scimitar and staring round, opening his mouth as if to say "Whosoever dares may try me!" He'd have said it aloud one day – except Dutoit was murdered by the mob before he could finish the voice-box.'

'And so you are making another Moor.'

'No.' Swiftly, Dédalon drew the plush curtain into place. 'I am making a woman.'

'The figure of a woman, you mean.'

'I am making a woman. Indistinguishable.'

'That's impossible, even for you!'

'Why should it be impossible?' the automaton-maker's eyes, flecked with yellow fire, held Flora's. 'Most people were certain Vaucanson's Duck was a real bird. They couldn't believe it had to be wound, to give it life.'

'But life isn't just movement! It's feeling and emotion—'

'And *love*?' demanded the automaton-maker scornfully. 'Is that what you were going to say? Or *sensibility*, that pretentious nonsense which makes poets faint on mountain-tops?'

359

'Yes – even anger!' cried Flora in a passion. 'Why not? It's just as real as flapping wings and rolling eyes!'

The automaton-maker dismissed the idea with a sweep of his hand. 'Anger is simply an increase in magnetic energy within the body. Heat and agitation of the particles. It's quite unnecessary for the continuance of existence.'

'What about hope, then? Hope – trust – and, yes, *love* if you like.'

'I do *not* like!' stormed Dédalon. 'My creation—' he indicated the closed curtain. 'My masterpiece will sigh and languish and make cow's eyes as well as anyone, and you may call it love if it pleases you. She'll do all of that – and it will mean as little to her as it should mean to you, Flora.'

For a moment, they glared at one another in silence.

'But will she make new life for you, Dédalon?' Flora asked softly. 'Will she make a child for her lover, do you suppose?'

'A child? Sired by a monster like Newsome?' The automaton-maker snorted scornfully. 'Are you so proud of the tyrant's son?'

Lydia has kept my secret. As swift as a cloud-shadow, astonishment flitted across Flora's face. The automaton-maker, who knew everything, did not, after all, know everything about Flora.

'What's the matter?' he demanded at once. 'Why are you looking at me like that?' He sidled closer, and peered up into her face. 'Do you mean to tell me the child is *not* Newsome's? That you meant exactly what you said – "a child for her lover"?' He stroked the black fringe of Flora's pelisse, like a man seducing a distrustful cat. 'Do you have a lover, *ma petite?*'

'No, I don't.' Flora leaned away from him.

'But you did have?'

'Yes.'

'And the child is his?'

Dédalon's eyes consumed her face, and it seemed pointless to deny the truth.

'So this man who imposed his child on you – who used you for his pleasure – has run off, leaving you to take the consequences?'

'No. Yes . . . I suppose in a way he did. He had a wife,' Flora added with finality, hoping to bring the subject to a decent close.

She was startled by the automaton-maker's ferocity.

'They all have wives!'

'What nonsense!'

'They all have wives, or regiments, or ships at anchor – how often have I warned you?'

'I believed I loved him.' Flora was angry at having been made to justify her actions.

'Romantic foolishness!' Dédalon's eyes glowed like the heart of his forge. 'Who is he, this brigand – this blackguard?'

'That's none of your business.'

'Tell me!'

'I will not.'

For a moment she believed Dédalon was about to attack her.

'After all I've said to you!' he shouted, whirling in the dimness. 'After all I taught you about the way things really are between men and women!'

'You're ranting at me like an outraged father, for heaven's sake!'

'And why not? You're as good as a daughter to me.'

'But I'm not your daughter, and you've no right to scold me as if I were.'

A furious silence fell between them.

'Very well.' Dédalon swallowed hard and held up his hands once more, this time in a plea for an end to hostilities. 'I beg your pardon for scolding, *ma petite*. It's just that . . . I hate to see you here, talking about *love*, when I've taken such care . . . I thought we understood one another, Flora.'

Flora watched him narrowly, her breathing heightened by annoyance, ready to turn and run from the house if he said another word of reproach. Only the inescapable fact that she needed his help kept her there at all – her restless, relentless compulsion to attack the Elders in some way.

Dédalon looked contrite.

'Forgive me, then, for my temper . . . yes?' Beguilingly, he plucked her sleeve. 'There now – we're friends again, aren't we? Why don't you tell me what's brought you back to me today, if it wasn't simply for the pleasure of seeing my ugly old face again.'

'I need your help,' Flora confessed, partly mollified, and proceeded to tell Dédalon about Felix Elder, and Mr Wesley, and her mother's blighted dream.

'Nothing could be simpler.' The automaton-maker seemed quite unsurprised by her request. 'What are these things, but pictures to be copied? I'm always amazed how readily people will exchange good, solid gold for scraps of worthless paper.'

'And you don't mind the risk?'

'My dear, I've taken far greater risks in my time. It's enough that you've asked me.' He waved his hands in the air. '*Voilà* – it's done.'

'I won't give you away,' she vowed, 'even if something goes wrong.'

'But nothing will go wrong.'

Flora glanced at him curiously. 'I wish I were as certain of that as you are.'

'Nothing will go wrong – provided you truly want to succeed. If the wanting is strong enough, that will carry it through.'

'Oh, I *want* to make fools of them!' Flora's pent-up resentment found its way into her voice. 'The Elders have taken everything from us, and left us with no honour, no self-respect – only disgust for the way we've allowed ourselves to be cheated.'

She stopped speaking, conscious of the hot colour which was mounting to her cheeks.

Dédalon was watching her shrewdly.

'And yet I seem to remember, many years ago, that you were especially interested in one of the Elders – the man who became your sister's husband.'

Flora turned her head away, pretending to watch Solomon noisily crunching cherries by the workbench.

'Darius Elder is every bit as bad as the others. Worse!'

'So he's condemned himself too, has he? Sinned, and been found out? You seem to dislike him very passionately.'

'I loathe all the Elders. You know that as well as anyone.'

'Indeed, indeed . . .' The sharpness in her voice warned the automaton-maker not to pursue the matter. 'And now, with my help, you're going to make fools of these people you hate, and steal all their money.'

'No—' Flora corrected him at once. 'Only eight thousand, three hundred and thirty-three pounds.'

'But what kind of revenge do you call that? These vultures of yours count their carrion in hundreds of thousands! Break them, my dear! Leave them crying for mercy! That's the only way to teach them a lesson.'

'I won't steal,' said Flora doggedly. 'I've told Lydia again and again. I only want what's rightfully Mamma's. Otherwise – if we steal from them, are we any better than they are?'

'A tooth for a tooth – pain for pain . . .'

'No!' Flora shut her eyes tightly, keeping out temptation. 'That kind of revenge destroys everything it touches.'

Dédalon raised his hands in deference to her scruples.

'As you please, as you please. I'll do whatever you want, *ma petite*.

You know you only have to ask. Though . . . there is something – a very little something – which you might do for me in return.'

'If I can.' Flora regarded him warily.

'It's nothing! Hardly anything at all, I promise you.' Dédalon sidled, crow-like, across the floor to touch a fold of the rust-coloured curtain. 'My masterpiece – this woman of mine who will dazzle the world – she must have the face of perfection. At first I thought of Lydia, but . . .' He shrugged apologetically. 'For my miracle I require purity and innocence, and there is none of that any more in our Semiramis, only greed and luxury. But you, my dear . . . I cannot think of a face I would rather have for my masterpiece.'

Flora laughed in disbelief. 'I'm hardly a great beauty, Dédalon.'

'Sometimes you are, I promise you. There is innocence in your face – and innocence is beauty.'

'Dédalon, I'm an old married lady! I'm hardly an innocent.' Yet Darius Elder had described her so – and the memory disturbed her. 'Sophie was always the pretty one in my family,' she murmured.

'*Pretty* is not what I want. I can find a dozen pretty women any day of the week. What I need is beauty.'

'Then why don't you create a face out of your own imagination? Then you can make your lady as pure and as innocent as you like.'

Dédalon made an awkward little gesture, and his glance strayed round the room.

'One may recognize innocence, but not be able to reproduce it.'

'Why ever not? I thought you could copy anything, *maître*.'

Dédalon avoided her eye. 'Once, I could have done it, perhaps. But not now.'

He held out his brown-spotted hands, splaying his sharp fingers as if examining them for the cause of their disobedience.

'Once – but not now.' He let his hands fall to his sides.

'But how could you "take" my face for your mechanical woman? Do you expect me to sit for a sculpture?'

Dédalon shook his head. 'Nothing so difficult. I'd take a cast of your face, in plaster – a perfectly simple operation. Haven't you heard of Madame Tussaud and her wonderful waxworks?'

'But surely her casts were made from corpses!'

'Oh, it isn't necessary to be dead.' The automaton-maker smiled persuasively. 'I can make a perfect cast from a living face, as long as the subject lies very still while the plaster is setting. Then from the mould I make up a mask in *cartonnage* sealed with gesso – or perhaps covered in fine leather, I haven't decided yet. But your part would be

363

so simple, Flora!' With a wave of his hand, Dédalon swept away any possible doubt. 'All you have to do is lie still for ten minutes, or perhaps a little longer, while the cast is setting.'

'Won't it hurt?'

'Not at all. But you must keep your eyes firmly closed, and not even try to whisper. It isn't as easy as it sounds.'

'And if I do it, you'll engrave the plates for our railway shares?'

'I've told you – I'll do that anyway, simply because you are my Flora.'

Flora's glance strayed to the plush curtain. He'd asked for very little. Ten minutes' discomfort, and her part of the bargain would be over.

'You'd better tell me when you want to make your cast, then.'

Dédalon spread his hands. 'I could do it now – if that's what you wish.'

4

He bound Flora's hair with a bandage which encircled her brow and covered her ears. Reflected in a sliver of looking-glass, she resembled a nun, all personality condensed into the small area of flesh which remained. Over this he spread a film of oil, coating her eyebrows and lashes so that the plaster would come away cleanly once it had set.

Lydia's old sofa stood against the wall, sprouting horsehair, and he made Flora lie down on it, covered to the chin with a piece of flowered cotton. For several minutes she lay there listening to him prepare the plaster, shooing Solomon from the water-jug as he mixed the ingredients vigorously in a bowl.

'Be kind enough to fix one of these in each nostril.' He rolled two pieces of card into short cylinders and passed them to her.

'What are these for?'

'So that you can breathe – otherwise your nose might become blocked.'

Less confidently now, Flora hoisted herself on one elbow to examine the tubes which were to be her lifelines.

'Lie back and close your eyes, please. The plaster will not wait.'

The automaton-maker touched her shoulder, and, reluctantly, Flora did as he'd instructed.

'Now, from this second until the cast is finally taken off, you must keep your eyes closed and your mouth also. Not screwed up tightly like a child eating a lemon, but without making a single blink, nor a whisper either. Raise your hand if you understand me.'

Again Flora did as she'd been told, and felt Dédalon grasp and squeeze her fingers.

'There's nothing to be afraid of, I promise you, but you must trust me absolutely. I shall stay by your side all the time, and talk to you so you'll know you aren't alone.' He released her hand, and she heard the bowl of plaster grate on the bench as he picked it up. 'I fancy this will feel a little cold at first, and then warmer as it begins to set.'

He began at her brow, smoothing and spreading. The sensation was cool, though not unpleasant – a light, steady pressure which, after the first few moments, became almost hypnotic. Flora began to relax – until the encroaching plaster suddenly weighted her closed eyelids like leaden, overwhelming sleep: but this sandman brought no sweet oblivion – only total and frightening darkness.

'Lie still,' warned Dédalon. 'A single frown, and the cast will be spoiled.'

Helpless on the sofa, Flora retreated inside her own thoughts. Then out of the darkness she heard Dédalon's voice, as silken as the liquid plaster.

'You must forgive my bad temper earlier, *chérie*, when you told me about the baby and your lover who went away. I didn't mean to scold you, but . . . you must understand, it makes me angry to see someone treat you badly.'

He continued to slide the cold wetness over the bridge of her nose, until Flora found to her dismay that she couldn't have opened her eyes even if she'd been allowed to; the plaster pressed down on them solidly now, like broad, heavy thumbs.

For a moment a wave of panic swept over her. Could she drown in plaster, blind and voiceless?

Determinedly, she fought down her fear. *Concentrate on reason*, she told herself – and clung to the sound of the automaton-maker's voice.

'You see,' it was saying, 'my daughter, too, made just such a mistake as yours. She fancied herself in love, and forgot everything I'd taught her.'

He was working the plaster down Flora's nose now, packing it round the two slender tubes which supplied her with air. She could smell the sweet, chalky scent of the plaster mixture, perilously close.

In the darkness, she reassured herself: Dédalon would never make a mistake. Not with her.

'Ah, yes,' his voice continued above her head, 'these fine gentlemen have no thought for the wretched women who are left to bear the consequence of their amusement.'

Amusement? The word was a humiliation in itself; Flora's breathing quickened, forcing up her chin.

'Lie still!'

Entombed, she could do no more than raise a protesting hand. But the automaton-maker simply pasted more plaster over her mouth and chin.

'My poor daughter . . . She believed the rogue, when he promised to divorce his wife and marry her. "We shall be faithful for all eternity," he said. "You shall be buried in my arms, like a second Héloïse." Oh, he spoke his lines well, that gentleman.'

Dédalon paused to scrape his spatula on the edge of the bowl.

'But of course, after a while his new toy was no longer a novelty. No doubt his Héloïse had become a little tarnished in his eyes, just like the last. So all at once he decided to be a repentant husband, a naughty boy devoted to his wife – until the next pretty face should come along to begin the game again.'

Flora was becoming aware of a tightening sensation in the region of her forehead where the plaster had begun to set.

'He couldn't wait', Dédalon continued remorselessly, 'to be rid of a lost girl and her baby.' With a final few strokes of his spatula he walled Flora up entirely. 'There you see the arrogance of the children of wealth – taught to help themselves to whatever takes their fancy without a thought for the consequences.'

Shut up in the prison of her stiffening, warming darkness, Flora raised an anxious hand. She felt Dédalon's fingers entwine with her own, and this time returned the pressure, grateful for his touch.

'Don't worry,' he said softly. '*I* won't leave you.'

She was only distantly aware of the spreading of the final layer over the mask – a layer which made itself felt as an increasing weight of plaster bearing down like a hand on her flesh. Buried alive: it was all she could do not to tear off the numbing slab and fill her lungs with great gulps of air.

'You're a brave girl, *ma petite*,' whispered the automaton-maker in her ear. 'You deserve to be cherished – not cast aside like the rubbish of the gutter. What kind of man could do such a thing?'

Darius Elder humiliated me . . . Flora repeated in the silence of her mind. *He lied to me . . . He read the paper and tricked me with kindness, like a beaten dog . . .* Impatiently, her hand rose to investigate the surface of the mask, but Dédalon turned it away.

'He cheated you with an empty fantasy.' The automaton-maker's voice was as smooth as milk and honey.

Darius knew from the start how lost I was . . . Defenceless in his hands . . .

'And where is he now?' Dédalon's words slid into her ear like quicksilver. 'Where is he now, with his promises and his passion? Do you believe he's thinking of you? Or is he lying with another woman at this very moment – promising her what he once promised you?

'The man who caused my daughter's death . . .' Dédalon's stool creaked as he moved. 'I hunted him down – I watched him suffer, exactly as I watched the fine gentlemen suffer in Paris, when they knew the guillotine was to be their last, gentle lover.

'That man, too – he knew there was no forgiveness for him in this world, only judgement. When the time came, I made sure he died.'

Set me free! Oh, set me free of this! Flora's chest rose in spasms as she fought for breath against the plaster shell tightening round her heart – round her mind, and round every living piece of her. Out of the suffocating darkness, the clear blue eyes of her baby son looked searchingly into her own. *Help me! What must I do to be free?*

Dédalon had taken her hand again.

'You're a little afraid? I think you were afraid, even before we began, *n'est-ce pas*? But you wanted so much to hurt the Elders . . . You must hate them a great deal, to put aside your fear.' The automaton-maker's hard thumb was massaging the back of Flora's fingers.

'Such passion! Such fierce anger, in a slender woman's body. Now – that makes me think. And do you know . . . I have a strange feeling . . . that this man Darius Elder is the father of your child.'

Anguished, bewildered, Flora couldn't bear Dédalon's touch any longer, and wrenched her hand away.

'So . . .' murmured the automaton-maker to himself. 'Well, now – I think we might be able to take this off.' With infinite care, he inserted his fingers under the edges of the plaster, sliding them so sinuously over bone and muscle that for a bizarre instant Flora found herself wondering what he must have been like as a lover. Then the pale plaster shell was raised, returning her, blinking, to the dim light of the workshop.

It was another world – and yet echoes of the old one lingered.

'You had no right to question me like that!'

'Did I question you?' Dédalon's eyes widened innocently. 'Surely not! How could I question you, when you were incapable of answering?'

'Questions . . . insinuations . . . You don't need answers, you make those up for yourself – and sometimes you frighten me, with all your talk of death and revenge.' There was a lump in Flora's throat, as solid as the plaster, and for a dreadful moment she thought she might be about to weep from sheer relief at being free.

'You're imagining things, *ma petite* – there's nothing to be afraid of in old stories. How can you possibly believe I'd ever harm you? Here – sit, sit . . .'

He insisted on washing her skin clean of plaster and oil before he'd allow her to look at the cast, stroking the contours of her face with a scrap of damp cotton while Flora stared fixedly over the top of his head.

'Now you may look.'

She looked.

'Is that really me?'

Somewhere in the depths of a milky, oily bowl, Flora's face was swimming. The bowl was a crucible of blue shadow and yellow light – a matrix – a white womb for her own features. She stared wonderingly into the smooth indentations, trying to assemble them into a living likeness.

'Half-close your eyes and reverse the image. Picture it rounded instead of hollow, and then you'll see how it should be.'

Flora frowned at the cast, forcing her mind to reinterpret the image. After a few moments, as if by magic, the concavity miraculously turned itself inside out, and her own features swam towards her, disembodied and ethereal, like a face drained of colour, glimpsed under water.

'Beautiful . . .' Dédalon was so close that Flora could feel his breath on her ear. He reached out to take the cast from her, cupping it reverently between his hands. 'What sin, to spoil such perfection! What blasphemy!'

A strange, irrational curiosity slid, snake-like, into Flora's mind.

'Dédalon . . .' she whispered. 'You never told me how your daughter died.'

The automaton-maker was still dreaming over his plaster cast, and answered almost absently.

'My daughter . . . drowned herself. A long time ago.'

368

CHAPTER TWENTY-TWO

I

Fortunately, Mr Theodore Wesley leaped at the chance of breaking
the law. His eyes danced with delighted wickedness: he clashed his
teeth and clapped his freckled hands like a man at a play until Flora
stared at him, astonished. Somewhere behind Mr Wesley's sober
tweed coat and jack-towel neckcloth there evidently lurked the heart
of a master criminal. It didn't seem to daunt him at all that the whole
business might stand or fall on his skill at passing himself off as a
railway engineer. Have no fear! Theodore Wesley would prove
himself a greater actor than Kean, if that was what it took to be
revenged on the Elders and to restore to dear Mrs St Serf her all-
important allowance.

'You mustn't say a word to Mamma,' Flora warned him. 'I'll find
a way of explaining the extra money to her somehow, but she must
never know the real story.'

In a gilt, griffon-backed chair with his coat buttons strained across
his comfortable paunch, Mr Wesley resembled nothing so much as a
prosperous seraph, innocently tickled by the prospect of mischief
ahead.

'Mr Wesley – you do realize . . . If we're found out, it could be
disastrous for all of us.'

Mr Wesley drew himself up. 'Did St George give a thought to
becoming supper for the dragon?' he enquired with dignity. 'Let
those scoundrelly Elders prosecute us if they dare! Let them prosecute, and look like simpletons in the eyes of the whole of London!
Let them see what it's like to be cheated and despised, and laughed
at by their friends!'

Mr Wesley proved to be a born conspirator, who adored his
clandestine meetings in the Zoological Gardens in Regent's Park with
two veiled ladies – one in profound black, and the other wearing the
largest diamond girandole earrings Mr Wesley had ever seen.

'Is she married?' he whispered, temporarily carried away.

'Many times over, you might say, Mr Wesley.'

'Ah, well. Never mind.'

After Mr Wesley had gone on his way, Flora remained walking with Lydia round the perimeter of the garden, where a new hedge screened the carriage-horses on the Outer Circle from the outlandish sight of kangaroos and 'Dr Brooke' the griffon vulture.

'Remember to pay your respects to the Arctic bear.' Lydia jerked her chin in the direction of a massive white bulk in a nearby cage. 'If it wasn't for his cousins at the Polar Sea, you'd still have a husband. What have you found there, sweetness?'

Flora had come to a halt in the middle of the path, staring at something a short distance away.

'What is it – a kangaroo?' Lydia shaded her eyes.

'Monkeys,' said Flora. 'Look – there they go! Did you see that one swing from the bars? It was just like Solomon, except its head was dark.' She watched for a moment before setting off once more, her face preoccupied behind her veil.

'Lydia,' she asked after a moment, 'how much do you really know about Dédalon? I've known him for so long, and he's taught me so much . . . made me think about things I'd never have questioned . . . and yet . . . Dédalon himself is still such a mystery in some ways.'

Lydia slowed to peer into a nearby cage.

'Dédalon? Oh, I don't reckon he's so much of a mystery. Didn't he tell us himself he was apprenticed to an automaton-maker in a castle in Picardy – and then he went to Paris during the Revolution, and stayed there during the Terror, which must have been dreadful, though Dédalon says it wasn't so bad. He's such an appalling old revolutionary!'

Lydia rattled her fan on the bars of the cage in an attempt to wake the sloth bear from its afternoon nap.

'And I remember him saying he worked for a while for Breguet the watchmaker.' Lydia stopped rattling as the hunched animal lifted its long, naked snout to blink at her reproachfully. 'Do you know – I'm told Napoleon himself used to go to Breguet's shop to talk about engineering?'

'Lydia!' exclaimed Flora reprovingly. 'What about Dédalon?'

'Oh, well, no doubt after all the fighting had stopped, Dédalon decided to come to London. His wife had died, I think he said, and he thought there might be a demand for his clever toys among the *émigrés* and the British nobility. And so he came to Shoe Lane, I suppose.'

Lydia abandoned the sloth bear, and came to link her arm with Flora's.

'But you can trust him absolutely, I do know that. He loves you like his own daughter. There's nothing he wouldn't do for your sake.' She halted, staring. 'Flora? What's the matter, my dear?'

'Nothing.' Slowly, Flora shook her head. 'Only . . . I'm afraid you may be right.'

2

Dédalon had appointed a date by which the railway certificates would be ready, and, reluctantly, Flora had agreed to call for them.

Reason told her she'd given nothing away by letting the automaton-maker copy her face for his mechanical woman. How much was it worth, a face which changed day by day and minute by minute? Yet she couldn't forget the sight of Dédalon with the cast in his hands like a crucible, or the suspicion that she'd given up something precious without even understanding what it was. Most of all, she dreaded being confronted by a perfect double of herself – her own head lying helpless under the automaton-maker's scalpel.

Yet when she got to Gough Square she was relieved to find only a rough, untrimmed mask of *cartonnage* which might have represented anyone at all.

Dédalon was full of unusual good humour, escorting Flora downstairs as she left and pointing out to her the almost complete quarter-size model of a steam locomotive which stood by the forge in the room which had belonged to Mrs Moss. The glow of the coals glittered like a bloodstain on its brass fittings and on the sides of its cylinders. Its goose-neck funnel was banded with more brass, and the journeyman who'd constructed it was hard at work on its matronly body, polishing it to perfection. Locomotion had hardly looked better when it drew its coal-wagons into Stockton.

'Railways!' snorted the automaton-maker. 'All of a sudden, everyone wants railways!'

Flora hugged her parcel of counterfeit certificates to her chest.

'Oh, I do hope so!' she breathed.

Two weeks later, in the early hours of one morning, Felix Elder was finishing a foray among the gaming establishments of St James's when he found himself in the company of the Honourable Frederick

Rosangle, one of Lydia Seaward's wealthy lovers and the nephew of the Marquis of Highbury. Quite how the Honourable Frederick had come to be sitting next to Felix was a mystery, but not only did this gilded youth address Felix as an old and valued friend, but he carried him off to Brooks's, filled him with excellent claret, and in the course of the next few hours, lost a considerable sum of money to him at the card-table.

Nobleman or not, Frederick Rosangle was still a minor, and answerable to trustees for his gambling debts. However, by a fortunate chance he'd ended the previous night richer by ten thousand pounds' worth of stock in the newly constituted Hull & Nottingham Railway, and since each share was presently paid up to half of its twenty-pound value, the untidy pile of certificates young Rosangle pulled out of his pocket would conveniently cover the five thousand pounds he'd just lost.

Smoothing the top certificate between his hands, Felix inspected it as carefully as his claret-soaked brain would allow.

'Handsome,' he rumbled, stubbing his finger on a fine engraving of a steam locomotive passing a church and a lake which headed the copperplate script.

Taking a long draught of wine from his glass, he frowned over the inscription.

'*These are to certify*', he read aloud, '*that the Bearer is Proprietor of the Share No. 892 of the Hull & Nottingham Railway Company, subject to the Rules and Orders of the said Company*, et cetera, et cetera . . .' For another few moments he breathed intently over the lines of script while Frederick Rosangle watched him through the wreathing smoke of a fine Havana cigar.

'Made out to the bearer,' Felix remarked at last. 'Isn't the building of the line authorized yet?'

Frederick Rosangle shrugged elaborately. 'Just a detail, I understand. Some hold-up to do with getting the King to sign the Act. They say Parliament authorized the railway quickly enough, but King George's eyesight is too bad at the moment for him to put his name to the bill, and they're waiting for His Majesty to have his cataracts peeled.'

Frederick Rosangle leaned over to fill Felix's glass.

'Should be a good little line, though,' he went on in the same careless tone. 'Part of it cuts across my uncle's land, and he seems pretty hot for it to start running. But if you'd rather have cash—' He reached out for the certificate. 'You can have my note-of-hand for the present, and I'll square it tomorrow with my trustees. There's a rumour the Hull & Nottingham will pay thirteen per cent this year, so no doubt the trustees will be happy to tuck this pile of stock away in their vaults.'

'*Thirteen per cent*, eh?' Felix snatched the printed page out of Frederick Rosangle's reach. 'Now that's what I call an excellent rate of interest.' Fortunately, the fact that a substantial river lay in the path of the line hadn't occurred to Felix any more than it had occurred to Flora. He inspected the certificate for another few moments, then slapped it down decisively on the table.

'Well, now, I'd say – *Fred* – that your misfortune tonight was a fine piece of luck for me. I'll accept your railway stock as the spoils of war, and thank you kindly for losing it to me.' He leaned forward, stretched his arms round the pile of certificates, and gathered them to his chest.

'Thirteen per cent from a provincial railway . . . Well, I'm damned!' Happily, he hugged his booty to his frilled shirt-front. 'Well . . . I'm . . . damned!'

Felix's discovery carried him into the bank next day in a jaunty mood which nothing could budge. Even when one of the junior clerks upset a column of sovereigns over his feet, Felix simply cursed mildly and went on his way, leaving the astonished youth on his knees among the rolling coins, wondering what in the world had made Felix so benign that morning.

'Never neglect provincial railways!' Felix barked at the Chief Clerk as they passed in the corridor a few minutes later. 'Long Annuities were all very well in my father's day – but for a quick, safe return, never neglect provincial railways!'

'Oh, indeed, sir,' murmured the startled Chief Clerk, and went off to confide in the Senior Cashbook Writer that Mr Felix must definitely have fallen in love, to be acting so very strangely.

Precisely at noon, the Keeper of the Shop Cashbook tapped on Felix's door to say that a gentleman in the Front Office wished to put a railway locomotive in the Elders' vault for safekeeping, since he'd heard it was the safest in London. The locomotive seemed quite a small one of its kind – although the Keeper of the Shop Cashbook, of course, was no expert – but since he'd heard of such items being prone to explode, he'd thought it best to consult Mr Felix before giving a definite reply.

373

Swollen with importance, Felix swept down from his lair to view the locomotive with the seasoned eye of a railway proprietor. As he entered the office there was a scuttling of clerks back to their desks and a snatching of pens from behind ears – and no wonder. There, in the middle of the public part of the floor, stood a magnificent scale-model of a railway locomotive, its brass fittings glittering in the thin sunshine of the bank windows, its wheels aflame with fancy paintwork and its funnel glossy as a jet bead.

Two young men in blue coats stood guard over this marvel, which they'd evidently carried in on a wooden stand; and leaning on its highly polished side – actually leaning on the phenomenon as if such things were commonplace to him – was a round, red gentleman in a strange snuff-coloured wig who introduced himself as Mr Augustus Brink, Chief and Contracting Engineer to the Hull & Nottingham Railway Company.

'And what did he say to that?' An hour later, by the puma's cage in the Zoological Gardens, Flora tried impatiently to extract the story of Mr Wesley's adventures.

'Mr Wesley,' cooed Lydia sweetly, 'won't you tell us what Felix did next?'

'Ah . . .' With an effort, Mr Wesley dragged his attention away from Lydia's earrings and back to his tale. 'Ah, well, after that Felix said I was precisely the fellow he most wanted to meet. Damned if he didn't slap me on the back and haul me off to the bank parlour for a glass of port and a discussion of the prospects of the Hull & Nottingham Railway.' Mr Wesley chuckled, and executed a little dance of delight.

'I don't mind telling you, I nearly burst from wanting to laugh in his face! *And your father called me imprudent!* I thought to myself. *Wait a bit, my lad, and we'll wipe that smug smile off your phiz.*'

'What a mercy you didn't say it!' Lydia fanned herself briskly. 'I never know what some of you gentlemen are going to say next!'

'Well, I assure you I'm not one of those loose-talking fellows!' Mr Wesley bridled at the very suggestion. 'Not in the slightest! I told Felix exactly what we agreed beforehand. I said I'd brought the model locomotive to London for the inspection of some of our investors, but that while it was here I wanted it locked up safely so none of our competitors could steal its secrets. "Very sensible," said he. "I'm pleased to see you taking such good care of my assets." *Of my assets!*' exclaimed Mr Wesley scornfully. 'Of *his assets*, by heaven!' Mr Wesley raised his hands to the puma in mute appeal.

'"Your assets, Mr Elder," I said to him – keeping my temper as well as I could – "Your assets are in good heart, I promise you. The company has a share capital of three hundred thousand pounds in half-paid-up shares, we have more mayors and aldermen on our board than you could shake a stick at, and all the landlords in the path of our line are ranked behind us to a man. Now that's healthy, you must agree!"

'I told him the signing of our Act had been delayed by the King's blindness – which he already knew, of course – but I pointed out that the delay was all to the good, since our scrip had been changing hands in the local towns as if money were going out of fashion.

'"As you'll have gathered," said he, "I happen to have come by a little of your stock." "Oho, well then, you're a lucky man!" I told him.' Mr Wesley nodded significantly. '"Since our incorporation will go through in a week or so, we've already surveyed our line and begun to break turf for the longest cutting. You should take up more stock, sir, before the whole country is clamouring for it."'

Mr Wesley beamed. 'That was when I had my brainwave.'

'What brainwave?' demanded Flora suspiciously.

'Aha!' A foxy expression spread over Mr Wesley's face. 'Now, I ask you, Mrs Newsome – what do *real* railway companies do as soon as they're decently able?' He paused, waiting for an answer.

'They build a railway line?' enquired Lydia innocently.

'Pooh!' Mr Wesley waved a hand. 'It's easy to see you aren't a woman of the world, Mrs – ah—' He halted, waiting for a name to be supplied.

'Pray go on, Mr Wesley – do.' Lydia favoured him through her veil with her most winning smile. 'What is it that railway companies do, if they don't lay down railway track?'

'They borrow money, ma'am!' exclaimed Mr Wesley triumphantly. 'They borrow – hugely and unwisely. So I thought to myself, "If we're really to make this fellow believe in the Hull & Nottingham, I'd better ask him for a loan.'

'So I told him I'd already been to Child's and Hoare's and a few others besides, but that they all wanted interest at five per cent, since our railway land is already fully mortgaged. I hinted that I thought the Exchequer Loan Commissioners might settle for four and a half, but Felix wouldn't hear of my trying them. Good heavens, no! Elder's Bank would be happy to oblige! He was quite insistent he'd give us whatever we needed at four per cent, and take company stock as security on the loan.'

'How much credit did you ask for?' Apprehensively, Flora waited for the answer.

'Sixty thousand pounds!' declared Mr Wesley with a flourish which sent the puma racing for the back of its den. '"Swear you're good for sixty thousand," I told him, "and I'll speak to my directors tomorrow."'

'Sixty thousand pounds!' echoed Flora in horror. 'But, Mr Wesley, that's an enormous sum! I thought we'd agreed we only wanted enough capital to make up Mamma's allowance – eight thousand, three hundred and thirty-three pounds?'

'But railways want a great deal more, Mrs Newsome – and that's what matters! Railway companies aren't interested in a few sovereigns here or there. If they borrow, they borrow magnificently, like princes. And if they crash,' he added proudly, 'they crash like emperors.'

'Mr Wesley does have a point,' agreed Lydia. 'Only a real railway company would ask for such an outrageous amount. Remember what I said – the bigger the lie, the more likely it is to be believed.'

'Yes, but still – sixty thousand pounds! And do you mean to tell me Felix agreed to all this?'

'Well, he gulped a bit at first, and said he'd have to think about it. I told him I'd be in London again in two weeks' time, and I'd call again to see what he'd made of it.'

'But if he asks questions in the City—' exclaimed Flora, 'he's bound to find out that Coutts' and the other banks have never heard of the Hull & Nottingham Railway!'

'Then we must give him someone whom he *can* ask,' Lydia put in imperturbably. 'Someone guaranteed to give him the right answers.'

Next morning the Honourable Frederick Rosangle sent his servant to Elder's Bank to present his master's compliments to Mr Felix Elder, and to enquire whether, since Mr Elder was now an investor in the Hull & Nottingham Railway Company, he might care to inspect the building work already in hand on the Marquis of Highbury's estate near Lincoln, where the Honourable Frederick was bound next day.

The two men set off by post-chaise soon after dawn – and since everyone knew that travelling was thirsty work, they made a determined sampling of every White Hart and Swan along the way, whenever the chaise put in to change horses. They spent the night in Leicester, toasting steam locomotion in porter and claret, and spent all next morning attempting to cure their hangovers with a mixture of malmsey and raw egg.

By afternoon, when a hired barouche at last carried them out across the Marquis's broad acres, Felix Elder couldn't have sworn where he was – in Heaven or in Hell, or in some part of England lying between the two.

Fuddled and blinking, he applied himself to the inspection of a long, raw gash in the landscape which ran across several fields, and where an army of men were digging as if their lives depended on it.

'D'you see? The line goes between those two small hills yonder.' Standing up in the carriage, Frederick – who seemed remarkably steady on his feet – pointed into the distance.

Felix attempted to pull himself up, lost his balance and slumped back heavily on the cushions, setting the carriage rocking like a rowing-boat and making him feel decidedly queasy.

Solemnly, he peered in the direction Frederick had indicated. Something was happening on the Marquis's land, certainly – something large and important which caused labourers to dig and surveyors to survey, and aristocratic nephews to grin like cats before a mouse-hole.

Felix's head lolled over the side of the carriage, more like a bull in a stall.

If this was what a half-built railway looked like, then everything seemed well in hand. The directors of the Hull & Nottingham Railway Company clearly had no intention of allowing the grass to grow under their feet: instead, they grubbed it up and tossed it aside, taking trees and hedges with it.

Felix beamed. There was something very appealing in the idea of ripping one's way through the countryside, barging through pig-pens and flattening fowl-coops, all in the name of unstoppable progress. The longer Felix gazed at the diggers, the broader his beam became, and his heart warmed to the directors of the Hull & Nottingham Railway, all of them fearless and far-sighted men.

An hour later he set off again for Leicester, alone in the post-chaise but delighted by what he'd seen. Arriving in Leicester at ten o'clock he discovered that fifteen shillings would not only secure the inn's finest bed, but also a chambermaid to put in it: and by half-past ten Felix was sound asleep, his brain suffused with dreams of the riches to be made in the English countryside.

Never neglect provincial railways! Let timid fellows stick to their desks in the City, if they were afraid to venture beyond its bounds. Felix Elder, with his hawk-like eye for profit, had discovered a potential goldmine in country railway stock.

Meanwhile, the Honourable Frederick Rosangle, not at all ashamed of having misrepresented a canal-cut designed to connect the River Trent with the limestone works on his uncle's estate, travelled back by another route to London and his grateful mistress's arms.

CHAPTER TWENTY-THREE

I

As Constance had observed, Felix Elder's word was now absolute law within the walls of Elder's Bank. By the end of the week he'd not only bullied his ancient partners into making sixty thousand pounds of the bank's money available for the Hull & Nottingham Railway Company to draw on, but had agreed to sink another ten thousand immediately into their highly promising stock.

'I trust you'll do your best for us, Mr Brink, when you get back to Nottingham.' Felix threw an arm round Mr Wesley's shoulders and wheezed in his ear, 'But not a word to the other fellows in the City, hey? We don't want the price flying up, simply because Elder's are known to be taking an interest.'

'Not a word,' promised Mr Wesley with feeling. 'Not a whisper to anyone.'

Next day, Mr Wesley set off by public coach for Nottingham, where he banked Felix's ten-thousand-pound draft in the name of the Hull & Nottingham Railway Company – and promptly drew it out again in untraceable Bank of England notes. In London, Flora counted out the exact sum which, invested in government stock, would restore her mother's original income, and sent Mr Wesley off to lodge the rest in a country bank, to be restored to Felix as soon as the coast was clear.

'It must all be fair and square,' she told Lydia afterwards.

'Well, I think you're mad.' Lydia shook her head over such scruples. 'And I warn you, my dear – in spite of all your honourable intentions, I suspect you've started something you may find very hard to stop.'

In fact, the imaginary locomotive of the Hull & Nottingham Railway Company was already running too fast on its course to be turned back. With ten per cent of the exciting H & N in his pocket, Felix Elder was utterly eaten up with railway fever. Every waking hour was spent dreaming of the day that the line – his line – would run straight and true from Hull to Nottingham, taking up passengers here and freight there, filling the Elders' coffers with every passing mile.

Mr Wesley, too, was enjoying himself hugely.

'We can't call a halt to it all, just like that.' He pouted like a child deprived of a favourite toy. 'Felix is bound to smell a rat if the company disappears overnight, and we don't want him sending to Nottingham for information. No—' He held up a plump and chairmanly finger. 'I propose we keep Felix warm for a bit, and then – if you absolutely insist on it – we can quietly let the whole thing vanish away.' A woebegone expression spread over his face. 'And just as I was beginning to have some fun.'

A few days later, to Felix's joy, the Hull & Nottingham confirmed a dividend of a thumping thirteen per cent, sending Felix gleefully off to his club to drop mysterious hints about eight-arch viaducts and fish-belly rails until he found himself drinking alone.

Unfortunately, Mr Wesley couldn't resist returning to the bank to measure the success of his inspiration.

'You've done *what?*' Flora demanded later that day.

'I've agreed to take up part of the loan.' Mr Wesley spread his hands helplessly. 'What else could I do? He was so insistent – and I had to think so quickly!' Mr Wesley fished in his pocket for the all-important pieces of paper. 'I made up a tale about starting work on an enormous tunnel, and said I'd need at least twenty thousand pounds over the next four weeks to pay my labourers.'

Bewildered, Flora scanned the papers he spread out before her.

'Who's Joseph Hardwick, for any sake?'

'He's Chairman of our Board of Directors,' Mr Wesley informed her proudly. 'That's me, of course.'

'And Robert Ellison, Company Secretary?'

'That's me, too.' A blissful smile spread over Mr Wesley's face, and he threw out his arms. 'You see before you an entire railway company, Mrs Newsome – directors, clerical staff, contractor and engineers all rolled into one, but equal, I flatter myself, to the burdens of them all.

'Yes—' Mr Wesley gave a short, preoccupied sigh, and clasped his hands behind his back. 'I told Felix I'd need six thousand pounds straight away, and none of it in these five-pound banknotes they insist upon nowadays. "I need gold", I said, "to pay my labourers – sovereigns and half-sovereigns, and a few shillings and pence, too, but chiefly gold."'

Flora pressed a hand to her brow to reassure herself she wasn't dreaming.

'And Felix believed all this?'

'Certainly he did!' Augustus Brink, engineer and contractor, thrust his chin into the air. 'My word's as good as the next man's, isn't it? I told him I'd be waiting in Fleet Street tomorrow noon, with a travelling-chariot and an iron-bound box. "Six thousand pounds, and the bulk of it in gold," I said. "And if Elder's Bank can't rise to that figure, then say so at once and I'll go off to the Bank of England for my money in future."'

'Now I'm sure I must be dreaming!' Flora stared at Mr Wesley, aghast. 'And what are you going to do with all this money when you get it?'

Mr Wesley shrugged with casual magnificence. 'I shall drive it up to Nottingham, I suppose, like the rest.'

'But you can't go careering about the country with a box full of gold! What if you're robbed, or the carriage breaks down? No, Mr Wesley, this has got to stop. You'll have to find an excuse for not taking the money.'

'But we must take it, or Felix will become suspicious at once.'

Flora flung up her hands in frustration.

'Then drive it to a bank somewhere just outside London. Lodge it in Felix's name like the last payment, and we can make sure he gets it back in the end.'

Mr Wesley's mouth hung open in disappointment. 'Why should we do that?'

'Because we aren't bank robbers, Mr Wesley – and this whole business seems to be running away with itself. I'm terrified it's all getting completely out of hand.'

2

From the days when the first Elder lent out gold angels from his shop at the Sign of the Spider, it had been a rule of the house that large withdrawals in coin must always be balanced by gold in the vault. Paper money was all very well, but each of the bank's paper notes carried a promise to pay its own value in solid gold whenever it might be demanded; and at the first hint of trouble that gold would be demanded, loudly and more menacingly by the minute.

If Felix's Chief Clerk had known in advance of the Hull &
Nottingham's enormous cash withdrawal, he'd have sent round to the
Bank of England for enough extra sovereigns to leave a comfortable
surplus in the Elder's strongroom. But Felix didn't bother to tell him,
trusting the day's deposits to supply whatever was needed. What was
six thousand in gold to a mighty banking-house whose notes were
considered as safe as those of the Bank of England itself?

Yet even as Mr Wesley rolled up to the door in his travelling-
chariot, Felix was about to learn what happened to banks which left
themselves short of sovereigns.

Four and a half thousand miles away from London's Fleet Street,
the old-established Calcutta trading house of Baird & Barragait had
failed – and like one of Mr Wesley's railway companies, had crashed
like a maharaja with debts exceeding a million pounds. Elder's Bank
stood to lose three hundred thousand in the crash, but due to the
oddities of the India mail, Felix Elder was one of the last men in
London to know. The news broke half an hour after the Hull &
Nottingham's gold had left the premises, when one of the bank's
largest depositors rushed in, breathlessly demanding to draw out his
entire funds in coin of the realm.

Felix gaped at the man, his mouth slack with horror.

'But, my dear sir, that's impossible! Surely not all at once – or
not all in gold!'

'Are you telling me you haven't got the coin to cover it?'

'Well – that is to say – of course we'll cover it – but in an hour,
perhaps—'

'I thought as much!' The customer slammed his fist on the counter.
'Thank God I came in time! I'll have none of your hours, Mr Elder –
nor your weeks or months, either. Give me my money here and now,
in Bank of England notes if you have 'em, or Child's, or Gosling's, or
Coutts' if you haven't, and I'll change them myself into good, solid
coin. No gold, eh! I knew it, as soon as I heard the news from Calcutta.
No gold in Elder's Bank, and their paper worth nothing at all.'

His face brick-red with rage and fear, Felix Elder watched the
man sprint out into Fleet Street, his pockets bulging with Bank of
England paper. For ten solid minutes, while the cashiers listened in
awe, Felix cursed the railway company which had run off with his
sovereigns at that critical moment – blasted it to Hell and back again –
reviled its directors, its contractors, its track-layers and surveyors too,
but principally Mr Augustus Brink and his iron-bound box, who'd left
Elder's bank dangling over the pit of disaster.

'A bank's credit', old Mr Elder was fond of saying, 'is like a woman's honour. One hint – one wink – its enough to destroy it beyond any hope of repair.'

Now at last Felix sent off to the Bank of England for more gold. But word had spread, and his messengers returned empty-handed to say that the Bank had refused to accept Elder's notes under the present circumstances. Perhaps when the full effect of the Calcutta collapse was known . . .

Already the dignity of the Front Office had been shattered by a mob of depositors demanding the return of their funds. With a groan, Felix thought of the hundreds of thousands of Elder's banknotes in pockets and shop cash-drawers throughout London and the neighbouring counties, each one bearing the awful legend 'promise to pay the bearer on demand'. Where were the assets to support that boast? In Long Annuities or Naval Annuities, or safe-as-houses East India Stock? No, they were where Felix had put them in daring adventures into coal and lime, or lent out to piratical American states or to high-spending noblemen whose estates were tied up in Chancery – wherever Felix was least able to lay hands on them in a crisis.

'Perhaps, if Mr Darius had been here . . .' observed the Chief Clerk wistfully. But Darius and his wife were now in Geneva, pursuing yet another cure for Sophie's irrational moods. Even with Felix's threats ringing in his ears, the bank's messenger would take four days to reach him, and Darius would need another four to return. By then there might be no bank to come back to.

The next day was Sunday, and the doors of Elder's Bank could decently remain closed: but Felix sped round London like a demented wasp, frantically arranging the mortgaging of Elder property so that the bank could open again the following morning. Deeds to houses and land were torn from the furious hands of Elder cousins: cash-boxes were raided, diamonds given in pawn and rents reassigned. Raging sisters and uncles and in-laws called down vengeance on Felix's head. The Elders were fighting for survival, all on account of the Hull & Nottingham's gold.

And yet when Felix tried to sell the H & N stock he'd acquired, no one seemed to have heard of the company – or of Joseph Hardwick, or Robert Ellison, or even of Augustus Brink himself, last seen disappearing down Fleet Street with six thousand pounds of Elder's sovereigns in his iron-bound box.

But before Felix could investigate further, Monday was upon him, and a surly crowd waited noisily for the bank to open. Felix stationed himself in the Front Office, pink and prosperous, braced to laugh at his customers' fears and assure them that Elder's could weather the crash of a dozen Calcutta houses without turning a hair.

Somehow the bank staggered on until midday, though by then the only gold left on the premises was in the owlish rims of the Chief Clerk's spectacles.

Already the infection had spread across London. In Downing Street, the Cabinet discussed the matter, and in Paris and Amsterdam distinguished bankers pored over documents rushed to them by mud-spattered couriers. Meanwhile, in the English shires twenty-five country banks for whom Elder's were agents tottered towards ruin, and the price of peas in Sleaford market halved to 1/4d a peck.

Oh, where was Darius when he was needed? Darius would have thought of something, surely! With ruin staring him in the face, Felix fell back on desperate measures.

At noon the Front Office was cleared for ten minutes. When customers were readmitted, they discovered a small wooden cask standing on the counter, brimming with gold.

'See that?' Felix demanded, jerking his thumb at the stout little barrel. 'That's just been brought in by a ship-owner wishing to deposit, but the blessed thing's so heavy we'll need three men to move it, and we've been too busy counting our cash to bale it out piecemeal.'

The crowd gazed at the cask in awe. One man, stronger than the rest, even put his shoulder against it, but failed to move it by so much as an inch. The crowd murmured amongst themselves, clearly now in two minds, and several put their banknotes back in their pockets and left, reassured.

Yet a burly drysalter who'd been watching from the doorway remained suspicious. Striding forward before anyone could stop him, he plunged his hand into the brimming barrel – only to pull it back sharply, nursing bruised fingers.

'Dammed if it ain't a fraud!' he exploded. 'The cask's upside down, nailed to the counter. There's no more'n a handful of sovereigns spread on the base.'

'The bank's broke, and they're trying to hide it!' yelled a man at his elbow. 'Grab what you can, before they go down altogether!'

The crowd hurled itself in a body at the counter, brandishing worthless Elder notes, shaking fists, banging angrily on the smooth-worn wood, bawling for gold or Elder blood.

From the mouth of the corridor, Felix watched the mêlée, his face ashen.

'Clear them out somehow,' he muttered to the Chief Clerk. 'Clear them out, and lock the doors. There's nothing more we can do for the present.'

3

'Serves them right,' observed Constance over dinner that evening. 'I still haven't forgiven Felix for threatening to reduce me to beggary, even if it's all been settled, as you tell me.'

'Are you sure it's as bad as they say?' At the opposite side of the table, Flora regarded her mother anxiously.

'Catastrophic,' confirmed Constance with relish. 'And now, apparently, two banks outside London have discovered secret accounts in Felix's name with thousands of pounds in them – money he claims he can't explain.'

'Oh my goodness . . .' Guiltily, Flora recalled Mr Wesley's country deposits, and the notes which lay at that moment, wrapped up in paper, in the bottom of her wardrobe.

'Obviously, Felix was planning to bolt to America.' Constance folded her hands with prim satisfaction. 'They say he's quite worn to a shadow over it all, and the whole Elder family are fighting like cat and dog—'

'Sophie's married to an Elder,' snapped Flora, her nerves suddenly on edge. 'Have you forgotten that?'

'Yes – to an Elder who wouldn't lift a finger to help me in my time of need.' Constance glared across the table. 'A fine son-in-law Darius turned out to be!' She dismissed the matter with a flick of her hand. 'You don't need to waste any sympathy in that quarter. Chillbourne's held in trust for Sophie, so even if Darius loses everything else they can still live comfortably on his wife's inheritance.'

'Could the Elders really lose everything, do you think?'

'Every penny, so Sybil Ivory says. Let's see how they like being poor for a change.'

Lydia, at the Zoological Gardens next day, was equally unconcerned.

'This is exactly what you wanted, isn't it?' Deftly, she speared a bun on the end of a long cane for the benefit of the Russian black bear. 'The Elders are in trouble, everyone's far too busy to worry about a non-existent railway company, and you and I and Mr Wesley are as safe as crows in a gutter. Here you are, Toby, my boy . . .'

The cane slid through the bars, and the bear snatched the bun off the end with a single swipe of his enormous claws.

'Here, Flora – you give him the next one.'

'No, please . . . You go on, if you're enjoying it.'

In truth, Flora couldn't bring herself to meet the animal's eye. Hunched in the centre of his heavily barred cage, the bear gazed dispiritedly at those who'd come to view him, a squat, diminished caricature of ferocity. His black coat was threadbare in patches from scratching, and matted by hours of motionless contemplation; when a bun was offered on the end of a cane, the bear took it mechanically, without enthusiasm, as if resigned to his abject role in life.

What had the poor creature done to deserve such punishment? Flora felt ashamed to be the unwitting cause of the animal's suffering.

'All this . . .' she murmured, 'just for being what he is.'

'Simple beasts,' remarked Lydia, who'd been thinking thoughts of her own.

'Bears?'

'Men.'

To Flora's amazement, when she returned to Montagu Square she found her mother's respectable front door wide open to the common gaze, and Constance sitting half-way up the stairs, her lace cap askew and its strings undone, and her face as pinched and grey as the thin strand of hair which had wriggled down over one shoulder.

'What's the matter, Mamma?' Hastily closing the door behind her, Flora gathered her skirts and hurried up the first few steps.

Feebly, Constance flapped a hand, and for the first time Flora saw that her mother's cheeks were wet with tears.

'But what's wrong? What on earth's happened now?'

Behind her mother, Maggie rumbled heavily down from the landing, a small flask of smelling-salts in her hand and her eyes almost as red as Constance's.

'Mr Elder was here—' she began in a low voice. 'Mr Darius Elder, that is—'

'Darius was here? But why—'

'Sophie's dead!' cried Constance suddenly, pressing the smelling-bottle to her nose and sniffing hard. 'My poor child – dead more than a fortnight, and I never knew . . .' She began to sob again, dropping the bottle and burying her face in her hands.

'Come you upstairs to the drawing-room, mistress.' With gentle insistence, Maggie hauled Constance to her feet, and the two women stumbled up the steps, each supporting the other, while Flora scrambled dazedly in their wake. There must be a mistake: how could Sophie possibly be dead? Sophie was in Geneva, and Darius with her. It was impossible for Darius to be back in London . . .

But there was no mistake. In the drawing-room, Constance subsided into an armchair, and in fits and starts and prompted by Maggie, poured out the pitiful story.

Mentone, it seemed, had suited Sophie no better than Nice, and in desperation Darius had taken her to Geneva, where mountain air and exercise had been known to work miracles in the past. But Sophie was consumed by irrational fears; before long she'd taken it into her head that Darius was having an affair with her maid, and with her nurse, and even with the half-witted girl who watered the flowers on the terrace, until the rooms of their rented villa rang with her accusations.

Carried down to the lake, she'd walked into the water fully clothed, and might have drowned herself, had Darius not prevented it. And still the rows went on, until one day, hysterical, she flew at him, scratching and slapping; when the nurse tried to pull her away, she fled from the room and dashed straight out of the house.

'And just at that moment,' said Constance sadly, 'there was a carriage passing the door . . . The driver said Sophie never looked right nor left, even when the horses were almost upon her.'

'Oh, poor Sophie . . .' Flora tried to conjure up an image of her sister's face, calm and at peace, but failed. All she could think of was the bright-haired child who'd sat on her father's knee, playing with the braid on his military coat. What if Flora had been the one to go to Chillbourne, and Sophie had stayed . . .

Darius had waited long enough to see Sophie buried in the cemetery of the Plain-Palais, and had then set off for home to break the news. At Calais, after four days on the road, stopping only to change post-horses, he'd at last learned of the bank's collapse, and pushed on to London at once.

'He only stayed here a short time,' gulped Constance. 'He had to go off to see Felix. He says if he can only persuade the Bank of

England to help, he may yet save them all.' She gave a desolate sniff. 'And, of course, Chillbourne is his now to offer as security.'

'But your allowance—'

'Will be paid, he says, whatever happens.' Constance raised her eyes tragically to Flora's. 'Can you believe it – Darius did write to Felix after all, ordering him to pay my allowance in full. He has Felix's reply to prove it.' She shook her head, trying to blink back fresh tears. 'So Felix was lying when he claimed never to have seen any letter.'

'Darius wrote to him?' A cold, hard stone turned over in Flora's stomach.

'The moment my letter reached Mentone, apparently.' Constance sighed again. 'I don't blame Darius for any of this. He's had enough trouble for a lifetime, these last few months.'

'He asked if you were at home, dearie,' Maggie put in. 'And then, when no one could find you, he asked if he might take a peek at the baby.' Maggie's face folded itself into an expression of sorrowful pride. 'Edmund was fast asleep, the poor little mite, when we went in to see him. "Ralph Newsome's son", said Mr Elder – and said it so sadly, too.' Maggie wiped her eyes with the corner of her apron.

Flora was already on her feet, running out of the drawing-room and upstairs to the nursery, suddenly consumed by a desperate need to be with her son. Sophie was dead – her sister, dead – and Darius was in London, overwhelmed by a disaster of Flora's making: the world was surely mad, and spinning out of control . . .

Safe in his cradle, Edmund slept on, blissfully unaware of the turmoil raging round his pale, faintly glowing head with its sprinkling of dark hair. Gently, Flora lifted him into her arms, confining the tiny hand which thrust out in alarm and watching him settle again, his lips sucking rhythmically in a cushiony, maternal dream.

His cheek was cool against Flora's fingers, and softer than cream. All at once, the anger and resentment which had consumed her until that moment seemed utterly inexplicable. What had possessed her? What injury had been great enough to drive her to such a wasteland of hatred?

Dédalon had been utterly wrong – she was sure of that now. Hope, trust, even love – those were reality, held in her arms at that moment. It was revenge, which destroyed the avenger as surely as the victim, which was the real illusion.

*

Soon after dawn the next day, Flora opened the wardrobe in her bedroom and pulled out her hoarded parcel of banknotes: eight thousand, three hundred and thirty-three pounds, wrapped in anonymous paper like a pair of boots or a new hat. For an hour and a half she laboured over a letter to go with it, and at last, still unsatisfied, sealed her final version with a wafer and made herself ready to leave.

The sun had still hardly risen high enough to bleach the stucco of the square when Flora slipped out of the house and set off through streets ringing with the morning calls of the milk-sellers. At the corner of York Place she found a hackney-carriage, horse and man still half asleep.

'New Road, and wait.'

Laying her parcel on the doorstep that had been Sophie's, she rapped hard with the knocker and waited for a moment, holding her breath, ready to leave her letter and run back to her carriage as soon as she heard the rapid footfalls of a maid on the floor of the hall.

Instead, from some distant corner she heard a step she knew – a step which still had the power to bring a lump to her throat and make the blood drum in her ears. Behind the door, the footsteps grew louder; in the street her carriage was waiting, the horse tossing its head to scatter a cloud of flies. Flora took a step towards it, and stopped, and turned to fling an anguished glance at the door, and another at the carriage, waiting to carry her away . . .

But by then the door had opened, and Darius Elder, in shirt-sleeves and black trousers, was staring at her in astonishment.

'Flora – I didn't expect . . . I mean, it's so early . . .' He ran a hand through his dark, uncombed hair. 'Forgive me – come inside, of course. I'm all alone here, except for the caretaker. No servants – not a soul.' He indicated the hall behind him, where the chandelier hung shrouded in a storage bag of brown holland.

For an instant, Flora hovered on the threshold, ready for flight, knowing all she had to do was push her note into his hand and run back to her carriage. Yet Darius looked so weary, so unresistingly hopeless, that her heart went out to him. He would hate her so, when he knew what she'd done – and yet now that he stood there before her, the urge to confess, to make everything honest between them, was too strong to resist.

'Darius, I'm so sorry . . . so dreadfully sorry—'

'Sophie . . . yes . . .' He made a gesture of helplessness. 'If only there'd been a cure – but there were no more doctors. We'd tried them all.' He opened the door a little wider. 'But come inside, won't you?'

'Darius – you must listen to me—'

'Ah . . .' He saw the note in her hand. 'I suppose you have appointments elsewhere. Things to do. You're a famous lady these days, so I hear.' He looked away, towards the waiting carriage, and when he turned to her again there was bitterness in his voice. 'Though I hoped you might spare me a few minutes, at least. Please, Flora – is that so much to ask?' For a moment his eyes met hers directly, then his glance fell on the paper-wrapped package at his feet.

'What's this?'

'It's money. That's what I've been trying to tell you. Last night I realized I couldn't keep it. I had to bring it back to you.'

Puzzled, he bent down to pick up the parcel. 'You're offering me money? That's generous of you, Flora, but—'

'It isn't my money, Darius. It's yours – the bank's. I stole it, you see,' she added softly.

Framed in the doorway, Darius stared at her in disbelief. 'You did *what*?' He glanced down again at the parcel in his hands, as if he almost expected it to dissolve into thin air as he watched. 'Flora, for heaven's sake, I don't know what this is all about, but let's not discuss it on the doorstep. You must come inside.'

There was a bloom of dust on the table in the hall, and the echo of bare boards underfoot. Sophie's house was hushed and neglected, and Sophie was gone. Flora had a sudden vision of her sister, brilliant in silks and feathers, chatting animatedly with her society painter, her eyes as bright as the diamonds in her hair. Sophie had had so much – but it had never been enough.

At the end of the hall the morning-room was in darkness; Darius flung open a pair of shutters, sending a shaft of sunlight to splash its dancing dust-motes over the sheet-covered furniture.

'I spent most of last night at the bank.' Apologetically, he indicated his open shirt collar. 'I imagine you're used to better these days. Your mother said—'

'The Hull & Nottingham Railway.' Flora's voice cut through his apologies, not entirely steadily. 'Please, Darius – I'm trying to tell you something, and it isn't easy.'

'I beg your pardon.' He straightened his back, formally polite. 'I didn't realize I'd interrupted you.' He gestured for her to speak. 'Please go on, Mrs Newsome.'

'The Hull & Nottingham Railway.' Flora took hold of a sofa-back to give her courage. 'Felix must have told you about it. He bought some shares in the company, and lent it money – except that the railway never existed.'

On a sudden impulse, she held out the crumpled letter. 'Here – read about it for yourself. I don't even know where to begin any more.'

Frowning, Darius took the letter, and turned away with it towards the light of the window. He read it swiftly, his frown deepening as he made his way down the single page; gradually, a baffled expression replaced the frown, and he leaned back on a console-table for support. He only glanced up once, to examine Flora disbelievingly – then his gaze passed on to the paper-wrapped parcel she'd brought with her.

In the middle of the room, Flora clung to her sofa-back and waited, wondering how she'd ever imagined herself his victim, this weary, embattled man whose hollow shoulders told their own story of misery and wasted hope. His face was gaunt and blue-shadowed from lack of sleep; from time to time he passed a hand over his eyes, as though he no longer trusted his mind to make sense of what he saw.

'You weren't alone in this, I imagine.' At last he finished the page and looked up.

'It was entirely my idea.' Flora lifted her chin. 'If anyone's to be punished, it should be me.'

For a few moments Darius considered what she'd said.

'You didn't have to tell me any of this,' he observed at last. 'Felix has no idea where his money went to – or how some of it came to be in these secret accounts. You covered your tracks well, Flora. If you hadn't told me now, I'd never have known.'

Flora flinched from the coldness of his tone. 'It wasn't meant to be stealing – just getting back what Felix had taken from Mamma. And now . . .' She looked down, twisting her gloves between her fingers. 'I suppose Felix, at least, will want to have me arrested.'

Darius sighed, and studied the ceiling above her head.

'What Felix wants isn't important any more – nor even why you took the money. At this present moment, the only thing that matters is saving Elder's Bank – and I don't imagine it would help our case with the governors of the Bank of England, if you were hauled into court to tell the world how easily Felix was taken in. I should think they'd wash their hands of us after that.'

Flora studied him, puzzled, searching his face for a clue to what he thought of her. She'd expected anger – or reproaches, at the very least – not this bleak analysis of the bank's position.

391

'And in a way,' Darius continued, 'I suppose you could say Felix brought it all on himself by persecuting your mother and pretending I had a part in his mischief.' He hesitated, and then added, 'In Felix's place I might have guessed you'd do something rash in return – but then, Felix doesn't know you as well as I do.'

He smiled, sadly and a little crookedly; then, after a moment, he glanced away.

'It was the crash of that Calcutta trading company which brought us down – your little fraud was simply the fuse that lit the powder. So I think it would be best for everyone if the truth about the Hull & Nottingham Railway never went outside this room.' His eyes swept back to meet Flora's. 'Will you promise me that, Flora? Will you keep it a secret between us?'

'Of course – I give you my word.' There'd been a challenge in his voice, daring her to forget past secrets between them: for an instant the sensation was so strong that Flora almost expected to hear her mother's footsteps overhead, counting out their seconds together. She hesitated to speak, unwilling to banish precious memories.

He was watching her again, with the same curious, appraising expression he'd worn when he'd finished her letter.

'You can keep your liberty then, Mrs Newsome. Your reputation is safe.'

'You've been far more generous than I deserve.'

Flora began to draw on the gloves she'd just removed. There seemed nothing more to stay for, except the disturbing, unsettling effect of his presence: no doubt after what she'd done he'd be glad to get rid of her.

Then, as she turned to leave, she heard his voice again.

'You must have hated me a great deal, to believe I'd let Felix harm your mother, and do nothing to stop him.' This time when Flora looked back, she saw Darius's eyes alive with resentment; the two livid spots she remembered of old had appeared on his cheekbones. 'Didn't you trust me at all?' he demanded. 'Simply because I had to take Sophie abroad, and you refused to understand? Wait—' he instructed, seeing her turn away. 'You still haven't told me what I want to know.' His gaze held Flora's relentlessly.

'The very words you used in your letter – *justice – doing what's right* . . . Did you really expect me to run off with you like a coward, leaving Sophie to the mercy of every medical charlatan in London? What would you have thought of me, if I had?'

Flora spread her hands, helpless to defend herself. 'I never wanted it to end like this – I didn't expect Sophie to die.'

'I tried to explain to you – I promised that as soon as Sophie was well again, there'd be a divorce, and we could be married . . . I swore it, Flora, but you wouldn't listen.'

Flora put her hands over her ears. 'Why should I believe you? I trusted you with the papers I left, and yet you betrayed me shamefully—'

'What papers?' He stared at her, suddenly motionless, both hands gripping the table behind him. 'Which papers, Flora?'

'You know perfectly well *which papers*. The document I sent you when I was married to Ralph – the packet sealed with green wax, which you weren't to open unless my voice was silenced—'

'I never opened it.'

'But the seals were broken!'

'Not by me, I swear it.'

Flora hesitated, unsure of her ground.

'Felix has read it. He told me you'd read it before him.'

'*Felix* said that? And you took his word for it?' Darius closed his eyes in disbelief. 'Flora – how could you trust Felix, sooner than me?'

'I don't know . . .' Flora wrung her hands, distressed. 'I remembered when we were in Rupert's Land – you seemed to understand so much – you seemed to know how it had been, with Ralph . . .'

'Because I loved you, for heaven's sake! I loved you, and watched you suffer, and suffered myself – don't you think it was obvious how that man Newsome had treated you?'

Flora put a hand to her cheek. 'I didn't want anyone to know what happened. And now Felix knows – and all his friends, I suppose . . .'

'You leave Felix to me. But, oh, Flora—' A sudden despairing silence fell, and then all at once Darius made up his mind. In two strides he crossed to where Flora stood, and pulled her, unresisting, into his arms. 'Didn't you understand how much I loved you?'

'It hurt so much to see you go away,' whispered Flora, hiding her face in his shoulder. 'I couldn't think of anything else but the pain of being alone again . . .'

He tilted her chin until he could look into her eyes.

'You were never alone. I thought about you every minute of every day – nothing but you, and how soon I could come back to London. But Sophie needed me, and heaven knows, I tried everything I could think of to make her well again.' Darius sighed, and Flora sensed his frustration in the hand which caressed her cheek.

'Then the months began to pass – so many empty months . . .' His hand moved to Flora's hair – softly, as if she might dissolve again into the creature of his imagination. 'And then your mother wrote to say Ralph Newsome had died, and you'd become a celebrity, no longer the Flora I remembered. I tried to picture you in black – the hero's widow, raising the hero's son.'

He hesitated for a moment, and then added quietly, 'Edmund's a fine boy, Flora. He's far more than Ralph Newsome deserved.'

The sadness in Darius's face was too profound to be borne, and Flora lowered her eyes.

'Edmund isn't Ralph's son.' At once she felt the arms which enfolded her stiffen. 'Edmund isn't Ralph's son,' she repeated steadily. 'It's true. He was born in May, not in February. He's your son, Darius – yours and mine.'

There was a long silence, and then a dawn of hope almost as unbearable as the sadness had been.

'Are you sure?'

'Well, of course I am.'

'*My* son?'

Flora glanced up, suddenly shy. 'He even looks like you sometimes. When he's staring at me – just as you're staring now.'

'I can hardly believe it.' All at once Darius let out a great whoop, and spun around, carrying Flora with him. 'My son . . . My son, and yours . . . Born of summer nights by a lake in Rupert's Land – do you remember, Flora? Do you remember what it was like when everything in the world seemed so miraculous and so simple?'

'I could never forget – no matter how hard I tried.'

He bent his head then, and kissed her, holding her tightly against him until he was sure that in Flora, too, memories had kindled of warm flesh relishing cool darkness, and smooth, grass-scented skin whispering under the fingers like the endless twining of the river.

'You'll have to marry me now, Flora.' For a moment Darius relinquished her lips, but didn't slacken his hold of her. 'For Edmund's sake, if for no other reason.'

'For my own sake, my love, whenever you wish – if you don't mind marrying a bank robber.'

'I'll reform you.' Lingeringly, he kissed her again.

'But are you sure it's legal for us to marry – sister and brother-in-law?'

394

'As the law stands, no one can stop us. Though I warn you – you may be the wife of a pauper before long. Even Chillbourne may go, by the time this is over.'

'I don't care about Chillbourne. I don't care whether we're rich or poor.' Flora stretched like a cat in the luxury of his arms. 'All I ever wanted was you.'

'Damn the bank?'

'Damn the bank!' she repeated happily.

'Except . . . there's my son to think of, now.'

4

Eventually – reluctantly – Darius did leave for the bank, where the cashiers eyed him in astonishment, amazed that a widower staring ruin in the face could stride out with such vigour, and issue instructions as if he'd just made a fortune instead of losing one.

Flora, at home in Montagu Square, said nothing to her mother: Darius had agreed that their marriage should be delayed until Constance had recovered a little from Sophie's death, and the crisis at the bank had been resolved, one way or another.

But Edmund, a little over three months old, was the soul of discretion, and Flora spent the rest of the morning secretly whispering to him about his newly acquired Papa, who was surely the kindest, cleverest, and most steadfast papa in the world.

If things had only been otherwise . . . If only Sophie and Darius had never been married, and Sophie had been there to share Flora's happiness . . .

For Flora had meant what she'd said – rich or poor, she'd be content, although for her mother's sake she hoped Darius was right to be confident of saving something from the wreckage. Mr Wesley, whose snuff-coloured wig was still smouldering in the kitchen copper, had promised to propose to Constance as soon as a suitable opportunity arose.

From the soft hollow of his cradle, Darius's son smiled up at his mother, and cooed an assurance that all would be well.

A sharp knock at the street door brought Flora running to her window in time to see a tousled head bobbing away towards town above the cropped jacket and shapeless trousers of an apprentice craftsman.

'Message for you, Miss Flora.' Maggie appeared at the door with a note in her hand.

Quickly, Flora unfolded the single page.

'The police have been here. It's vital I see you, for the sake of someone very dear to your heart. If you can call here this afternoon at two o'clock, all may still be well.'

Underneath was a name. *Dédalon*.

By the time Flora reached Gough Square, the afternoon had become thundery and plum-coloured, casting a false twighlight over the cobblestones and making them glisten like a lizard's scales.

As Flora passed the door of the forge-room, the apprentice she'd seen earlier glanced up, wiping his hands on his apron.

'Can I help you, ma'am? The master's upstairs, if it's him you're looking for.'

'The last room on the right. I know it.'

'Yes, ma'am . . . the last room on the right.'

As she turned away, Flora noticed the boy watching her strangely, as if her face seemed unexpectedly familiar to him. Disconcerted, she climbed the stairs: this was the price of crime – to be haunted by a vision of spies on every street corner.

The door of Dédalon's workshop stood open as usual, but to Flora's dismay the automaton-maker wasn't alone. An unknown woman in black had settled herself on a draped, throne-like chair with her back to the door – hatless, with her dark hair caught up on the top of her head much as Flora did her own, and fixed with a pair of tortoiseshell combs. Flora hesitated on the threshold. Here was a widowed lady, calling to enquire about the progress of a commission; how long would Flora have to wait before she could speak to Dédalon alone?

'Ah, Flora!' The automaton-maker had heard her step in the hall, and hurried to usher her inside. 'Come in, come in! Don't stand in the doorway.'

'But you have a visitor—'

The lady in the chair had fixed her attention on the rooftops beyond the grimy window, too well-mannered to turn and stare.

'A visitor? Ah – you mean my dear friend here . . . Come in, *ma petite*, and meet her.'

Dédalon tilted his head and held out a hand in a gesture of invitation.

All, at once, with a lurch of the heart, Flora guessed the identity of the automaton-maker's caller.

'Come!' Dédalon swung his arm wide, his eyes as bright as needles. 'What are you afraid of? An old man and his voiceless daughter?'

When Flora still didn't move he reached out, took her hand, and gently guided her into the room. 'Here is my child, as you see.'

He led Flora forward, unresisting, and turned the draped chair towards her. It spun slowly on its brass castors, and the pale, bland face of the seated woman turned with it, her gaze sweeping in an arc across the room to rest with cool indifference on Flora's breastbone – and to penetrate far beyond it, as if Flora were as transparent as glass or had ceased to exist altogether, less substantial than the automaton-woman herself.

'Do I . . . look like that?'

The shape of the woman's face was Flora's; the nose and brow were hers, and the colouring, too; the automaton-woman's skin even possessed a faint, glowing translucence, as if quickened by real emotion. Flora was seized by a desire to touch that tranquil cheek, to reassure herself that the gently blushing flesh was really as cold as the wax which covered it.

Yet she resisted the impertinence. The woman's lips hung slightly apart, tensed to speak if she could only capture the words.

The automaton-maker leaned away, comparing the two of them, his eyes darting between reality and replica.

'You tilt your chin a little more than I thought,' he murmured after a moment. 'I can see that now. And when you speak, you arch your left brow, opening the left eye wider.' He nodded, satisfied with his discovery. 'We made our cast, you see, with your face relaxed as if in sleep, and alas, this is the price of it. But wait! Watch how she moves!'

He pressed a hidden lever in the base of the chair, then stepped back, his head a little to one side, a father admiring his pretty daughter.

'Isn't she graceful? Isn't she remarkable?'

Somewhere deep within the automaton, a mechanism betrayed its presence with a steady, whirring hum. For a moment nothing happened; then with a smooth, elegant movement the woman's head began to lift and turn as if an acquaintance had called her name. Her

397

chest rose and fell in a rush of feeling, while the fan in her delicate fingers suddenly flew open, shuddered, and began to flutter to and fro coquettishly. Her stare grew passionately intense; her lips opened to a soft, inviting 'O' like the pink heart of a rose; her heavy eyelids drooped – once, twice – sweeping her cheek with dense lashes before her head turned away once more, her fan hissed shut, and the audience was over.

The performance was slight – hardly anything, compared with the vanishing coins and rippling organ-keys of the smaller automata. Yet the subtlety of each movement, of each tilt of the head and sway of the shoulders, was the work of a dozen little springs and cams, regulated to perfection; the turn of the wrist which guided her fan was as eloquent as the gesture of her free hand . . . Impossible – but for that faint, persistent whirring – to believe one had not just watched a lady signal to her lover across a crowded room.

'She's . . . remarkable.' Shocked, Flora could say no more.

'Oh, she's better than remarkable.' Dédalon bent to rewind the automaton-woman's mechanism with a ferocity startling in such a shrivelled frame.

'Dédalon,' Flora asked uneasily, 'why did you ask me to come here today? Was it for this? To see your automaton?'

'Of course not!' Dédalon's voice was scornful. 'I sent for you to set you free. To save you!'

'But you don't have to do that. We're all quite safe – you and Lydia and Mr Wesley, too. I've owned up to forging the railway shares, and it doesn't matter any more.'

'Pah!' Dédalon waved an impatient hand. 'I mean the other business – the *affaire* with this man who fathered your child.'

Flora stared at him, suddenly apprehensive. 'I told you before, that's none of your concern.'

'Of course it's my concern! Because this morning I heard that Darius Elder is back in London – and his wife is dead. Your sister – dead. You didn't think I knew that, did you?' He peered up into Flora's face. 'Do you imagine I'm going to let that scoundrel steal you away from me again?'

'I won't listen to any more of this!' Flora began to move towards the door, but the automaton-maker sprang into her path.

'You mustn't go.'

'Stand aside, Dédalon – I warn you.'

'But you mustn't go to him! You mean nothing to this man, I promise you. He'll destroy you again, if you let him.' When Flora tried to push past him, Dédalon's voice rose to a desperate pitch. 'Listen to me, Madeleine – please!'

Silence fell like the dropping of a curtain, broken only by the squabbling of crows on the rooftops outside.

'*Madeleine*?' Flora stared at the automaton-maker, thunderstruck. 'Your daughter – the one who was drowned . . . Her name was Madeleine?'

'Dédalon made a gesture of resignation. 'Madeleine Mallier.'

'Not Dédalon.'

'No.' He was watching her warily now, his head slightly tilted. 'My name is Mallier, also.'

'And you lived in Paris . . . when Wellington was ambassador there . . .'

'After I left the château.'

'Madeleine Mallier . . .' Softly, Flora repeated the syllables. 'Madeleine was the girl who drowned herself in the river at Péronne.'

'My daughter – and her lover's child. Your father's child!' Dédalon snapped savagely. 'After your father lured her away from me – and then abandoned her!'

'And died of it, here in this room.' Stunned, Flora gazed round the room, seeing it once more with her mother's davenport in place of the workbench, and the round table in the centre with a patch of white shirtsleeve and her father's blood drying blackly around it.

'The music-box! The box with the little dancer—'

'My daughter danced – oh – like a feather in the wind. No one who saw her dance could forget it.'

'You killed him! You killed my father, as directly as if you'd pressed the gun to his head.' Flora stared at the automaton-maker in horrified bewilderment.

'He killed himself, when he abandoned Madeleine! He was a father too – he should have understood.'

'You followed him to London—'

'To make sure he died! Edmund St Serf deserved death – just as this man who wants to steal you away from me deserves death.'

The automaton-maker curled the fingers of one hand softly round Flora's arm, drawing her away from the door.

'In half an hour, Darius Elder will come here to see you. I sent him a note – and I fancy he'll come.'

'I won't let you harm him!' Desperately, Flora tried to tear herself away, but the automaton-maker's grip was too strong. 'Let me go!'

'Oh, he has you in his power, this libertine.' Dédalon gave Flora's arm a shake. 'He's seduced your reason – and he'll ruin you, just as your father ruined Madeleine, and left her to die.'

'That's a lie!' Flora twisted in Dédalon's grip to bring her face squarely to his. 'Tell me this, Dédalon – why did Madeleine have no one to turn to, when my father abandoned her? Why couldn't she have stayed with you in Paris?'

Seeing him hesitate, Flora plunged on.

'She couldn't stay because you'd turned her out into the street – that's why! You couldn't bear poor Madeleine to fall in love with another man – and when you saw the proof of it, you threw her out. You're every bit as much to blame for her death as my father!'

'No!' Dédalon's hands were trembling now. 'I wanted to keep Madeleine safe for ever! Safe with me.'

He glanced round the room, and with a sudden shove, pushed Flora into a wooden chair by the bench. Caught off-balance, she struggled to rise, but with a strength she'd never suspected, Dédalon had already dragged her wrists together and begun to bind them with cord.

'Safe,' he muttered. 'Safe from lovers and flatterers, and young men with lies in their mouths . . .'

'Let me go!' Flora kicked out, hampered by the fullness of her skirt. 'Let me go, Dédalon!' Yet in a few seconds the cord had been looped round and round, binding her to the chair.

Perhaps there were journeymen and apprentices within earshot: Flora opened her mouth to scream, but Dédalon smothered the sound with his hand, and swiftly gagged her with a strip of cotton from the bench. At the other side of the room the automaton-woman watched serenely, as if it pleased her to see her rival overthrown.

'It's for your own good.' Panting from the effort, the automaton-maker regarded Flora sternly while she rolled her head, glaring at him in mute fury.

'Now – you shall wait here with me, out of sight.'

Tipping Flora's chair on to its rear legs, Dédalon dragged it, squealing, into the corner behind the rust-coloured curtain. Then he disappeared, and Flora heard the twittering of brass castors in the dimness. From where she sat, she could only see that portion of the room nearest to the window; after a moment Dédalon came into view again wheeling her automaton self.

'Just . . . here, I think.'

He positioned the automaton with her back to the recess, almost within touching distance, her face turned towards the grimy panes of glass. After a few seconds' rummaging amongst the debris on the workbench, Dédalon stationed himself next to her to keep watch, and as he leaned on the sill, Flora saw the dull gleam of a pocket-pistol in his hand.

Her mind raced wildly in the silence. Perhaps, if fate was kind, Darius wouldn't come; yet her heart told her he'd come at once, if he believed she needed him. *Oh, please be delayed, or somewhere far away!* Bound and gagged, she groaned inwardly in helpless despair. It was impossible that their happiness should be destroyed, after all that had happened . . . Yet the pistol in Dédalon's hand was real enough, and she knew with chilling certainty that death was no stranger to him.

With a low whistle and dragging his chain, Solomon the capuchin came to share the automaton-maker's watch, examining Flora with curious eyes before turning to find out what interested his master so much beyond the window.

'He's coming.' The automaton-maker moved back from the glass. 'He's at the mouth of the lane – at least, I assume it's him, from the way he's looking up at the house.'

Flora wriggled again, mumbling frantically behind her gag and trying to beg Dédalon with her eyes to let her speak.

'Any moment now . . .' He cleared Solomon from the workbench with a sweep of his hand, and slid behind the curtain at her side, his head cocked, listening.

After a few seconds, voices drifted up to them from the street door – and then footsteps in the stairwell, hard soles grating on stone. Confined behind the heavy, musty curtain, Flora heard the footsteps slow at the top of the stairs, and then advance, a few paces at a time, as Darius glanced through the open doorways of the other rooms.

Behind her gag, she began to mumble again, and instantly found Dédalon's hand on her throat.

'Be silent! My daughter will make your excuses.'

The footfalls grew suddenly clearer – and then halted altogether somewhere nearby: Flora guessed Darius was standing in the workshop doorway, staring in at the dim and rigid figure of her mechanical self.

Dédalon's fingers tightened on her throat until it was as much as she could do to breathe.

'Flora?' Darius seemed uncertain, puzzled by the automaton-woman's stillness.

Behind the curtain, Flora heard him take a step forward.

'Flora?' he asked again. 'What's the matter? Why won't you look at me?'

Now Flora understood: Dédalon was waiting for Darius to come into clear view in the thin light of the window. The automaton-maker was half-crouched beside her, his eyes glittering and his lips drawn back, enchanted by the success of his automaton daughter. Flora, whose head was buzzing from the fierceness of his grip on her throat, could only beg silently *Go away! Oh, Darius, if you love me, go away!*

But, disconcerted by that stubbornly averted head, Darius had begun to stride forward.

'Flora, whatever's happened, at least speak to me—'

Beyond the curtain, Flora heard a sudden sharp scream as Solomon fled from the impassioned stranger, and hurled himself against the base of the automaton, looking for shelter. There was a click, and then the faint whirr of the automaton-woman's mechanical heart as slowly, coquettishly, the other Flora began to turn her head.

'What in the name of heaven—'

'Don't move!' Like a spider, Dédalon scuttled out from behind the curtain, raising the pistol in his hand.

She heard Darius's voice: 'Where's Flora? What have you done with her?'

Freed from Dédalon's grip on her throat, she tried to croak into the cloth that bound her mouth, but Solomon's screams and the purr of the automaton drowned out the sound.

'What have you done with her?' Darius shouted again.

'She's safe! Safe from you and your kind!'

Directly in front of her, Flora saw Dédalon level the pistol.

'Between the fifth and sixth ribs—' he murmured to himself, 'and a fraction to the left of the breastbone . . .'

'Madman! Tell me what you've done with Flora!'

As if time was suddenly suspended, dragging out a second to infinity, Flora saw Dédalon's finger tighten to whiteness on the trigger; she saw the automaton-woman peep out invitingly from behind her fan, and Solomon huddled under the workbench . . . and drew her legs back as far as they would go.

Flora kicked out with a force that hurled her chair forward, sending her crashing to the floor, but not before her booted feet had caught the automaton-maker's knees and knocked him off-balance. As she flew forward there was a bright flash of light and the crack of a shot echoing from wall to wall, drowning everything in its roar.

And then there was silence. Flora craned upwards to see her rival paralysed in her chair, her head bent back at an unnatural angle and her throat torn open in a tangle of rods and broken chains.

With a howl which sent Solomon careering to the end of his leash, Dédalon dropped the pistol and threw himself on the shattered body of his automaton.

'Ma précieuse! Oh, mon dieu . . . Qu'est-ce que j'ai fait? Non, non, ce n'est pas vrai, ma petite . . .' He crooned over the damage, stroking the broken throat with passionate fingers.

'Flora! Thank God!'

Snatching a knife from the workbench, Darius flung himself on his knees beside Flora's chair, slicing at the cords which bound her and somehow managing to hold her to him at the same time.

'The pistol! Oh, Darius – get the pistol!'

But the automaton-maker had lost all interest in his weapon. He'd turned his back on them, oblivious to anything but the task of restoring his damaged masterpiece.

'Quick – this way.'

As they ran for the door, Solomon darted out from under the bench, flailing his chain in a paroxysm of rage and terror. Shrieking, he rushed at them, dragging over a pot of glue on its iron trivet by the fire.

Startled by the clatter, the monkey scooped up an armful of wood-shavings and hurled them at the hearth. Instantly a stream of fire leaped out from the grate into the glue-soaked litter which lay in drifts on the floor. In a matter of seconds the boards were alight, unfurling a carpet of flame across the room to scorch the walls and lick at the legs of the workbench.

Already the doorway had disappeared in the smoky shadows, but Flora, gathering her skirts with one hand and dragging Darius by the other, ran to it by instinct. Somewhere behind them, the automaton-maker struggled to wrench the broken figure of his automaton free of her chair.

'Wait—' At the door, Flora turned. 'Solomon – he's chained to the wall. We can't leave the poor creature to burn!'

'Stay here, then.'

Shielding her face with one arm, Flora saw Darius stride back through the flames, wind a loop of the capuchin's chain round his hand and jerk it from its staple. The petrified animal flew at once, screeching, towards the door.

'Darius! The ceiling's burning! Oh, quickly!'

The house had always been a tinder-box. While a miasma of damp hung about its cellars, the upper floors were as parched as a wasps' nest, creaking and rustling in the least wind.

Fire had hold of it now: the room which had once been Constance's symbol of gentility was already picked out in flame and glowing wainscot, and hot enough to force Flora back from its threshold.

Behind the plaster and lath, the fire found a filling of straw and raged through it, exploding into the next-door rooms with their stores of cotton and card. As Flora was driven back towards the stairwell she heard a voice scream in terror – hers, it seemed.

'Darius!'

Figures emerged at last, black against the painful light of the fire, Darius followed by the bent, scuffling, haunted figure of the automaton-maker, the skin of his face red-raw, dragging the smouldering remains of his mechanical daughter.

'Hurry – down the stairs, before the fire takes them.'

The stairwell groaned as they ran down it; overhead, the fire had begun to devour the boards of the landing, and the glowing pieces showered down in an incandescent storm as they dashed through the hall.

Then all of a sudden they were outside in the thundery warmth of the square, blackened and dishevelled, clinging to one another, their feet skidding on the flagstones.

'Are you hurt?' Darius halted at last and clasped Flora in his arms.

'No – just a scratch or two. But look at your hands!'

'It's nothing. Not as long as I can hold you.'

'Your coat smells of burning.'

'And your hair.'

Flora was suddenly aware of her legs becoming boneless, unable to support her alone.

'If you let go of me, I'll fall.'

'There's no fear of that.' He pulled her closer. 'I don't ever intend to let go of you again.'

A crowd had gathered, faces upturned and lit by the great lamp of the burning building.

All its life, the house had been ugly; now, in its final moments, it became a thing of dreadful beauty. Men and women poured silently from doorways all around with babes in their arms and awe-stricken children round their knees. In the gutter, a river of rats flooded away to new quarters in the channels and ditches of the city.

At Flora's side one of Dédalon's apprentices was gazing upwards, open-mouthed, his shining eyes reflecting the rage of the fire. Flora lifted her cheek from Darius's shoulder, and glanced from face to face among the crowd.

'Where's Dédalon?' she demanded suddenly. 'Darius – where's Dédalon? He was behind us, surely, as we ran downstairs.' She reached out to touch the apprentice's arm. 'Have you seen Dédalon? He should have come out after us.'

'You were the last.' Reluctantly, the young man dragged his eyes from the blazing building, but not for long. 'Solomon ran out, and then you two.' He turned back, fascinated by the blaze. 'If the master was behind you, then he's in there still with that automaton of his. He'd never have left without saving her.'

Far above Gough Square, a fantastic serpent of smoke was coiling into a sky the colour of dull steel, rearing higher and higher on its crimson tail. As it climbed, it was transformed. One moment it piled up as a fortress – more outlandish, even, than the ice-turrets of Hudson Bay; then with a plunge the fortress became a ship, or perhaps a canoe; until the canoe dissolved in a writhing of vapour, and grew into a locomotive, and then a monkey . . . or a bishop . . . or a little organist . . . or candlesticks, and an inkstand minus its taper-snuffer.

Defiantly, the smoke drifted up to challenge the heavens and become something for the whole of London to wonder at.

Alison McLeay
After Shanghai £15.99

Don't miss the stunning new novel from Alison McLeay, just published in hardback

Shanghai . . . in the twenties and thirties its name signified glamour, intrigue, and bizarre self-indulgence. Born there into a wealthy English ship-owning dynasty, Clio Oliver's childhood is as cloistered and lavish as that of any Chinese princess within the high walls of her garden until, one day, she finds herself trapped between two cultures when her grandfather's death summons her to England and the rest of her warring family.

Shanghai has taught her about sensuality and obedience, but nothing about love – or the poignant loneliness which could haunt the brittle life of wealth and privilege between the wars. Now, in old age, revisiting the magical, mysterious city of her birth, she recalls her search for that passionate truth – with Igor, the Russian refugee and her aunt's lover, who taught her an erotic fox-trot as a child; with the dashing Ewan McLennan, who carried her back to Shanghai, where seduction, heartbreak and danger waited in equal measure; and with Stephen Morgan, tied to the family by the strands of ancient scandal and as much of a stranger in their ranks as Clio herself – a man whose disturbing presence would ensure that after Shanghai, nothing could ever be the same again.

Yet it was only when the falling bombs signalled the end of the city as she had known it that Clio began to understand the true nature of the choices which lay between her and the realization of her dream.

Praise for *The Wayward Tide* by Alison McLeay, also available in Pan Books with *Sweet Exile*

'Utterly captivating from beginning to end: a winner' KIRKUS REVIEWS

'Imaginative, fluent . . . dazzlingly evocative of time and place' REAY TANNAHILL

Christine Harrison
Airy Cages £5.99

A tender and evocative first novel by an acclaimed short story writer, about a woman of an age to know better, who falls in love on sight with a stranger.

Maisie Shergold is an attractive forty-something art historian; Michael Curran, a young, drifting musician from Ireland. Michael loses his ticket on the platform of Paddington Station. In an instant, Maisie – up till then apparently sensible and independent – is smitten to the point of obsession.

The mystery of a beautiful icon, whose religious significance has stirred the Russian Monarchist movement into action, takes the lovers from contemporary London to St Petersburg, and later to Michael's home in Ireland where Maisie makes a shattering discovery about him.

This is a novel that explores falling in love as a revolution of two. What causes it? Where does it come from? What is love worth? Is it imprisoning or freeing with its shifting contradictions and ambiguities? In the end, Maisie will emerge stronger, and irrevocably changed.

All Pan Books are available at your local bookshop or newsagent, or can be ordered direct from the publisher. Indicate the number of copies required and fill in the form below.

Send to: Macmillan General Books C.S.
            Book Service By Post
            PO Box 29, Douglas I-O-M
            IM99 1BQ

or phone: 01624 675137, quoting title, author and credit card number.

or fax: 01624 670923, quoting title, author, and credit card number.

Please enclose a remittance* to the value of the cover price plus 75 pence per book for post and packing. Overseas customers please allow £1.00 per copy for post and packing.

*Payment may be made in sterling by UK personal cheque, Eurocheque, postal order, sterling draft or international money order, made payable to Book Service By Post.

Alternatively by Access/Visa/MasterCard

Card No. ☐☐☐☐☐☐☐☐☐☐☐☐☐☐☐☐☐☐

Expiry Date ☐☐☐☐☐☐☐☐☐☐☐☐☐☐☐☐☐☐

Signature _____

Applicable only in the UK and BFPO addresses.

While every effort is made to keep prices low, it is sometimes necessary to increase prices at short notice. Pan Books reserve the right to show on covers and charge new retail prices which may differ from those advertised in the text or elsewhere.

NAME AND ADDRESS IN BLOCK CAPITAL LETTERS PLEASE

Name _____

Address _____

_____

_____

_____

3/95

Please allow 28 days for delivery.
Please tick box if you do not wish to receive any additional information. ☐